THE NOVEL IN THE VIOLA

THE NOVEL IN THE VIOLA

Natasha Solomons

WINDSOR
PARAGON

First published 2011
by Sceptre
This Large Print edition published 2012
by AudioGO Ltd
by arrangement with
Hodder & Stoughton Ltd

Hardcover ISBN: 978 1 445 88784 5
Softcover ISBN: 978 1 445 88785 2

British Library Cataloguing in Publication Data available

Printed and bound in Great Britain by
MPG Books Group Limited

For Mr S

‘Please treat the church and houses with care; we have given up our homes where many of us lived for generations to help win the war to keep men free. We shall return one day and thank you for treating the village kindly.’

Notice pinned to the door of Tyneford church by departing villagers, Christmas Eve, 1941

CHAPTER ONE

General Observations on Quadrupeds

When I close my eyes I see Tyneford House. In the darkness as I lay down to sleep, I see the Purbeck stone frontage in the glow of late afternoon. The sunlight glints off the upper windows, and the air is heavy with the scent of magnolia and salt. Ivy clings to the porch archway, and a magpie pecks at lichen coating a limestone roof tile. Smoke seeps from one of the great chimneystacks, and the leaves on the un-felled lime avenue are May green and cast mottled patterns on the driveway. There are no weeds yet tearing through the lavender and thyme borders, and the lawn is velvet cropped and rolled in verdant stripes. No bullet holes pockmark the ancient garden wall and the drawing room windows are thrown open, the glass not shattered by shellfire. I see the house as it was then, on that first afternoon.

Everyone is just out of sight. I can hear the ring of the drinks tray being prepared; on the terrace a bowl of pink camellias rests on the table. And in the bay, the fishing-boats bounce upon the tide, nets cast wide, the slap of water against wood. We have not yet been exiled. The cottages do not lie in pebbled ruins across the strand, with hazel and blackthorn growing through the flagstones of the village houses. We have not surrendered Tyneford to guns and tanks and birds and ghosts.

I find I forget more and more nowadays. Nothing very important, as yet. I was talking to somebody just now on the telephone, and as soon as I had replaced the receiver I realised I'd forgotten who it was and what we said. I shall probably remember later when I'm lying in the bath. I've forgotten other things too: the names of the birds are no longer on the tip of my tongue and I'm embarrassed to say that I can't remember where I planted the daffodil bulbs for spring. And yet, as the years wash everything else away, Tyneford remains—a smooth pebble of a memory. Tyneford. Tyneford. As though if I say the name enough, I can go back again. Those summers were long and blue and hot. I remember it all, or think I do. It doesn't seem long ago to me. I have replayed each moment so often in my mind that I hear my own voice in every part. Now, as I write them, they appear fixed, absolute. On the page we live again, young and unknowing, everything yet to happen.

When I received the letter that brought me to Tyneford, I knew nothing about England, except that I wouldn't like it. That morning I perched on my usual spot beside the draining board in the kitchen as Hildegard bustled around, flour up to her elbows and one eyebrow snowy white. I laughed and she flicked her tea towel at me, knocking the crust out of my hand and onto the floor.

'*Gut.* Bit less bread and butter won't do you any harm.'

I scowled and flicked crumbs onto the linoleum. I wished I could be more like my mother, Anna. Worry had made Anna even thinner. Her eyes were huge against her pale skin, so that she looked more than ever like the operatic heroines she played. Anna was already a star when she married my father—a black-eyed beauty with a voice like cherries and chocolate. She was the real thing; when she opened her mouth and began to sing, time paused just a little and everyone listened, bathing in the sound, unsure if what they heard was real or some perfect imagining. When the trouble began, letters started to arrive from Venice and Paris, from tenors and conductors. There was even one from a double bass. They were all the same, *Darling Anna, leave Vienna and come to Paris/London/New York and I shall keep you safe . . .* Of course she would not leave without my father. Or me. Or Margot. I would have gone in a flash, packed my ball gowns (if I'd had any) and escaped to sip champagne in the Champs Elysées. But no letters came for me. Not even a note from a second violin. So I ate bread rolls with butter, while Hildegard sewed little pieces of elastic into the waistband.

'Come.' Hildegard chivvied me off the counter and steered me into the middle of the kitchen where a large book dusted with flour rested on the table. 'You must practise. What shall we make?'

Anna had picked it up at a second-hand bookstore and presented it to me with a flush of pride. Mrs Beeton's *Household Management*—a whole kilo of book to teach me how to cook and clean and behave. This was to be my unglamorous fate.

Chewing on my plait, I prodded the tome so that it fell open at the index. '*General Observations on Quadrupeds . . . Mock Turtle Soup . . . Eel Pie.*' I shuddered. 'Here,' I pointed to an entry halfway down the page. 'Goose. I should know how to cook goose. I said I knew.'

A month previously, Anna had walked with

me to the telegraph offices so that I could wire a 'Refugee Advertisement' to the London *Times*. I'd dragged my feet along the pavement, kicking at the wet piles of blossom littering the ground.

'I don't want to go to England. I'll come to America with you and Papa.'

My parents hoped to escape to New York, where the Metropolitan Opera would help them with a visa, if only Anna would sing.

Anna picked up her pace. 'And you will come. But we cannot get an American visa for you now.'

She stopped in the middle of the street and took my face in her hands. 'I promise you that before I even take a peek at the shoes in Bergdorf Goodman's, I will see a lawyer about bringing you to New York.'

'Before you see the shoes at Bergdorf's?'

'I promise.'

Anna had tiny feet and a massive appetite for shoes. Music may have been her first love, but shoes were definitely her second. Her wardrobe was lined with row upon row of dainty high-heels in pink, grey, patent leather, calfskin and suede. She made fun of herself to mollify me.

'Please let me at least check your advertisement,' Anna pleaded. Before she'd met my father Anna had sung a season at Covent Garden and her English was almost perfect.

'No.' I snatched the paper away from her. 'If my English is so terrible that I can only get a place at a flophouse, then it's my own fault.'

Anna tried not to laugh. 'Darling, do you even know what a flophouse is?'

Of course, I had no idea, but I couldn't tell Anna that. I had visions of refugees like myself, alternately fainting upon overstuffed sofas. Full of indignation at her teasing, I made Anna wait outside the office while I sent the telegram:

VIENNESE JEWESS, 19, seeks position as domestic servant. Speaks fluid English. I will cook your goose. Elise Landau. Vienna 4, Dorotheegasse, 30/5.

* * *

Hildegard fixed me with a hard stare. 'Elise Rosa Landau, I do not happen to have a goose in my larder this morning, so will you please select something else.'

I was about to choose Parrot Pie, purely to infuriate Hildegard, when Anna and Julian entered the kitchen. He held out a letter. My father, Julian, was a tall man, standing six feet in his socks, with thick black hair with only a splash of grey around his temples, and eyes as blue as a summer sea. My parents proved that beautiful people don't necessarily produce beautiful children. My mother, with her fragile blonde loveliness, and Julian so handsome that he always wore his wire-rimmed spectacles to lessen the effect of those too-blue eyes (I'd tried them on when he was bathing, and discovered that the lenses were so weak as to be almost clear glass). Yet somehow this couple had produced me. For years the great-aunts had cooed, 'Ach, just you wait till she blossoms! Twelve years old, mark my words, and she'll be the spit of her mother.' I could spit, but I was nothing like my mother. Twelve came and went. They held out for sixteen. Still no blossoming. By nineteen even

Gabrielle, the most optimistic of the great-aunts, had given up hope. The best they could manage was: 'She has her own charm. And a character.' Whether this character was good or bad, they never said.

Anna lurked behind Julian, blinking and running a pink tongue-tip across her bottom lip. I stood up straight and concentrated on the letter in Julian's hand.

'It's from England,' he said, holding it out to me.

I took it from him and with deliberate slowness, well aware they were all watching me, slid a butter knife under the seal. I drew out a creamy sheet of watermarked paper, unfolded it and smoothed the creases. I read in slow silence. The others bore with me for a minute and then Julian interrupted.

'For God's sake, Elise. What does it say?'

I fixed him with a glare. I glared a lot back then. He ignored me, and I read aloud.

Dear Fraulein Landau,

Mr Rivers has instructed me to write to you and tell you that the position of house parlour maid at Tyneford House is yours if you want it. He has agreed to sign the necessary visa application statements, providing that you stay at Tyneford for a minimum of a twelve-month. If you wish to accept the post, please write or wire by return. On your arrival in London, proceed to the Mayfair Agency in Audley St. W1 where ongoing travel arrangements to Tyneford will be made.

Yours sincerely,
Florence Ellsworth
Housekeeper, Tyneford House

I lowered the letter.

'But twelve months is too long. I'm to be in New York before then, Papa.'

Julian and Anna exchanged a glance, and it was she who answered.

'Darling Bean, I hope you will be in New York in six months. But for now, you must go where it is safe.'

Julian tugged my plait in a gesture of playful affection. 'We can't go to New York unless we know you're out of harm's way. The minute we arrive at the Metropolitan we'll send for you.'

'I suppose it's too late for me to take singing lessons?'

Anna only smiled. So, it was true then. I was to leave them. Until this moment it had not been real. I had written the telegram, even sent the wire to London, but it had seemed a game. I knew things were bad for us in Vienna. I heard the stories of old women being pulled out of shops by their hair and forced to scrub the pavements. Frau Goldschmidt had been made to scrape dog faeces from the gutter with her mink stole. I overheard her confession to Anna; she had hunched on the sofa in the parlour, her porcelain cup clattering in her hands, as she confided her ordeal: *'The joke is, I never liked that fur. It was a gift from Herman, and I wore it to please him. It was much too hot and it was his mother's colour, not mine. He never would learn . . . But to spoil it like that . . .'* She'd seemed more upset by the waste than the humiliation. Before she left, I saw Anna quietly stuff an arctic rabbit muffler inside her shopping bag.

The evidence of difficult times was all round

our apartment. There were scratch marks on the floor in the large sitting room where Anna's baby grand used to sit. It was worth nearly two thousand schillings—a gift from one of the conductors at La Scala. It had arrived one spring before Margot or I were born, but we all knew that Julian didn't like having this former lover's token cluttering up his home. It had been lifted up on a pulley through the dining room windows, the glass of which had to be specially removed—how Margot and I used to wish that we'd glimpsed the great flying piano spectacle. Occasionally, when Julian and Anna had their rare disagreements, he'd mutter, 'Why can't you have a box of love letters or a photograph album like any other woman? Why a bloody great grand piano? A man shouldn't have to stub his toe on his rival's passion.' Anna, so gentle in nearly all things, was immovable on matters of music. She would fold her arms and stand up straight, reaching all of five feet nothing and announce, 'Unless you wish to spend two thousand schillings on another piano and demolish the dining room again, it stays.' And stay it did, until one day, when I arrived home from running a spurious errand for Anna to discover it missing. There were gouges all along the parquet floor, and from a neighbouring apartment I could hear the painful clatter of a talentless beginner learning to play. Anna had sold her beloved piano to a woman across the hall, for a fraction of its value. In the evenings at six o'clock, we could hear the rattle of endless clumsy scales, as our neighbour's acne-ridden son was forced to practise. I imagined the piano wanting to sing a lament at its ill treatment and pining for Anna's touch, but crippled into ugliness. Its rich, dark tones once mingled with Anna's voice, like cream into coffee. After the banishment of the piano, at six every evening Anna always had a reason for leaving the apartment—she'd forgotten to buy potatoes (though the larder was packed with them), there was a letter to post, she'd promised to dress Frau Finkelstein's corns.

Despite the vanished piano, the spoilt furs, the pictures missing from the walls, Margot's expulsion from the conservatoire on racial grounds and the slow disappearance of all the younger maids, so that only old Hildegard remained, until this moment I never really thought that I would have to leave Vienna. I loved the city. She was as much a part of my family as Anna or great-aunts Gretta, Gerda and Gabrielle. It was true, strange things kept happening, but at age nineteen nothing really terrible had ever happened to me before and, blessed with the outlook of the soul-deep optimist, I had truly believed that all would be well. Standing in the kitchen as I looked up into Julian's face, met his sad half-smile, I knew for the first time in my life that everything was not going to be all right, that things would not turn out for the best. I must leave Austria and Anna and the apartment on Dorotheegasse with its tall sash windows looking out onto the poplars which glowed pink fire as the sun crept up behind them, and the grocer's boy who came every Tuesday yelling 'Eis! Eis!' And the damask curtains in my bedroom that I never closed so I could see the yellow glow from the streetlamps and the twin lights from the tramcars below. I must leave the crimson tulips in the park in April, and the whirling white dresses at the Opera Ball, and the gloves clapping as Anna sang and Julian wiped away proud tears with his embroidered handkerchief, and midnight ice cream on the balcony on August nights, and Margot and me sunbathing on striped deckchairs in the park as we listened to trumpets on the bandstand, and Margot burning supper, and Robert laughing and saying it doesn't matter and us eating apples and toasted cheese instead, and Anna showing me how to put on silk stockings without tearing them by wearing kid gloves, and and . . .

'And sit, drink some water.'

Anna thrust a glass in front of me while Julian slid a wooden chair behind me. Even Hildegard looked rattled.

'You have to go,' said Anna.

'I know,' I said, realising as I did so that my luxuriant and prolonged childhood was at an end. I stared at Anna with a shivering sense of time pivoting up and down like a seesaw. I memorised every detail: the tiny crease in the centre of her forehead that appeared when she was worried; Julian beside her, his hand resting on her shoulder; the grey silk of her blouse. The blue tiles behind the sink. Hildegard wringing the dishcloth.

That Elise, the girl I was then, would declare me old, but she is wrong. I am still she. I am still standing in the kitchen holding the letter, watching the others—and waiting—and knowing that everything must change.

CHAPTER TWO

In the bathtub, singing

Memories do not exist along a timeline. In my mind everything happens at once. Anna kisses me good night and tucks me into my high-sided cot, while my hair is brushed for Margot's wedding, which now takes place on the lawn at Tyneford, my feet bare upon the grass. I am in Vienna as I wait for their letters to arrive in Dorset. The chronology laid out upon these pages is not without effort.

I am young in my dreams. The face in the mirror always surprises me. I observe the smart grey hair, nicely set of course, and the tiredness beneath the eyes that never goes away. I know that it is my face, and yet the next time I glance in the mirror I am surprised all over again. Oh, I think, I forgot that this is me. In those blissful days living in the bel-étage, I was the baby of the family. They all indulged me, Margot, Julian and Anna most of all. I was their pet, their *liebling,* to be cosseted and adored. I didn't have remarkable gifts like the rest of them. I couldn't sing. I could play the piano and viola a little but nothing like Margot, who had inherited all our mother's talent. Her husband Robert had fallen in love before he had even spoken to her, when he listened to her perform viola in Schumann's *Fairytale Pictures*. He said that her music painted lightning storms, wheat fields rippling in the rain and girls with sea-blue hair. He said he'd never seen through someone else's eyes before. Margot decided to love him back and they were married within six weeks. It was all quite sickening and I should have been unbearably jealous if it hadn't been for the fact that Robert had no sense of humour. He never once laughed at any of my jokes—not even the one about the rabbi and the dining room chair and the walnut—so clearly he was deficient. The possibility of a man ever being besotted with my musical gifts was highly improbable but I did need him to laugh.

I entertained the idea of becoming a writer like Julian, but unlike him I'd never written anything other than a list of boys I fancied. Once, watching Hildegard stuff seasoned sausage meat into cabbage leaves with her thick red fingers, I'd decided that this would be a fine subject for a poem. But I'd not progressed any further than this insight. I was plump while the others were slender. I had thick ankles and they were fine boned and high cheeked, and the only beauty I'd inherited was Julian's black hair, which hung in a python plait all the way down to my knickers. But they loved me anyway. Anna indulged my babyish ways and I was allowed to sulk and storm off to my room and sob over fairy-stories that I was far too old for. My never-ending childhood made Anna feel young. With a girl-child like me she did not admit her forty-five years, even to herself.

All that changed with the letter. I must go off into the world alone, and I must finally grow up. The others treated me just as before, but there was self-consciousness in their actions, as if they knew I was sick but were being meticulous in giving nothing away in their behaviour. Anna continued to smile benevolently upon my sullen moods, and slip me the fattest slice of cake and run my bath with her best lavender-scented salts. Margot picked fights and borrowed books without asking but I knew it was just for show. Her heart wasn't in the rowing, and she took books she knew I'd already read. Only Hildegard was different. She stopped chiding me, and even when it was probably most urgent, she no longer pressed Mrs Beeton upon me. She called me 'Fraulein Elise', when I'd been simple 'Elise' or 'pain of my existence' since I was two. This sudden formality was not out of respect at some newfound dignity on my part. It was pity. I suspected Hildegard wanted to give me every mark of rank and social status during those last weeks, knowing how I must feel the humiliation in the months to come, but I wished she would call me Elise, box my ears and threaten to pour salt on my supper once more. I left biscuit crumbs on my nightstand in clear contravention of her no-biscuits-in-the-bedroom policy, but she said nothing, only gave me a tiny curtsy (how I crawled inside) and retired into her kitchen with a wounded expression.

The days slid by. I felt them pass faster and faster like painted horses on a carousel. I willed time to slow, concentrating on the tick-tick of the hall clock, trying to draw out the silence between the relentless beats of the second hand. Of course it did not work. My visa arrived in the post. The clock ticked. Anna took me to receive my passport. Tick. Julian went to another office to pay my departure tax and on his return disappeared into his study without a word and with the burgundy decanter. Tick. I packed my travel-trunks with wads of silk stockings, while Hildegard stitched hidden pockets into all of my dresses to secrete forbidden valuables, sewing fine gold chains along the seams.

Anna and Margot accompanied me on coffee-drinking excursions to the aunts, so we could eat honey-cakes and say goodbye and we'll meet again soon when-all-this-is-over-whenever-that-will-be. Tick. I tried to stay awake all night so that morning would come slower and I would have more precious moments in Vienna. I fell asleep. Tick-tick-tick and another day gone. I took the pictures down from my bedroom wall and slid a knife under the mounting paper, slipping into the lid of my trunk the print of the Belvedere Palace, the signed programmes from the Opera Ball and my photographs of Margot's wedding; me in my muslin dress with the leaf embroidery, Julian in white tie and tails, and Anna in shapeless black so she wouldn't upstage the bride and still looking prettier than any of us. Tick. My bags lay in the hall. Tick-tick. My last night in Vienna. The hall clock chimed: six o'clock and time to dress for the party.

Rather than going to my bedroom, I drifted into Julian's study. He was at his desk scribbling away, pen clasped in his left hand. I didn't know what he was writing; no one in Austria would publish his novels anymore. I wondered if he would write his next novel in American.

'Papa?'

'Yes, Bean.'

'Promise you will send for me the minute you arrive.'

Julian stopped writing and drew back his chair. He pulled me onto his lap, as though I was nine rather than nineteen, and clutched me to him, burying his face in my hair. I could smell the clean scent of his shaving soap and the cigar smoke that always lingered on his skin. As I rested my chin on his shoulder, I saw that the burgundy decanter was on the desk, empty once again.

'I won't forget you, Bean,' he said, his voice muffled by the tangle of my hair. He clutched me so tightly that my ribs creaked and then with a small sigh, he released me. 'I need you to do something for me, my darling.'

I slid off his lap and watched as he crossed to the corner of the room where a viola case rested, propped against the far wall. He picked it up and set it down on the desk, opening it with a click.

'You remember this viola?'

'Yes, of course.'

I had taken my first music lessons upon this rosewood viola, learning to play before Margot. She took lessons upon the grand piano in the drawing room while I stood in this room (a treat to encourage me to practise) and the viola squealed and scraped. I even enjoyed playing, until the day Margot stole into Julian's study and picked it up. She drew the bow across the strings and it trembled into life. The rosewood sang for the first time, music rippling from the strings as effortless as the wind skimming the Danube. We all drew in to listen, hearing the viola like a siren's song; Anna clutching Julian's arm, eyes wet and bright, Hildegard dabbing her eyes with her duster and me lurking in the doorway, awed by my sister and so jealous I felt sick. In a month all the best music masters in Vienna were summoned to teach my sister. I never played again.

'I want you take it to England with you,' said Julian.

'But I don't play anymore. And anyway, it's Margot's.'

Julian shook his head. 'Margot hasn't used this old thing for years. And besides, it can't be played.' He smiled at me. 'Try.'

I was about to refuse, but there was something odd in his expression, so I picked up the instrument. It felt heavy in my hands, a curious weight in the body. Watching my father, I placed it under my chin and picking up the bow drew it slowly across the strings. The sound was muffled and strange, as though I had attached a mute beneath the bridge. I lowered the viola and stared at Julian; a smile twitched upon his lips.

'What's inside it, Papa?'

'A novel. Well, my novel.'

I peered inside the f-holes carved into the body of the instrument and realised that it was stuffed full of yellow paper.

'How did you manage to get all those pages in there?'

Julian's smile spread into a grin. 'I went to a string maker. He steamed off the front, I placed the novel inside and he glued it shut.'

He spoke with pride, pleased to confide his secret, and then his face became serious once again.

'I want you to take it to England, for safekeeping.'

Julian always wrote in duplicate, writing out his work on carbon paper in his tiny curling hand, so that a shadow novel appeared upon the pages underneath. The top layer on watermarked white paper was sent to his publisher, while the carbon copy on flimsy yellow tissue remained locked in his desk drawer. Julian was terrified of losing work and the mahogany desk held a word-hoard. He'd never permitted a copy to leave his study before.

'I'll take the manuscript with me to New York. But I want you to keep this copy in England. Just in case.'

'All right. But I'll give it back to you in New York and you can lock it inside your desk again.'

The hall clock chimed the half hour.

'You must go and dress, little one,' said Julian, planting a kiss on my forehead. 'The guests will be arriving soon.'

* * *

It was the first night of Passover and Anna had dictated that it was to be a celebration, a party with champagne and dancing like there used to be before the bad times. Crying was absolutely forbidden. Margot came round early to dress and we sat in our dressing gowns in Anna's large bathroom, faces flushed with steam. Anna filled the tub with rose petals and propped the dining room candlesticks beside the washbasin mirror, like she did on the evening of the Opera Ball. She lay back in the tub, her hair knotted on the top of her head, fingers trailing patterns in the water. 'Ring the bell, Margot. Ask Hilde to bring a bottle of the Laurent-Perrier and three glasses.'

Margot did as she was bidden, and soon we sat sipping champagne, each pretending to be cheerful for the benefit of the others. I took a gulp and felt the tears burn in my throat. *No crying,* I told myself and swallowed, the bubbles making me choke.

'Be careful there,' said Anna with a giggle, too high pitched, striking a note of false gaiety.

I wondered how many bottles of wine or champagne were left. I knew Julian had sold the good ones. Anything expensive or valuable was liable to be confiscated; better to sell it first. Margot fanned herself with a magazine and casting it aside, marched to the window, opening the sash to let in a cool breath of night air. I watched the steam trickle outside and the gauze curtain flutter.

'So, tell me about the department in California,' said Anna, lying back and closing her eyes.

Margot flopped into a wicker rocking chair and unfastened her robe to reveal a white lace corset and matching knickers. I wondered what Robert thought of such exciting underwear and was instantly filled with envy. No one had ever shown the slightest interest in seeing me in my underthings. Robert could be quite dashing in the right sort of lighting, although he always got rather too animated when talking about his star projects at the University. I had once grievously offended him when I'd introduced him at a party as 'my brother-in-law the astrologer' rather than 'the astronomer'. He'd turned to me with a haughty glare, asking, 'Do I wear a blue headscarf and dangling earrings or ask you to cross my palm with silver before I tell you that with Venus in retrograde, I see a handsome stranger in your future?' 'Oh no, but I wish you would!' I replied, and as a consequence he'd never really forgiven me, which was a pity, because before that he used to let me take puffs on his cigar. 'The university at Berkeley is supposed to be very good,' Margot was saying. 'They're full of kind things about Robert. They're so pleased he's joining them and so on.'

'And you? Will you play?' said Anna.

Margot and Anna were the same; they were caged birds if they couldn't have music. Margot lit a cigarette and I saw her hand tremble, ever such a little.

'I shall look for a quartet.'

'*Gut. Gut.*' Anna nodded, satisfied.

I took another gulp of champagne and stared at my mother and sister. They would make friends wherever they ended up. In any city in the world they could arrive, seek out the nearest cluster of musicians and for as long as the sonata, symphony or minuet lasted, they were at home.

I watched my sister, long-limbed and with golden hair, like Anna, falling in damp curls on her bare shoulders. She sprawled in the wicker chair, robe dishevelled, sipping champagne and puffing on her cigarette with an air of studied decadence. A film of perspiration clung to her skin and she smiled at me with dreamy eyes.

'Here, Elsie, have a puff.' She held the cigarette out to me, letting it dangle between her fingers.

I knocked her hand away. 'Don't call me that.'

I hated being called Elsie. It was an old woman's name. Margot laughed, a rich tinkling sound, and at that moment I hated her too and was glad I was going far, far away. I didn't care if I never saw her again. I retreated to the window, unable to breathe through all the mist. Despite the heat I clutched my robe around me, not wanting to take it off in front of them and display my big white knickers and schoolgirl brassiere or the small roll of baby-fat oozing around my middle.

Sensing a round of bickering about to start between Margot and me, Anna did the one thing she could to make us stop. She began to sing. Later that night Anna performed before all the assembled guests, while the garnet choker around her neck trembled like drops of blood, but it is this moment I remember. When I think of Anna, I see her lying naked in the bathtub, singing. The sound filled the small room, thicker than the steam, and the water in the bath began to vibrate. I felt her voice rather than heard it. Anna's rich mezzo tones were inside me. Instead of an aria, she sang the melody to *Für Elise*; a song without words, a song for me.

I leant against the window frame, feeling the cool air against my back, the notes falling on my skin like rain. Margot's glass sagged to the ground unheeded, the champagne trickling onto the floor. I saw that the door was ajar and Julian lingered in the doorway, watching the three of us and listening. He disobeyed Anna's rule for the night. He was crying.

CHAPTER THREE

AN EGGCUP OF SALTWATER

The guests arrived for the party. A manservant had been hired for the evening, and he stood in the hallway, collecting coats from the gentlemen and assisting the ladies with their hats and furs. Robert was the first to arrive; he came before eight and I fixed him with a stare to display my disapproval. According to Anna, extreme punctuality was a terrible habit in a guest, although to my irritation, when I complained about Robert, she said that it was acceptable in family or lovers. Some guests didn't arrive at all. Anna issued thirty invitations the week before. But people had started to disappear, and those who remained decided it was best not to draw attention to oneself, to live quietly and not make eye contact in the street. We understood that some would prefer not to come to a Passover soirée at the home of a famous Jewish singer and her avant-garde novelist husband. Anna and Julian said nothing about the missing guests. The table was silently re-set.

We all gathered in the drawing room. Those who had chosen to attend the party had apparently decided by unspoken accord to dazzle in their finest. If coming to the Landau party was dangerous, then they may as well be resplendent. The men were dashing in their white tie and tails. The ladies wore dark furs or dull raincoats down to the floor, but when they removed their chrysalis-coats we saw that beneath them they sparkled like tropical butterflies. Margot's dress was shot silk, indigo blue as a summer's night and studded with silver embroidered stars, which twinkled as she moved. Even fat Frau Finkelstein wore a plum-coloured gown, her white, doughy arms puckered by tight gauze sleeves, grey hair plaited into a crown and studded with cherry blossom. Lily Roth conjured a feathered fascinator from her bag like a magician, and fastened it in her hair, so she resembled a bird of paradise. Every lady wore her jewels, and all of them at once. If in the past seeming garish or extravagant or petty bourgeois had troubled us, now, as we felt everything sliding away into blackness, we wondered how we could have worried about such things. Tonight was for pleasure. Tomorrow we would have to sell our jewels—grandmama's spider-web diamond brooch, the gold bracelet studded with rubies and sapphires that the children had teethed upon, the platinum cufflinks given to Herman when he made partner at the bank—so tonight we would wear them all and shine beneath the moon.

Julian sipped burgundy and listened to Herr Finkelstein's stories, smiling easily in all the right places. I'd heard them all—the time he met Baron Rothschild at a concert, and the Baron, mistaking him for someone else, had tipped his head and the Baroness her sherry glass, *'and who on earth would have dreamt there was a smart fellow as bald and round as me? I must find my double and shake his hand.'* I rolled my eyes, bored from a distance. Julian saw me and gestured for me to join them; I shook my head and edged away. Julian stifled a laugh. Margot exchanged pleasantries with Frau Roth, Robert hovering beside her, awkward and incapable of small talk. He could discuss only his passions: astronomy, music and Margot, while Frau Roth's sole topic of conversation was her seventeen grandchildren. I hoped they were not sitting next to one another at dinner.

I knew this was my last party as a guest. I studied the manservant in his black tie, and impassive face, and tried to imagine myself as one of them, refreshing glasses and pretending not to hear conversation. Pity I'd never said anything worth eavesdropping upon when I'd had the chance. I tried to think of something now—some profound insight upon the state of the nation. No. Nothing. I smiled at the servant, attempting to convey some sense of solidarity. He caught my glance, but instead of smiling back, glided over.

'Fraulein? Another drink?'

I looked down at the full glass in my hand. 'No.

Thank you. I'm fine. All topped up.'

A flicker of confusion showed on the man's face—clearly I had summoned him for my amusement. I flushed, and muttering some apology hurried out of the drawing room. I lingered in the hallway, listening to the snatches of chatter floating from the next room. *'Max Reinhardt is to leave for New York next week, I hear . . . Oh? I thought it was London.'*

I closed my eyes and fought against the impulse to stick my fingers in my ears. The kitchen door was firmly shut but emanating from it was a series of clatters and bangs and some of Hildegard's more colourful curses. No one, not Rudolph Valentino, not Moses himself, could have persuaded me to enter the kitchen at that moment.

From my vantage point, I saw Margot and Robert whispering in the corner, hand in hand. I had it on good authority that flirting with one's spouse in public was the depth of ill manners (with someone else's husband it was perfectly fine, of course) but once again, Anna informed me that within the first year of marriage it was quite acceptable. I hoped Margot had written their first anniversary in her diary along with a note to 'stop flirting with Robert'. She would be in America by then, and with something like regret I realised I would not be able to tell her to behave. I must write and remind her. Although, I mused, it was possible Americans had different rules, and I wondered if I ought to point this out to her. At that moment, I was feeling charitable towards my sister. While at most parties I watched as the men swarmed around Margot and Anna, tonight I had caught little Jan Tibor surreptitiously glancing at my bosom, and I felt every bit as sophisticated as the others. In the darkness of the hall I puffed out my chest and fluttered my eyelashes, imagining myself irresistible, a dark-haired Marlene Dietrich.

'Darling, don't do that,' said Anna, appearing beside me. 'The seams might pop.'

I sighed and deflated. My pink sheath dress had once belonged to Anna, and although Hildegard had let out the material as much as she could, it still pinched.

'It looks lovely on you,' said Anna, suddenly conscious that she may have wounded my feelings. 'You must take it with you.'

I snorted. 'For washing dishes in? Or for dusting?'

Anna changed the subject. 'Do you want to ring the bell for dinner?'

The bell was a tiny silver ornament, once belonging to my grandmother, and tinkled a 'C' sharp according to Margot, who had perfect pitch. As a child, it had been a great treat to put on my party frock, stay up late and ring the bell for dinner. I would stand beside the dining room door, solemnly allowing myself to be kissed good night by the guests as they filed in for dinner. Tonight, as I rang the bell, I saw all those parties flickering before me, and an endless train of people walking past me, like a circular frieze going round and round the room, never stopping. They chattered loudly, faces pink with alcohol, all obeying Anna's dictate of gaiety.

My family was not religious in the slightest. When we were children, Anna wanted Margot and me to understand a little of our heritage and at bedtime told us stories from the Torah alongside tales of 'Peter and the Wolf' and 'Mozart and Constanze'. In Anna's hands, Eve was imbued with the glamour of Greta Garbo, and we pictured her lounging in the Garden of Eden, a snake draped tantalisingly around her neck, a besotted Adam (played by Clark Gable) kneeling at her feet. The Bible stories had the wild and unlikely plots of operas and Margot and I devoured them with enthusiasm, mingling the genres seamlessly in our imaginations. Eve tempts Adam with Carmen's arias and the voice of God sounded very much like *The Barber of Seville*. If anyone had asked Anna to choose between God and music there would have been no contest, and I suspected that Julian was an atheist. We never went to the handsome brick synagogue in Leopoldstadt, we ate schnitzel in non-kosher restaurants, celebrated Christmas rather than Chanukah and were proud to be amongst the new class of bourgeois Austrians. We were Viennese-Jews but, up till now, the Viennese part always came first. Even this year, when Anna decided we would celebrate Passover, it had to be a party with Margot in her wedding sapphires and me wearing Anna's pearls.

The long dining table was covered with a white monogrammed cloth, the plates were gold-edged Meissen and Hildegard had polished the remaining family silver to a gleam. Candles flickered on every surface, a black rose and narcissi posy (rose for love, black for sorrow and narcissi for hope) rested on each lady's side plate, and a silver *yarmulke* on each gentleman's. Anna insisted that the large electric lamp be left off and candles provide the only light. I knew that it was only partly for the atmosphere of enchantment that candle glow casts, and more practically to hide the gaps on the dining room walls where the good paintings used to hang. The family portraits remained: the one of me aged eleven in my flimsy muslin dress, hair close-cropped, and the images of the sour-faced, thin-lipped great-grandparents with their lace caps, as well as great-great-aunt Sophie oddly pictured among green fields and a wide blue sky—Sophie had been agoraphobic, infamously refusing to leave her rancid apartment for forty years, but the portrait lied, re-casting her as some sort of nature-loving cloudspotter. My favourite was the painting of Anna as Verdi's Violetta in the moments before her death, barefoot and clad in a translucent nightgown (which had fascinated and outraged the critics in equal measure), her eyes beseeching you wherever you went. I used to hide beneath the dining room table to escape her gaze, but when I emerged after an hour or more, she was always waiting, reproaching me. The other paintings had gone, but they left reminders—the sun-bleached wallpaper marked with rectangular stains. I missed most the one of the bustling Parisian street in the drizzle; ladies hurried along a tree-lined boulevard, while men in top hats clutched black umbrellas. The shop-fronts were red and blue and the ladies pink-cheeked. I had never been to Paris but this had been my window. I shrugged—it shouldn't matter now whether the paintings were here, since I would not see them. But when leaving home one always likes to think of it as it ought to be, and as it was before, perfect and unchanging. Now, when I think of our apartment, I restore each picture to its proper place: Paris opposite the painting of breakfast on the balcony (purchased by Julian as a present for Anna on their honeymoon). I have to remind myself that the pictures had vanished before that last night, and then, with a blink, the walls are empty once again.

The chairs scraped on the parquet floor as the men helped the ladies into their places, gowns catching on chair legs and under feet, so that the hum of chatter rippled with apologies. We all peered round the table with interest, hoping that ours would be the amusing end of the party and the others did not have better dinner companions. Herr Finkelstein adjusted his *yarmulke*, so it neatly covered the bald disc on his head. The men alternated between the ladies, stark in their black and white, ensuring that none of the women's rainbow dresses clashed beside one another. Anna and Julian sat at opposite heads of the table. They exchanged a look and Anna rang the silver bell once more. Instantly the diners fell silent and Julian rose to his feet.

'Welcome, my friends. This night is indeed different from all other nights. In the morning my younger daughter, Elise, leaves for England. And in another few weeks, Margot and her husband Robert, depart for America.'

The guests smiled at Margot and then at me, with envy or pity I could not tell. Julian held up his hand and the hum of conversation dulled once again. He was pale, and even in the half-light I could see beads of perspiration on his brow.

'But the truth is, my friends, we already live in exile. We are no longer citizens in our own country. And it is better to be exiled amongst strangers than at home.'

Abruptly he sat down, and wiped his forehead

with his napkin.

'Darling?' said Anna, from the other end of the long table, trying to keep the note of anxiety from her voice.

Julian stared at her for a second, and then recollecting himself, stood up once more, and opened the *Haggadah*. It was strange—until this year we had always hurried through the Passover Seder. It had become a kind of game, seeing how fast we could race to the end, reading quickly, skipping passages so that we could reach Hildegard's dinner in record time, preferably before she was even ready to serve it, causing her to puff and grumble. This night we paused and, by tacit agreement, read every word. Perhaps the God-fearing among us believed in the prayers and hoped that due to their diligence, He would take pity. I did not believe this, but as I listened to stout Herr Finkelstein singing the Hebrew, double chins trembling with fervour, I was torn between scorn at his religious faith (I was Julian's daughter after all) and a sense of congruity. His words licked around me in the darkness, and in my mind's eye I saw them shine like the lights of home. I pictured Anna's Moses, a hero of the big screen (James Stewart, perhaps) leading the Jews into a rose-red desert and then something older, a glimpse of a story I had always known. As a modern girl, I fumbled with my butter knife, embarrassed by Herr Finkelstein's chanting. He gazed heavenward, oblivious to the dribble of *schmaltz* wobbling at the side of his wet lips, and I wanted him to stop, never to stop.

We murmured the blessings over the cups of wine, and the youngest, Jan Tibor, started the ritual of the four questions: 'Why is tonight different from all other nights? Why tonight do we eat only matzos?'

Frau Goldschmidt pushed her reading glasses up her nose and recited the response: 'Matzos is used during Passover as a symbol of the unleavened bread that the Jews carried with them when they escaped out of Egypt, with no time for their uncooked bread to rise.'

Margot snorted. 'A Jewish household with empty cupboards? Not even a loaf of bread? Seems unlikely to me.'

I kicked her under the table, hard enough to bruise her shin, and I felt a small pulse of satisfaction as she winced.

'Elise. The next question,' said Julian, in his no-nonsense voice. He held up a sprig of parsley and an eggcup brimming with saltwater.

I read from the worn book in my lap: 'Why is it that on all other nights we eat all kinds of herbs, but on this night we eat only maror, bitter herbs?'

Julian placed his book face down on the table, and looked at me as though I had really asked him a question to which I wished to know the answer. 'Bitter herbs remind us of the pain of the Jewish slaves, and the petty miseries of our own existence. But they are also a symbol of hope and of better things to come.'

He did not glance at the *Haggadah*, and as he continued I realised that the words were his. 'A man who has experienced great sorrow and then has known its end, wakes each morning feeling the pleasure of sunrise.'

He took a sip of water and dabbed his mouth. 'Margot. The next.'

She stared at him, and then glanced down to her book. 'Why is it that on all other nights, we don't dip our herbs at all, but on this night we dip them twice?'

Julian dipped a sprig of parsley in the pot of sweet *charoset* and leant across the table to hand it to me. I popped it into my mouth and swallowed the sticky mixture of apples, cinnamon and wine. He bathed a second piece of parsley in the saltwater and gave it to me, watching as I ate. My mouth stung with salt, and I tasted tears and long journeys across the sea.

CHAPTER FOUR

Enough clouds for a spectacular sunset

After dinner, Margot and I stole onto the balcony. The rich beef stew had been one of Hildegard's best; I wanted to cram myself with the taste of home while I still could. Margot tossed a few cushions onto the floor, and we sat side by side, looking at the shaking leaves on the top of the poplar trees.

'You will write, Bean,' she said.

'Well, I shall try. But I expect to be rather busy with bridge parties, lawn picnics and such.'

To my surprise, Margot clutched my hand. 'You must write, Elise. No joking.'

'Fine. But my handwriting's terrible and I don't plan on improving it.'

'That's all right. It will give Robert something else to complain about. And you know how happy that makes him.'

My litany of faults had provided Robert with another source of interest, and consequently I felt he ought to show a little more gratitude towards me. The balcony doors creaked and Anna stepped out. Margot and I shuffled along to make room for her on our bed of cushions. I kicked off my shoes, which were starting to pinch, and wiggled my toes in the cool night air. Anna had painted my toenails scarlet, and I thought they looked very fetching—it seemed a shame to wear shoes at all.

'You are to take the pearls with you, Elise. Hildegard will sew them into the hem of your dress tonight.'

'No Mama, they're yours. I have the gold chains if I need money.'

I reached for Anna's hand, wishing that she would be quiet. Lights glinted in the apartments across the street, and where the curtains were not drawn we watched a marionette show of silhouettes perform rituals of daily life: maids drew baths or cleared away the supper trays, an elderly lady took three tries to climb into her raised bed, a dog sat in a chair by an open window, and a man all alone and naked except for his hat paced to and fro, hands clasped behind his back. This vantage point had been my and Margot's favourite for many years, and we had glimpsed countless dramas play out across the street. When we were children we would squabble and scratch at one another's faces, but dusk produced an inevitable truce, and we would creep out onto the balcony and sit beside one another in companionable silence and watch the show. It seemed almost inconceivable that it could continue without me. I looked down at my beautiful red-painted toes for comfort.

'The pearls are yours,' said Anna. 'I gave the sapphires to Margot as a wedding gift and it is right that you should have the pearls.'

'Stop it,' I snapped. 'Give them to me in New York.'

Anna fiddled with the hem of her gown and said nothing.

'Why do you want me to have them now?' I asked. 'You're not going to forget to send for me, are you? How can you forget me? You promised, Anna. You promised.'

'Darling! Calm, please.' She laughed at my outburst. 'Of course I won't forget you. Of all the silliest things.'

'Elise, you're not easily forgotten,' said Margot. 'You're her daughter, not a pair of gloves.'

I folded my arms across my chest, shivering in the crisp night air and struggled against the urge to cry. My family did not understand. They might be leaving, but they had each other. Only I was alone. I fretted that they would forget about me, or worse, discover that they liked it better without me.

From my position on the cushions I edged closer to Margot, greedy for her warmth.

'Oh look,' she said, pointing at a balcony on the top floor, where a prim, uniformed maid held a curly-haired poodle over the edge of the parapet so it could tinkle. A yellow arc rained down on the pavement below.

Anna hissed her disapproval. 'Ach, have you ever seen such laziness!'

'I think it's highly original, and as such I applaud it,' I said.

'God help the family you end up with,' said Margot.

My retort was cut short, as Julian called us to come inside: 'Darlings, the photographer is here.'

I can't help wondering if perhaps I remember that last night so vividly because of the photograph. We all gathered in the drawing room, the tables pushed back against the wall, chairs laid out in higgledy rows. Lily Roth used her feather fascinator as a pointer to organise us into position, and barked at the gentlemen to extinguish their cigars and cigarettes. Margot and I allowed ourselves to be directed to low stools near Julian and Anna. I still wasn't wearing any shoes, and hid my bare feet under my long dress. Margot and I huddled conspiratorially, giggling as the elderly ladies fussed and fidgeted and insisted that they be seated with their husbands or sons or nearer the back where their wobbling jowls would be less on display.

Photographs are so strange; they are always in the present tense, everyone captured in a moment that will never come again. We take them for posterity, and as the shutter blinks, we think of the future versions of ourselves, looking back at this event. The photograph I have of the party is one snapped while we were waiting for the official picture to be taken. The flash exploded in a burst of light and caught us unawares. Margot and I sit whispering together, paying scant attention to the others, perhaps laughing at Lily conducting the crowd with her feather or the unnoticed gravy stain on Herr Finkelstein's white shirt. I only realised when I looked at the picture how alike Margot and I were. Her hair is pale, and mine dark, but our eyes are the same, and except for a slight babyish roundness to my face, we are mirror sisters.

Jan Tibor watches us from the edge of the

crowd. Anna and Julian are side by side, close and yet not quite touching, both watching some forgotten drama that is taking place outside of the frame. Anna wears her arctic fox jacket fastened with a diamond clasp, snow-white fur brushing her throat, silk gown spilling out from underneath. Her brown eyes are uneasy, and brow slightly furrowed. Julian leans towards her, handsome, unsmiling. His legs are crossed, and his left trouser has ridden up, showing a flash of unseemly sock, which I remember as virulent yellow. He disliked wearing black tie or tails, so always sported some small rebellion. By some trick of the photographer, only Anna and Julian are in sharp focus; the rest of us cluster around them, mortals at the feet of the white queen and her black-haired, cross-gartered prince.

*   *   *

I couldn't sleep. I knew the moment I closed my eyes it would be morning and time to leave. I kicked off the bedcovers, climbed out of bed and crept into the silent hall. A pair of stray brandy glasses lay discarded on the windowsill at the far end, catching the light as dawn sneaked into the east, peeking between the gaps in the terraces. 'Busy old fool, go back to bed,' I grumbled at the sun, and padded into the kitchen, closing the door. Hildegard's kitchen faced west, so it was comfortingly dark, and night-time still. It was a cramped room, built without regard to the convenience of the chef, but Hildegard was a sorceress when it came to cooking, and an endless stream of delicacies flowed from her lair. She had cleaned away the debris from the party, the wooden tops were scrubbed and leftovers carefully removed to the pantry. I decided upon a midnight—or rather five in the morning—snack and slipped into the larder.

On the top shelf, a large bowl of creamy custard rested under a glass dome, and beside it lay a tray of herb potatoes. I decided that these would do very well, and unfolding the creaking steps, climbed up to retrieve my prize. I carried them back to the kitchen table and settled down with a large spoon. I was less than halfway through the custard and hadn't even begun upon the potatoes, when the door creaked open and Hildegard appeared in her flannel nightie and cap. She drew up a chair and sat with me as I licked the back of the spoon. She did not chide me for my nocturnal raid (I'd had my ears boxed for less) and instead seemed to consider that this was the last time she needed to worry about her pigtailed thief.

She surveyed me from under hooded lids. 'I've some marzipan. You want it on toast?'

I nodded and pushed the custard bowl aside. She heaved herself to her feet, unwrapped a loaf of bread, sawed off a thin slice and lit the grill.

'You're to take Mrs Beeton's *Book of Household Management* with you,' she said, with her back to me. 'I've circled my favourite passages.'

'But it's huge.'

'The English are different from us. Mrs Beeton will help you.'

I knew that this was not an argument I could win. I may refuse to take the book. I might refuse to pack it. I may even padlock my trunk. But I knew, with the same certainty I had that it would take two bowls of creamy custard before I was sick, that when I opened my trunk in London, the red-bound Mrs Beeton would be nestled among my knickers.

'Fine. I'll take it.'

There was a thud and the book landed on the table next to the bowl. I toyed with the idea of dropping yellow cream on it, but the truth was I knew it would take more than this to defeat Hildegard. I was too tired to read, but as I turned the pages a musty stench seeped into the kitchen. I suspected this was also the smell of old English houses. Sandwiched between two leaves was a thin piece of worn paper. I pulled it out and read the English inscription: '*To Mrs Roberts and her Sweetheart and House-band from a sincere and hearty well-wisher, May there be just sufficient clouds in one's life to make a spectacular sunset.*'

I closed the book in disgust, hiding the paper. Hildegard was right: the English were different. On the occasion of a wedding, they wished one another unhappiness. And to talk about sunsets at the beginning of a marriage—it was all very distasteful. I was certain that such behaviour broke all sorts of rules of etiquette. Hildegard slapped in front of me a plate of toast with melting butter, thin slivers of marzipan sliced on top. I took a large bite and closed my eyes in contentment. Anna and Julian were asleep across the hall; the water pipes whined and groaned. I wanted to stay here forever, eating toast while my parents slept.

I have thought about that last night a hundred, no a thousand times since, but I have never written it down before. And I find I like the permanence of the words upon the page. Julian and Anna are cradled safely in my words, caught up in paper dreams. I could leave memory aside and slide into fiction. There is nothing to prevent me from writing them a whole other story, the one I wished for them. But I don't and I steal away, returning to the clamour of the present, the gardener asking about the geraniums, the postman arriving with a package, and I leave my parents asleep on a cool spring morning in Dorotheegasse long ago.

CHAPTER FIVE

THE WRONG DOOR

London was cold. I'd left Vienna as spring was creeping into the city parks—pools of fallen blossom lay on the grass, while tulips and forget-me-nots filled the flowerbeds, shining under the cool morning sun. A rancid layer of coal fog encased the whole of London and the city was bathed in yellow dark; a perpetual half-light, neither dawn nor dusk. The sun lost its heat and London lingered in a false winter. To my eyes, the people were grey and covered in a film of smog. They hurried everywhere, eyes downcast in the streets, never pausing to take in the beauty of a morning like they did in Vienna, but scurrying about their business, eager to escape into their houses.

I don't recall much about the hostel where I spent my first night in England, except that it was in Great Portland Street, beside the synagogue, and filled with frightened girls from Vienna, Berlin, Frankfurt and Cologne. We'd all been terrified into speaking only English, but since we could not, we were silent. The mute girls watched me as

I darted from the hallway to the shared toilet, eyes following me like Anna's portrait at home. The hostel was funded by some Jewish philanthropists and provided free bed and board to girls newly arrived from Europe. We were permitted to take no valuables or money with us as we left, and arrived on the doorstep of the hostel with nothing but our clothes and bags stuffed with books and letters and stockings—a lifetime of mementos of things left behind. The landlady insisted that my trunk be locked in a store on the ground floor, complaining that it was far too heavy to lug up to the top of the house. At least, that was what I'd understood when she'd surveyed my battered trunk and suitcases, and hissed words at me in a torrent as harsh and baffling as the squawk of an angry goose. I didn't have the English to argue, so I clasped my satchel and the viola case and shuffled up the stairs to bed.

Undressing, I discovered every part of my skin that had been exposed to the air was coated in a slick of grime. I stood at the washbasin in the narrow room, scrubbing at my hands, face and neck with a bar of marble soap until my flesh was red raw. The bedroom curtains were stained and the windows nailed shut, but through the tiny gap in the casement the fog snuck in like wisps of smoke, and when I coughed, it was black in my linen handkerchief. Anna had urged me to visit the sights, to walk along the Mall, explore Trafalgar Square and peek at the great opera house in Covent Garden, but I did not want to leave my tiny room, fearing that outside I would choke. Once, in a science class, my teacher had sliced open the lungs of a pig. They glistened pink and I'd imagined the pig living happily in the countryside breathing in lungfuls of grass-laced air, until its unfortunate end. My first night in London, I perched on the edge of the wooden bunk, and thought of my own lungs, no longer pig pink but slowly turning black, like a bruised fingernail.

I had only a small leather satchel with my wash things and a change of underwear, but when I opened it, I found Margot had stuffed chocolate bars and a romance novel at the bottom. I knew it was she; Hildegard never approved of shop-bought sweets, and the book smelt of Margot's violet perfume. As I breathed in the familiar scent, I experienced a pang of homesickness so intense that it made me retch. I did the only thing I could to make myself feel better—I ate the chocolate bars. Not one, but all of them. I curled up on the hard bunk, too afraid to remove my clothes, having heard the tales of lice and gruesome bed bugs, and crammed the chocolate into my mouth, two bars at once. I knew Margot or Anna would have saved them, nibbled a corner, careful to preserve for as long as possible this little relic of home. At this thought of my more sensible mother and sister I began to cry, but my mouth was still full of chocolate and I wept with dribbles of brown trickling down my chin, and felt the indignity of my fate. I determined not to leave the room until it was time to go to the Mayfair Private Service Agency and lay on the bed reading, eating chocolate and craving home so badly that I thought I might die.

* * *

After breakfast (weak tea, stale bread, orange-coloured jam) I walked to Mayfair. I clutched the letter from Mrs Ellsworth in my hand; I had read and re-read it a dozen times, but could glean nothing about the writer. Her instructions were quite clear: I must go to Audley Street. I did not know how far it was and I did not know how to ask for a ticket for one of the trams or omnibuses that clanked up and down the streets. I had visions of either being ejected from a moving vehicle for having paid the wrong fare and landing on the ground in a crack of broken bones, or being whisked away to another part of the city, where I would be lost forever, unable to find my way back to Great Portland Street. I buttoned up my coat and adjusted my favourite emerald silk scarf (the one that Anna told me brought out the colour in my brown-green eyes) and made sure that I had on a clean pair of gloves.

I lingered outside the black door on Audley Street. It was freshly painted and a brass knocker gleamed, the front steps still wet from having been newly scrubbed. I closed my eyes and thought of how Anna had to play all different kinds of women, and resolved that I would do the same. Yes, I should be Violetta, the courtesan/whore adored by men, indifferent to the undignified flurries of public opinion—and also my favourite heroine of all time. Thus, imagining myself to be a debonair nineteenth-century harlot, I entered the Mayfair Private Service Agency.

I found myself in a room decorated in white and gilt, red velvet sofas piled high with tasselled cushions and a thick, plush pile carpet. There was a delicious aroma of coffee and freshly baked pastries, and my mouth watered. I stood there, as I considered Violetta would have stood, haughty, impervious, and I must have been quite good as a smart woman in a staunch black frock sailed towards me across the carpet, her face fixed with a practised smile—polite, professional, with a twist of subservience.

'Madam, may I take your coat?'

Not deigning to speak, I allowed her to remove my jacket from my shoulders and usher me to one of the sumptuous sofas.

'Some coffee? A little cake perhaps?' she asked, as soon as I was comfortably settled.

I felt a little puff of relief. These were questions I had answered many times in my English lessons with Anna.

'Yes, if you please. I would very much like some café.'

She froze. Her tight smile, no longer quite so polite, contracted even tighter.

'You are from Germany?'

'Austria. Vienna.'

'And you are looking for a maid?'

I smiled at her pleasantly, practising indifference and fished out the crumpled letter from my skirt pocket.

'I am Fraulein . . . excusing me . . . Miss Elise Landau, and I am to Tyneford House.'

The woman's smile disappeared altogether and she reached out and hauled me up from the sofa with a strong hand, as I realise now, clearly furious at her mistake. How could she have been tricked into treating a refugee, a servant, with the grovelling respect due to an English lady? It was outrageous.

'You came through the wrong door. This entrance is for ladies only.'

She thrust my coat at me. 'Go outside and enter through the other door.'

I stared at her, rooted to my spot on the carpet, left arm in the right sleeve of my coat, and tried to remember that I was not Elise but Violetta. I remembered that envious women were always trying to humiliate Violetta (as well as steal her boyfriends, all while she was dying of consumption) and felt a little better. My coat trailing across the ground behind me, I performed my best flounce, and left.

Standing outside on the pavement, I leant against the railings and looked about for another entrance. A flight of steps led down into a basement, and at the bottom, set into a flaking wall, was another black door. It had no brass knocker, only a sign saying PLEASE WALK IN. I descended the stairs, taking care not to slip on the rotting leaves caught in the treads.

There were no sofas, plush carpets or gilt mirrors in this room. Peeling brown linoleum covered the floor and low wooden benches were set against each wall. Girls sat on one side and a few men on the opposite. Glancing along the row, I realised that all the girls looked like me: pale-faced refugees, anxious and yet remembering mother's command to sit up straight, expensive gloves clasped between damp fingers. An older couple, he in a well-cut suit and she in a fur stole, sat together on the women's bench, hand in hand. They looked like they were about to go out for lunch, rather than serve it. I wondered what he had been before: a banker? A violinist? Would she set down her fur on the counter before setting to peeling carrots?

At the end of the room a grey-haired woman

in half-moon spectacles sat conducting interviews behind a plain wooden desk. As I wondered if I ought to stride over, slide my letter onto the desk and demand the promised assistance, a pimply faced boy of about fourteen winked at me and, catching my eye, slid his tongue across his teeth in a slow curve. In Vienna I would have slapped him or, more likely, he would not have dared make such a lascivious gesture to a girl like me. But I was not in Vienna and I shrank against the wall, suddenly exhausted. I was no Violetta. I was only Elise, and defeated I took my place at the end of the bench beside the other girls.

I must have sat there for several hours, watching a moth bash its paper wings against the dangling electric light fitting. Every twenty minutes, the woman behind the desk would call out 'Next maid!' or 'Next manservant!', taking care to alternate between the sexes. I watched the couple go up to the desk together and managed to eavesdrop the odd word: 'a situation together . . . butler . . . housekeeper . . . yes, I suppose, gardener and cook would do . . .' When the pimple-faced boy walked past me to take his turn at the desk, I glared at him, doing my utmost to radiate cool disapproval. Hildegard was an expert in this, especially when Julian left cigar butts beside the bathtub; afterwards she'd leave them in a soggy heap in an ashtray outside his study—she couldn't scold him but she let her disgust be felt. But I clearly lacked Hildegard's genius, because when the boy sauntered by me on his way back to the door, he blew me a kiss. I was outraged at his cheek. Frustrated by my inability to issue the tirade of chastisement that he deserved, I stuck out my tongue. Our eyes met for a moment, and I saw in his a light of triumph.

'Next maid . . . You. To the desk.'

It took me a moment to realise that the woman with the half-moon spectacles and the ramrod back was calling to me. My cheeks burning, I hurried to the desk and sat down. She peered at me with small blue eyes.

'Manners, please. You may be appointed to one of the finest establishments in all of England. Or Scotland,' she added, as an afterthought. 'Do you have any experience in domestic service?'

I stared at her, slowly translating her words in my head.

'Well,' she demanded, impatient. 'Cat caught your tongue?'

This was such a strange expression that I giggled in spite of myself, and then realising my mistake, slapped my hand in front of my mouth. Hastily, I pulled out Mrs Ellsworth's crumpled epistle from my pocket and pushed it across the table. She read in silence and then looked up at me.

'Well, you are a very lucky girl, Elise. Mr Rivers comes from a fine old family. Not titled, but ancient nonetheless. You must try to be deserving of his faith in you,' she said in a tone that revealed she thought this most unlikely. 'I don't want to see you back again in a week or two because the work was hard. I had a woman in a month back who said she'd been a countess or something. Said she'd never even put on her own stockings before and if we wasn't in the midst of such a servant shortage, I would have sent her packing. But then this morning I got a note from Mrs Forde, saying that Mrs Baronstein was the best char she'd ever had.'

She gazed at me across the table and I realised that some response was required, but once again I found myself imprisoned by my lack of language, unable to utter a word. Realising that I had nothing to say, and presumably taking me for an impertinent wretch, she stood up very straight and pushed back her chair. It squealed against the linoleum like a kicked dog. She disappeared into a side room, returning a minute later with an envelope, which she thrust at me. 'Here. Take this. There are sufficient funds for your journey and instructions. You are to take the 8:17 train from Waterloo to Weymouth tomorrow morning. You will be met at Wareham station.'

She studied me for a moment, before adding, 'I know exactly how much money is in that envelope so don't go telling Mrs Ellsworth that it was not enough, or I shall find you out, so-help-me-God.'

I snatched up my letter and, stuffing it into my coat pocket along with the money, strolled past the benches of waiting refugees and former countesses.

* * *

Lying on the narrow bed that night, still wearing my now crumpled clothes, I sobbed myself to sleep. I had never really cried before coming to London. Several months ago, trying to avoid Hildegard's wrath after having stolen a wing off a cold chicken intended for Anna's bridge ladies' luncheon, I had stubbed my toe so hard on the kitchen table that it made my eyes water, but not actually cry.

After the meeting at the Mayfair Agency I had gone to the post office to send Anna a wire, like I had promised. While I waited in yet another queue (I had experienced more standing in polite, shuffle-legged lines in my first thirty-six hours in England than ever before in my life), I composed the telegram in my head:

ENGLISH FRIGHTFUL STOP COMING HOME STOP

Or perhaps:

AM ACCUSED OF THIEVERY STOP ESCAPING TO NEW YORK STOP

And yet, somehow the message I sent when I reached the counter was:

ALL WELL STOP DEPART FOR TYNEFORD TOMORROW STOP ENGLISH CHARMING STOP

At eight-nineteen the next morning, I sat in the third-class carriage of the Weymouth train as it chugged out of Waterloo. My trunk and suitcase were stashed in the luggage car, while I sat sandwiched between two matronly ladies, and to my chagrin, every time the train lurched left or right I was propelled into the bosom of one or other. Neither lady appeared to notice, but I was extremely glad when one disembarked at Croydon and I was able to slide up to the window seat. I pressed my face against the glass, and through my own reflection I watched the sprawl of London stretch on and on. I had never seen so much grey in my life; the only pinprick of colour was the odd red sweater or yellow frock, fluttering amongst the dull whites on the washing-lines. The small terraced houses backing onto the railway, with their ragged patchwork gardens and dirt-encrusted windows, reminded me of the glimpse into my old neighbours' lives in the apartment across the street. Boys in shorts scrabbled in the dust and lobbed pebbles at the passing train as women scolded them from doorways. All the chimneypots belched smoke and the leaves on the stunted shrubs beside the tracks were black instead of green. I kept my ticket anxiously clasped in my palm, and it grew sticky with sweat, the ink starting to run.

My stomach growled. I had eaten the meagre breakfast provided by the hostel, but had no money for lunch, except for the remaining coins in the envelope. I shuddered as I recalled her threat—I couldn't possibly spend a halfpenny of that money on a bread roll. I wasn't sure what would happen if I ended up in prison—I rather doubted Julian could help me here. I regretted having eaten all of Margot's chocolate.

A young man in a cheap suit smelling of cologne and cigarettes climbed onto the train and, slamming the carriage door, settled opposite me. He gave me a little smile and a nod before unfolding his newspaper. I tried to read the headlines. In my quiet cocoon of unhappiness I had forgotten the outside world for a day or two and had heard no news. *London smog reaches record level . . . Royal Family embark on voyage to America . . . Is Czechoslovakia next?* I tried to read more, but the print was too small.

'Miss, you want to read?'

I looked up, and saw that the young man proffered the newspaper. I hadn't realised, but I was perched on the edge of my seat.

‘Thank you. Please. Yes. I would like very much.’

I took the paper and began to read the article, slowly and yet fairly fluently. I could understand written English quite easily. I felt him watching me.

‘Your mouth moves when you read.’

I blinked, startled by such an intimate observation.

‘I’m sorry. Didn’t mean to be rude. I’m Andy. Andy Turnbull.’

I wasn’t sure whether this was usual or not, strangers telling one another their familiar names on trains. Perhaps it only occurred on the Waterloo to Weymouth line. I neither wanted to cause offence nor encourage his attentions.

‘Elise Landau,’ I said curtly, returning to the paper.

‘Is you from Czechoslovakia then, Miss Landau?’

I lowered the *Daily Mail* in surprise. ‘No, Austria. Vienna.’

‘Ah Vi-enna. I’ve heard of that. Beautiful canals. The Doodge Palace.’

I sighed—the English were as ignorant as Margot had claimed. ‘No, that is Venice. In Italy.’

From his expression, I could see that this meant nothing. I tried again. ‘I am from Vienna. Austria?’

He stared at me, smiling blankly, and it was quite apparent that he hadn’t the slightest idea about Vienna. I didn’t know why I should care, and yet it irked me that this overly familiar young man in a shiny suit with a dried egg stain on his left trouser leg knew nothing of my city.

‘*Vienna is a city where you can see the sky. There are a thousand cafés lining the pavements, where we sit and drink coffee and chatter and the old men argue over chess and cards. In spring there are balls, and we dance till three in the morning, the ladies a swirl of white dresses like apple blossoms spiralling to earth in the night. We eat ice creams in the summer by the Danube watching boats hung with lanterns drift along the water. Even the wind waltzes. It is a city of music and light.'*

'Beg your pardon?'

I blinked at him again, realising that I'd been speaking in German. 'Please excusing me. My English language is not so good. Vienna is best city in all world.'

He gave me an odd look. 'Why you here then?'

I had neither the words nor the inclination to answer. I racked my brains for a suitable phrase. 'I am explorer. In-tepid.'

I raised the paper, and he did not speak to me again for a full half hour. I studied the stories closely, trying to understand the nuance. I suspected that one or two of them were intended to be mildly humorous but the detail was beyond me.

'May I fetch you something from the buffet?' asked Andy, interrupting my lesson.

I was dreadfully hungry, and thought guiltily of the envelope of cash in my pocket. Anna insisted that one should never accept offers of refreshment from unknown gentlemen. On reflection, I decided I must be cautious.

'No, thank you.'

He tipped his hat and ambled along the carriage, bouncing against the benches on either side of the aisle as the train clattered and rocked. A few minutes later he returned with two bottles of milk and two paper bags filled with chocolate biscuits. He pushed one of each into my hands.

'Sorry, miss. Felt awful uncomfortable munching across from you,' he said, holding up his own bag of biscuits. 'Scuse the impertinence.'

'Thank you,' I said and sipped at the milk. It was slightly sour, just on the turn, but I didn't care. I drank greedily in gulps and tried not to cram the biscuits into my mouth. It was the first time in two days that someone had been kind to me.

'You was hungry,' he observed.

I swallowed my mouthful of crumbs, suddenly self-conscious. I folded up the newspaper and returned it to him. 'I thank you, Mr Turnbull. Most kindly.'

He grinned. 'You're funny, you are.'

I turned back to the window—perhaps in England I was funny. I didn't know. I wasn't sure when, but we had left London and rushed through a verdant land. It began to rain and drops hammered against the windows. We hurtled past cows sheltering beneath clumps of trees and wool-soaked sheep and brimming rivers slopping against their banks. The stations became smaller and the time between them lengthened. The metalled roads winding beside the railway were replaced by dirt tracks, turning to muddy soup in the deluge. I wished I had not packed my raincoat at the bottom of my trunk. The carriage began to empty; Andy clambered out at Salisbury, tipping his hat.

The train travelled more slowly. I could see vast country houses, each the size of an entire apartment building, marooned in swathes of meadow like ocean liners. After the drab squalor of the city, I felt I was not gazing upon reality but a stage set daubed in make-believe colours. The grass was too green, and the banks of primroses beside the tracks bright as fresh butter. The rain vanished as suddenly as it had arrived, and the sun slunk out from behind a cloud, so that the sky was streaked with blue and the green ground glistened. I listened to the strange place names called by the guard: 'Next stop Brockenhurst . . . Change here for Blandford Forum and the slow train to Sturminster Newton . . . Next stop Christchurch . . .'

I felt drowsy, and my limbs were stiff, while my temples pulsed with the rhythm of the train. It was stuffy inside the carriage and I wrenched open the window and leant out, enjoying the wind rushing against my cheeks and tearing at the pins fastening my hair. I opened my mouth and tasted salt. The air was clean and heather-scented, and I scoured the horizon for a glimpse of the sea. We hurtled along wild heath tangled with scrub and black swathes of forest. The trees stretched endlessly into the distance, a mass of swaying green, rippling up and down the sloping hills.

'Next stop Wareham. Wareham next stop,' called the guard, hurrying through the train.

I stood in a rush, heart beating in my ears, and snatched up my satchel and the viola case. I wobbled on my feet as the train shuddered to a halt, fumbled with the door, hands shaking, and climbed out onto the platform. Frightened that the train would leave with my belongings, I shouted for the guard and ran to the luggage car.

'Which one is it, miss? Hurry up now. Train needs to be off.'

Thirty seconds later, I was standing alone on the station platform. A torn poster commanding the reader to DRINK ELDRIDGE POPE'S INDIA PALE ALE flapped in the breeze, and far away a dog barked. I watched as the train became snail-sized and disappeared into the woods, sat down on my trunk and waited.

CHAPTER SIX

Seventeen gates

'Elise Landau?'

'Yes?'

I looked up and saw a lean man of at least seventy years, shoulders slightly stooped, standing at the end of the platform and chewing on a pipe with extreme concentration. He ambled across to me in no particular hurry and glanced at my luggage.

'Yorn?'

I stared at him, uncomprehending. He spat the pipe out of his mouth and enunciated with exaggerated clarity.

'Them baggages is what be belongin' ter you?'

'Yes.'

Muttering something under his breath, he disappeared down the platform again at the same slow lope, reappearing a few minutes later with a trolley. With surprising ease he heaved on the bags and trundled it towards the front of the station.

'Mr Bobbin don't like ter be kept waitin',' he said gruffly.

I attempted to smooth my dress and hair, while scurrying to keep up. In my experience chauffeurs were invariably impatient. The old man led the way to a cobbled yard, where a smart motorcar waited, engine running, but my companion walked past it, stopping instead beside a ramshackle wooden cart attached to a massive carriage-horse, nose buried in a stash of hay.

'Ah. Mr Bobbin,' he said, letting out a small, satisfied sigh.

In those days, carriages and carts were still a common sight in Vienna, but they belonged to tinkers and coal-merchants, or farmers bringing goods to market. I had understood Mr Rivers to be a wealthy man and presumed him the owner of at least one motorcar. I experienced a strange feeling in my belly, as I realised that Mr Rivers may indeed have a smart motorcar and simply did not choose to send it and his chauffeur to collect the new housemaid. As I idled, my luggage was unceremoniously tossed in the back of the cart and after clambering onto the driving seat, the old man reached down and hauled me up with a strong arm.

'Yer can sit in the back or yer can sit next ter me.'

The back of the cart was littered with empty grain sacks, assorted pieces of farming equipment and smashed crates. I saw the glint of a scythe and was almost certain that something was wriggling under a piece of tarpaulin. I chose the seat at the front.

'What is your name?' I asked, settling on the wooden bench.

'Arthur Tizzard. But yer can call me Art.'

'Like painting?'

He gave a chuckle, a low sound that started in his chest. 'Aye. That's right.'

We proceeded through the little town of Wareham, my first glimpse of an English village.

The buildings were low, mostly faded red brick with tiled roofs, some in peeling lime-wash and here and there a brown thatch. Along the high street, the upper storeys protruded above the pavement, like Frau Schmidt's overbite. It was afternoon and most of the shutters were drawn, few people were about and those there were seemed in no hurry. A boy pushed a bicycle, his basket filled with dappled eggs. A woman sat on a front step and smoked, a baby playing peek-a-boo beneath her skirts. The wheels of the cart ground along the road, and the horse's hooves clack-clacked. We crossed a bridge where a dozen sailing boats bobbed on their river moorings, and passed a handsome public house with men dawdling outside, arguing idly over a pack of cards, as though none of them much cared about the outcome but took slow pleasure in the disagreement. In a few minutes we left the town and plodded along a straight road across a marsh; birds swooped in and out of the reeds and the air stank of damp mud. The ground was flat and riddled with small pools of dark water, filled with paddling fowl. I saw a flash of white wing and a black-beaked swan came into land, its cry hollow on the wind. The wetlands were edged by a bank of sloping hills, some covered with swaying meadow grass and others woodland dark.

At a crossroads, and needing no instruction from Art, Mr Bobbin took a sharp right turn and in a short time the marshland was behind us and we crept up a steep track into hilly country once more. I still could not see the sea and, standing up in my seat, tried to peer beyond the ridge of green hills.

Art chuckled. 'Jist you wait. Yerl see soon enough.'

The banks on either side of the road became tightly wooded, and I only glimpsed flashes of the sloping fields and a blue and white marbled sky. At the top of the rise, I saw a graceful stone manor half concealed by towering rhododendrons studded with crimson flowers.

'Creech Grange,' said Art.

Mr Bobbin's back was steaming with sweat, and saliva bubbled around his bit; Art leant forward and crooned words of encouragement. 'Com' on yer ol' loplolly, jist dawk arn.'

The track became steeper and steeper, and the horse wheezed and coughed, the cart inching slower and slower, until we reached a passing place hewn out of the hillside, and Art stopped the cart.

'Right, missy, out 'ere. Mr Bobbin needs a breather.'

I jumped off the cart, grateful to stretch my legs, landed on a damp patch of moss and slipped straight onto my behind, scraping my hands as I tried to break my fall. Art pulled me up and dusted me down like I was five years old, tutting like Hildegard.

'Aw. Yers not wearin' right shoes. Need some clod'oppers. 'Ere, rub this on them scritches.'

He handed me a glass bottle and unstuffed the cork. I took a sniff and inhaled whisky fumes.

'Nope, don't whiff at 'im. Splash it like. Sting like buggery, but stop it gettin' nasty. Learnt that in the big war.'

I did as I was told—sprinkling drops all over my grazed palms, and let out a gasp as the alcohol seeped into them, my cuts tingling with fire.

Art chuckled. 'An' now take a gulp, right enuff.'

Anna was most particular about a lady drinking

spirits. They did not. But then Anna was far away. I swallowed and felt my throat tingle like I had swallowed red-hot needles.

We walked up the hill, Art resting his palm on Mr Bobbin's sodden flank, and me hobbling, feeling the ache of my bruised shins. I wondered what Margot would say if she could see me—bedraggled, mud splattered, hair tumbling down from the pins. Our progress was slow, as every few minutes the way was barred by an ancient wooden gate. The horse halted, standing well back as Art clicked the catch and swung it open. In less than a mile I counted eleven gates leading up the road, and yet I felt quite content at the slowness of our pace. The air was full with unfamiliar smells of damp earth and strange flowers. Insects hummed and crawled, falling from the low branches into my hair and onto my cheeks. I brushed them away, smearing black across my skin. The tree tunnel bathed everything in a green glow, and I slipped and skidded on the broken stones underfoot. It was humid beneath the canopy, and I felt clammy and damp, slightly embarrassed about the dark patches of sweat showing through my blouse. Eventually, a white hole of daylight appeared at the end of the line of trees, blocked by another gate. The horse paused once more, Art unfastened the latch and ushered us into the sunshine. The air changed instantly. Salt wind whipped around me, flinging my hair into my face, and I saw we were perched upon the open backbone of the hill range. The landscape fell down to the sea on both sides. To the right lay a lacework of silver-grey rivers running through small green fields, spotted with the brown and white backs of cattle. Ponds glimmered like ladies' hand mirrors, growing larger until they rushed into the vast grey sea. The breakers foamed on the distant beaches and I imagined the rush of noise in my ears was not the sound of the hilltop wind but the crash of the sea. On my left, coarse heath grass rolled down into a shaded valley nestled between the banks of hills, which formed the vale like a pair of cupped hands.

Art chewed on his pipe and the horse huffed and sighed.

'Tyneford valley,' said Art. 'Can yer feel it?'

I looked at him, and then at the yellow beach beyond. I smelt heather and wood smoke and something else, something intangible that I did not yet have the words to express. Art chuckled.

'Aye. Gits everyone. Spell o' Tyneford.'

He turned to face me and gave me an odd look. 'Don't talk much, do yer? Some of them new maids, won't stop their rattlin'.'

I smiled, wondering what Julian would think of this assessment of me—a quiet girl, not chattering on like the others. It had only been a week and already he would not know me. I was not quiet—my lack of English imprisoned me in silence. I was longing to question Art about Mr Rivers and Mrs Ellsworth and Tyneford and the name of the bay that I could see glimmering in the distance, and if it was safe to swim out to those rocks where the gulls rested and the kind of bird with the long tail feather that burst out of the bush, singing a flurry of honeyed song. Questions tumbled over one another in my mind, and yet I could form none of them into sentences. So I walked beside the horse in dumb silence, and allowed Art to believe me a nice, quiet kind of girl.

He steadied my elbow as I clambered back onto

the cart, grateful for the rest. I had been travelling all day, and my head was starting to ache. The track was narrow and tufts of dusty grass or thistle sprouted in the middle in a dull green stripe. Mr Bobbin plodded along as birds soared to and fro, or twittered frantically from the low gorse bushes. The sky stretched vast and open from the hills to where it merged with the sea in a grey-blue line, and I tilted my head back to gaze at the racing clouds, feeling myself reel, dizzy at the thought of my own smallness; I realised I was nothing more than a feather on the wing of one of the brown-backed geese that swooped overhead.

The horse turned to the left, down an even narrower track leading into the valley of Tyneford itself. The path sloped steeply, and he edged forward, hooves slipping and catching on the loose pebbles. Wild flowers and shrubs brushed the cart on either side, and tiny heads of cow parsley ripped from their stems and lodged in the wheels of the cart and the wooden side slats. A tiny speckled bird hitched a lift on a battered milk crate in the back. Another series of gates barred our descent, and Art leapt down again and again to open them. Cattle and sheep grazed freely beside the road, or dawdled in front of the cart, causing Art to hiss and shout, 'Git, git. Yer bony good fer nuthins.'

Art steered us through the final gate and past a pair of low stone cottages, their walls darkly overgrown with ivy and smoke curling from their chimneys. I saw more cottages and a scattering of larger houses all cut from the same rough grey rock, lining a narrow street leading to a water pump and a small church, but the horse, needing no direction from Art, turned to the left and ambled along an avenue of waving lime trees. The leaves sprouted new green, bright and soft, and the trees towered above me, their branches a mass of clasping hands and limbs.

I did not see the house itself until we were nearly upon it. Poking above the trees on the lime walk were the chimneystacks and a brass weathervane in the shape of a ship, tacking and jibing in the wind; it appeared to be sailing across a sea of green leaves. Then a flash of light, and the windows on the north gable glinted through the trees. I stood up in my seat, eager for a better view and there, as we emerged from the avenue, was Tyneford House. I will never forget that first sight. It was a handsome manor, at once elegant and easy; the stone a different colour from the cottages—a warm yellow which glowed in the sunshine. A gothic porch stood at the side of the house, a family shield carved into its sandstone façade, a pair of stone roses in each corner, and around the westerly windows grew an ancient wisteria with a profusion of heavy blossom, shaking in the wind. It was not merely the beauty of the building itself that struck me on that afternoon or on the many since, but the loveliness of its position; there are few places in England where nature has done more. Beech woods edged the gardens and the house stood on rising ground, the bank of hills behind. A smart terrace ran along the length of the house, with a few stone steps leading to a velvet-striped lawn, sloping down towards the sea. Every window at the front gazed out upon the water which glittered, calm and beguiling. I breathed in that strange scent again: thyme, freshly turned earth, sweat and salt.

Art guided the cart to brick stables in a large

yard at the back of the house, and set about unfastening Mr Bobbin and hosing him down. I climbed down and stood awkwardly in the cobbled yard, listening to the crash of the sea.

'In there,' said Art, pointing to a wooden door at the back of the house. 'Git now. I'll bring yer stuff in a bit.'

I frowned, realising that Art spoke to me in exactly the same tone he used to address the wayward cows. Only later did I discover that this was in fact a gesture of great trust and affection; there were very few two-legged creatures that Art esteemed. A pair of young stable lads appeared from one of the loose boxes and one started to brush down Mr Bobbin, while the other hauled a large bucket of water. One of the boys stared at me, mouth agape, and slopped the water all over Art's boots.

'Ninnywalling clod 'oppin' turd . . .' Art started to yell, and I decided to vacate the yard, before any of his wrath was directed at me.

The back door led into a dark passageway smelling of damp and mouse—a sickly stench, rather like urine. The walls were whitewashed but the slit windows cast almost no light. Voices came from behind a closed door at the end of the passageway, along with wisps of steam. I tapped on it with my knuckles, unsure whether I actually wished anyone to answer. While at home I was cautious on entering Hildegard's domain, there was always the unspoken restraint—my mother was her employer. The kitchen door flew open, and I was knocked back against the wall.

'Oh, what you standin' there fur?' said a stout girl in a white apron and a matching cap.

'May Stickland. Stop idling, get them potatoes an' come back inside.'

'Aye. There's a girl lurkin' in the passageway,' said May.

'Well, bring her in then.'

I followed her into the kitchen—what seemed then a large modern room, with gleaming expanses of tiled counters and a huge wooden table in the centre covered in flour and littered with pastry cutters. Racks of utensils hung from hooks above a vast cast-iron cooking range, and armies of wooden spoons huddled in jars beside twin butler sinks. The windows were set high into the wall so that I could not see outside, but light streamed in, illuminating the particles of flour that hovered in the air like floating snow. I knew Hildegard would have wept with joy to even glimpse such a kitchen—this would be her Xanadu. The housekeeper, Mrs Ellsworth, sat in state at the table, surrounded by baking trays, a round pat of butter, flour bucket, packets of spice and yeast. Her grey hair was drawn back into a neat bun, her skin tanned and lined, suggesting a life out of doors, despite being monarch of the kitchen. She wore a starched white shirt and full black skirt with a crisp apron fastened around her middle.

'Elise Landau.' She made this a statement, not a question, and I was unsure how to respond.

I reached into my pocket and produced the envelope from the Mayfair Private Service Agency, and gave it to Mrs Ellsworth. She opened it and glanced at the contents: several coins and a receipt for my train ticket.

'Did you have nothin' for lunch? I hope you didn't let some young man purchase you refreshments, missy.'

I said nothing and willed my cheeks not to redden. Mrs Ellsworth huffed, and waved at May. 'Get the girl some bread and butter. She must be hungry. No dinner, indeed. I hope you're not one of them continentals what doesn't eat. I'm too busy for skinny girls.'

She scrutinised me with grey eyes. 'Well, you don't look like one them meal-skipping wenches. There's too much work for you to pine away, mind,' she warned.

'She don't speak much,' said May, dumping in front of me an enamel plate with some bread and crumbling cheese.

'Well, *you* could do with talkin' a good deal less,' said Mrs Ellsworth, and May slunk to the sink, where she could wash the dishes and spy without being criticised.

Mrs Ellsworth turned back to me. 'In the morning I'll show you your duties. Tonight you can 'ave an early night.'

I nodded dumbly, my mouth full of bread and cheese. She pushed a small pile of laundry across the table at me.

'Tomorrow I want to see you wearing these. And we're goin' to have to talk about your hair.'

I wiped my hands down my skirt and picked up the clothing: a white cap and apron. The symbols of my new life and I hated them already.

CHAPTER SEVEN

Mr Rivers

I went to bed early, in a small room under the eaves. It had sloping ceilings, and I couldn't stand up in two thirds of it, so I lay down on the bed (in my cotton pyjamas, finally having the confidence to remove my dress without fear of fleas) and stared at the rough wood beams. They had jagged saw marks all along the side and had never been sanded—why bother to smooth beams in a maid's attic? Yet the room was scrupulously clean and newly whitewashed and if there had only been a small fireplace, it might have been cosy. I set the pictures of my family and Vienna on the single chest of drawers. The Belvedere Palace looked rather incongruous in the spartan surroundings. There was no radiator or light switch, and I sprawled by candlelight, feeling like one of Anna's operatic heroines, save for the fact I was cold, miserable and without an applauding audience. From a tiny window, I glimpsed a sliver of slate-grey sea, turning to shining black as daylight faded into dusk. There was a knock at the door, and a white envelope slid underneath.

I shot up, and clutching the sheet around me, waddled to the door, but when I opened it no one was there. I stole into the corridor and glanced about. Empty. Shrugging, I padded back into my bedroom and, picking up the letter, closed the door. The envelope was postmarked Vienna and I recognised Margot's curling handwriting. I ripped it open, and began to read.

I thought you might like a letter as you arrive. As I write this, you've not yet left. I can hear you arguing with Papa in his study—you've been cheating at backgammon again. But I miss you. You've not gone and I miss you. I hope you liked the chocolate. I've not packed it yet, but I will. And I know that by the time you read this, you'll have eaten it all. Probably all at once so you felt sick and then were hungry the next day.

I heard that there are conch shells in Dorset that sing a perfect middle C. I want you to find one—then we can play together. I'll play viola and you can whistle on the conch.

I snorted. Margot was always so desperate to include me in her music—to her it was like I was blind and she needed to find ways of showing me how to see. I'd given up explaining that I loved listening to music and felt no longing to play. I'd find her the conch, and I'd take it to America then she'd realise what a ridiculous idea it was. At the word 'America' I felt a pain in my chest. It was even further from me than Vienna, across a wider sea.

Do as Hilde says, and read Mrs Beeton. All the English ladies use it, Anna says. You must try to behave, Bean. Try not to get dismissed from Mr Rivers' service. At least not until we have an American visa for you. Then you can prance into the living room at teatime and pick all the cherries off the cake and cheek everyone as though you are at home and you can be expelled from the house and come to California in a hurry and I shall be oh so pleased to see you and we shall drink champagne. But until then, you must be good.

I pinched my arm to stop myself from crying. It was Margot's lack of commas that did it—she sounded breathless, chattering without a pause like she did when she was excited. Sometimes I hated her, but I enjoyed hating her from nearby. From this distance I'd soon forget how much she annoyed me, and I'd miss her so much, it would become unbearable. I screwed up my eyes and concentrated on all the things about my sister that tormented me: she filched my books, underlining the passages she liked with purple ink; she strutted around my bedroom in her silky underthings displaying her superior bust; sometimes when we fought, she pinched the rolls of baby-fat around my middle between her fingers; and she always looked better in my clothes than I did. No, none of this made me miss her any less—despising my sister was a luxury belonging to the old life. I looked forward with greedy anticipation to the moment when I could hate her again.

I picked up the white maid's cap and sauntered over to the small mirror propped on the plain wooden dresser and held it up to my hair. Even Margot couldn't make this look good, not even if she spent an hour in the bathroom with peach lipstick, powder and the rouge sent from Paris. I dropped it on the floor in disgust, kicking the apron with my bare toe.

Art had lugged up my trunk and bags while I was in the kitchen with Mrs Ellsworth, and I decided to unpack. I had never unpacked my belongings before; we always had maids of our own to perform such tasks, and after we were forced to dismiss them, Hildegard and the Jewish daily kept our drawers tidy, and our clean linen continued to appear monthly, starched and folded. For the first time since I had departed Vienna, I unlocked the trunk and folded back the lid. Sure enough, the vast volume of Mrs Beeton's *Household Management* rested on the top, like a brooding hen. I felt almost glad to see her, like I had a piece of Hildegard with me. I still had no intention of actually reading it. I shoved the undergarments into various drawers, and pulled out my skirts and dresses, spreading them carefully upon the bed. I had a tiny razor blade amongst my wash things, and sitting cross-legged on the blankets, I set about retrieving the valuables from their hiding places, trying not to slice my fingers and bleed over the clean clothes. I felt along the hem of each skirt before hanging it up in the wardrobe, and soon I had a small stash of gold, which I placed inside a stocking and shoved in the back of a drawer. Anna had packed in layers of tissue paper the soft pink evening gown I'd worn that last evening. I didn't know when she had sneaked it in and, while I realised that I would never have occasion to wear such a dress, I should be glad to see it hanging in my wardrobe, a memento of better times. When I lifted it, I noticed that the hem was rumpled, as though something was concealed within. Taking the razor blade, I unpicked the extra layer of stitching, and carefully drew out a snake of white pearls. Anna's pearls.

I sat on the bed as the evening dulled into darkness, and listened to the breakers on the beach. The string of pearls shimmered in the candlelight and I ran my fingertips along the smooth beads, pale as drops of milk. The stowaway pearls revealed Anna's doubt that I'd ever see her in New York. I pulled them through my fingers, again and again, unwilling to fasten them around my neck, in case they choked me.

*   *   *

I fell into a fitful sleep, but the sound of the sea kept invading my dreams. I was carried on a ship into a far-off land, but it was not America, and I knew we sailed the wrong way to reach Anna and Julian and Margot. I howled at the captain to turn the boat around, but two muscled crewmen with wolfish faces picked me up by my arms and cast me into the sea. I thrashed and tried to scream, but my lungs filled with burning saltwater. I awoke with a cry, and found myself soaked with sweat, the bedcovers as wet as if I had drenched them with a bucket of water. My candle had burnt out and it was pitch dark. I took deep breaths, in and out, in and out, until I felt my heartbeat slow to a steady thud, and decided to go and wash my face.

I padded along the corridor in bare feet, feeling my way like I was playing a lonesome game of blind man's bluff. I had never been afraid of the dark or night-time noises, and willed myself not to be scared now. I had not noticed the bathroom on my way upstairs, and had been directed to an outside privy when I'd requested the toilet. Several doors led off the corridors, but not wanting to disturb May or any other maids who might be sleeping, I decided to creep down to the yard and splash my face outside in the cool air. The back stairs lay in total darkness and I groped my way down keeping one hand on the banister, managing not to stumble on the narrow treads. I emerged in the corridor beside the kitchen and hurried along to the back door. It was unlocked and I stepped straight out into the moonlit yard.

The cobbles were cold beneath my feet and slippery with dew. As I skidded, stubbing my toe on a broken stone, I realised that it might have been sensible to put on my shoes, but then I only ever thought of sensible things when it was too late. Mr Bobbin's brown and white dappled head rested on the stable door; his eyes were closed and he snored softly. I smiled; I'd never heard a horse snore before—only Julian when he'd had too much brandy from the decanter in the dining room after a good dinner.

The night air held a chill and I shivered in my damp pyjamas, but I liked the quiet. There was no one around but me and I experienced a rush of satisfaction. For now I was free from worrying about how to behave, what to say, which words to use and, if I wanted, I could skip around the silent yard without anyone scolding me for inappropriate displays. I stretched luxuriously, revealing my belly to the night and gave an unladylike yawn. My hair was sticky with sweat and clung to my face and I decided that I would wash, despite the cold. An old-fashioned water pump with an iron handle stood in the middle of the yard. I'd watched the stable boy use it earlier before scrubbing Mr Bobbin, and I mimicked his movement, pushing the handle up and down, until a steady stream of water sluiced my feet and gushed over the cobbles. Kneeling, I shoved my head under the flow, trying to pump at the same time and managed to rinse my hair as well as spray myself with freezing water. The cold took my breath away, emptying my mind of all thought, save for the sensation of icy liquid washing through my hair, over my cheeks and trickling down my neck. It was not unpleasant, and the rush of water crowded out my tumbling worries. The pump squealed and whined, filling the empty yard with the sound, so that it took me a moment to realise someone was speaking to me.

'Hullo?'

I scrambled to my feet, banging my head against the pump. A pain exploded above my eye and I crouched, rubbing my forehead. The next moment, a man was kneeling beside me, pushing my wet hair out of my face with his fingers.

'Are you bleeding? Or is this water? I can't see. Come into the light.'

I allowed myself to be led into the corner of the yard, where a yellow oil lamp rested on a mounting block. The man touched my forehead, where I'd cracked it against the pump. I was too embarrassed to look into his face, and stared at my bare, slightly grimy toes.

'No, you're all right. I'm sorry. Didn't mean to frighten you like that.'

I looked up and saw in the gloom a man of about forty with dark hair, and a slight smile playing around his eyes. Anna would have called him handsome, but I knew that men of forty were far too old to be considered any such thing.

'Christopher Rivers,' he said.

'Elise Landau,' I said, offering him my hand.

He glanced at my proffered hand for a moment, before clasping it warmly between both of his. I reddened, suddenly remembering that I was a maid now, and didn't shake hands with gentlemen. I realised how strange I must appear to him, standing in the middle of his stable yard in the middle of the night in a pair of drenched pyjamas. When he released my hand, I folded my arms tightly across my chest.

'It is very pleasant to be making your acquaintance Mr Rivers . . . sir,' I added as an afterthought, recalling that this was the way English maids addressed gentlemen.

'Charming to make yours, Elise,' said Mr Rivers, doing his best to repress the smile that was spreading from his eyes to his mouth.

I glanced back down at the cobbles. No man other than my father had ever addressed me by my first name before. In Vienna, only fathers, brothers and lovers used a lady's familiar name. The few men I knew always called me 'Fraulein Landau' or 'Fraulein Elise' at the very most, and when this tall man called me by my first name alone it sounded intimate.

'May I suggest that you go back inside? You are rather wet, and I would not like you to catch cold.'

'Yes . . . erm. Mr . . . erm. Sir.'

'Mr Rivers is just fine.'

I nodded and squeezing out the water from my long plait onto the yard, I turned to go inside the house. As I reached the back door, he called out to me.

'Elise?'

I hesitated, my hand on the door handle.

'I think it best that neither of us mentions this meeting to Mrs Ellsworth. We meet in the morning as strangers.'

'Yes, Mr Rivers.'

I can't be certain that the moon was full, but if it wasn't it ought to have been. Whenever I think back to that night, I see a white lantern of a moon hanging over the stable yard, the wind shivering in the marram grass. As in a dream, I am both the girl in the scene and some other self, watching her. I see Mr Rivers sliding back the girl's hair, and I feel the warmth of his fingers on my forehead. I watch that other Elise cross the yard and slip into the dark house.

And then I lay in the dark, staring up at the blackened ceiling beams of my little attic room, twisting my wet plait round my arm, twisting, twisting.

CHAPTER EIGHT

Like Samson I will not cut my hair

Mrs Ellsworth ushered me through the green baize door and into the main part of the house. That door was the dividing line between our domain and theirs, as inviolate as any national boundary. She walked me around the west drawing room, pointing out an alarming array of precious china bells and antique netsuke that I was not to break. A collection of stern-faced ancestors glared down upon me from shadowed walls, the curtains tightly closed to preserve the Chinese silk wallpaper and a Turner seascape of the rocks in Mupe Bay. The painted sea crashed noiselessly against the glistening rocks, as storm clouds swirled. Mrs Ellsworth informed me in a voice heavy with pride that this was the most precious painting in the house, insured for more than a thousand guineas. She paused by the vast stone-carved fireplace, inset once again with the family crest and twining ivy. The yellow sandstone was blackened at the back with soot and smoke, and the ashes of an old fire fluttered in the grate.

'Each mornin' you're to clean out the fireplaces in the main sitting room, the dining room and the mornin' room. If ladies are visiting in cold weather then you are to go quietly into their rooms and put a match to their fire. Fire must be laid the night before, mind.'

'Yes, Mrs Ellsworth.'

I stifled a yawn. I had never been so bored. The list of tasks stretched endlessly before me, and I knew with quiet certainty that I would never remember half of them, and a fierce scolding was inevitable.

'Did you understand how to use the beeswax on the floor?'

'Yes, Mrs Ellsworth.'

'An' you saw how to polish them ornaments without breakages?'

'Yes, Mrs Ellsworth.'

'You can come back and finish cleaning in here later. Mr Wrexham likes to show new housemaids how to light a fire properly.'

I hurried after Mrs Ellsworth out into the panelled hall and into a cheerful dining room laid for breakfast. My first lesson had been upon the importance of walking fast: a maid is never idle, and dawdling is idle. For the next twelve months, I must proceed everywhere at a jog, as though upon urgent business of state, even if I were merely returning an eggcup to the pantry. I learnt that a stroll was a privilege of the wealthy. When I thought about it, I had never seen Hildegard amble; she hurried everywhere with the same expediency as Mrs Ellsworth, and even in our quiet hours chattering together in the kitchen, her hands were never still—her knitting needles click-clicked, she darned the tears in my clothes, or dusted sugar over buns plucked from the oven.

In the morning room, a silver coffeepot rested on a hotplate, releasing a delicious aroma and my mouth watered—since my arrival in England I'd had nothing but thick black tea, which I found quite revolting. These curtains were open and the bright sunlight streamed through the tall casement windows. Outside lay a terrace with stone balustrades woven with tangled vines. Low terracotta pots brimming with scarlet geraniums were set at regular intervals beside white-painted tables and chairs, while beyond the terrace, smooth lawns sloped down towards the sea. It was so beautiful that I couldn't help but smile.

'Harrumph. Another dawdler,' said a voice.

I looked around and saw a white-haired man, with the deportment and authority of a conductor, standing beside Mrs Ellsworth. I suppressed a giggle; I'd never actually heard a man say 'harrumph' in real life before. It was a word I'd only ever read in storybooks, while trying to improve my English.

'Elise, meet Mr Wrexham. Mr Rivers' butler, valet and the head of staff here at Tyneford.'

I hesitated, far more awkward before this austere old man than I had been last night when confronted with Mr Rivers himself. Was I supposed to shake his hand? To curtsy?

'Most pleased and delighted in the . . . shaping of your . . . acquaintance, sir,' I said, keeping my hands firmly at my sides.

He stared at me with narrowed eyes. 'Is the girl attempting humour?'

'No, I don't believe so, Mr Wrexham. I think her grasp of the English language is a trifle peculiar.'

'Well. Give her some improving books. This won't do. She must be able to wait on English ladies and gentlemen, without causing confusion or *embarrassment*.' He pronounced this last word as though it was a capital offence.

'Yes, very good, Mr Wrexham,' said Mrs Ellsworth.

The next quarter of an hour was spent with Mr Wrexham schooling me in how to lay and light a fire. I worked my way through most of a box of matches, several sheets of newspaper and all of his patience, but by the time the morning room door opened and Mr Rivers entered, a hearty blaze roared in the hearth. He bade a good morning to the senior servants and, ignoring me entirely, seated himself at the table with his morning paper.

'Will you be needing anything further, Mr Rivers?' inquired Mrs Ellsworth.

'No thank you.'

'Well, this is the new house parlour maid, Elise,' she said.

'Very good. Nice to meet you, Elsie,' said Mr Rivers, not looking up from his paper.

I felt irritation prickle along the back of my neck. Elsie, indeed. I wanted to grab the top of his wretched paper and crumple it. I'd never been so rudely ignored in all my life. Mrs Ellsworth ushered me outside and thrust a box of cleaning utensils into my arms.

'Now. You can go and clean the sitting room properly. When you've done that, you can start on the bedrooms. Make sure you make them beds up properly, like I showed you.'

I started to walk away at a brisk pace, until she called me back and issued a further slew of instructions in a low voice.

'Elise. Remember, you must not be visible from the outside. When cleaning the windows, you must duck down and walk away if you ever glimpse any ladies or gentlemen outside on the lawn or terrace. If Mr Rivers enters, you apologise, collect your cleaning things and leave. You must be invisible. You understand?'

'Yes, Mrs Ellsworth. I am to be invisible.'

* * *

My hands bled. My nails split and the fingertips on each hand were raw and sliced with tiny cuts. My legs ached like I'd been running for miles across the hills and I'd pulled every muscle in my shoulders and arms. All I wanted was to lie in a hot bath filled with Anna's lavender salts and then disappear to my soft bed, with a cup of Hildegard's special kirsch-laced hot chocolate. Instead, I had to clean and scrub and polish and hurry between chores. The house was vast, many times the size of our sumptuous Viennese apartment, and entirely lacking in modern comforts—certainly none that would make the life of a maid a little easier. I found myself sighing like a lover over the memory of Hildegard's smart new vacuuming machine. Mr Wrexham caught me gazing out of the small arched window above the side porch, staring at the feathered clouds tumbling across the sky like a clutch of ducklings.

'Chop chop, girl! If you've time to idle, I've a list of jobs for you.'

As he clapped his hands at me, I picked up my rag and bottle of vinegar, ran into the nearest bedroom, and set to dusting the mirror and dressing table. A photograph of a pretty young woman in a drop-waist gown, the kind that had been the height of fashion in the twenties, rested on the table beside a tortoiseshell comb and a dish for earrings. I picked it up to dust the glass, and looked at the face. She had a sweet smile, not quite straight, and she squinted shyly at the camera, as though reluctant to have her picture taken. The other things on the table were incongruous: a stash of gentlemen's magazines, an old copy of *Sporting Life* and a silver cigarette case. On second glance, I realised that the dish was filled not with earrings but cufflinks. A brown leather armchair was positioned next to the window, and on the sill rested an ashtray. This was a gentleman's room, not a lady's. I heard the door open behind me, and whirled round expecting to see Mr Rivers, but Mr Wrexham had glided in, with the smooth grace belonging to the most proficient butlers.

'This is Mr Christopher Rivers' room.'

'Yes. Mr Rivers.'

Mr Wrexham frowned. 'No, Mr Christopher Rivers. Mr Rivers' son. He's up at Cambridge presently. He returns in a few days. May shall clean the room then. You are not to come up here while Mr Christopher is in residence.'

'Why?'

The question slipped out, before I realised it. Mr Wrexham reddened with displeasure, and I could see that he was debating whether to even answer me.

'Because Mr Rivers is making a generous concession to your circumstance. Mr Rivers does not think it proper that you should be in a young gentleman's room, when he is in the house.'

Mr Wrexham reached out and took from me the photograph of the girl, which I hadn't realised I was still clasping, and replaced it tenderly on the table.

'The late Mrs Rivers. A fine lady,' he said quietly, half to himself.

I studied the gentle figure in the frame with her wispy pale hair and tried to imagine her married to the vigorous Mr Rivers. I wondered why it was that all old photographs seemed sad.

* * *

The day disappeared in a whirl of dust and exhaustion. May and a gap-toothed girl from the village assisted in the drudgery. I glimpsed a manservant lugging buckets of coal, while a liveried footman carried trays into the library or study. I cleaned four guest bedrooms but none of them seemed to be in use, and held the musty stench of neglect, despite their daily airings. At five o'clock I descended the back stairs to the servants' hall and tea. A long oak table had been set for supper, and Mr Wrexham sat at one end and Mrs Ellsworth at the other. This was the first time I had encountered all the servants together, and there were fewer of us than I had imagined. At ten to five, the two daily housemaids disappeared away to their own dinners in the village so that there were only eight live-in staff seated around the wooden table, cradling bowls of steaming stew and mash. Two low benches rested on either side of the table, with matching high-backed chairs for the butler and housekeeper. The dark panelled hall was thirty feet long, the table running nearly the length of the room, and easily could have seated a staff of forty. The hall echoed with our voices and I wondered when it had last been full. We would have been much more comfortable in the airy kitchen rather than sitting on the hard wooden benches in the gloom. A faded sampler nailed above our heads proclaimed the dreary motto 'Work and Faith', while the wall was studded with little brass bells, each corresponding to a label: 'study', 'drawing room', 'master bedroom' and so forth. More modern electric service bells had been installed in the kitchen and servants' corridor, and this antique system lent the hall a dismal air. I sat beside Henry the footman (his real name was Stan, but the footman at Tyneford was always called Henry), while Billy the gardener (wild hair unpruned, in contrast to the neat shrubs in his domain) sat shovelling food and speaking to no one. Jim, the kitchen boy, chattered to Peter, the general manservant. May, scullery maid, general busybody and personage most put out by my appearance at Tyneford, sat opposite and watched me with round, piggish eyes, and I felt that if it hadn't been for the others, she would have snarled at me with her small, yellow teeth.

'I were supposed to be housemaid. Bin scullery drudge fer five year,' she said.

I said nothing and scrutinised the brown steaming contents of the bowl before me.

'You're not ready for promotion. I can't have you chirpin' away to the ladies an' gentlemen,' said Mrs Ellsworth, drumming her fingers against the table, and I gained the distinct impression this was an argument that had been underway for some time.

'Enough,' commanded Mr Wrexham, eyes narrow with outrage. 'Elise was engaged under a direct order from Mr Rivers. I will not have his orders questioned in this house. Is that quite clear?'

May bent her head and began to sob noiselessly into her dumplings. Mrs Ellsworth moved to comfort her, but on catching Mr Wrexham's furious gaze, thought better of it and reached for her napkin instead.

'Mrs Ellsworth, would you say Grace?' he said.

All the servants bowed their heads, pressing their hands together, forming triangles above their plates. I did not know what I ought to do. I could not pray. I had been forced to leave my family but I would not become a Christian. I knew that every prayer I uttered would carry me further away from them. I closed my eyes, and sealed my lips tight shut.

'For what we are about to receive may the Lord make us truly thankful. We ask you Christ our Saviour to bestow your blessing upon Mr Rivers, Mr Christopher and bless all who live in this house. Amen.'

There was a murmur of 'Amens' from around the table and I opened my eyes. Mr Wrexham was looking at me, mouth pursed with displeasure.

'You do not wish the Lord to bless this house?'

'I cannot be praying with you.'

'And why not? Is our God not good enough for

you.'

I thought of Anna and Julian and the last night in Vienna. I had never really prayed before that night. I was not sure that I ever would again, but I remembered the honey chant of Herr Finkelstein and his song of the Promised Land. *Next year in New York.* Until I saw them again, that must be my last prayer.

'I am a Jew.'

The tone of my voice surprised me. It was strong and clear: an absolute declaration. I had never said those words before; I'd been driven out of my Vienna and across the sea because of them and yet I had never uttered them aloud. There must have been something in my expression, as neither Mr Wrexham nor anyone else ever mentioned my refusal to say Grace again.

There was a loud knock at the door and Art stomped in, wearing a pair of filthy outdoor shoes, caked in muck that stank distinctly like horse manure. Mrs Ellsworth scowled but did not scold him, saying only, 'Your dinner's on the warmer in the kitchen. You can go and fetch it yourself.'

I had forgotten about Art, and now wondered why he didn't dine with us. Peter leant towards me, confiding, 'Art don't like ter eat wi' two-legged uns. 'Ee likes ter munch 'is supper out wi' th' horses and cows. But Art likes a meat stew right enuff rather than a bit o' hay.' He guffawed loudly at his own joke.

'Mr Bobbin don't talk nearly as much poppycock as the rest o' yer,' said Art. 'Can't blame a man fer wantin' a bit o' peace wi' his dinner.'

I couldn't blame him at all, and wished I could take my bowl and sneak outside to eat beside

Mr Bobbin in the quiet yard. I smiled at Art, and he gave me a quick wink as he left. I felt a flush of happiness at the feeling I had an ally amongst the household. May gazed at me with ill-concealed dislike.

After the meal, we cleared away the dishes into the sink in the back scullery, where May stood up to her elbows in soapsuds, scrubbing and complaining under her breath. The other servants vanished to their duties, while I trailed after Mrs Ellsworth and Mr Wrexham into the kitchen. I hovered in the doorway, not knowing what I ought to do next.

'Elise. You are to wait at table tonight,' said Mr Wrexham. 'Mr Rivers has a guest and it's Henry's evening off.'

'And I'm very happy to take his place, Mr Wrexham,' said Mrs Ellsworth.

'No thank you, Mrs Ellsworth,' he replied. 'The child must learn. She has been engaged as house parlour maid and she shall fulfil those duties.'

I watched the pair of elderly servants. I guessed that they had lived in this house together for twenty years, and yet they never spoke to one another without using a formal title. Mrs Ellsworth stifled a little sigh and sat down at the kitchen table. Mr Wrexham laid a fresh place setting around her, and handed me a pair of forks and a willow-patterned dish filled with dried peas.

'Now serve Mrs Ellsworth her vegetables.'

Every night at supper, one of the maids, or later Hildegard herself, had elegantly placed vegetables and potatoes on my plate. Now that it was my turn, I did not find it so easy. The peas tumbled onto Mrs Ellsworth's lap, or else I dropped the forks. I was scolded for leaning in too close (*this is not a common public house, girl*) and for standing too far back (*how can you wait on a lady from such a distance? A little common sense, please*). After half an hour, Mrs Ellsworth stood up.

'Excuse me, Mr Wrexham. I have a dinner to cook.'

She walked over to the vast cooking range and clattered pots, while Mr Wrexham returned the dish to its place on the dresser and poured the dried peas back into a jar. He handed me a clean apron.

'Tonight, Elise, you shall serve the water and collect the empty plates.'

I frowned; I had succeeded in placing nearly all of my last forkful of peas smoothly on Mrs Ellsworth's plate—only one had disappeared down the back of her neck. I felt quite cheated at being relegated to water duty but decided it was best not to argue.

'Now sit down,' said Mr Wrexham.

I sat, wondering what was to be the next lesson. Perhaps the art of the wrist flourish when unfolding a napkin? But then, I felt Mr Wrexham's hands in my hair. I whipped around to come face to face with a gleaming pair of scissors.

'No hysterics, please. Your hair must be cut.'

'No. No. I cannot.'

I backed away from him towards the oak dresser at the far end of the kitchen. My heart pounded in my ears and the stew in my belly bubbled. I kept my eyes fixed on the long blades. I must not blink. Must not blink. In my mind I saw the scissor-man in *Struwwelpeter* coming at me with his cry 'snip, snip', ready to slice off my hair.

'I will not cut it,' I half shouted, half cried, edging

further into the corner.

'Elise. Stop making such a fuss,' said Mrs Ellsworth. 'And Mr Wrexham, you're frightening the girl. She's turned quite white.'

Mr Wrexham lowered his scissors and folded his arms. 'I cannot have anyone waiting in my dining room with long hair. It's undignified and unsightly. And unclean.'

Mrs Ellsworth turned to me, her face almost sympathetic. 'In England, dear, all maids must have their hair cut short. It's a mark of position. And hygiene,' she added, as though we Austrians knew nothing of cleanliness.

I closed my eyes, blinking back the threatened tears. Margot had admonished me to be good. I must not be dismissed, not over something so silly.

'Then I shall cut the hair. But I shall cut. Not him,' I pointed to Mr Wrexham, now lurking behind the hulking table.

Mrs Ellsworth gave a curt nod. 'Very well. Give Elise your scissors, Mr Wrexham.'

He placed them on the table and slid them towards me. I stared at them, glinting as the light from the high windows fell across the blades. I knew Mrs Ellsworth and Mr Wrexham both watched me, doubting my nerve. Taking a breath, I seized the scissors and stalked to the door.

'Above the collar, Elise,' called Mr Wrexham.

I ran helter-skelter up the back stairs to my attic room and slammed the door. I perched on the end of the narrow bed, steel scissors on my lap. The dressing table mirror was tilted so that it reflected my pale face and tight mouth. Mr Wrexham had not unfastened my cap when attempting to cut my hair, and it remained pinned behind my ears.

With trembling fingers, I removed the lace, and then drew out each pin holding my long black hair. It tumbled in dark waves down my back and I ran my fingers through it, feeling the softness against my cheek. My hair, my one beauty. I was vain over nothing else. Margot used to tease me when we were small that I was a changeling. Anna and Julian could not be my real parents; they were too clever and beautiful and I was round and ugly and couldn't play music. I knew she lied. My black hair was the exact colour of Julian's. At bedtime when I was a child, he snuggled beside me on my bed, our two heads touching, dark as a night river, and he wrapped my long plait around his wrist while he recited stories. Once he whispered the tale of Samson and Delilah. Samson, the Hebrew prince, who ripped open a lion with his hands and pulled a comb of honey from its chest. Samson's strength was hidden in his straw-coloured hair, until Delilah came with her wine and her treachery and her scissors and cut her prince into a mortal. I stared at Julian with wide eyes, until he laughed and goosed me, but I could not understand the joke and promised him with childish solemnity, 'Like Samson I will not cut my hair.'

I picked up my brush. It had real boar bristles sewn into a sponge mounted on a mahogany paddle, a present from Anna for my birthday. I drew it through my hair, slowly teasing out the tangles and knots, until my hair shone in the gloom. Setting the brush aside, I parted my hair and plaited it for the last time. Staring into the mirror, I picked up the scissors and cut. I gasped, before I realised that it did not hurt. My braid was so thick, I had to hack and slice. After a minute, I sat staring at my plait lying discarded on the floor. I scooped it up and walked over to the wastebasket, but hesitated before tossing it in. I held a timeline in my hands: I had been growing my hair since I was nine years old. The feathery ends belonged to the plump child racing barefoot around the apartment, hiding from her sister. I'd played with Margot's porcelain doll and she pulled my hair so hard, my eyes watered. In revenge, I ran my fingertips along Hildegard's filthy floor rag and then stole into Margot's room and, opening her viola case, stroked my dirty fingers along the bow hair. When she came to play, the instrument shrieked a moment before Margot herself. I hid myself in the laundry room, feeling guilty about the damage to her viola bow and tried to appease my conscience by recalling the stinging pain of her pulling my hair.

I opened an empty drawer and, coiling the plait round, placed it inside. There was something faintly macabre about the detached hair lying in the cardboard container, but I could not quite bear to throw it away.

* * *

When I returned to the kitchen an hour later, eyes red from crying, Mrs Ellsworth was careful not to say a word. She pressed a mug of hot tea and a ginger biscuit into my hands and continued to fuss over her pastry. Recognising this token of kindness, I accepted the tea and tried to eat the biscuit, but it scratched my throat.

'Now, go through to the dining room. Remember to stand on the gentleman's left, just beside his elbow and keep your left arm folded behind you as you lean. Don't smile. Not that there's any danger of that,' she muttered, adjusting my cap and brushing a crease from my apron. 'Don't mind Mr Wrexham. He's not a bad man; he just likes things done in the old ways.'

Leaving the warm kitchen, pots bubbling, the sound of May banging pans from the scullery echoing behind me, I hurried along the passageway into the panelled hall. It was perfectly quiet and empty. I tried to remember which door led to the dining room. All were shut, and a series of wooden doors faced me on every side. I listened and hearing movement behind one, concluded that this was the dining room and slipped inside, looking for Mr Wrexham.

Mr Rivers leant over a billiard table, a tumbler of whisky beside him. I mumbled an apology and tried to slide out before he noticed me.

'Your hair.'

'What?'

'You cut your hair.'

'Excusing me, I must be finding Mr Wrexham.'

Mr Rivers lowered his billiard cue and took a step closer, reaching out as if to touch me, and then stopped, reaching for his whisky instead. He took a deep draught. Setting his glass down on the table, he gave a little wave, dismissing me. He adjusted his cue and leant low over the green baize, narrowing his eyes as he aimed for the white.

'Wrexham will be in the dining room. Second door on the right.'

I made to leave and then, hesitating, addressed him in a most un-parlour maid like manner.

'Why me, Mr Rivers? I know nothing where things are. There are dozen of advertising-ments in

Times newspaper every day. Why you hire me to be maid and not some other girl?'

He straightened, studying me for a moment and then smiled.

'I was glancing through the paper and saw that ridiculous message you'd placed—"I will cook your goose" or some such. It made me laugh.'

It struck me that Mr Rivers was an unusual man. I couldn't imagine many men hiring maids according to their comedic possibilities. He bent over the billiard table once again, lining up the red.

'Then, by chance I noticed your name—*Landau.* There's a curious novelist with the same name. Seemed an auspicious coincidence. Told Mrs Ellsworth to write to you. She's always complaining that it's impossible to find new staff.'

'Julian Landau?'

'Yes. You know of him?'

'He's my father.'

'Really?'

He stood up, setting his cue on the table, game forgotten.

'I've all his books. Come and see.'

I followed him into the library, where he pointed to a series of bound books, lined up in symmetrical rows above his desk. In the strange house, they appeared to me as old friends, and I felt the pleasure of recognition as I saw them. I supposed in a way my father had saved me—his books had brought me to Tyneford. I thought of Julian's new novel hidden away in the viola, and wondered when it would be bound in smart leather and join the others on the shelf.

'You may read them, if you like,' said Mr Rivers. 'They must make you think of home.'

I thanked him politely; Anna always said that a man with an excellent taste in literature was a man to be trusted.

Dinner passed without incident. I poured water and stacked plates and stood in the corner and was miserable. The two men sat at opposite ends of the dining table, separated by a desert of polished mahogany, so that all conversation had to be yodelled from one end to the other. Mr Wrexham shuttled between them, carrying trays of vegetables and pouring wine. I could not understand why they did not sit together at one end of the table like Julian and Anna did when they had no guests to entertain. It was absurd English manners and tradition over commonsense—if this was Mrs Beeton's advice, I didn't think much of it. Mr Rivers neither looked at me nor acknowledged my presence. His guest was a jowly man, with a red beard coating his double chins. They spoke of politics and war and Chamberlain, but I was too unhappy to eavesdrop. Mr Wrexham was pleased with my performance, and sent me up to bed with a cup of cocoa as a reward. I could not understand why the English used food to communicate. In Vienna Frau Finkelstein trained her pug with treats.

Upstairs in my attic room, I poured the dregs of cocoa out into the yard, watching it spatter down the brickwork. Pulling on my pyjamas, I settled onto the bed and drawing out a scrap of writing paper and a pencil began to compose a letter home.

Dear Margot (and Julian and Anna and Hildegard since I know you will all be reading this letter),

I have not yet had a chance to search for shells. They made me cut my hair. But please don't be sad. I look quite sophisticated. And thinner. I'm not sure which of these is best. I shall go to an excellent hairdresser in New York and have it properly trimmed, and then I shall look very fine indeed.

When do you leave for America? Do you all go together? Remember to send for me straight away. But don't worry—it is not terrible here, so much as dull—there is no one to talk to. I don't think the other servants like me very much. Mr Rivers is all right—he likes Papa's books. I love you all.

I read through the letter, which seemed to hold a lightness that I did not feel, pulled out the viola from its hiding place beneath my bed and cradled it in my arms.

'What's your story? Do you have a name yet? I think you are about a girl stranded on a rainy island. A girl with green eyes and a weakness for chocolate.'

In my mind I heard a snort, as Julian shook his head.

'I'd never write that sort of story. Not in a million years.'

I rattled the viola, listening to the stack of pages inside knock against the wood.

'Pirates, then, Papa. I hope there are pirates and a tall ship.'

Julian laughed, a deep rumble. *'Far too romantic.'*

'Give me a hint?' I pleaded to the imaginary Julian, and tried in vain to shake a page loose from its hiding place and out through the f-holes. It was

no use and I stashed the viola back in its case. I closed my eyes and pretended that I was at home in Vienna, listening to Hildegard fuss in the kitchen, while Anna and Julian slept across the hall. If I tried very hard, I could almost hear Julian snore.

I awoke in the middle of the night. I sat up in bed, listening to the unfamiliar creak and tick of the old house and feeling utterly alone. I needed comfort. In a daze I padded downstairs and into Mrs Ellsworth's larder. I reached up to the top shelf and helped myself to the elderflower syllabub left over from the gentlemen's desserts. Thinking back, I was lucky that no one caught me. Then, I did not consider my midnight snack as theft. I only wanted to gorge like I did at home, but the sweetness was sickly and unfamiliar. All this time later, the taste of syllabub is still the taste of homesickness and if, in early summer, I catch the scent of elderflower, I am nineteen again, sitting cross-legged on the larder floor, clasping a basin of creamy dessert, refusing to cry.

CHAPTER NINE

Kit

The next few days passed in a haze of polish. I dusted in my sleep and my clothes smelt of spilt vinegar. The only respite from loneliness was stolen minutes in the yard, feeding apple cores or lettuce scraps to Mr Bobbin. The yard was situated at the side of the house away from the sea, but I could hear the crash of the surf, while coarse marram grass sprouted at the edge of the cobbles. Each night I lay in bed listening to the water rush and smash on the rocks below, promising myself that in the morning I would walk down to the sea. Yet, when dawn came, I was always too tired, and wriggled under my blankets, desperate for another few minutes of sleep.

I had no free time. In the five minutes before dinner, when I was supposed to be washing my hands and face, I wandered into the yard. I fed the horse from my palm, feeling his warm breath upon my skin, and listened to the rhythmic grind of his large yellow teeth. He never made any noise but huffed out of his nostrils and bumped his stable door with his nose whenever he saw me. I realised that I was becoming like Art, my only friend having four legs, and decided it was imperative that I improve my English. Mr Wrexham was similarly determined although for a different motive: he had high hopes for me in the dining room. I must not speak, nor eavesdrop and yet I must be capable of impeccable English conversation. He thrust upon me *The Shorter Oxford English Dictionary in Two Volumes*, as well as *Debretts: Baronetage of England 1920.* He attempted to add Mrs Beeton to my pile, and his lip twitched in approval when I explained I already owned a copy.

'You would do well to study it, Elise. Devote one hour a day to the wisdom of Isabella Beeton. She writes for the lady of the house, but her insight is universal. Universal.'

I would have laughed at his familiarity with 'Isabella', whispering her name in the dreamy tones of an old lover, but I knew by now that Mr Wrexham was a man entirely without humour, who did not take kindly to the smiles of others. I stashed his books in the corner of my bedroom, resolving never to read them.

Early one morning in my second week, while cleaning the blue guest room, a sun-filled space with sky-coloured curtains, I encountered a stack of novels on the windowsill. They were clearly provided for the entertainment of female guests, set apart from the leather-bound volumes in Mr Rivers' library. I perched on the window seat overlooking the rolling lawns. It had been pouring for hours, and the gardens were soaked, the snapdragons and hollyhocks lay stooped and battered in the beds, but now a streak of sun made the wet grass glisten, while the black storm clouds raced across the hills like smoke from a band of dragons. The sky drifting above the sea was empty and pale blue. I longed to walk down to the beach, sit on the rocks and breathe gulps of salt air. I'd been inside the house for days, and I felt caged and cross. Picking out a novel with a tattered orange cover, I determined to escape for a couple of hours. I concealed the filched book at the bottom of my cleaning box, and disappeared up to my room to collect a volume of the *Oxford English*, before returning to the service corridor. I paused outside Mr Wrexham's open door. It was not yet eight o'clock, and he stood in his perfectly pressed tails, ironing Mr Rivers' newspaper. I entered in silence, peering around his elbow as I tried to read the headlines. I needed to find a way of obtaining the discarded papers; I'd been in Tyneford for nearly a fortnight and I was starved of news. Mrs Ellsworth had a wireless in her parlour, and allowed May and me to listen as a treat some evenings, but she only liked the light programmes. The old papers were meticulously stored in the butler's room, but I suspected that Mr Wrexham would class borrowing discarded newspapers from his room as theft. He did not approve of females taking any interest in politics; newspapers were the preserve of men, while only gentlemen were permitted opinions upon their contents.

'Mr Wrexham?'

He jumped, nearly dropping the iron.

'Elise! You almost made me scald Mr Rivers' *Times*.'

'I am most sorry, Mr Wrexham.'

'No, it's "I am *very* sorry". You must learn.'

'I am *very* sorry.'

He set the iron beside the stove in the corner. 'Almost. It's "v-very". Not a "w-wet wellington". Ah. Good, I see you have the dictionary.'

'Yes, I have the headache, Mr Wrexham. Please, I go and study English in fresh air?'

He scowled. 'But your duties?'

'I have cleaned guest rooms. Fires are laid. With air I be better by lunchtime.'

He hesitated, and then shrugged. 'Very well. One hour. But this is not to become a habit, mind. You need to be strong in service, yes?'

I nodded and gave a smile, which I hoped appeared sincere. 'Yes, I am strong girl.'

'Very well, then. Off you go.' He returned to ironing the newspaper.

I hesitated, and then cleared my throat. 'Mr Wrexham? I can put newspaper in morning room. I know. *Times* placed on side plate, headlines facing Mr Rivers.'

'Yes. All right. Don't crease it,' he said, handing

me the paper with reverence.

I scurried out of his room before he could change his mind, slowing down to a forbidden dawdle as soon as I left the servants' corridor, so that I had time to read the headlines.

Cabinet meet over Refugee Crisis . . . Unemployment Fears . . .

There was insufficient time for me to do anything but scan the first few lines, and I wanted to search inside for any snippets about Vienna. I ambled into the morning room and placed the paper on the side plate of the single place setting. Since my first night serving in the dining room, Mr Rivers had had no other guest. He appeared to live in the house in quiet solitude, save for the staff. He went into the study in the mornings, and then walked out each afternoon. The only regular caller was Mr Jeffreys, the estate manager, a gentleman invariably clad in muddy breeches and accompanied by a wagging red setter. I wondered why we scrubbed and polished the half-dozen guest rooms each day, when no guest ever stayed.

I lifted the front page of the paper, peeking for any scraps of news. I'd had no letter from Vienna since Margot's, and I was desperate for word. The brass clock on the mantelpiece chimed the hour and I scurried out, not wanting to be found rifling through the newspaper by Mr Rivers. It was a habit my father detested. 'A man's newspaper is his own. It's a thing of sanctity.'

I exited through the back door into the yard, but for once I did not pause to pet Mr Bobbin, even when he thudded his nose against the stable door to draw my attention. I hurried along the footpath leading off the beech grove, and headed towards the village. The hedgerows trickled with rain, and my shoes were instantly sodden from the dripping grass, but I did not care. For the first time at Tyneford, I was free, even if it was just for an hour. The track was slippery with liquid mud, gnats slapped into my face, and white butterflies flitted amongst the honeysuckle, which smelt sickly sweet in the damp air. I emerged in front of a cluster of houses and a neat row of stone shops: a bakery, a butcher's and post office cum general store, with a scarlet-painted letterbox set into the wall outside. Behind the shops lay a small church, built out of the same grey limestone, and in the distance the low bank of the Purbeck hills. The ancient roof and chimneystacks of the great house peeked out from above the beech copse like the masts of a command ship amongst the fleet of cottages.

From behind a netted window, an old woman sewed and stared. I smiled and she almost waved, before sealing the gap in the curtain. Several women in floral dresses, cardigans and galoshes walked past me and filed into the shop, the door clattering and brass bell jangling. Peeping through the glass frontage, I saw piles of boxes heaped on top of one another containing flour, polish, sugar, soap flakes, combs, chocolate, suet, envelopes, toilet tissue, bottles of rum and lemon cordial, paperback books, razor blades and balls of wool. I had never seen a shop so tightly packed; it appeared to sell everything, so that the customers were forced to clamber carefully over the stacked goods. In my pocket, I clasped a whole shilling (a reward for having helped Art scrub the interior of the Wolseley) and with only a slight twinge of guilt, I entered the shop. Five minutes later I rushed out, my pockets stuffed with three bars of chocolate.

The village nestled at the foot of the valley, the ring of hills enclosing it on three sides, and in front the grey sea stretched away into the horizon. I turned away from the clutch of houses and walked along the unmade road towards the beach. The tinkle of cowbells was carried on the wind, and filled the air with an eerie music. On the sloping hillside, two men in shirtsleeves selected pieces of flint from a large pile, stacking it into a curving wall to mark a new field boundary. A solitary rook perched on a gatepost, surveying their progress with lazy curiosity. As I walked further along the track it became rougher, too narrow for cart or car. The roar of the sea grew louder and I started to run.

In ten minutes, the village lay behind me and I reached the edge of the curving bay. Just above the tide-line lay a tumbledown hut, half concealed by bramble and blue sea-grass, like a fisherman's cottage in a story. It almost appeared to be growing out of the rock. An old man, his hair as white as dandelion feathers, sat on a lobster pot mending a piece of netting with a rusted knife. He looked strangely familiar, but I couldn't think where I had seen him before. I smiled and he gave me a curt nod before returning to his net. I scrambled over the rocks leading down to the beach, holding my books under one arm and trying not to drop them in the dirt. It was growing warm, and sweat made my top lip itch. Several fishing-boats lay propped upon the rocks beside a cobbled causeway out of the reach of the high tide. The painted bottoms were speckled with barnacles and stinking scraps of seaweed. Even from several yards away, I could smell the stench of fish.

Before me, the sea foamed and crashed upon the pebbles. The water cracked against the stones, and there followed a creak as the tide surged and the pebbles rattled and ground together. I glanced back at the cottage. The old man was busy with his lobster pots and no one else was to be seen. I squatted down and drew off my shoes and stockings, and with one last glance behind me, stripped off my skirt as well, weighting my clothes with the books. The breeze was cool, despite the early summer sunshine, and my skin prickled with goose bumps. Barefoot, I picked my way across the pebbles down towards the sea. The wet stones sparkled in the sunlight, while the wind whipped my short hair into my mouth, and I held it back with one hand, muttering crossly. When my hair had been long, I pinned it tightly and it did not flap into my eyes. As my toes touched the cold water, I let out a gasp. A chill tingled up and down my legs and I shrieked.

No one could hear me. I could shout and stamp and cry out and it did not matter. I waded out into the surf and banged my fists against my thighs, until they were stinging red. I shouted at the sea and my voice was lost.

I hate it here. I hate it. Hate it. Anna. Julian. Margot. Hildegard. AnnaJulianMargot. Annajulianmargotannajulmaanna . . .

I chanted their names over and over, until they became a pulp of sound and lost their meanings. Salt spray battered my face and I licked it away. I was tired of behaving and being silent. I wanted more words. Bad words. I tried swearing in German, remembering all the profanities I had heard Julian use, especially those that made Anna wince and mutter, 'Oh, darling.' Yet, it was oddly unsatisfying. I wanted English words. The more terrible, the more they would please me. I glanced back at the dictionary lying on the beach. Out of curiosity I had looked up some forbidden words. What was it? *Testes.* Yes, that must be a very dirty word. But I needed more. I must try and remember. I screwed up my eyes, and recalled a word I'd seen daubed in paint on a wall in London. Yes. I could almost see it. It was like the word belonging to those stinking shellfish in vinegar that Henry the footman had offered me. I filled my lungs with air and hurled my words at the sea.

'Testes! Testes and cockles!'

My cries were absorbed in the pounding of the surf. I looked up at the racing clouds and shouted again, so loudly that my voice cracked and rasped in my throat.

'Shit. Hell. Hate. Testes and cockles! Cockles.'

'Titties. Titties and fishcakes!'

I whirled around and saw a tanned young man, trousers rolled up to his knees, hopping across the rocks towards me. I stared at him, open-mouthed. He raised a hand in greeting and then dropped it as he reached my side.

'Oh, I'm sorry. Is it a private game? I rather fancied joining in.'

I was too startled to be embarrassed. I gaped at him. He must have been my age, perhaps a year or two older. He had dark blond hair, and had apparently not shaved this morning as his chin was coated in straw-coloured bristles. Margot would declare him a 'slovenly sort of person' while Anna always warned me to beware of young men who did not shave. A smile played around his lips. I was suddenly conscious of the fact that I was standing in the surf in my knickers. I tugged my woollen sweater down low to cover myself and without acknowledging his presence, turned around and stalked across the beach to my clothes. I sat down and quickly pulled on my skirt. He came and settled beside me. I shuffled away, leaving a space between us and picked up my books, placing them as a further barrier. He glanced at my defensive heap, clearly amused and turned to gaze out at the sea.

'I'm Christopher. Christopher Rivers. Though everyone calls me Kit.'

I looked at him in surprise. 'But you're not supposing to be coming till Thursday.'

'Well, it's Tuesday and here I am.'

'Mr Wrexham will be being most annoyed. He is liking to be prepared.'

'Wrexham is always annoyed. He was born cross. And goodness, your English really is dreadful.'

I shot him a furious glance, picked up my books and scrambled to my feet. He caught my wrist and tried to draw me back down. I wrenched my arm away from him, to my shame feeling tears prick my eyes.

'Let me go! Stop you.'

'I'm sorry. I'm only teasing. Honestly. I'm a bit of an idiot. Really didn't want to upset you. Here.'

He offered me a dirty handkerchief. I looked at it in disgust and he shoved it back into his pocket.

'See? Told you I was an idiot.'

I found myself repressing a smile. His hair fell across his eyes, and there was a large hole in the elbow of his navy sweater, which was rather endearing. Although, I suspected, he would not be short of girls eager to darn his sweaters, socks or anything else.

'You're working up at the big house?'

'Yes. I am Elise Landau. New house parlour maid.'

He fumbled inside his pocket and produced a damp packet of cigarettes. He placed one between his lips, and offered me another. I shook my head. Anna did not approve of young men smoking, especially before four in the afternoon. I tried to disapprove of Kit.

'Ah, yes. *Elise.* I know all about you. You're from Vienna. And I'm sorry to say, you're terrible at polishing silver. Oh, yes, and your father is the rather serious novelist Julian Landau.'

I stared at him in surprise, and he preened, clearly gratified by my reaction. I must learn to disappoint him. And it was all true—only the day before Mrs Ellsworth had reprimanded me for leaving polish residue on the silver and not buffing the spoons.

'You've read my father's books?'

Kit tried to light his cigarette. The matchbox was soggy and he tried several times before he finally discarded the sodden box and struck the match against a rock.

'No. I'm afraid I haven't. Though, now of course, I must.' He exhaled a puff of smoke. 'My father is an avid reader. And since he only reads very earnest, and I'm sorry to say, rather dull books, I must therefore deduce that your father's books are . . . serious.'

'They are most serious. And also . . .' I reached for the dictionary and thumbed through the pages, while Kit watched, 'profound.'

'Profound? Oh, well, in that case I rescind my

offer to read them. *Sporting Life* is as profound as I can manage.'

I laughed. 'You are not so stupid. I am very sure.'

'Not stupid, Elise. Idle.'

He leant back on his elbows in an elegant sprawl, and I found myself wishing my hair were still long. I felt awkward beside this English man-boy. Not wanting to seem childish, I sat back down, maintaining my careful distance. He pointed at the cliffs behind us—sandy brown and heather cropped. Tufts of coarse grass and purple thistle sprouted amongst the crumbling rock face. 'This is Worbarrow Bay. And that snout-shaped rock just there is the Tout.' Then he gestured to the sweeping curve of the beach, curling for a mile to a precipitous cliff of jagged yellow stone, which bookended the bay. He wriggled upright a little more and leant closer to me, so that I could follow the tip of his finger. 'And that is Flower's Barrow.'

I squinted, the round disc of the sun dazzling my vision, and saw a stark outline of rock on the pinnacle of the hill towering above the sea. Running back from it were grass ridges cut in sprawling rows, all trailing down the slope and back towards Tyneford. Kit closed his eyes and lay flat on the pebbles. 'Yes, you need a tour guide. And someone to teach you proper English.'

I scowled at his audacity. 'I have dictionary. And books to learn me.'

'Oh yes? What books?'

I pulled out the battered paperback from inside the dictionary and handed it to him, daring him to laugh. Kit opened one eye and studied the first instalment of the *Forsyte Saga* with a serious expression, and returned it to me, giving a helpless shrug.

'Well, you're quite right, Elise. I can't do better than that—the first family of England is not the Windsors but the Forsytes. I think we ought to read together.'

I looked at him, trying to discern whether he was teasing, but he shot me an easy smile. Only this morning, I had been silently bemoaning my loneliness and poor English. Lessons with Kit sounded fun.

'Yes. Very well, Mr Rivers.'

He rolled his eyes. 'My father is Mr Rivers. I told you, I'm Kit. Anyway, I'm going to call you Elise, although I must admit "Fraulein Landau" has a lovely ring to it. Stern and exotic all at once.'

I giggled and held up the book. 'Who is to read him first?'

'It. Not him. And I've read it. You shall read the adventures of the beautiful Irene and the dastardly Soames tonight and we'll discuss tomorrow.'

As I gathered up my books, I dropped my chocolate bars onto the ground. Kit rolled his eyes.

'Can't eat all of those. Give yourself a bellyache.'

I shrugged and stuffed them into my pocket, suddenly not wanting them at all. 'I must be travelling back to the house.'

Kit yawned, stretched and stood, offering me his hand and when I took it, he hauled me to my feet. 'I'll walk with you,' he said, and I found to my surprise I was glad.

We strolled past the pair of stone cottages, the old man still busy with his lobster pots. The space outside his hut was littered with nets, some tangled and torn waiting to be mended, others neatly folded. Kit waved to him.

'Morning, Burt.'

The old man looked up from his broken lobster pot and grinned at us.

'Mornin', Mister Kit.' Comin' boatin' soon?'

'Course. This afternoon if the weather holds.'

Burt shook his head. 'Nope. Rain comin' in later. Jist after luncheon's my guess. Tomorrow'll be fine. But Sunday's best.' He winked, and grinned at Kit showing a mouthful of bare gums, brown and pink like an earthworm. 'Yup. Sunday's the day. I can feel it.'

Kit studied the old man, appearing to read something in his expression. He thrust his hands in his pockets, and gave a curt nod, as though to mark he understood. 'Sunday then. And I'll bring Elise.'

'Righty ho.'

Burt bent his head back over his pots and we continued up the lane. The muddy surface was drying in the sunshine, and cloudy puddles formed in the dips.

'Did you recognise him?' asked Kit.

I frowned. 'He is seeming familiar but I cannot think . . .'

Kit laughed. 'He's Burt Wrexham. Wrexham the butler's elder brother.'

I thought about the two men and suddenly realised the likeness between them was striking: they could almost be twins. 'But they sound so different. Were they both birthed in Tyneford?'

'Yes, both born and bred here, sons of Dick the fisherman and Rose Wrexham—I suppose that made Rose a fishwife.' He gave a chuckle. 'They called their first son Burt, but Rose insisted on calling their second son Digby. Don't know why. Rumour has it that Lord Digby did her a kindness, picked her up in his coach when she was pregnant and walking back from market or something. Nonsense probably. But people here believe that the name Digby gave the younger Wrexham boy airs and graces. Aspirations above his station.'

I gave Kit a suspicious look.

'Oh, I'm permitted airs and graces. I'm a son and heir, you know.'

He held up his hands in mock surrender, giving me an innocent smile, before he paused to light another cigarette, puffing smoke happily into the breeze. 'Anyway, Digby Wrexham vanished from Tyneford on his thirteenth birthday—day he was supposed to be apprenticed to his dad. All Wrexham men are fishermen. But he came back five years later with no trace of his Tyneford accent and knocked on my grandfather's door and asked for a position as upper footman.'

I tried to imagine Mr Wrexham growing up in the tiny hut on the beach and running away so he wouldn't have to become a fisherman. I couldn't really understand it. Burt exuded contentment as he pottered in the sunshine, surrounded by his nets.

'He still goes fishing with Burt on his afternoon.'

I pictured Mr Wrexham perched at the bow of the small rowing boat in his black coat and tails, like an oversized seasick crow, and giggled.

We walked along the lime avenue and into the empty stable yard. The cobbles were almost dry, although a dribble of water trickled out of the pump and sluiced between the stones, forming a miniature river system.

'Wait,' said Kit, catching my arm. 'Your cap.'

I stood quite still as he adjusted my white maid's cap, squaring it neatly on my head. He brushed down my apron and picked a burr from my sleeve.

'There. Now Flo won't complain.'

'Flo?'

'Mrs Florence Ellsworth. Although I wouldn't recommend that you try calling her that.'

As I scurried through the back door and along the servants' corridor, I could hear Kit shouting after me, 'Hurry up and read about the Forsytes. Then we can start our English lessons.'

I raced up the stairs to my room under the eaves, shoving the books onto the dresser, and smiled for the first time in several days.

* * *

As I suspected, Mr Wrexham was exceedingly put out by Kit's unanticipated arrival. He was fully prepared for Kit's disembarking the 11:43 train from Basingstoke on Thursday morning. Art had been told to prepare the car; the appropriate brand of cigarette had been sent from London, *Sporting Life* had been ordered into stock at the general store, and additional marmalade taken down from the high shelves in the pantry. However, May was in the middle of washing the curtains in Kit's room, and presently they lay draped all around the scullery and laundry, and the room was not ready. If he had been able, Mr Wrexham would have reproached Kit, but since he could not, he made do with scolding me. He somehow connected Kit's early arrival with me, and though he could not quite deduce why, I was deemed responsible.

'These things should not happen. How is a butler to be prepared in such circumstance? And with such a small staff. It's not to be borne. Not to be borne.'

All my work was found to be at fault: the knives were dirty, the mirrors smeared and the fires did not draw properly. Mr Wrexham was so dissatisfied with my duties that he banned me from serving at dinner, a dishonour he was certain I must feel keenly. 'Go upstairs to bed early tonight, girl. Study your English and let us try to do better tomorrow.'

That night I lay on my bed watching the evening sky turn orange, then black, and wondered if I was disappointed to be banished from dinner. I was grateful to have another hour of freedom; usually I crept into bed wanting nothing but sleep. Yet I experienced a pang of disappointment at the thought that I would not see Kit again until tomorrow. And perhaps not even then: I knew from watching Anna's operas that foreign gentlemen were inevitably fickle and not to be trusted. And yet, life at Tyneford already seemed less awful than it had that very morning when I had raged at the sea. When I thought of Kit, I felt a fulsome glow in my belly, as though I had eaten a large helping of Hildegard's goulash and dumpling stew.

CHAPTER TEN

FISH AND A ROSE-PATTERNED TEACUP

Kit's presence seemed to breathe life into the old house. Everyone woke up: the daily housemaids dusted each nook with fanatical care, humming as they rubbed beeswax onto the stone floors or beat the ancient rugs with hazel brooms. It was as though the manor and its inhabitants had been covered with an invisible dustsheet and Kit had shaken it off. The scent of Mrs Ellsworth's baking pervaded the service corridor and wafted into the musty hall. Mr Wrexham retreated into a dark pantry that I hadn't known existed, and began to fill cauldrons with water pulled from the spring in the kitchen garden. He appeared to have forgiven Kit his premature arrival as first thing after breakfast the pair disappeared into this pantry. Sounds of bubbling emitted from behind the closed door, while sweet yeast-filled steam trickled from underneath the seam. Even May seemed less resentful of my presence, going as far as to offer me a humbug from a newspaper twist.

I did not speak to Kit again until Saturday. During the week I tried to linger outside the pantry, waiting for him to emerge but Mrs Ellsworth pounced, hurrying me away with a list of chores as endless as Penelope's web. Every moment was occupied with tasks and Mr Wrexham did not choose to reinstate my privilege of waiting at the dinner table. But on Saturday morning, as I cleaned the sitting room windows, I glimpsed Kit pacing on the lawns with his father, their heads bowed in earnest conversation. Deliberately ignoring Mrs Ellsworth's instructions to withdraw from view, I watched the two men. Mr Rivers' face was grey and he looked tired and unhappy. Kit turned away from his father, his expression blank and unreadable. He saw me watching from the window and met my gaze for a second, before walking back towards the house. I continued to stare, cleaning forgotten, as Mr Rivers paced upon the grass, and then disappeared down the path leading to the sea. It occurred to me that Mr Rivers was the only member of the household apparently unmoved by Kit's arrival. The porch door banged, and a second later Kit himself appeared in the sitting room, treading damp footprints across the polished floor. I frowned, ready to reproach him and then remembering my place, bit my lip, but he must have seen my look of displeasure. 'Sorry. I'll take them off.'

I stared at him, saying nothing as he sat down in the middle of the floor and removed his shoes. He padded across the room in his socks to where I stood beside the windows clutching my rag and, opening the glass wide, threw out his shoes so that they sailed through the air, landing on the lawn with a thud-thud. He slammed shut the casement.

'There. I'm sorry.'

He smiled warmly, eyes blue and beseeching. 'Did you meet the Forsytes?'

It took me a moment to realise that he meant the paperback novel hidden beneath my pillow.

'I have not had time,' I said, standing stiffly beside a worn sofa. I had intended to read the book every night, but the moment I climbed into bed, I slipped into an exhausted sleep.

He sank into an easy chair and swung a leg over the armrest, revealing a large hole in his sock. A toe peeped through.

'Oh.' He sounded so sad, as though my not reading the book were a personal rejection.

'I am wanting to read. But I am finding so very busy.'

'Oh, all right. But try and hurry up.'

I studied Kit for a second, wondering if I'd ever been so impatient with Hildegard. Probably. I was always tired now. Every morning, I woke up with May banging on my door, wishing I could go back to sleep. I liked cleaning the large drawing room, as I could sit down on the Persian rug behind the sofa and daydream. If Mr Wrexham or anyone else came in, I was concealed from view and if discovered could pretend I was polishing the brass feet of the sofa or a mark on the parquet floor. 'So will you come?'

'I'm sorry? Beg pardon.'

Lost in thought, I hadn't heard a word Kit had said.

'Church tomorrow.'

I swallowed, and instinctively ran my hand through my hair. 'I cannot. I do not go to church.'

Kit sat up straight in the overstuffed armchair. 'Just this week. I promise it will be fun.'

'Fun?' I thought it odd that church was so different to synagogue; the few occasions I had been dragged along by the great-aunts, I'd been dazed with boredom. On Yom Kippur, with the ban on teeth brushing, I'd spent all day avoiding the sour stench of the old ladies' breath, ducking to avoid kisses.

'Yes. Fun. Don't come all the way in. Stand by the door, just this once. Trust me.'

'I think about it.'

The door swung open and Mr Wrexham stood in the doorway. Seeing me in conversation with Kit, his eyes narrowed with displeasure. I picked up my cleaning box and hurried out into the hall.

'You are not to talk to Mr Kit.'

'He speaking first.'

Mr Wrexham frowned. 'Yes, well. Mr Kit is most good-natured. They must not see you cleaning. It's improper. Next time, you make your apologies and exit.'

'Yes, Mr Wrexham.'

The butler and housekeeper were quite determined the illusion be maintained that the house was cleaned by magic or elves. Fires should be laid and lit, curtains opened and closed, floors swept, rugs cleaned, silver polished, pictures dusted but the act of cleaning must never be seen. I found it very odd. Even Hildegard and our maids in Vienna scrubbed in our presence. Hilde especially huffed and puffed and muttered as she went. She was neither silent nor invisible.

Mr Wrexham drew me into the corner of the hall, speaking in a low voice. 'Elise, post arrived for you. It was a little late this morning. The fault of a flat bicycle tyre, I believe. So, if you wish, you may come to my little ro—'

He stopped mid-sentence, face setting into his passive butler's smile, as Kit wandered into the hall in his socks.

'How's the brew this morning, Wrexham?'

'Coming along most pleasingly, sir. Would sir like to come and taste?'

Kit grinned at me. 'Wrexham is a dark horse, Elise. He's a master brewer. Makes the best beer in Dorset.'

'Sir is very kind.'

Kit checked his watch. 'Ten fifteen. A good time to sample the latest batch. Want to taste, Elise?'

Mr Wrexham's smile remained firmly pinned. 'Elise has a great deal of work this morning.'

Kit shrugged, and began to follow Mr Wrexham out of the hall and along the service corridor leading to the back pantry. I watched them for a second, and then, not caring if I was to be scolded later, called out, 'Mr Wrexham?'

He froze and turned around, fixing me with a look of cold displeasure.

'My letter? Please. My letter.'

'I am with the young gentleman, Elise. Remember your manners.'

His voice held a note of warning, but Kit was oblivious.

'Oh give Elise her letter, Wrexham. The beer can wait a minute.'

I felt a rush of gratitude towards Kit, even though I knew the butler would be furious with me later.

'Very well,' said Mr Wrexham, without looking at me.

We walked along the service corridor in silence, until we reached his room. I waited outside, while Kit continued along to the beer pantry. Mr Wrexham slipped inside, retrieving not one but two letters propped upon a plain side table beside the door. Wordlessly, he passed them to me.

'Thank you.'

I shoved them into my apron pocket and started to back away, desperate to disappear upstairs and read in peace.

'Wait,' commanded Mr Wrexham. 'Take this polish and these cloths. The china in the library is in urgent need of cleaning. I will inspect it before lunch. I expect perfection. I would strongly suggest that you put these upstairs, and read them later.'

Stifling a sigh, I bowed my head. As I glanced up, I met Kit's sympathetic eye. He lurked in the gloom of the corridor, just out of Mr Wrexham's sight. Thankfully, this time he said nothing, apparently realising that any more interference on my behalf would only incense the butler further. Having absolutely no intention of setting aside the letters for later, I took the cloths and scurried to the library, grateful that Mr Rivers was out on one of his walks and I could be assured of solitude.

The library was situated in the north wing of the house, the drive and porch outside one window, and the front lawns outside the other. Unless Mr Rivers was present, the curtains were kept drawn to protect the fragile bindings of the ancient books. The sea air, so beneficial for rude human health, corroded the Rivers' family library, so that when some of the books were opened the pages sloughed away to nothingness. I once ran my finger along a leather spine and a layer of crimson flaked away onto my skin. Mrs Ellsworth instructed me to burn pinecones in the grate each morning and dip candles in lavender oil, but the fragrance of musty books pervaded. The daily housemaids detested the room, complaining it was 'duckish dark an' puts us all in a bother', and I earned their profuse gratitude when I offered to take over its cleaning. I liked the proximity of Julian's novels, and I found the permanent twilight soothing rather than eerie and I liked it best at dusk. Then I would trim the scented candles while the orange sun lowered in the west, making the spines of the books appear to blaze for a minute and then dull, as the sun slipped behind the shadow of the hill.

I knew Kit and his beer would keep Mr Wrexham busy, and Mrs Ellsworth was busy preparing luncheon, so I had a few minutes to read my letters. I borrowed the silver letter knife from the Victorian desk and settled on the hearthrug. I opened the one with the earliest postmark first. It was inscribed with Margot's breathless scrawl.

> *Tomorrow Robert and I leave for America. I hadn't wanted to leave until Mama and Papa's visa arrived and we could all go together, but Papa had a talk with Robert and afterwards they both insisted that we must take the next boat. I cried and so did Mama but the two men ganged up on us. So please don't be worried if you don't hear from me for some time as I will be on the boat and then I don't know how long it will be till I can write again oh Bean how I miss you and how much worse it will all be when I am away from Hilde and Mama and Papa and even the aunts. I wish we could stay as it must all blow over soon and even Mama says so and I don't want to go so far away and surely they will be only a month behind. I hope all is well with you and try not to eat too much.*

The ink was smudged with what I could only assume were Margot's tears. I took a deep breath, feeling a little sick. My sister was always the one prone to hysteria, or what Julian called the 'artistic temperament' (since I was not an artist of any kind, my own moods were classified as childish immaturity). If Julian wanted her to leave, there must be a good reason for it. And Robert had been fired from the University a week after the *Anschluss*, and there was a well-paid job waiting for him in California. It made no sense for them to stay in Vienna any longer. We would all return in a year or two, until then there was no point in being sentimental. I gave a snort—when had I become so practical? My family would not recognise me.

I reached for the next letter, postmarked one week later than Margot's.

Thank you for your telegram. But next time you write, you must use our new address. Your father, Hildegard and I left the apartment in Dorotheegasse for a smaller one in Leopoldstadt. Please don't be upset, or worry about us in the least. The new place is bright and pleasant and much more sensible for the three of us. With you girls gone, Julian and I were rattling around in such a big place. We are really very cosy.

All is well here. We miss you and Margot, even grumpy Robert, to tell the truth. But we are very glad that you are safe. You shouldn't worry—I don't think they are interested in old people like us. You must write and tell me what the English countryside is like. I've heard that it is very beautiful. I hope the food is all right, even if it's not up to Hilde's standards. You are not to get skinny.

Your loving mother,
Anna Julie Landau

I slid the letter back into my apron pocket, unease gnawing at me. Anna, Margot and I always told each other everything but Anna's letter clamoured with things unsaid. Why had they moved? Surely, with their American visas coming so soon, they could have waited a few weeks. I didn't like being unable to picture my parents. Usually I thought of them in my childhood home: Julian scrawling in his study, Anna returning pink-cheeked from the shops, laden with parcels wrapped up in striped paper. Now I didn't know how to think about them. Instead of a picture, there was blankness.

*   *   *

That afternoon, Mr Wrexham instructed me to serve tea to the gentlemen on the terrace. He clearly felt that this was a treat I did not deserve, but Kit had requested the beer be bottled in time for lunch on Sunday and while I ought to be punished for my cheek ('requesting a letter and delaying the young master is a household crime—their needs above yours, every time, missy') he could not risk inconveniencing the gentlemen. I might be in disgrace, but tea must not be late.

I stood in the kitchen, holding the vast tea tray, willing my arms not to shake as Mrs Ellsworth placed upon it the china teapot and strainer, a kettle of hot water, milk jug, scones, clotted cream, raspberry jam, a plate of lemon peel biscuits, and a pile of salmon and cucumber sandwiches. Henry the footman accompanied me, opening all the doors, guiding me through the Tudor porch and finally out onto the terrace.

'You all right from here, Elise?' asked Henry.

'Yes, thank you.'

The footman vanished inside. Mr Rivers and Kit sat on cast iron chairs, before a white-painted table. Kit was smoking, flicking ash into a terracotta flowerpot. His father ignored him and pretended to read his newspaper. I knew he was not actually reading as his routine was invariable: breakfast and the headlines at eight fifteen, afterwards, open the day's post and study the news until ten thirty. The paper was always ready to be placed on the pile in Mr Wrexham's study before lunch. As I placed the tray on the table and re-arranged the spoons, I wondered why Mr Rivers did not wish to talk to Kit.

I picked up a rogue sugar-lump with the tongs and plopped it back into the bowl, hoping neither gentlemen noticed. Mrs Ellsworth had given me very precise instructions on how tea must be served, and only when I had practised the routine twice without fault on her and May was I given permission to serve the gentlemen. I set a porcelain cup before Mr Rivers and Kit, placing a tiny silver spoon on the edge of each saucer at two o'clock; then, picking up the teapot, I stood on the left-hand side of Mr Rivers.

'Tea, sir?'

'Yes, please, Elise. Pour away.'

I sloshed tea into the cup, decided it was a touch dark and added a splash of hot water from the silver kettle.

'Sugar?'

'Ah, no thank you.'

I looked at Kit. I wasn't sure how to address him in his father's presence. He smiled at me lazily from across the table.

'Yes please and two sugars,' he said, saving me the embarrassment.

In less than a minute, there were two steaming cups of tea, without a drip spilt in either saucer, and plates laid with scones and jam. I felt rather pleased with myself.

'Anything else, sir?'

Mr Rivers lowered the paper, folding it in half and setting it down on the table. I eyed it greedily, hungrier for news than for any of Mrs Ellsworth's cakes.

'No thank you. That will be all.'

As I picked up the tray, ready to return it to the kitchen, Mr Rivers took a sip of tea. A split second later he spat it out. A mouthful of leaves swam in the saucer. I'd forgotten to use the strainer. My hands flew to my cheeks in horror.

Kit laughed out loud, and took a glug of his, swallowing it with a shudder. 'Ah, so this is how they drink tea in Vienna, yes? Trying to teach us some manners?'

'I'm so sorry, Mr Rivers,' I said, attempting to grab the cup from him.

Mr Rivers smiled and gripped the teacup firmly; there was a crack and the handle snapped off. I looked at him, and then at the fragile rosebud handle in my fingers and wondered if it would be bad manners to cry.

'I'm a terrible maid,' I said, eyes downcast.

'Honestly, we've had much worse. Here,' Kit passed me a handkerchief, clean this time. 'It really doesn't matter.'

Mr Rivers gently prised the broken handle from me.

'Please, of all the silly things to be upset by. The truth is, neither Kit nor I even like taking tea. It's Mrs Ellsworth who insists upon it.'

'Yes,' said Kit. 'Even father's afraid of Flo.'

I couldn't help but smile. Mr Rivers stood up and tossed out the contents of both cups onto the grass, leaving a black smudge of tea leaves.

'I'll tell Mrs Ellsworth that I broke it. I can take her scolding, I assure you,' he said with a glance towards Kit.

'Thank you,' I said.

'We'll ring if we need anything else,' said Mr Rivers kindly, dismissing me.

'Yes, sir.'

I'd seen the other girls perform a little bob or half curtsy as they said this, but I couldn't bring myself to do it. Julian had taught me to bow to no man. The Emperor was dead, the Empire rightly disbanded, and in a republic no one was greater or lesser than anyone else. I wondered how he reconciled this with Hilde washing his socks and making his breakfast and drawing his bath, but decided these were disloyal thoughts when Julian was not able to defend himself.

On hearing the tinkle of the service bell, I returned to the terrace to discover that Mr Rivers had gone, and Kit sat alone. His food remained untouched, but a pile of spent cigarettes lay in a small heap beside his chair. I piled the tea things back onto the tray, trying not to clatter too loudly.

'How is your family?' he asked.

'Most well, thank you. They have moved to a smaller apartment.'

I swallowed and licked my dry lips. 'Kit?'

'Yes, Elise?' He raised an eyebrow.

'I am very much liking to read Mr Rivers' paper *Times*. I am having no news of Vienna. When he is finishing, maybe I can be reading? And also good for my English improvements.'

He smiled. 'Of course. I shall ask Father. He won't mind.'

'Thank you very much.'

Kit waved away my gratitude and flicked a stray crumb from the table.

'Come to church tomorrow. Take your mind off

things. It's nothing to do with God, I assure you. It's to do with fish.'

'Fish?'

'Yes. See, now you're intrigued, but you'll only find out if you come.'

'Fine. I shall come if Mr Wrexham permits it.'

Kit snorted. 'Course he will. Chance to convert a Jew. He'll be perfectly delighted.'

CHAPTER ELEVEN

Balaam and Balak

Kit was quite correct. Mr Wrexham had to refrain from rubbing his hands together with glee when I informed him the following morning that I wished to attend the Sunday service with the other servants.

'Ah, good. I'm gratified Mr Kit persuaded you. That boy has a pure soul.'

I remained silent, confident that my presence in church had nothing to do with anybody's soul.

I was sent upstairs to find a hat, but on discovering my pink cloche cap flattened at the bottom of the wardrobe, I tied a silk scarf over my hair instead. Margot always used to tease me that in a headscarf I resembled one of the frumpy Yiddish housewives arrived from shtetls in the east. They jostled in unhappy gaggles before the counter in the Jewish deli, jabbering in their rough German. We were embarrassed by these peasant Jews, who had nothing to do with us. At school, they kept to themselves at the other side of the playground, huddling in their brown wool coats and crude headscarves while Margot, I and the other bourgeois, assimilated Austrian Jews, played tag with the Catholics and giggled at them from afar. But according to Margot I was secretly one of them; even in Hermès I looked like I ought to be selling potatoes.

By the time I returned downstairs, the household had already left for the small church at the foot of the hill. This suited me fine; I preferred to walk alone, free from Mr Wrexham's litany of behavioural suggestions, and it also meant I could linger by the door, without pressure to sit with the others. I did not want to venture all the way inside and I would not pray.

I remember that Sunday with absolute clarity—it was one of those perfect June mornings that make one certain Eden was a summer's day in southern England. The bells rang out across the hillside, chiming with the tinkle of the sheep bells in the field beside the churchyard. Swallows zoomed across the empty sky, while on a stone wall a black cat watched yellow ducklings dabble on the pond with greedy eyes. I took a deep breath and filled my lungs with summer. The air was laced with the fragrance of a thousand wild flowers and the sunlight made the snapdragons and foxgloves in the cottage gardens shine vermillion pink. The entire countryside was smeared with colour; the sky a bold throbbing blue and beneath it the meadows sprinkled with buttercups, shining like gold coins. Back then I didn't know the names of the flowers—they came later—but now instead of patches of orange and yellow petals, I recall cowslips and creeping jenny. In the distance the sea sparkled and glittered, white spray crashing on the shore. It was tempting to forgo church entirely and disappear to the beach, but knowing this would only get me into trouble with Mr Wrexham and Mrs Ellsworth I hastened through the churchyard. I hesitated beside the oaken door leading into the nave. The congregation crowded in tight rows, singing a dreary hymn, and Mrs Ellsworth's large black hat, perched on her head like a bedraggled rook, was visible above the swaying mass. At the front on a raised pew stood Mr Rivers and Kit.

I waited at the back, propped against the cool lime-washed wall, keeping my lips tightly sealed. I would not sing. What would Julian or Anna think if they knew I was here? I felt my cheeks redden and was nearly resolved on slipping away, when Kit caught my eye and smiled. It was a look of pure delight. To my amazement, he appeared genuinely glad that I had come. I decided I must stay, if only for fifteen minutes.

I half-closed my eyes and listened to the soft drone of the vicar as he mumbled through prayers and parish notices. He was a balding man in a long black frock-coat and white cassock, and seemed ill at ease as he stood muttering beside the altar. There was a faint scent of mothballs mingling with the damp in the church, as though the men and women were all dressed in outfits stored at the back of wardrobes for six days a week. The service was every bit as tedious as my rare visits to synagogue, and I felt oddly reassured. I did not find God or his worship spectacular in any language or incarnation. On a shelf in his study Julian kept a hand-painted Indian prayer book, containing hundreds of fantastical illustrations edged in gold; blue-skinned gods with many hands cavorted across yellow cities or hunted howling tigers through green forests. I suspected that even if I should attend one of the exotic Hindu services with incense and marigolds and blue gods, I would still be bored. I surveyed the parishioners, and while a few studied the vicar with careful concentration, most fiddled with their prayer books or stared up at the open window, where a butterfly with brown and purple wings fluttered in a draught, frantic for an escape. In the backmost pew, Burt and Art engaged in a surreptitious game of cards. When a particularly loud chorus of 'Amens' distracted Art, Burt slid an ace of clubs into his trouser pocket and shot me a conspiratorial wink.

I fidgeted, toying with the ends of my silk scarf, and swallowed a yawn. I couldn't understand why Kit had told me to come, and was just about to slip away when I noticed a girl at the front of the church with red hair. She wore no hat or head covering of any kind and her long hair fell down her back in scarlet waves, like a blood-red sea. She stood in the row directly behind Kit, and he swivelled around to whisper some secret, holding up his prayer book beside his mouth so no one else could eavesdrop. She giggled and blinked. I decided to stay.

The congregation grew restless and Burt and Art each tucked his cards inside his jacket. As I watched, I realised that every man was silently unfastening his tie or cravat, shoving it into a pocket or handing it to his wife. There was a low hum of anticipation. Now, every set of eyes watched the vicar. He was patently aware of his parishioners' sudden focus, and beads of sweat began to trickle down his forehead, and he stumbled over the next prayer. The people were coiled, drawn back like the hissing tongue of a snake, and I was glad to be beside the door. The vicar tottered towards a vast leather tome laid open on a wooden lectern, brushing his damp brow with the back of his hand. He cleared his throat twice, his voice catching as he began to speak.

'Today's lesson is from Numbers . . .'

There was a collective intake of breath.

'Balaam . . .'

All the men in the congregation rose to their feet.

'. . . and Balak'.

At the word 'Balak' all the men ran towards the door. I flattened myself against the wall as they sprinted past me, heart beating wildly, terrified that I would be carried away in the throng and trampled. The noise of fifty pairs of hobnail boots clattering along the stone flagstone reverberated around the small church. Suddenly I felt fingers entwined in mine, as Kit hissed in my ear, 'Come on!'

He tugged me outside into the river of sprinting men. I saw he also clutched the hand of the redheaded girl. I narrowed my eyes and started to run.

We rushed down towards the sea, the stony path echoing with the sound of a hundred pounding feet. As we reached the beach, two fishing-boats bobbed frantically on the waves, while men gathered beside half a dozen more, heaving against them with broad shoulders and staggering forwards to the surf.

'Mr Kit, come!' called a voice.

I turned to see Burt hollering from outside his hut, where a small blue- and white-painted boat rested on a wooden platform.

'Help me push 'er down,' commanded Burt.

We scrambled back up the rocks and Kit, the girl and I heaved at the small boat. She was cripplingly heavy, and I nearly crumpled under her weight. The next moment I felt the load lighten and saw a broad young man with sandy hair pushing at the bow of the boat.

'Git away Poppy, yer'll hurt yerself,' he said to the girl. 'Yoos too,' he added, with a nod in my direction.

We stepped back and watched the three men dash down to the surf, dragging the small fishing-boat, feet sinking into the pebbles like mud. They waded out into the water, trousers instantly black wet, the boat tossing in the breakers.

'Well, are you coming?' Kit yelled.

The redhead grabbed my hand and hauled me along the beach to the boat. She hitched her skirt up high, tucking it into her knickers, and pulling off her shoes tossed them onto the deck. I raised my dress up over my thighs, but drew the line at tucking it into my underwear. She leapt in, shaking her head as the tall man offered her a hand. I tried to do the same, and crashed into the wooden side, bruising my shins. The next moment, I felt hands around my waist, and found myself being thrown into the boat head first, like a catch of fish. Kit jumped in beside me.

'Sorry about that. No time for grace.'

He grabbed an oar and pushed off the beach, as the other men hoisted a battered brown sail.

'See? Aren't you glad you came?' Kit demanded.

I sat in a puddle on the bottom of the boat, my shin trickling with blood and did not answer.

'Oh, and this is Poppy,' he said, gesturing to the girl with scarlet hair. 'And that's Will.'

The young man gave a lopsided smile and raised a hand, before continuing to adjust the rigging.

'Didn't yer forget summat?' asked Burt, his voice holding a note of reproach.

'Ah yes. This great old gal,' Kit tapped the wooden mast, 'is *The Lugger.*'

Poppy sidled up beside me. 'Did he even tell you what today is?' she asked with a dark glance in Kit's direction.

I shook my head dumbly.

'He's such a beast. You must think us all barbarians.'

'It's to do with fish?'

'Yes. This is the first day of mackerel season. We go out looking for mackerel as soon as the vicar tells the story of "Balaam and Balak".'

'We could be startin' any time in June, mind,' said Burt, appearing from behind the sail. 'Jist isn't so much fun.'

'Yes. Running out of church really upsets the vicar,' said Kit. 'And it adds a certain sense of occasion.'

'Sawed a shoal this mornin'. Far out in Worbarrow. We'll head for there,' said Burt.

The Lugger was the last boat to launch, and all around us small fishing vessels joggled up and down on the waves. Some were already so far out that they appeared to be toy-sized, white sails like folded pocket-handkerchiefs. Above us the sky was streaked with herringbone clouds, while the green-blue sea stretched away into the horizon, curving around the earth. Salt spray battered my cheeks, and the wind lifted my headscarf and made Poppy's hair writhe, Medusa-like.

'Durst yer worry,' said Burt, pointing to the other

boats. 'They doesn't know nothin'. I don't git much but I does git fish. Ready about.'

Everyone ducked instinctively. Everyone except me. I was whacked cleanly on the back of the head as the boom whipped across *The Lugger*. I crumpled into the bottom of the boat, pain exploding at the base of my skull.

'You idiots!' Poppy screamed. 'She doesn't know what to do.'

She crouched beside me, wrapping her skinny arms around my shoulders. I felt dazed and a little sick, and wished she'd let go.

'Leave her be, Poppy. Give her a minute, she'll be fine,' said Kit, coming closer. 'You will be fine, won't you?' he said, eyeing me cautiously.

'If the girl is goin' ter up-chuck, over the side please an' I thank yer,' said Burt.

I lay down in the bottom of the hull, feeling the throbbing pain subside.

'Yes. She's all right,' said Kit. 'Her colour's coming back.'

He helped me sit up and ushered me to the bow, giving me a pile of sail covers and coiled lines to settle on.

'If someone says "ready about"—you duck. "Jive oh". Duck. "Bugger it". Duck. Understand?' asked Kit.

I nodded and then instantly regretted it, as my head started to pound. But despite the pain, I smiled. I had never been out on a boat before. The crossing on the ship from France did not count. I had sat hunched on my trunk in the belly of the liner, unable to see out, retching quietly into a paper bag. This was different. Grey-backed gulls and black cormorants circled us, hurling their whooping cries into the wind. I found that I rather liked the rocking sensation as the boat dipped up and down across the waves. The rushing air and pounding saltwater made me forget everything but the sound of the sea and the call of the gulls. I shrieked as a wave crashed over the bow, soaking me, and thinking it was a game Poppy, Will and Kit joined in, shouting for joy.

'Look,' said Burt, pointing to a dark shadow beneath the surface of the water. Above, a flock of gulls circled and swooped. 'Ready about.'

I squatted down, covering my head with my hands as the boom clattered across. The small boat hurtled towards the dark patch of sea, signalling wildly to the other fishing vessels. I hadn't realised, but we'd turned around and were heading back into shore, racing alongside the shadow in the sea. Will and Kit ladled stinking bait over the side, and the water writhed with glittering fish.

'Take the tiller,' said Burt, and Poppy took over the helm while he began to unfurl a net heaped at the stern. Another fishing-boat was now only twenty yards away, sailing parallel to us. Burt whistled, and a shrill echo came back.

'Yup. *Brandy Queen* is a comin'.'

The other boat tacked and sailed right towards us, and as it reached us, almost brushing the side, Burt tossed one end of the net to a bearded fisherman. He caught it effortlessly and as *Brandy Queen* turned again, Burt spooled his end of the net into the water, trapping the fish. *Brandy Queen* and *The Lugger* hovered where the bay began to shelve, waiting. Then the other boats swarmed us in a rush, oars thrashing, men shouting, all driving the mackerel into the shallows and the great stretched net, and away from the safety of the deep. The vast net now encircled the black shoal of fish, but they lay motionless in the water as *Brandy Queen* and *The Lugger* dragged them closer and closer to the shore. Waiting on the beach stood the rest of the village, dozens of women and children, all changed from their Sunday best into work clothes, and now poised to help gather in the catch. Along the narrow path leading to the shore, a caravan of wagons trundled down to the sea.

'Coastguard telegraphed the mackerel dealers,' said Kit.

'Won't be too happy ter be dragged away from Sunday lunch,' said Burt. 'But s' goin' ter be a goodun, I got a tingle in my toes.'

The Lugger was almost on the beach when the sea exploded. Rainbow fish leapt out of the water, breaking the surface in a thousand places, turning the shallows into a swirl of white foam. The sunlight caught the shining backs of the mackerel and they glittered red and brown and green and black. The gulls shrieked and dove, catching wriggling fish in their beaks as the women and children beat them away with brooms and sticks. Women surged forward, splashing into the sea in their clothes and grabbing the nets, as men bounded from the boats to help. The sea was alive with dancing, flapping fish, and they soared into the air in high curves before crashing back into the waves. Fifty people lined the shore, clutching the heavy net, and heaving it inch by inch up the pebbles and onto the shelving beach.

The fish sprawled on the strand, twitching in the sunlight, while bare-legged children raced up and down, hurling stones to keep away the gulls and greedy cormorants. Everyone was there: Mr Wrexham and Mrs Ellsworth lobbed pebbles at the birds; May chattered to a fisherman, tugging half-heartedly at the net. Mr Rivers helped haul it into the breakers so that the seawater washed over the fish, keeping them fresh until the dealers could load them into their ice carts. He had removed his tie and rolled up his shirtsleeves, and stood barefoot in the shallows, trousers soaked to the knee. Seeing Burt's boat, he waded deeper, and grabbed the painter.

'Shall I pull you to shore?' he asked.

'Aye,' said Burt. 'Them ladies durst want a soakin'.'

Kit climbed out to help his father, and the two men towed *The Lugger* through the water away from the mackerel, before dragging her a few yards up the beach. Poppy hopped out with ease and raced back along the beach to the netted fish. Mr Rivers offered me his hand, and helped me clamber onto the pebbled shore.

'Well, I expect this is something you don't see every day in Vienna.'

'No sir.'

'And, Elise, I shall inform Wrexham that you have permission to read my newspaper.'

Before I could thank him, shouts boomed behind us, as the mackerel dealers swarmed the beach.

'Excuse me,' said Mr Rivers. He turned away and jogged along the strand to the cluster of dealers, gesturing to the catch with a broad smile. A moment later, Kit joined him. The two men shook hands with each dealer in turn and appeared to listen patiently, before shaking their heads and pointing back to the haul.

'Gooduns, them,' said Burt. 'Squire Rivers and Master Kit will make sure as a spring tide that we gits a good price. Dealers haggle us ter hell, won't dare wi' Squire.'

An agreement appeared to be reached, hands were shaken once more, and as Kit whistled, men, women and children rushed to the mackerel and began piling them onto stretchers, into buckets and barrels and ferrying them onto the dealers' carts. The sound of the gulls was deafening. I soon lost count of the number of loads I helped to carry. Poppy and Will sprinted up and down with endless hauls, never seeming to tire. Among the dozens of bobbing heads, Poppy stood out like a single holly berry in a basket of hazelnuts. I felt brown and dull with my cropped hair. Some of the carts were able to edge down onto the pebbles, and as the net became emptier, the fish could be deposited directly from the net into the wagons and trucks. The process took several hours, and it was nearly three o'clock before the last cart rolled away up the stone road. Stray fish lay scattered along the beach and Mrs Ellsworth directed the children into the final clear-up, plopping the fish into a vast steel saucepan. I lay down on the strand and closed my eyes, exhausted. Kit collapsed beside me.

'I hope you like mackerel,' he said.

His arm brushed mine but I was too tired to obey decent etiquette and did not push him away. His skin felt so warm and I wondered that in all her lectures upon proper behaviour, Anna had failed to mention that behaving improperly was much more fun.

*   *   *

Later that evening the village held a feast upon the beach. The air grew cool but the dappled stones retained the heat of the day, and even as the light dimmed we walked barefoot across the warm pebbles. Small boys pelted to and fro gathering armfuls of wood and piles of dry sea-grass and, under Kit's direction, built a vast bonfire on the shore. In the darkling light, he lit the fire, pushing a discarded cigarette into a cocoon of dead leaves. Within a few minutes, orange flames licked the sky and sparks flew into the waves, like vermillion fireflies.

'Don't dawdle, Elise; come and help,' called Mrs Ellsworth.

I padded across the stones to the edge of the dunes, where she and a small army of women had set up a field kitchen. Red coals glowed in the rocks, and resting directly on top of them were dozens of cast-iron pans filled with mackerel. The fish had been scaled and gutted, but that was all. They squeezed together, eyes unseeing, sizzling in spoonfuls of butter, handfuls of dark green samphire and hunks of peppered fennel. I knelt down between Poppy and Mrs Ellsworth and took over a frying pan, turning the gleaming fish as the sun sank into the sea. A crowd gathered around the bonfire, several of the children clutching bunches of flowers: ragged robin, honeysuckle, lavender, rosemary, ladies bedstraw and burnet rose. Burt and Art helped them decorate *The Lugger* with the flowers, until the battered fishing-boat was transformed into a fairy tale craft, more suited to Tennyson's Lady of Shalott than a stubbled fisherman with mismatched boots. Art, Will and Kit bore *The Lugger* down to the shore and out into the shallows. Burt picked up a small girl, not older than seven or eight, and carried her in his arms, placing her tenderly on the sail covers in the bow. As we all watched, they sailed towards the mouth of the bay.

'It's an old custom,' said Poppy, leaning over and turning my fish with a fork. 'We must give thanks to the sea. After the first catch, we make a sacrifice of flowers. Though, personally, I'd be quite happy to see Sally Hopkins go overboard as well. That child's a menace.'

'Don't say such a thing,' scolded Mrs Ellsworth.

'Sorry, Aunt Florence,' said Poppy.

I looked up at them in surprise.

'Oh, she's not my real aunt. She's from Bristol. I grew up in the bungalow on the cliff.'

She pointed with her fork to where a yellow light twinkled on the headland.

'Aunt Florence has known me all my life, that's all. Tyneford's an odd place, you know. It's not like anywhere else.'

We ate the fish with our fingers, picking out the bones and discarding them onto the strand, where they would be eaten by gulls or washed away by the tide. Poppy, Will, Kit and I all sat together on a large driftwood log, eating in contented silence. I realised that for the first time since I'd left Vienna, I was happy. The fishermen drank beer and sang dirty songs to the moon, while the children shouted and played in the dunes.

'Have you ever seen a saltwater log burn?' asked Kit.

I shook my head and instantly he jumped to his feet and jiggled our log, knocking the rest of us onto the ground in a tangle of limbs.

'Stop it.' Poppy tried to sit back down, holding fast to her fish.

'Wretched dung-squab,' said Will, sending a pebble whizzing past Kit's ear.

'Elise needs to see,' said Kit, apparently unconcerned that he had nearly lost a piece of his ear.

He dragged the giant piece of driftwood onto the bonfire. It crackled and flared and tongues of bright blue flame rose up hissing. The fire was quite unreal, like a magician's furnace, and I half expected a fishtailed genie to emerge from the sapphire flames. The blue was almost as bright as Kit's eyes. He was so different from the boys I had known in Vienna—not that I had known very many. There was little Jan Tibor, small for his age, bespectacled and terribly clever at playing the piano, according to the chorus of great-aunts. Sadly he never gave me the opportunity to marvel at his musical intellect myself, as whenever we met he stammered with nerves, his eyes bulged behind his thick spectacles and he looked like he wanted nothing more than to be sick, let alone play a little Chopin. Great-aunt Gabrielle was quite convinced he was going to be a famous composer one day. Nonetheless, he was too short for romance. Margot's Robert was handsome enough, but more serious than the dour ancestors on the wall in the Tyneford dining room. And I did not like men who scolded me. Robert, I decided, would make an excellent butler, austere and disapproving. He and Mr Wrexham could have a scintillating afternoon, comparing my shortcomings.

Kit was different. He had confidence, but lacked the preposterous swagger of some of the Austrian boys. I liked it when he laughed. I found myself wanting to do things that would make him laugh again.

'Are you in love with Kit?' said Poppy, suddenly appearing at my elbow.

'I'm begging your pardon.'

'Oh, it's all right. Everyone is in love with him. I used to be too. Until I was fourteen and then I grew out of it.'

'You're not in love with me anymore?' said Kit, returning from the bonfire to perch beside her.

'No,' she said, turning her back on him and facing me. 'Well? Are you?'

I stared at her, too shocked to speak. Will fiddled with his boots, suddenly very busy with his laces, while Kit was seemingly mesmerised by two small boys cheerfully toasting snails on sticks in the bonfire flames.

'Don't worry,' said Poppy. 'He likes it. Kit needs all women to be in love with him. I think it's because of his mother. She died when he was very young.'

I looked at Kit, who smiled back at me with good-natured ease, apparently unconcerned at Poppy discussing him and his dead mother as though he were not here. I recalled the photograph in Kit's bedroom of the blonde girl with the shy smile, and wondered how she had died.

'I am very sorry,' I said.

Kit smiled. 'It's all right. I don't remember her.'

I wasn't sure how not remembering her made it all right. To me, that made it worse.

'That psychoanalyst. Mr Freud. He's from Vienna. Did you know him?' asked Poppy.

I exhaled a tiny sigh of relief at the change of

topic. 'No. But once I seeing his daughter Anna in a stationery shop.'

'Oh, really. What did she buy?'

'I cannot remember. Envelopes I think.'

'Oh.'

Poppy did not conceal her disappointment, clearly hoping for some unique insight. She spied an upturned barrel and climbing upon it, sat swinging her legs in the moonlight; her pale skin was speckled with golden freckles, like biscuit crumbs on a white tablecloth. The sea glinted beneath the stars, and lights on a ship far out on the channel blinked in the darkness. The fishermen's song grew frantic, they stamped and clapped as they chanted, the grind of the pebbles beneath their feet like a growl coming from the earth. I found myself swaying to the rhythm of their melody, and imagined Anna singing with them, a silver song to their chorus. The ship on the horizon disappeared around the curve of the earth, and I waved, pretending it was Margot on her voyage across the sea. Art jumped upon an upturned boat and began to play a melancholy tune on a fiddle to accompany the singers. The strings had a rich dark tone, and in my mind it became Margot playing on the vanishing ship, the sound muted and strange because of Julian's pages stuffed inside the belly of the rosewood viola.

CHAPTER TWELVE

DIANA AND JUNO

Kit and I sat on the bluff in the cool November dawn. Summer had bloomed and withered into autumn. We huddled side by side on the pinnacle above Flower's Barrow, staring down at the churning sea. I shivered and wrapped my arms around my waist as the weak sun rose behind the hill.

'Come on. You're being mean now. It wasn't that bad,' said Kit.

'No, all right. I still like the *Forsyte Saga* best, though. It's more elegant.'

Kit snorted. 'Nonsense. Just your English was so bad then, you didn't notice how hammy it is.'

'Perhaps. But, I tell you—I'll always have a place in my heart for them. They're the first English family I ever knew.' I smiled and blew onto my hands. 'Come on, I'm getting cold and I have a thousand glasses to polish.'

Kit clambered to his feet and then pulled me up beside him, so that I staggered and fell into him, laughing. Whenever he was home from Cambridge he'd been giving me early morning English lessons. With all our reading and his tutelage, I was now fluent. I still stumbled over the odd word and when I got excited or upset my sentence structure became a little eccentric, but conversation was effortless. With a pang, I realised that I now dreamt in English, even while dreaming of Vienna. I wasn't the girl with the python plait who had arrived in

Tyneford all those months ago—I was someone new. If history hadn't forced me across Europe, would I have discovered that I loved the sea and big sky and fields of grass? It must have been hidden inside me like an oak tree in an acorn, or bluebells beneath the soil. Once upon a time, my ancestors had lived in the shtetls and farmed in the east. Perhaps this love of the wild was a folk memory, buried within the heart of every bourgeois city Jew. I tried to imagine Anna striding across the top of the tout, dressed as a picturesque peasant. I suspected that her love of countryside and wild things ('dirty and foul-smelling things, darling') was buried rather deeper than mine. Something must have shown on my face.

'Have you heard from them yet?' said Kit.

'No. Still nothing. I don't understand it.'

'I thought they were leaving for New York.'

'They were supposed to. Months ago. But the visa never comes.'

'It will be all right, Elise,' he said.

'Will it?' I said, thrusting my hands inside the warm wool of my coat. I started to trudge down the hill.

'I hope you've got me a decent birthday present,' said Kit, hurrying after me.

'No. I've nothing.'

'Good. Because there's something I want from you.'

'Oh?' I looked at him suspiciously. Kit's favours inevitably ended up with me being scolded by Mr Wrexham.

'Don't look so worried. Meet me, Poppy and Will in the yard after supper.'

'All right.'

We hastened down the hillside, picking our way along the sloping ridge. The hedgerows had been battered by centuries of ocean gales, and the branches on the hawthorn and blackthorn grew only on one side of each tree, the bare twigs streaming out like a girl's windswept hair. The bushes were studded with crimson berries, not yet stripped by the greenfinches or pied wagtails flitting across the grey skies. Ropes of black bryony lay tangled between the bushes, while triangles of stinking iris lurked at the bottom of the hedgerows. The damp grass had faded to a dull green, dappled with patches of dark mud.

'Let's run,' said Kit, grabbing my hand.

He tore across the ridgeway, hauling me alongside him, scattering stray sheep out of his way, the bells around their necks chiming in the wind. The bitter air slapped against my cheeks, numbing them, and my lungs burnt with exertion and cold. Kit could run for hours. He was usually so sedentary—he liked nothing more than to nestle in a padded armchair, one leg slung over an armrest, cigarette in one hand and book in the other, chatting idly as I dusted or cleaned out the grate. He could barely stir himself to fetch another glass of sherry or empty his ashtray. But when he decided to run, he would hurl himself across the hills like one of the golden roe deer with the hounds behind, and he'd sprint tirelessly for an hour or more. I'd watched him from the drawing room window, running for the sheer exhilarant pleasure of it, and then he'd return spent, and flop into his usual battered leather armchair in the sitting room, light a cigarette and then not stir again for a day or two.

'Kit! Slower. I can't,' I said, trying to get the

words out between gasps.

My skirt was too tight for his bounding strides and unless I stopped to yank it up, I would fall. There was a loud rip, as the seam tore.

'Kit!'

He took no notice and continued to pull me along beside him as we began the steep descent into the village. A speckled kestrel hovered overhead, wings motionless, as it glided above some invisible prey. The scree path was slippery and I bounced and slid, terrified every moment I would tumble. We reached the bottom and Kit turned to me laughing, but I was furious.

'Don't ever . . . do . . . that . . . again,' I shouted, between gasps. 'I . . . thought . . . I'd . . . fall.'

'But you didn't,' he said, not riled in the least. 'And now you won't be late for Wrexham.'

I clasped Kit's wrist and turned it over so that I could see his watch. It was not yet seven, and I had time to go and start my daily tasks. The elderly butler had agreed to Kit's English lessons, as long as they did not interfere with my duties. 'The girl is a maid, not a houseguest, I don't care if she was a royal countess in Vienna.' This was the strongest language Mr Wrexham had ever used with Kit; in his own surly way the old man adored him. Kit took the proviso seriously, and ensured that my lessons took place before the lighting of the household fires. This was all very well in summer, but by the beginning of November it meant that I was up before dawn, and a full hour before May hammered upon my bedroom door.

'I think we can have no more lessons until after the party,' I said.

'Can't you try and manage? Just get up a little

earlier, lazy-bones.'

He gave me a gentle nudge in the ribs.

'No.' Contradicting Kit was almost impossible. Especially when denying him something that he wanted. 'I'm already having to get up at five.'

'So do I.'

'Yes. And then you sleep all morning. I have to work.'

'My poor Cinderella.'

I picked up a burr and lobbed it at him, so that it lodged in his golden hair. He tugged at it for a second, then, realising it was stuck, shrugged and gave up, letting it dangle. Kit was not vain.

'You have friends arriving this morning.'

The following day was Kit's twenty-first birthday and his coming of age. Mr Rivers had agreed to a house party at Tyneford, a full three days of celebrations with half the young ladies and gentlemen of Dorset in attendance. Mr Wrexham and Mrs Ellsworth had existed in a state of acute anxiety for several weeks. They tried and failed to hire extra staff; endless plans had been drawn up and distributed by the butler, only to be discarded in disgust a few hours later. Mrs Ellsworth and a girl from the village had spent the best part of a week baking endless cakes and preparing jams and pickles and marinades. For his part, Kit ordered crates of liquor from London, along with stainless steel cocktail shakers, and took time each evening before dinner to teach Henry, Art and Mr Wrexham the art of cocktail making. The butler did not approve. Cocktails were an American abomination, but it was the young master's coming of age and he must be denied nothing. So, when he was not busy poring over the staff plan, Mr

Wrexham could be found studying with excruciating care the technique for the 'Tom Collins', the 'Gin Sling' and the 'Harvey Wallbanger', like a schoolboy swotting over Latin verbs.

The first guests arrived after lunch. I was busy arranging flowers or, more precisely, being told by Mrs Ellsworth that my arranging was hopelessly inadequate, whilst she tugged teasels, ivy and a rosy spray of herb robert into an appealing posy.

'Did your mother never teach you?'

I shrugged. Anna loved to buy flowers, armfuls of them from the market every week—bouquets of black roses, white lilies or orange blossom, which she spread out across the kitchen table in glorious patterns, cooing over the colours and scents with childish glee, all the while humming Delibes' *Flower Duet*. The practicalities of arranging she left to Hildegard.

'There. You see?'

Mrs Ellsworth thrust at me a pretty china vase decorated with blue swimming fish, and now filled with the precisely disarranged flowers.

'Put them upstairs in Lady Diana Hamilton's room.'

'Yes, Mrs Ellsworth.'

Taking the vase, I hurried along the corridor and up the back stairs to the blue guest room. For the week I was to act as lady's maid for the Hamilton sisters. They were titled but not rich, or not sufficiently rich to travel with a maid. Mr Wrexham was quite determined that I must fulfil this role. He claimed that my Viennese past qualified me for the task—'you have been to balls and operas or assisted your mother in her preparations I am sure'—but Henry confided that after a Parisian lady's maid, an Austrian was considered the most fashionable. Apparently, Mr Wrexham took great pleasure in the fact that Tyneford House was to provide an Austrian lady's maid for Mr Kit's privileged guests. I had no idea that my nationality made me so exclusive. I wondered if my appeal would be diminished if they realised Austria no longer classed me as a citizen.

I set the vase down on the dressing table and glanced around the room. The soft blue curtains matched the November sky and through the windows the grey sea glinted and thrashed. I wondered what it would be like to stay here as a guest rather than as staff, to have Kit pull out my chair at dinner and call 'Wrexham, another soda and lime for the lady.' When I remembered the Elise in Vienna with her easy life of concerts, scented baths and familial love, I felt that I remembered someone else. Outside there was the sound of tyres on gravel, then a minute later voices in the hall and the flurry of arrival. I slid out of the blue room and watched from the shadows at the top of the staircase. Two girls with cherubim cropped blonde curls prowled the hallway below. I knew they waited for Kit. They wore pale fur coats and Mrs Ellsworth took their gloves, but the taller refused to let the housekeeper help her with her mink.

'Oh, no. I'm always so cold and this place is positively glacial. Where on God's earth is Kit? I mean he drags us down to this forsaken place, the least he can do is be around to greet us,' she said, in a tone that I am sure she believed was wry and disarming, but to my ear was rude.

The sitting room door opened and Kit wandered

out in his socks to be embraced by both girls.

'So sorry. I was asleep. Was awake at five.'

'Excitement at our arrival?'

The doll-like girl pawed him, smoothing his ruffled collar.

'What else, Diana?' he said, helping her off with her coat. Apparently Diana was no longer concerned about being cold.

'Diana. Juno. It's a pleasure to see you again.'

Mr Rivers appeared in the hall, and both girls presented him a cheek; he placed a cool kiss on each. The banter ceased in Mr Rivers' presence; even Diana and Juno appeared to be in awe of him.

'Mrs Ellsworth will show you to your rooms, and then perhaps you will join Kit and me for tea?'

'Yes, thank you, Mr Rivers,' said Diana.

He gave her a warm smile. 'I think you are quite old enough to call me Christopher.'

'Yes, Christopher,' she said, in the tone of a child who has discovered that her teacher has a first name.

Suddenly meek, the two girls followed Mrs Ellsworth up the stairs. I shot along the corridor towards the back stairs. I was a split second too slow.

'Elise!' called Mrs Ellsworth.

Reluctantly, I turned and walked back.

'Your ladyships, this is Elise. She will be your maid during your stay.'

The girls looked me up and down. There was a long pause, during which I believe they expected me to curtsy. I did not. Mrs Ellsworth cleared her throat and then opened the door to the blue room.

'I hope your ladyships will be quite comfortable. Please ring if you need anything.'

Mrs Ellsworth gave a little nod and disappeared. I turned to hurry after her but Juno called out, 'Elly-ease. Wait a minute. We might need something.'

Repressing a sigh, I followed them into the room.

Diana sat down at the vanity table, gazed into the mirror and rolled her eyes.

'Lordy! I am such a mess. Can you fix hair—what-was-your-name?'

'Elise, your ladyship. And I can try if you like.'

I picked up a brush and a couple of pins and reached out for a stray blonde curl. She slapped my hand away.

'Stop it. You'll only make it worse.'

I bit my lip with the effort of not answering back.

Juno sank down on the window seat. 'This weather is awful. Why he's having the party now, Christ only knows. He could have waited till June or July and some decent chance of sun. This place is absolutely horrid in winter.'

Diana fluffed her curls. 'The countryside is a hobby, not a place where one actually lives.'

I chewed my tongue. Had I ever been like this? I hoped not, though Hilde would have spanked me if I'd tried. Diana looked at me in the mirror.

'So Ellis, you are a German Jewess?'

'Austrian.'

'Oh yes. Same thing,' she snapped, impatient.

'I am from Vienna.'

'The Viennese are very fashionable.' She turned to her sister. 'I heard that Jecca Dunworthy was waited on by a Viennese countess when she stayed with the Pitt-Smyths in Bath.'

I said nothing and picked blonde strands from

the hairbrush. Diana reapplied her lipstick.

* * *

During dinner, I stood behind Diana, my back flat against the wall. As the elder sister, she received the marks of attention. A girl drafted in from the village loitered behind Juno. She was under strict instructions to say and do nothing except carry dirty crockery. Several young ladies and gentlemen had arrived during the afternoon, and the dining room now echoed with laughter. Mr Rivers sat at the head of the table beside a slight girl in a lavender frock. She was so thin that she reminded me of a leaf curl, hardly there at all. She ate nothing, however much Mr Rivers pressed her, and sipped only white wine. I had never been at a party with so many young people; with the exception of his father, all the diners were friends of Kit and the air crackled with flirtation. Mr Wrexham silently refilled the glasses. It was stifling beside the fire. I had stoked it into a blaze before dinner, and now I could scarcely breathe. I wished I could sit, and felt sweat tickle my forehead. Must not fall. I tried to inhale air through my nose and out through my mouth. The candles flickered against the dark wallpaper and made the family portraits appear oddly lifelike. Their faces dripped like waxworks.

'Ellis. You.'

Diana snapped her fingers at me and I realised that she was pointing to her napkin, which had fallen on the floor. I stepped forward, willing myself not to faint, and bent to pick it up. My fingers were not working properly and it took me two attempts. I straightened, swaying, and steadied myself on the back of her chair.

‘What are you doing?’ she hissed.

‘So sorry, your ladyship.’

I replaced the napkin on her lap with a little flourish and retreated to the back of the room. I saw Mr Rivers watching me. A look of concern slid across his face. He called Mr Wrexham to his side, and a moment later the elderly butler propped open the dining room door and opened the window. A stream of cold air blew across my cheeks and I smiled at Mr Rivers, but he had turned back to Juno, his serious blue-grey eyes fixed upon her. Across the room, Kit was building a bread roll tower and laughing with Diana and a bosomy girl in a green dress. A few minutes later, as I glanced along the table, I saw that Mr Rivers’ chair was empty.

‘You. Again.’

Diana’s napkin sprawled at her feet once more. The fabric on her dress must be very slippery. I knelt to pick it up and, as my fingers touched it, she moved her foot, pinning my skirt to the floor with a sharp heel. I crouched at her feet, trapped like an idiotic pageboy. I tugged at my skirt but she dug in further, so that I could not free myself without making a scene. After a half minute, she allowed me to stand and replace the fallen napkin onto her lap.

I retreated to the wall, remembering not to lean, as per Mr Wrexham’s precise instructions. Apparently leaning was as bad as dawdling. Diana fed spoonfuls of her syllabub to Kit, who ate one or two and then batting her away, lit a cigarette. He never would have dared smoke during dinner with ladies in his father’s presence, but after Mr Rivers left, any restraint amongst the party evaporated. Juno rested her head on a young man's shoulders, his fingers toying with her hair. The butler disappeared to fetch another bottle from the cellar. The gentlemen unfastened their bow ties.

'Elise,' called Kit.

'Yes, sir?'

He dangled his black bow tie between his fingers.

'Put it on.'

'No.'

'It's my birthday.'

'No, your birthday's tomorrow.'

As I looked up, I realised that the entire party was watching us argue. I tried to grab the bow tie from him.

'No. I want to put it on you.'

'Kit,' I pleaded in a low voice.

His eyes were glassy with drink. I decided it would be best to humour him before Mr Wrexham or Mr Rivers returned. I could shout at him later. I crouched beside his chair and he slipped the silk around my neck. His breath smelt of alcohol and his lips were red with wine. I felt my cheeks colour as he tied the bow around my throat, his fingers brushing my skin. I swallowed and he did not remove his hand. I knew I ought to move away, but I stayed for a moment, feeling the warmth of his fingers, watching the half-smile crease around his eyes.

'Shall I ring the bell for coffee?' said Diana, voice shrill, her painted fingernails drum-drumming on the tablecloth.

I pushed Kit away, scrambled to my feet and half ran out of the room in my haste to fetch the tray.

*　　*　　*

After serving coffee I slipped away into the stable yard. Poppy and Will sat side by side on the mounting block. In the last couple of months they had quietly started courting, and Poppy's small freckled hand rested in Will's large one.

'How's the party?' she asked.

'Kit's drunk.'

'In front of his father?'

'Mr Rivers left after the dessert.'

I kicked a stray piece of flint and it shot across the yard, hitting the water pump with a crack.

'What do you know about Diana Hamilton?'

Poppy sat swinging her legs, tossing pear drops up into the air and catching them on her tongue. 'Well, their father, Lord Hamilton, lost the family fortune on a horse. Tragic really. Diana was named after his first big win. Juno after his second. Then he went and lost it all on Afternoon Delight.'

'I think she's sweet on Kit.'

Poppy shrugged. 'Most girls are. Shame if she's set her cap at him, though. Flirting and making eyes is one thing, but really he ought to marry someone with money. This place needs a fortune spent on it.'

I looked away, avoiding her eye.

She tossed another pear drop and Will pushed her out of the way, catching it himself. She laughed, throwing back her head and gobbled the next sweet straight from the paper bag. I forced myself to smile and leant against the stable door.

'What does Kit want to talk to us about anyway?'

Poppy shrugged and jumped down off the mounting block, wandering over to Mr Bobbin's door. The old horse poked his nose out and she fed him a pear drop.

'You're all better now, aren't you,' she crooned, stroking him behind the ears.

Kit ambled into the yard, hands thrust in his pockets, and puffing on his usual cigarette.

'Sorry,' he said as soon as he saw me. 'Bit much to drink. You've always known I was an idiot.'

I had wanted to yell, chide him over his stupidity, but he looked so full of remorse that my resolve waivered. I pulled the wrinkled bow tie out of my apron and thrust it at him, saying nothing. He took it from me and fixed me with bloodshot eyes.

'I'm sorry, Elise. Really I am. Sometimes I forget. That . . . you know . . . you're not one of us.'

I stamped my feet and rubbed my hands together. A frost was beginning to form along the cobbles and the ivy clinging to the stable's brickwork glittered in the darkness. A few months ago in Vienna, I had been one of them. Now I wasn't sure what I was. The other servants barely spoke to me. They knew I wasn't one of them either. I belonged nowhere.

'What is it that you want?' I asked, careful to stand away from him, on the other side of the yard.

Poppy stopped feeding sweets to Mr Bobbin and looked back at Kit, who cleared his throat and stubbed his cigarette out on a cobblestone.

'Well, I thought it would be fun. You know, shake things up a bit. If you and Poppy came to my party dressed as chaps. I'll lend you each one of my old tuxes. It'll be fun.'

I stared at Kit, feeling myself redden with anger for the second time in as many hours.

'You are mad. Quite mad. I'm a maid. I serve drinks. I fill glasses. I clean things. I am not some cabaret girl. This is not the *Simpl.*'

Kit remained unfazed by my rage. He watched me through his too blue eyes and gave a tiny shrug.

'No need to shout. Thought it would be fun. Thought you were the kind of girl who liked to break a rule or two.'

I had to admit that it did hold some appeal, as did the prospect of annoying Diana, but the rational part of me realised it was not sensible. I recalled Margot's warning: I must behave. There was no visa waiting for me in New York.

'No. I am going to bed. Do you need anything, sir?' I used the 'sir' to irritate him, remind him of the difference in our positions.

Kit looked at me, and for the first time in our six-month acquaintance, I saw a flash of anger glide across his face. His eyes narrowed.

'Yes, thank you, Elise. I would like a brandy and a cigar.'

I glared at him, but after my little barb, I couldn't very well refuse.

'And you, Poppy?' he said, turning to her. 'Can I tempt you into a tux? You'd look very fetching, I'm sure.'

She shook her head. 'No thanks. I have a new dress. I want to wear that.'

'Good,' said Will. I'd actually forgotten he was there. Will was so quiet; he sat and he watched Poppy, eyes big with love, saying nothing. 'I maint be a gentleman like yoos, but it gives me a nasty feelin', this stuff. Don't think them folks will see it as a bit o' fun an' nonsense.'

'Tosh,' said Kit. 'What do you know? You won't even come to the party.'

'No. I doesn't need to be sneered at by yer

chums.' Will spoke slowly without raising his voice, watching Kit levelly and unafraid. 'I wish yer a very happy birthday and I'm right glad of yer friendship. But I ent comin' dancin' an' makin myself ridiculous. Them others won't git that things is different here. They won't git Tyneford ways.'

I had never heard Will disagree with Kit before. Kit didn't answer, only thrust his hands deep into his pockets and kicked at a piece of straw. He knew Will was right. He noticed me hovering beside the back door, staring at him.

'Aren't you supposed to be getting me a brandy?' he snapped.

Muttering under my breath, I slipped inside the house. When I returned a few minutes later, they were laughing again, peace restored. I couldn't imagine that Kit could stay angry for long, especially not with Will. The two had been friends all their lives. I knew very little about the England outside of Tyneford, but I suspected that in most places stone wall builders and son and heirs were not close friends. Kit, Will and Poppy had run together across the hills looking for wild duck eggs, and fishing for elvers as soon as they were tall enough to clamber over the stiles and wooden gates that divided the valley. Kit was at ease with Poppy and Will. When I watched him with his Cambridge chums and the society set, he pulled on a new personality like Diana donned her fur coat. He was rakish and charming and he drank and I wasn't sure whether I liked him or not.

'I'm goin' ter walk Poppy home,' said Will, draping a hefty arm around her shoulders.

Kit gave him a playful slap on the back and kissed Poppy on the cheek. She waved goodbye to me, and they walked away into the darkness, leaving Kit and me alone in the stable yard. I thrust the brandy into his hands.

'You can have this, but I'm keeping the cigar.'

He raised an eyebrow. 'You smoke cigars? That's new.'

He pulled a box of matches out of his breast pocket and struck a light. I sucked at the cigar, but couldn't get it right. Kit plucked it out of my mouth, lit it and placed it back between my lips. I sucked gently, drawing the smoke into my mouth and succeeded in not spluttering.

'My brother-of-law. Robert. He used to give me his cigar sometimes at parties.'

'I hope brother-of-law is the same as brother-in-law or I shall be jealous. And I'll have to fence him or something. And I'm appalling and he'll probably kill me.'

I laughed, but my heart was beating loudly in my chest. I wondered that Kit could not hear it. He drained his brandy.

'It's wicked, Elise, but sometimes I find myself wishing for war. Because then you'd have to stay.'

'Kit. Don't. My family.'

'I know. I'm sorry.'

'I wish you could meet Anna. She'd charm you in a second.' I passed him the cigar. 'What do you remember about your mother?'

'That's the thing, Elise; I don't.'

'I suppose you were very small when she died.'

'I was four—quite old enough to remember her. She died very suddenly. She drowned.'

'Drowned? Oh, Kit, how awful. I'm so sorry.'

He rubbed his nose, leaving a grey smudge on the tip. 'Funny thing was she was an excellent swimmer but she drowned in the bath. Had some kind of fit. My father found her. For years he was terrified I suffered from the same weakness. Wouldn't let Nanny bathe me. Insisted on strip-washes instead. I must have been a very smelly little boy.'

Not knowing what to say, I reached for his hand. He allowed me to squeeze it for a second and then disentangled himself, flicking cigar ash from his trouser leg.

'When they told me, apparently I fainted. Then, when I woke up, she was gone. Disappeared. I couldn't understand why everyone looked so sad. Why my father wouldn't stop crying. All my memories of her had vanished, you see. I look at family photographs and I see myself standing beside a pleasant-faced stranger. I remember parties, picnics, boat trips and I know she was there but she's not in my memory of any of them.'

'Do you dream about her?'

'No.'

I wished I could offer some words of comfort, promise him Anna's love, but I had no consolation and Anna was far away. I kissed him on the cheek, smelling the sandalwood of his cologne mingling with the cigar smoke.

We sat in silence, side by side, our fingers not touching, and listened to the huff of the horses, their breath steaming in the cold air like water vapour from a singing kettle.

CHAPTER THIRTEEN

The Birthday and Broken Glass

The next morning May woke me before dawn. It was Kit's twenty-first and the day of his party. Over a hundred guests were expected for dinner and dancing, and we had hours of preparation, plus eight houseguests to care for. I cleaned the living rooms and laid the downstairs fires before the sun crept up behind Tyneford hill. As I carried the basket of kindling upstairs, dawn blazed through the window above the porch. The hillside seemed to crackle and burn with light, the backs of the cattle shone rosy-red and the hawthorn bushes were licked with scarlet. I thought of Moses and smiled.

'Elise,' called a soft voice behind me.

I turned to see Mr Rivers in the hall, wearing his dressing gown and slippers.

'Have you been reading the papers?'

I scoured *The Times* every evening before falling asleep, searching for even the slightest piece on Vienna or Austria, but I had read nothing but the usual dismal stories on page fourteen: Jews harassed, property seized, arrests and inflammatory speeches by Herr Ribbentrot and Herr Hitler. Stories buried among notices about the planting of geraniums, the King opening Parliament and the famous Corry triplets needing their tonsils removed.

Mr Rivers frowned, worry lines appearing on his forehead.

'The attack in Paris? I hope Herr von Rath

survives. I fear it will be bad for the Jews if he does not.'

He gestured to me and I followed him down the stairs and into the library. Automatically, I went to the windows and opened the curtains, so that the early morning light trickled into the room. Mr Rivers sat at the desk and fiddled with the dials on his wireless. Static crackled as the instrument warmed. I felt a swirl of nausea and a pain thrum in my temples. I recited their names as a prayer: *Annaandpapannaandpapannaandpapapapapa.* Then the voice of the newsreader over the airwaves: '*The King opened Parliament yesterday. A grand ceremony . . .*'

We listened to the news in silence for a few minutes. The attack in the German embassy in Paris was not mentioned. As the shipping forecast began, Mr Rivers switched off the wireless.

'Well, it would appear the BBC does not share my anxiety. Perhaps they are right and all will be well. You will let me know as soon as you hear from your parents?'

'Yes, sir.'

He settled in his chair behind the desk and studied me without speaking. I was not sure if I should leave. Mr Rivers was always kind to me, but I never forgot that he was my employer. He possessed a cool reserve that demanded respect from even the fickle Diana and Juno. I always felt he was at a distance, as though he existed behind a pane of glass. He never slouched or spilt his whisky or made mess of any kind. His desk was meticulously ordered, envelopes stacked according to size and letters were responded to by return. He lacked Kit's ease and warmth, and rarely spoke to me unless it was a polite request for some refreshment. I sometimes wondered that he was Kit's father. I supposed Kit must have taken after his mother. I never knew what Mr Rivers was thinking. Sometimes I caught him watching me, though usually he looked away so quickly that I was not sure if I had imagined it. Mr Rivers gestured to the row of Julian's books on the shelf behind him.

'Is your father writing something new?'

'Yes, sir. But he won't find a publisher in Austria. His books are banned now.'

He watched me, not blinking. I wondered what he would think, if he knew that Julian's latest novel was hidden upstairs. For a moment, I was almost tempted to tell him. No. The novel was mine and I would not share its existence with anyone. The secret belonged to me and to Julian. It struck me that I had never seen Mr Rivers unshaven before. A shadow of black stubble grazed his chin and lip. I swallowed and licked dry lips—there was something I had always been curious about.

'Do you speak German, sir?'

'Yes. Though I speak her very poor. I am much the best at reading her.'

Despite the nauseous feeling in my gut, I smiled and clapped my hands. I felt a rush of happiness at hearing my mother tongue, even when slightly garbled.

'Sir, you speak wonderful German. You must tell me if you wish to practise. I would be so happy to help you. Really, I would. You can tell me which of Papa's books you like the best. The Minotaur's Hat *has always been my favourite.'*

'Slow down!' he said, laughing. 'I can't understand when you speak so fast.'

‘I’m sorry.’

‘I should very much enjoy some German conversation lessons. Perhaps after all this party chaos has dissipated?’

‘Yes, sir.’

‘And I shouldn’t have worried you. I am sure all will be well. If I hear anything more, I will tell you right away.’

* * *

After leaving the library, instead of lighting the fire for Diana, as I ought to have done, I ran up the stairs to my little attic. I fumbled through my drawers and pulled out Anna’s pearls. I don’t know why, but I wanted to wear them that day. I fastened them under my blouse, tugging the collar up so that they were hidden. I hastened to the guest room, and slipped inside to discover Diana already awake.

‘You’re late. I’m cold. I need tea right away.’

‘Yes, your ladyship.’

I stood up and started to hurry away to fetch the tea tray but Diana called me back.

‘Light the fire first. I can’t believe this place doesn’t have proper radiators.’

It was true; the house only had central heating in the downstairs reception rooms. None of the bedrooms had radiators. Kit explained that his father had been forced to sell one of the good paintings to pay for the ground floor heating to be installed. Mr Rivers decided that instead of selling the Turner seascape, family and guests alike could manage with old-fashioned fires. Except for the servants. We had neither radiators nor fires and suffered with chilblains from late October.

It seemed very odd to me that a man who owned such a large and magnificent house as Tyneford could not afford to heat it properly. Kit informed me that the profit on the estate was marginal and when faced with a choice of having staff or heating, his father always chose staff. He was a gentleman of the old school and believed it his responsibility to employ as many people from the village as possible. The two men rarely spoke and appeared to take little pleasure in one another's company, but when Kit discussed his father, his voice resonated with pride.

I put a match to the fire, blowing gently on the tiny flame, and in a minute there was a roaring blaze. I added coal and pine logs, and warmth spread into the room like reaching fingers. I stood up with a smile, taking satisfaction in my new skill. Before this year I had never lit a fire before, but now I reckoned I was as good as Hildegard.

'He can't help it,' said Diana.

She sat propped up on embroidered cushions, her tight blonde curls a halo around her head. In the morning light, her eyes appeared violet.

'I beg your pardon?' I said.

'You've cast some spell over Kit. You Jewesses. You're nothing special to look at. But men can't resist.'

I knew I oughtn't to, but I laughed out loud.

'Don't you dare laugh at me! Don't you dare.'

I attempted to swallow my laughter, tickled at the notion of myself as some species of exotic temptress. I supposed that with all the running up and down stairs I had lost a little of the baby-fat around my middle. I pictured myself as a turbaned seductress in an oriental fantasy and giggled.

Diana picked up a cushion and hurled it at me. It struck me on the cheek and flopped onto the rug. I scooped it up, fluffed it and placed it on the armchair by the window.

'I'll fetch your tea, your ladyship.'

'You were part of the smart set in Vienna?' said Diana, smoothing her silk nightgown.

I hesitated. Even in Vienna, my family was bourgeois, part of the new class of Jewish artists and liberals, but however assimilated we remained separate, like cream on milk. Anna was feted at the Opera Ball because all Viennese society wanted to hear her sing, but the Landau family name did not procure us a box, or the best table at Café Splendide. Diana did not need to know this.

'Yes,' I answered. 'Part of the smart set.'

'Oh,' said Diana, her voice soft and sad. 'Because I thought Viennese women were the height of fashion. And everybody knows that a lady doesn't wear pearls until after six o'clock.'

She burrowed into her pillows, a satisfied smile playing on her pink lips. Irritation prickling down my spine, I disappeared to fetch her breakfast tray.

* * *

The ladies and gentlemen had been invited to a shoot over at the nearby Lulcombe estate in order to give the servants time to prepare for the evening's festivities. For us, the day passed in a whirl of frantic activity. It was regimented by Mr Wrexham's staff plan, a document of military precision. The butler himself supervised the polishing of the silver; I cleaned the knives again and again, while Henry rubbed salt dishes, peppershakers, candlesticks and placeholders to a gleam. Mrs Ellsworth held the keys to the linen closet and watched closely as May and I carried the starched tablecloths to the dining room, and spread out specially hemmed cloths along the side table in the billiard room, which was to be set up as a bar. Lanterns were strung up across the terrace, and white roses sent from Harrods filled every room. Art and Burt laid out lines of candles across the lawns, ready to be lit at dusk. A pair of girls from the village assisted Mrs Ellsworth and the kitchen boy, and even Poppy appeared before lunch to help with the baking of game pies. In a corner of the heaving kitchen, she skinned pheasants, diced venison and wood pigeon, and hacked up chunks of honeyed ham. A tin bath was carried into Mr Wrexham's room, and packed with ice, then bottles of champagne. With great difficulty, three extra maids and another footman had been hired for the evening, borrowed from neighbouring estates, and the servants' corridor hummed with voices and scurrying feet, like a hive of honeybees. The larder brimmed with iced cakes: lemon sponges, chocolate truffle, cherry and oozing mandarin. Syllabubs rested beside trifles, while trays of poached salmon decorated with paper-thin slices of cucumber sat on low boxes. Cold chicken and exotic peach and cumin chutneys lined the pantry. I scurried to and fro with messages and cutlery and trays of water glasses; rolls of napkins and lists of guests; paper place cards from Liberty of London; sugar cubes and crushed sea salt; cocktail shakers, ice buckets, sprigs of mint and bottles of whisky, rum, gin and kirsch; painted fruit plates and porcelain coffee cups.

Unable to concentrate, I dropped a tray of

butter dishes on the kitchen floor, just after May had stamped them with the family crest, and was sent in disgrace to empty the compost. Even at the back of the house, the gardens were immaculate. White ribbons had been tied around the box trees and I glimpsed the stable boys sluicing down the yard, where space had been cleared for thirty cars. Art's room was filled with bales of straw and jugs of beer and sandwiches, so that the chauffeurs could wait in comfort. I wanted Mr Rivers to return, so that I could find out whether there was any more news, but they were not expected back until it was time for the ladies to dress for the party. There was nothing I could do, but fetch and carry and clean and wait and worry.

The servants' dinner was held early at four o'clock, and for the first time during my residence at Tyneford we filled the benches in the dining hall, squeezing in together elbow-to-elbow, as we spooned our soup and gobbled our bread and cheese. Excitement buzzed amongst us like electricity, and we listened to Mr Wrexham with something akin to pride.

'I know you are all very tired. You've been working hard for many weeks. Tonight is the culmination of all that effort. Tonight is the coming of age of Mr Christopher Rivers, heir to Tyneford. Let us ensure that all the ladies and gentlemen who attend the evening's celebrations speak in glowing terms of Tyneford service. Let us be a credit to Tyneford and the Rivers family.'

There were cheers as the assembled servants toasted Kit. Mr Rivers had given permission for a bottle of champagne to be opened, and we each had a drop in our glass, which we savoured like ambrosia. Even Henry and May smiled at me—tonight at least, I could be one of them. As I hurried upstairs to change into a clean uniform and a specially ordered lace cap and apron, I found myself tingling with anticipation, greater than anything I had experienced in Vienna when attending parties as a guest. The door to my attic room was ajar and I shut it firmly, wanting a moment's quiet. I re-tied the pearls around my neck and thought of Anna. Was she safe? Did she think of me?

Dusk darkened into night and there was a rumble of tyres on the driveway. Diana and Juno would be clamouring for me in a moment. I couldn't fathom how two grown women could be so helpless. They needed their clothes spread out on their beds, packets of soap unwrapped, towels warmed and scented. I hastened downstairs to the blue room and started to draw the curtains. I paused and opened the casement, peeping out across the house and gardens; lights blazed in every window, and on the lawns Art stooped to light the candles inside the storm lanterns, so that small flames flickered in the gloom. The night air was cool against my skin, and the wind sang in the larch leaves.

'Is my bath drawn?' said Diana, barging into the room and discarding her gloves on the floor.

Sighing, I drew the curtains and slammed the window shut.

'I'll run it now, miss.'

I slipped into the small tiled bathroom and turned on the taps. The water thundered against the sides like a screeching train in a tunnel, and I poured in handfuls of rose-scented bath salts which filled the closet with sweet smelling steam. I was exhausted, my limbs ached and my temples throbbed, and I wanted nothing more than to slip into the scalding water myself.

'I need unbuttoning,' called Juno.

I hurried back into the room and unfastened the bone buttons on the back of her riding cape. It was a ridiculous garment, and I could imagine few things less suitable for actual riding. Not that there was any danger of that with Juno. I couldn't recall her venturing outside unless it was to climb into a motorcar.

'Did you have a pleasant day, Lady Juno?'

'Don't talk to me,' said Juno.

'I should like a lemon cordial,' said Diana, who had at least undressed herself and now lounged in the chair beside the window flicking through a copy of *Vogue*.

Resisting the urge to say a bad word, I ran down to the kitchen to fetch a glass. I knew from experience that there was no point returning without ice, and so sought a cube from the bucket in the larder. It was all melted into slush, and so I was forced to take a piece from the champagne cooler in Mr Wrexham's room. It was a full five minutes later when I scrambled back up the stairs to the blue room. The sound of rushing water greeted me and, shoving the glass of stupid lemon cordial at Diana, I ran into the bathroom. Water poured from the tub and onto the floor. Wading through the puddles in my shoes, I turned off the tap. Furious, I stalked into the bedroom to face Diana and Juno. They sprawled in their silk chemises on the twin beds, discussing the drawings of this season's Dior dresses.

'Could you not have turned off the tap?' I said, almost shouting.

Diana turned to me with cold eyes. 'I could if I were a maid.'

'I was downstairs fetching you a drink.'

'Yes. Thank you. You remembered the ice.'

There was no point in arguing further. I cleared up the mess as best I could, and then called that the bath was ready.

'Jolly good. And my dress is hanging in the wardrobe, if you could be so kind as to lay it out on the bed. I believe it might need another press,' said Diana, flicking the page in her magazine.

I went to the wardrobe and unbolted the door. Before me lay a row of skirts, blouses, high-heeled shoes, and dresses in green, rose and cream silks.

'The emerald is mine,' called Juno.

I picked it out and hung it on the back of the door, examining the chiffon for creases.

'I shall wear the pink,' said Diana.

I pulled out a dress in pale pink water silk and lifted it up to the light. My heart began to hammer and rage swelled inside me.

'This is mine.' I held the dress close to me. 'You can't wear it.'

'Can't I?' She spoke very quietly. 'You'll tell Wrexham that it's yours?'

I knew Mr Wrexham would not care whether the dress was mine or not. It was all about their comfort. I was a maid and this was a minor humiliation.

'You could always run to Kit,' she whispered.

I stared at her. So this was about Kit. From downstairs, I heard the tinkle of breaking glass. I closed my eyes and thought of Anna. I felt as if I were walking on quicksand, the ground beneath my feet sank and sucked. I was so tired.

Dropping the dress to the floor, I left the room.

* * *

I checked my cap in the hall mirror and descended the grand staircase. The panelled reception hall was empty, the servants not yet in position. Everything was ready: tables laid, glasses prepared, drinks pleasantly chilled. I could hear clattering and muffled cries emanating from the service corridor and decided to stay well away. The door to the library was ajar, and I pushed it open. Mr Rivers sat beside his desk, toying with a brandy glass. Kit lounged by the window, for once not smoking. Neither man smiled.

'Many happy returns. Mr . . . Kit . . . sir,' I mumbled. I never was sure how to address him in his father's presence.

'Thank you, Elise,' he said, his face grim.

Mr Rivers poured a glass of brandy and slid it across the desk towards me.

'Herr von Rath is dead. He died several hours ago and there are reports of a pogrom in Germany.'

Feeling dizzy I snatched the glass, taking a glug of brandy. My throat burnt. 'And Austria?'

'All across the Reich,' said Kit.

'There are reports of arrests. Smashing of Jewish property. Synagogues burning,' said Mr Rivers, pouring me another drink.

'Elise, I'm so sorry,' said Kit, crossing the room and taking my hand.

Conscious of Mr Rivers' eyes upon us, I withdrew my fingers from his grasp. I drained the brandy and blinked.

'Is there anything else, sir?' I said, turning to his father.

Mr Rivers shook his head, his face full of sadness.

'No, Elise. You may go.'

'Thank you, sir.'

I bobbed my head and slipped out of the library.

* * *

The guests appeared in twos and threes, drifting into the billiard room for an exotic cocktail shaken by Henry or Art, who stood fidgeting in his special occasion suit. Ladies in feather boas sipped champagne in the drawing room, or lingered to gossip on the stairs and in the great hall. Waiters in white tie and tails scurried to and fro, refreshing drinks and carrying canapés on silver trays. A small band of musicians tuned up in the library, and breathy notes from a flute mingled with the chatter and laughter. The two glasses of brandy had been a mistake. I felt hot and my black wool dress clung beneath my arms. I wanted to unfasten a button, but knew I could not risk Mr Wrexham glimpsing the hidden pearls. Maids did not wear jewellery even after six o'clock. Juno giggled with Poppy, clearly oblivious to the fact that my friend was merely middle class and had grown up in a bungalow. I saw Kit talking to Diana, smiling at something she'd said. The flush in her cheeks perfectly matched the soft tones of Anna's dress. It was larger on her than it had been on me, and she'd tied a rope of crystal beads around the waist so that it clung to her figure. She looked much more beautiful in it than I ever had and, at that moment, I hated her. I wanted to be wearing the dress. I wanted to feel it wrapped around me, still smelling faintly of Anna's perfume. There had not been time to clean it after the last night in Vienna, and I imagined it to hold the scents of that party, a lifetime ago.

Guests clustered in small groups at round tables, nibbling Mrs Ellsworth's poached salmon and quail egg tarts. A woman in a lavender gown stroked the cuff of a tall man with a clipped moustache, as she perched upon his knee. Two girls, both in red dresses, ate slices of chocolate cake and drank virulent coloured cocktails from long glasses. I collected plates and helped ladies to slices of cold pie and chicken and watched out of the corner of my eye as Kit flitted amongst his guests. He stole closer and passed me an empty champagne flute.

'No more news.'

I refilled his glass and fought the impulse to drain the contents. I wanted to disappear with a bottle down to the beach, drink and shout and rage at the sea. Instead, I noticed Diana in Anna's dress, picking iced rose petals off a sponge cake and alternating smiles between two men.

'It'll be all right, Elise. Really it will.'

'Why do you keep saying that? You don't know anything.'

Kit looked so utterly dejected that I felt a nudge of guilt. This was his party, and what was happening in Europe was hardly his fault. I took a breath and forced myself to smile.

'Anna would love your party. She'd be furious if she knew that you worried about her and did not enjoy yourself.'

Kit stared miserably at his champagne, shaking

the glass so that golden bubbles rose to the surface like shooting stars.

'I promise you, she'd be very angry. If she were here, she'd be standing halfway up the stairs. Perfect acoustics, you see. And she'd have organised the band. And she'd be singing.' I gave a short sigh. 'I wish you could hear her sing.'

Over Kit's shoulder, I saw Mr Wrexham glowering at me. A parlour maid in conversation with the host was not acceptable. I hurried away and, grabbing an ashtray, made for a group of gentlemen smoking on the terrace.

'Ah, excellent, do you have a light?' asked a sandy-haired chap, brandishing an empty box of matches.

'Certainly, sir,' I said, pulling out a new box from my apron pocket. I'd learnt over the last several months that there were certain things I always needed to keep handy. Mr Wrexham was most gratified when he'd realised that I perpetually carried matches, a spare handkerchief, paper and pencil, a hair net and peppermints in my pocket, viewing it as a sign that I had finally accepted my role in life was to attend to their comfort. In fact, I detested having to hurry away in search of elastic bands or aspirin and found that I saved a good deal of time by keeping a supply of bits and pieces upon my person. It was for my convenience rather than theirs.

It was cold on the terrace, and several candles had blown out, even those inside the storm lanterns. A thick mantle of cloud blocked out stars and shrouded the top of Tyneford hill. The night was black dark and the crash and boom of the sea seemed to come from nowhere. The doors to the house had been thrown open, and music drifted into the air, wafting down towards the beach like an invisible haar. I hovered in the shadows, grateful for a moment's rest. Beneath the string of glimmering lanterns couples danced, girls floating to and fro in their pastel dresses like soap bubbles on the breeze. I was content to gaze upon them, and remembered the last dancers I had watched at the Opera Ball, the previous March. It was only a few weeks before the *Anschluss*, and on that night at least it appeared that nothing would ever change. Anna was invited to sing of course, and for the first time, I attended with my family. As it was my first ball, I wore white like all the debutantes. Great-aunt Gerda lent me her diamond earrings, which shone in my ears like slivers of ice. For the first half hour, I could not join the dancing. I was transfixed. The girls spun and whirled in their spotless gowns across the ballroom. It seemed that the whole of Vienna was in that one theatre, a thousand girls turning, turning. I grew dizzy. It was like watching snowflakes rushing in a blizzard. At Kit's party, as I watched a fair-haired girl lean back in her partner's arms, I saw Margot, her faced flushed with happiness. The church clock chimed the quarter hour and I willed time to turn backwards. I wanted the hands on the clock to rush the wrong way, and whisk me back to that other place. I did not care if I had to live it all over again, minute by minute, second by second; I wanted to return to Vienna and another time.

Diana and Mr Wrexham appeared at my side, half hidden in the gloom.

'Lady Diana requires your assistance, Elise,' he said, giving me a curt nod.

'I seem to have had an accident with my dress,'

said Diana with a giggle, feigning embarrassment. 'I've been such a silly thing. I've gone and spilt my wine.'

I examined her, and through the darkness saw a crimson stain down the front of Anna's dress. Diana watched me, a smile playing on her lips, daring me to complain. Not saying a word, I followed her into the house and up the stairs to her bedroom. We made our way through the throng, weaving through revellers lining the landing. I opened the door to the blue room and Diana slipped inside. She unfastened the dress herself, undoing the hooks along the right seam, and stepped out of it, leaving it in a heap on the floor. She stood in the middle of the bedroom in her high-heeled shoes and her silken underwear, perfectly unembarrassed, and shot me a look of pity.

'I hear there are problems for your kind at home. Such a shame for you. Not wanted there. Not wanted here.' She sighed deeply. Anyone who did not know her would believe her heart breaking in sympathy. She gazed at me with her dark eyes, the colour of bruises. 'I just can't imagine.'

Kneeling down, I scooped up the spoilt dress and ran upstairs to my bedroom. It was ruined. I buried my face in the fabric. It reeked of wine and Diana's sickly gardenia perfume. She'd stolen a piece of Anna from me. I was so angry, I scratched at my arms until little beads of red appeared on my wrists. I stuffed the dress into the wastebasket in my room and strode back down to the party. A girl with a long dark plait woven with silver thread stood on the landing, feeding strawberry ice cream to a young man. A half-drunk bottle of wine rested on the carpet beside them. I swept it up and hurried away, despite their protestations. Checking over my shoulder for Mr Wrexham, I darted into the bedroom at the far side and clicked the key in the lock.

The room was empty. Curtains drawn. I took a gulp of wine, and marched over to Kit's closet. The room smelt of his cigarettes. A damp towel hung over the back of a rail and a bottle of cologne left open on the vanity table emitted his scent of sandalwood and honey. I took another sip of wine, straight from the bottle, spilling a drop on my chin, and wiped it away with the back of my hand. Music drifted up through the floorboards like smoke. There was a shriek from outside the window but I did not open the curtain and I did not look. In the distance I felt the black sea, crashing, crashing.

Despite the chaos of the party, Mr Wrexham had still found time to tidy up the customary mess in Kit's room. All his trousers were neatly folded away into the large wardrobe. I tugged at a black pair. Not part of a dinner suit. I let them fall to the floor. I pulled out another pair and then another, dropping them all, until I came to a dinner jacket and matching trousers—deep grey with a matt black ribbon running along the fold. I unbuttoned my dress and hauled them on. Kit was slim, a lithe man-boy, and yet, to my surprise, they were loose around my waist. When had I become thin? Anna wouldn't approve. I found a white shirt with a starched collar and, slipping it on, stuffed the shirttails into the waistband. The jacket was big around my shoulders but the trousers were only very slightly too long and I supposed that the suit must have belonged to Kit some years ago, while he was still at school. I picked up his comb, and sitting down at the dressing table drew it through my short hair. His mother smiled at me from the brown photograph. Snatching up the wine bottle, I drained the dregs. It was Diana's fault. The ruined dress. Red stained. Blood stained. Frau Goldschmidt's spoiled fur. The disappeared. Not wanted here. The Jews killed Herr von Rath. Pogrom. Anna's dress. She stole Anna. The novel in the viola. Diana. It was all Diana.

I checked my reflection in the mirror. Eyes too bright. Lips marked with wine. Leaving my dress in a crumple in the middle of the floor, I unlocked the door and ventured out onto the landing. I half expected a gasp, cries of disgust. Nothing. The girl with the long plait had gone. A couple kissed in the shadows. Snatches of music mingled with the chatter and shouts of laughter but no one noticed me. I supposed they took me to be a boy with my short, slick, smooth hair. Sauntering down the stairs, I scanned the crowd for Kit. No one accosted me for drinks or cardigans or clean plates or the way to the powder room. For a few minutes I was one of them again. Despite the heat and the noise, and the girls banging into me as they danced up and down, up and down, I could breathe. I spied Kit on the terrace and made straight for him.

'Kit. Kit.'

He stared for a second, not seeing me. I tugged on his sleeve.

'Kit. It's me.'

A slow smile of delight spread across his face.

'You did it. You really did it.'

He grabbed my hand and drew me under a lantern so he could see me better, turning me first one way, then the other.

'You look fine. Jolly fine.' He tucked a stray curl behind my ear, smoothing it flat. 'Almost like a boy.'

'Well?' I demanded. 'Are you going to ask me to dance?'

Kit gave a snort. 'Or you could ask me. Doesn't make much difference right now, does it?'

'Will you dance, Kit?'

'Delighted. Wait here a mo.'

He ducked inside, leaving me alone on the terrace. I slunk into the shadows, not wanting to be discovered. Not yet. The music stopped. Then, as I listened, there began the lilt of a familiar melody, 'Tales from the Vienna Woods', Johann Strauss. Kit reappeared at my side.

'I thought a Viennese waltz seemed appropriate.'

Appropriate was not a word I would have used in the circumstances. He offered me his hand and, as I took it, led me towards the lights of the house and the swaying couples.

'One second.'

I grabbed a stray glass of champagne off a side table and drank it, the bubbles tickling my throat, before slapping it down empty on the tray of a passing waiter. The doors from the large drawing room leading to the great panelled hall were thrown open, and couples waltzed from one room to the next, weaving amongst each other in intricate patterns. I imagined silken threads connecting them all and the waves of dancers making some vast piece of embroidery. The men were all clad in their black tie and tails, while the women formed a bouquet of colours. Ruby dresses swirled and a girl in seawater blue arched back in her partner's arms, her long, sand-coloured hair brushing the floor.

'Come on,' said Kit, taking my hand and leading me into the throng.

I had never danced with Kit before, never would again. I stiffened as he clasped my waist with his left hand, and pulled me into a firm hold. He smiled down at me.

'Thought I'd lead? That all right with you?'

I was not an excellent dancer, but every Viennese girl can waltz just as sparrows can fly. I ignored the other dancers and moved with Kit. Rise and fall. Rise and fall. Glide and turn. Whispers behind me. The other couples began to notice that two men were dancing together. The girl in blue missed a beat. Her partner slowed. Only look at Kit. Rise and fall. And turn. He swept me round. Where was Diana? She needed to see. Couples fell back against the wall and watched us with a hiss of disapproval. *That's not a man, it's a girl.* And turn. Glide and sweep. *Isn't that the maid?* Kit dipped me in his arms. *I hear she's from Vienna.* Rise and fall. *Maid or Jew whore?* He held me close.

'It was called the "wicked dance", you know,' he whispered.

'And was banned in London.'

'Indeed. A waltz is supposed to be shocking.'

I saw our reflection in the long hall mirror as we sashayed past, two slim figures in black and white: Kit tall, golden head shining in the candlelight and me, small beside him, with dark hair and darker eyes. I glimpsed Diana standing at the foot of the stairs in a clean taffeta gown. She stared at us, lip curled in revulsion. I smiled at her, warm in Kit's arms. I heard the crack of breaking glass, as Kit stepped on a discarded champagne flute. It shattered and I skidded, the sole of my shoe sliding over the shards. Broken glass in the temple. Sorrow. Always remember the sadness. No joy without sorrow. We surged forwards on the music. I closed my eyes. Breaking glass. Kit's birthday and the temples are burning. Kit was speaking softly in my ear, but I had not heard him. Instead I listened to the echo of breaking glass.

'I think we should shock them a little more,' he said, loudly this time.

He dipped me again and as I leant back in his arms, he kissed me. For a moment I forgot Diana, the murmurs of disapproval and let him kiss me. He tasted of brandy and cigarettes.

'Let her go.'

I felt a hand on my shoulder. I opened my eyes. Mr Rivers stood beside us, eyes black with anger.

'What have you done?'

CHAPTER FOURTEEN

THE END OF US ALL

We stood in the library before Mr Rivers. From the other side of the door came the swell of chatter, a collective murmur of disapproval. The curtains were open and I could see the reflection of our pale faces in the windowpane. Outside, the last of the candles on the lawn puffed out and the garden vanished into darkness.

'You can't speak to me like that anymore. I'm twenty-one,' said Kit, angrier than I had ever seen him.

'Only a boy would do something so foolish.'

Mr Rivers paced up and down before the window, hands folded behind his back.

'You can't dress up the housemaid in men's clothes in front of half the girls in the county set. This isn't some cabaret or a pansy club. You've made a fool out of yourself.'

'It was fun. A piece of fun,' said Kit, shouting.

'No. You wanted to poke fun at them. Shock them. Make them think that you were "one of those". You invited half of the county to a party and then insulted them.'

Mr Rivers turned to me, his voice cold. 'I don't know what it is like in Vienna but in England amongst polite society young ladies do not dress up as boys outside of the pantomime.'

I thought of Anna dressed in breeches as Cherubino, her hair looped up in a boyish bob. But that was Mozart, not real life. Julian always said that Mozart was music hall for intellectuals.

Mr Rivers shook his head, words faltering in disbelief and looked back at Kit. 'Why did you kiss her? And in front of all the society girls.'

Kit met his father's eye, defiant. 'Because I wanted to.'

I was not sure which made Mr Rivers angrier: the fact that Kit had kissed me or that he had done it before the county. He paced up and down on the worn Persian rug, pausing beside me.

'How can I possibly fail to dismiss you after this?'

I shook my head and sat down on the wooden steps propped against the bookcase. The black tie choked me and I felt ridiculous. I wanted nothing more than to change back into my itchy maid's uniform. Even the white cap and apron would be a relief.

'No. It's my fault. I asked her to do it,' said Kit.

'She can't stay,' replied his father. 'Mr Wrexham and Mrs Ellsworth will demand her dismissal.'

'Whose house is it? Yours or theirs?'

Kit was so angry that bright red marks appeared on each cheek.

'My house, Kit. Until I die, it's my house.' Mr Rivers took a breath, trying to calm himself. 'I have to think of the good of the household. What's best for you. Your reputation.'

'Don't bother about me. What about Elise?'

'I can find her a suitable position elsewhere.'

Despite all Mr Rivers' kindness and attentions, I was still just the maid—whatever I used to be. My head throbbed. Sharp fingers of pain jabbed in my temples. As I remembered the brandy and the wine and the champagne, a sick feeling churned in my stomach. What had I done? Above Mr Rivers was a row of books with *Julian Landau* inscribed in gold letters along the spine. I felt that it was my father himself gazing down upon me, his face sagging with disappointment.

'Please. I shall go. I knew it was wrong. I leave.' Under the stress my English disintegrated. My voice choked and I swallowed a sob. Kit crouched beside me, and tried to take my hand.

'No. No.'

I shook him off, refusing to look at him. 'Don't do this,' said Kit, his face contorting with unhappiness.

I looked past him to his father. Mr Rivers stood with his back to me, his shoulders stiff with fury. He said nothing.

'Good night, Kit. I'm so sorry. I'm sorry, Mr Rivers. I told you I was a terrible maid. I really am very sorry.'

The French doors were open to the night, and I slipped outside and into the darkness.

*   *   *

Tears streaking my cheeks, I sprinted across the black lawns and down the steps leading to the cliff path. As I drew closer to the water, my sobs were drowned out by the smash of the sea. Why hadn't Kit followed me? He was supposed to pursue me into the night and plead with me to stay. Instead, I was alone. I shuddered and slowed as I reached the edge of the cliff. Beneath, the sea boomed and foamed, flecks of salt spray pounding against the chalk. A few hundred yards away a yellow light winked in the dark. The bungalow above the cliff. Poppy. I would go to Poppy. I started to run.

*   *   *

On reaching the house, I banged on the door, hoping that she would answer and not one of her aunts. There was a flicker of light and then a girlish figure in a white dressing gown appeared on the porch. I licked saltwater from my lips.

'I saw what you did. Oh, Elise.'

I scowled and dug the tip of my nail into the fleshy part of my thumb; I would not let her see me cry. 'May I stay here, tonight?'

'Of course.'

Inside, she ushered me to a small bedroom overlooking the beach and handed me a clean nightdress and a bar of soap.

'Try to sleep. We can talk in the morning.'

I remember that after she left, I stood for a while in the darkness clutching the bundle she'd given me. Eventually, I curled up on the bed, closed my eyes and listened to the rhythmic sound of the waves rumbling on the beach below. Now writing so many years later, I am tempted to ease into a different story. I take a sip of coffee and imagine a story where instead of lying hot and sleepless, I run down to the shore. I take out *The Lugger,* haul her along the pebbled shore and into the surf. I know how to raise the sail and use the oar to push off the beach. Under the light of the moon, I sail across the wide sea. Sail to France. Sail to Anna and Julian. I arrive in Vienna in the silent dark, drifting up the Danube, a ribbon of black silk. They are waiting on the shore, called down to the river by their dreams, and together we sail away. We float across the ocean to New York—and Margot—and arrive at the Statue of Liberty in our handkerchief sailboat in the rose-red dawn and no one turns us away. It is the storyteller's prerogative to try to write, every now and then, the ending she might wish for. Even if it exists only on the white page.

*　　*　　*

I awoke to knocking on the window. The curtains were open and in the half-light of daybreak I saw Kit. I threw off the covers and waving at him to be quiet, slipped out of the bedroom. Doing my best not to disturb Poppy or her aunts, I crept out of the front door. He was waiting for me in the patch of scrub that passed for the garden of the bungalow.

'I've come to—' he said.

I put my finger to his lips and led him further

from the house. In the midst of my disgrace, I did not wish to wake the others. I wore only Poppy's white nightgown, and the sand was cold beneath my bare toes. I wrapped my arms around myself and shivered.

'Everything's all right. You can go back,' said Kit. 'I've spoken to Father and you can go back.'

I shook my head. 'No. I can't. I have to leave.'

Kit looked exhausted. There were blue shadows beneath his eyes. He had changed into pale brown slacks and a navy sweater but I suspected he had not been to bed.

'After lunch I'm going to hitch a lift up to Cambridge,' he said, trying to make me look at him.

I said nothing, and traced patterns in the sand with my toe.

'I've spoken with Father. You can go back. When I'm gone,' he added.

'It's not fair, Kit. It's my fault. You shouldn't have to go.'

He chuckled. 'It was my idea. My birthday present.'

I swallowed and carried on making loops on the ground with my foot. I sighed. He needed to know the truth, even if he never spoke to me again. 'That's not why I did it, Kit. I did it because of Diana. She stole my mother's dress and ruined it. And I was angry with her. And I did it to spite her. It wasn't because of you at all.'

Kit ran a hand through his hair. It stuck up around his ears like strands of golden straw.

'You let me kiss you because of Diana?'

'Yes.'

He took a step closer. His eyes were angry now, pupils spreading into the iris like ink into blotting paper. He grabbed my shoulders, his hands warm on my bare skin.

'You're hurting me,' I said.

I tried to wriggle away but he held me firm.

'Because of Diana. Nothing else.'

'I told you. Yes.'

Instead of letting me go, he bent down and kissed me. The coarse stubble on his chin grazed my cheek. His lips tasted of cigarettes and salt, like he'd been walking along the beach. His mouth was warm and soft and then I was kissing him and thinking of Margot and Robert always kissing in the corner of the drawing room at evening parties with me wondering why do they do that, it's so very rude, and then I thought now I understand and then I wasn't thinking anything at all except let him keep on kissing me oh keep on kissing me. He drew away and cupped my chin with both hands.

'Just Diana, then,' he said, smile twitching.

I touched my mouth with my fingertips and blinked, too surprised to speak.

'Goodbye, Elise,' he said, taking my hand. 'I hope you hear good news from your parents.'

He leant forward and placed another kiss on my lips. Then he turned and walked away along the cliff path leading back to the big house.

* * *

I woke up several hours later, with Poppy sitting on the edge of my bed, holding out a cup of tea. I jolted upright, nearly knocking it from her hand, and stared at the streams of bright sunlight rushing in at the window.

'What time is it?' I asked, smoothing my rumpled

hair.

'Late. Past eleven.'

'Oh.'

I settled back into the pillows, remembering my disgrace. My lie-in was ignominious rather than luxurious. And yet, Kit had said I was free to return after lunch. I gulped a mouthful of scalding tea, finally reconciled to the revolting English habit of drinking it with milk and sugar.

'A message came from the house. You're to see the senior staff at one thirty,' said Poppy, taking the cup, which I had been dangling perilously over the white bedspread. She placed it firmly on the bedside table.

'There is no use brooding till then. Get dressed and we'll go down to the beach.'

Pulling on a pair of her slacks, and a red sweater that must have clashed horribly with her hair, I followed her down to the sea, racing along the cliff path. The aunts had already vanished for the day, and I experienced a pang of envy at the thought of her freedom. In Tyneford, every moment of my day was accounted for, but Poppy was at liberty to get up when she liked and do as she pleased. For me, today was an unexpected, disgraceful holiday. Poppy could sit and watch the waves whip across the shore every day if she liked. Her life seemed a veritable paradise.

The tide was out, and the beach lay bare, pebbles glistening under the cold November sky. We discarded our shoes and socks, raced down to the surf and skimmed flat, brown stones. I only managed three or four bounces before my pebble sank into the water, while Poppy, with a casual flick, sent them racing like frogs across lily pads, eight or nine jumps at a time. Growing bored, we wandered along the strand to Burt's hut. The old man sat out on his upturned bucket, mending lobster pots again. He gave a friendly wave and we strolled over, loitering awkwardly amongst the spooled fishing-nets.

'Mornin',' he called.

Poppy knelt beside him and grabbed a pot. She pulled out a small knife from her pocket and started to scrape barnacles from the metal.

'Heard there was a spot o' bother last night wi' yoos and Mr Kit?' said Burt.

I nodded dumbly.

'In trouble wi' Mr Rivers and Mr Wrexham?'

'Yes.'

He gave a low chuckle. 'Yer doesn't want ter go, does yer?'

I leant against the wooden fencepost, and for the first time considered leaving Tyneford. Last night in anger and humiliation I had promised to leave, but I had not really thought what that would mean. I imagined Art attaching Mr Bobbin to the ramshackle cart and driving me to the station, jogging slowly across the green hills. And then sitting on the grey train chug-chugging its way back to the grey, smoke-filled city. Perhaps if I were very lucky, I might gain a position with two old spinsters, serving tea and buttered crumpets on paper doilies, as they sucked on their dentures. There would be no more nightjars calling from the heather in the June dark, or the wind whispering in the larch leaves or the sugar scent of jasmine after the rain. No more listening to the sea hurtle and smash into the rocks during a storm. And there would be no more Kit. Not exile for a month or two or three, but never again. I swallowed and rubbed damp palms along my slacks.

'No. I don't want to leave this place.'

Burt smiled and paused fiddling with his lobster pot.

'What time is it?' asked Poppy.

Burt studied the sun above the sea. 'Bout quarter ter one or thereabouts.'

'You can tell that by looking?' I asked, awed.

'Nope. Jist heard them church bells.'

Saying our goodbyes to Burt, we hurried towards Tyneford House. I put on my shoes and socks and Poppy neatened my hair. I felt waves of trepidation as we walked through the stable yard, now empty of cars. All the guests had gone, and I saw Henry winding up the string of lanterns. He pretended not to see me.

'I hope . . . you know,' said Poppy, giving up on trying to say the right thing and hugging me instead.

'Thanks,' I said and headed to the back door. Now that I realised how much I wanted to stay, my heart rattled in my chest like a penny in a beggar man's cup. The servants' corridor was empty and freshly washed. I surveyed the panelled hall, the scene of last night's events. All signs of the party had been wiped away, and yet beneath the soap-scented cleanness, I detected a note of sadness. The house sighed and shrugged and like the partygoers themselves, placed her tinsel back into the drawers with the good china, and felt the sag and dullness of everyday life. The tiny holes in the oak panelling, made by generations of woodworms, suddenly seemed worn and drab in the afternoon glare. In the heavy beams overhead, I heard the ominous tick-tick of the death-watch beetle.

My shoes echoing in the wooden hall, I crossed back to the servants' corridor, feeling the censure of the Rivers ancestors as they peered down at me from their gilt frames. Even the spaniels poised at their sides watched me with haughty disdain. Save for the portraits, the house was empty. Twelve hours ago it had brimmed with dancing couples and legions of white-suited waiters and now the silence unnerved me. Much as I disliked Diana and Juno, they had filled the house with life and motion. When Margot and I visited the great-aunts in Vienna, we used to explode into their dainty apartment, careering around the lacework tables and porcelain displays with our stories of school and fresh air. We perched on overstuffed sofas, nibbling ginger wafers and chattering without pause, as the three aunts, Gretta, Gerda and Gabrielle, beamed at us through pince-nez spectacles and spoilt us with chocolate, or let us rifle through the jewellery box and use great-grandmother's diamonds and golden bangles as dressing-up trinkets. When Anna decided it was time to leave, Margot and I were buttoned into our coats and bundled back onto the street, but when I glanced up at the aunts' apartment, I always spied them in the window, waving. Always waving. Always sad. That is how the big house felt that afternoon—a maiden aunt in the window, waving as the children rush away.

My feet heavy, I walked over to the butler's door and knocked.

'Come in.'

Mr Wrexham and Mrs Ellsworth waited for me in the butler's pantry. They sat side by side on the two high-backed chairs, while I stood before them, a repentant schoolgirl. I studied the floor, noticing the flagstones were spick and polished. I waited for the scolding, expecting an outpouring of wrath and fully prepared to cry. I was used to men with tempers—Julian could rage like a drunken circus bear (usually when his writing was not going too well or Anna ventured a cautious criticism of his latest draft). But what Mr Wrexham said next, I was not prepared for. He did not shout. He did not appear angry, only sad.

'So,' he said. 'You are to be the end of us all.'

Mrs Ellsworth clicked her tongue against her teeth in tacit agreement. Mr Wrexham shifted in his chair and then stood to address me, words pouring forth from his very soul.

'This never would have happened in my father's time. Girl like you, sacked and gone. Good riddance. But the problem is, you're not one of us. You're not one of them either. You don't fit. In a house like this everyone has his place. And he needs to know it for the thing to work. We each have our roles to play and we've managed just fine for a thousand years. But you . . . you and your kind. Mr Rivers and Mr Kit they don't treat you like a maid. Any other girl would have been dismissed in an instant and not by the master—he wouldn't have interfered! This is my world. But he's interfering with the running of the household because of you.'

Tears trickled wetly down my cheeks unbidden and I wiped my nose with the back of my hand. Mr Wrexham passed me a crisp white handkerchief, but he could not stop. He gazed at me, unhappy.

'Mrs Ellsworth can't even school you like a proper housemaid. It's not about laying the fires just right, or pouring the tea, or keeping quiet during dinner. You've changed everything. Don't you see? You are neither one nor the other. This is the end of Tyneford, I promise you. And it's not your fault but you brought it with you.'

I sobbed into the old butler's linen handkerchief, not knowing what I could say, what defence I could offer. His accusation was not personal and was not intended to be cruel. I was merely part of something larger that threatened his world, and the world of his father and grandfathers. But I loved this place, and I had not meant to bring about its demise. I could not believe it was true. He was mistaken. He had to be.

CHAPTER FIFTEEN

Maybe tomorrow

I heard nothing from my parents except for a six-word telegram at the end of November: ALL WELL STOP DON'T FRET STOP LOVE ANNA STOP. I sent them weekly letters from the post office in the village, filled with chirping gossip and nonsense or scraps of stories told me by Poppy or Burt. They never replied, and I had no idea whether the letters actually arrived at their destination, but I sent them just the same. I liked to think of Anna and Julian toasting brioche in front of the fire and reading my letters, even if it wasn't true. The English winter was not as bitter as the Austrian one, no snow padded the rooftops or coated the hillside, but I was cold, colder than I had ever been in my life. I went to bed in my clothes, with my overcoat draped over the covers and a filched hot-water bottle to warm my frozen toes, and I was still cold. I longed for my feathered eiderdown—the English blankets were all too thin. I dreamt about the possible stories that the viola contained. I conjured musicians playing wild tunes on the rocks above Worbarrow Tout, while Julian and Anna danced upon the sea (Julian in his canary-yellow socks). The rosewood held an infinite possibility of stories, and in the darkness Viennese pedlars jostled with goose-stepping soldiers who emerged from apartment buildings with broken windows.

My fingers swelled with chilblains and I struggled to strike the match to light the living room fires. I had almost forgotten what it was like to be warm; I shivered before the kitchen range, my hands wrapped around a mug of tea, reluctant to venture out into the arctic house. And there was no Kit. I hoped he would be back home for Christmas, but Mrs Ellsworth gave no instructions for his room to be prepared. I crossed my fingers for New Year. December 30th came and went. New Year's Eve arrived, but not Kit.

1938 slipped into 1939 while I was sleeping. Mr Wrexham politely invited me to join the servants for a glass of sherry at five past midnight (when Mr Rivers' solitary glass of champagne had been tidied away) but I declined with equal politeness. I was a shadow in the big house. Mr Rivers barely acknowledged my presence, while the other servants studiously ignored me. Only Art tolerated me, giving me handfuls of hay to feed to Mr Bobbin, the only member of the household who took pleasure in my company.

On the third of January, a letter arrived from Margot. In the cool morning light, I crouched before the fire in the drawing room and tore it open.

Anna won't ask you to help so I decided that I must. The American visa never comes. Julian never writes, not a single word (you would have thought writers would be better correspondents) and Anna's letters are full of happy lies. I'd like to say that I didn't believe a word, but I wanted to, oh, little Bean, I wanted to. And then, Hildegard wrote to me:

'It is no good here for your parents. Every week it is more difficult. They go and they wait and they are told, "Maybe tomorrow. Maybe next week." But the visa never comes.'

'Herr Finkelstein was taken away the night of November 9th. He came back but without his teeth. And they were good strong teeth. I sent Herr and Frau Landau to a hotel that night. They were safe there. But the crazies came here and took Herr Landau's books and made a bonfire of them in the street. Then they threw his desk out of the window and they burnt that too. Now all his manuscripts are gone and he thanks the God he doesn't believe in that it was nothing worse.'

Elise, they cannot wait any longer. Can your Mr Rivers help get them to Britain?

I lowered the letter, and blew gently on the coals,

causing orange flames to flare for a second. I tried not to feel a nudge of jealousy that Anna wrote more often to Margot than to me—it was not important. I must speak to Mr Rivers today, even though he hardly tolerated my presence in the house. I was the reason his son was exiled from Tyneford and the source of the servants' mutterings, but I would beg him, if I must.

*   *   *

At half past twelve, Mr Rivers set out for his walk to the top of Flower's Barrow. From the window in Kit's room, I watched him trudge up the hill, the gamekeeper's spaniel wagging at his feet. The sky was grey flint and the grass beneath a virulent green. The grass really was greener in England; on a train through France that other life ago, I had passed through endless hot brown fields. Even the undulating meadows in the Austrian Alps were dull in spring, yellowed by the snow. Mr Rivers walked fast, a tall figure, overcoat flapping in the wind, reaching the top in a few minutes. I'd never noticed before, but he had Kit's stride, only slower, more deliberate. I settled into the leather armchair beside the window. Drizzle began to fall, spotting the glass and paving stones on the terrace below. I liked hiding in Kit's room. It smelt of him: sandalwood, cigarettes. A silver case rested on the windowsill, and I flicked it open, lighting one of his familiar Turkish blend. I coughed and wafted the smoke. I knew I should be in trouble if I were caught, but since the incident I had made certain my work was exemplary and Mrs Ellsworth rarely checked up on me anymore. I allowed myself a few puffs and then extinguished it, sliding it back into the case, half smoked. I decided it was not that I missed him—simply the house was empty without him. Without Kit, I had no one to talk to, so it was only natural I should feel his absence. It was nothing more. I ran through the memory of his kiss. I had played it through so often in my mind that it was becoming worn around the edges, his voice scratched and thin, like an overplayed gramophone record.

I picked up the picture of his mother. It was odd to think that she was as much a stranger to Kit as to me. No wonder she looked so sad. I studied the angle of her jaw, the pale gold of her hair. I saw Kit in her face. He might have forgotten her, erased her from his childhood, but she was still there, her likeness hovering beneath his skin.

Mr Rivers reached the open grassland and strode along the ridgeway, bent against the wind. I slipped out of Kit's bedroom and hurried down the back stairs, collecting my woollen coat from the hook at the back door, and ventured out into the yard. The cobbles were slick with rain. Pulling my collar up around my ears, I hastened up the hill path, in pursuit of Mr Rivers. I did not want to confront him in the library, the scene of my disgrace. I noticed that when he returned from his walks, blue eyes bright, he seemed almost happy. Sometimes I even glimpsed him smiling. Mr Rivers did not smile often. I frowned and tried to rub some warmth into my hands. When I first came to Tyneford, he used to smile—usually at my poor English, though he always tried to suppress it, so as not to hurt my feelings.

The rain was falling thickly now. I blinked away great droplets that landed on my eyelashes. My shoes sucked and squelched in the muddy bank. Disgruntled cattle huddled under the barren trees, fat raindrops dangling from their ears like jewels. A dappled cow watched me with sad eyes as I trudged up the hill. I was too high to hear the roar of the sea, but the green waves hurled themselves against the cliffs as gulls soared and screeched. I wished I were like one of the heroines in the orange-jacketed novels that Kit lent to me; they were always irresistible in their wet things, only occasionally catching a dash of pneumonia which inevitably served to drive them into the stammering hero's arms. I could feel my nose turning red and dripping and my short hair cling to my face. Not that I wanted Mr Rivers to find me irresistible, just pathetic and wan, and as he gazed upon my tragic eyes (like the stern father in *La Traviata* upon the dying Violetta) he would decide that he had to help me, hang the consequences. I sneezed. It seemed a trifle unlikely.

There was yapping at my feet as the brown and white spaniel surged towards me, bouncing up with muddy paws, licking at my hands.

'Down! Stanton. No.'

Mr Rivers grabbed at the spaniel, which slipped through his fingers, smooth as a fish, and started to chase after a squawking pheasant.

'Elise?' he said, startled by my presence on the rain-soaked hill.

If I were a proper heroine, I should have swooned or broken my ankle and wept as I pleaded with him to help my family. But my ankles were stout and my cheeks a healthy scarlet from exercise.

'I came up here to find you, Mr Rivers. Please don't tell Mr Wrexham.'

He said nothing but watched me with those blue eyes. I swallowed and felt my heart pound in my ears.

'They burnt his books, Mr Rivers. They took them outside and burnt them.'

The wind picked up strands of my hair and whipped them against my face, stinging my skin.

'And the American visa?'

'It never comes.'

He stood quite still, unconcerned by the pounding rain and the scream of the wind in the bare trees. I felt impatient, almost ready to stamp my waterlogged shoe. He must know what I wanted.

'Will you help me? Please.'

He remained silent.

'Please. I know I've behaved dreadfully. But I've done my best since then, really I have. And I don't know what else to do.'

He gave a slight nod to show he was listening. I took a deep breath and continued, meeting his level blue gaze.

'And if the war starts. And everyone says it must. Even Art and Burt and Mr Wrexham say so. Anna and Julian must be in America or France or here.'

Putting his fingers to his lips, he let out a piercing whistle and, in a flurry of wagging mud, the spaniel reappeared, its pink tongue flopping with happiness.

'We should return to the house. It's god-awful weather to be out.'

I stared at him for a moment. Was he going to help? I could not tell.

* * *

The whispers of war had built up to a cacophony, as a single leaf blowing in the wind becomes a forest floor spinning in a hurricane. Even Mrs Ellsworth tuned her wireless into the evening news, allowing May and me to sit in her little parlour and listen while we drank our cocoa before bed. I wanted war. I wanted my Austria back, as long as the fighting did not start until Anna and Julian were safely stowed across the sea. I tried to imagine them here in Tyneford: Julian striding across the hills beside Mr Rivers, gun slung over his shoulders, or Anna playing Mendelssohn on the grand piano in the drawing room. The tuning was spoilt from the salt air, but I knew Anna could make it sing. Mrs Ellsworth brought the sinister gas masks out of the basement, anxious despite Mr Rivers' endless reassurance, and quite certain that war could be declared at any second and German bombs would fall a minute later, gassing the entire household. At night, I had uneasy dreams of Anna playing the piano, her fingers rippling across the keys and her angel voice muffled by her rubber gas mask.

One morning in February, a flock of letters arrived from Margot. The post from America was proving terribly unreliable; there was nothing for weeks and then I would receive a packet of letters all at once. They spilt off Mr Wrexham's silver tray, and I caught them in my apron before they fluttered to the floor. This was my one afternoon a week off, and I saved the letters until after lunch, stowing them in my pocket to read on the beach. Poppy had promised to take me to Brandy Bay, then all the way past Wagon Rock, and onto the Tilly Whim Caves. At two o'clock she waited for me outside the bungalow, wrapped in oilskins and layers of woollen scarves.

'Come on. You ready?' she called, impatient.

I nodded and Poppy took off along the high cliff path, not down to the beach at Worbarrow, but sprinting along the narrow chalk track. It was sopping from the weeks of rain and slippery as ice, and I shrieked, terrified that she would fall down the cliff. The hungry sea smashed against the base of the rocks, foam tufting on the breakers. She laughed and slowed to a jog, so I could catch up. Her hair broke free from its swaddling, and flew around her face in red flames. The dark sea seemed to swallow all the light from the world, so that the sky glowered grey as it hovered over the water. Poppy's hair was unnaturally bright against the winter seascape. She tried to knot it back into place.

'I used to hate it,' she said. 'I was born with long hair. Not a good head of curls like some babies but long hair all the way down to my shoulders.'

There was a splutter overhead, gaggling and flapping, as a flock of geese, grey-blue with orange bills, skimmed the air above us.

'Greylag geese. Aren't they beautiful?' asked Poppy. 'Tell Art you saw them, and he'll get out the shotgun. Roast goose, damson jelly—delicious.'

I stared at the soaring birds, vast and dark as shadows, their pinkish legs drawn up underneath their bellies, neat as the ancient aunts on the sofa, hiding their feet beneath the puff of their skirts. I didn't want to eat the geese, I wanted to watch them fly. Poppy had raced on, and I ran to find her. My mind echoed with the call and crash of the sea, the wind whipping the swelling waves into an ever-increasing fury. In the distance a small fishing-boat danced and leapt on the water. We ran and walked in fits and bursts for an hour, watching as Brandy Bay appeared below us, the smooth sand lapped by low tide, and then disappeared as we turned the headland. On the horizon stood Lovell's Tower, a solitary stone folly perched on the cliff top above Kimmeridge Bay.

As we rounded the next bend, the cliff path split, one continuing up and over the headland on towards Kimmeridge, and the other leading to a rocky shelf and several black square caverns. I hurried after Poppy to the flat limestone shelf. The caves loomed dark and ominous, and I stifled a delicious shudder. Poppy disappeared into one and I followed. The cave smelt damp and the walls were coated with green mould the colour of spinach. They were hewn with square strokes, and vast slabs of rock lay strewn across the ground. Poppy selected one for a seat, and I chose another beside her. While Poppy lounged and smoked, I drew out Margot's packet, choosing her most recent letter to read first.

> *Have you heard from the parents? I get almost no letters from them anymore. But, I have discovered from Hildegard the problem with the visa—Julian and Anna cannot afford the exit tax. There is a bribe to pay, exactly how large I don't know, but they have run out of money. They cannot get a proper price for anything they sell. Robert has been trying to find a way to send them money from America but it is almost impossible—everyone comes here from Europe, there is no one going back. Please, Bean, please ask Mr Rivers to find a way to help.*

Then, when they are safe with you, I shall persuade Robert that we must come to England. I don't think it can be so different from America. It is so quiet with the two of us. Who would have thought that I could miss your noise and untidiness (I think of you every time I pick up Robert's clothes off the floor)? I even miss the stink of Julian's cigar and Hilde's huffing when he stained the sideboard with dribbles of burgundy. And Anna . . . how do you bear missing Anna?

I thought California was full of sunshine. Here, it rains all the time. I have umbrellas in every colour—I take my rainbow out into the rain. Robert's English is getting better. Though, it doesn't really matter as half the department is from Strasbourg or Vienna or Berlin, and mostly they speak Scientist anyhow.

I have joined a quartet at the University. Women play in public here, in actual concerts in halls with people paying money to hear them. I wonder if I dare? The aunts would never approve. Can you imagine their faces? A great niece who is a professional musician in a proper orchestra! Only harlots perform for money. But do you know, Bean—I think I should rather like to be a harlot. It has always rather suited Anna.

I knew nothing about exit taxes. Julian used to have plenty of money. I remembered the large, flat banknotes in his wallet, but now no one would take his books. I thought of the stash of gold chains, hidden in the stocking in my attic bedroom and felt a ripple of guilt. I resolved to speak once again to Mr Rivers. I kicked at a pebble and it flew against the cave wall, causing a tiny avalanche to rain down.

'Careful,' said Poppy. 'It's not very safe in here. Bits of roof are always falling in.'

She studied me for a minute, her feet tapping against the rock. 'I am sorry about your family. I'd help if I could. And I might, you know. I'm off to London. For something secret.' She glanced over her shoulder as if someone might be eavesdropping and whispered, 'For the government—in case there is a war.'

'You are?'

I was torn between curiosity and misery that she was leaving.

'Yes. I decided not to take up my place at Cambridge. I really don't see the point for girls—all that work and then not allowed to collect your degree. It's like being in an egg and spoon race only you aren't allowed to win or even eat your egg at the end, if you know what I mean.'

'Yes. I think I do.'

'And if there is a war, I'm sure they won't let girls fight. They never do, you know, it's most unfair. But in this job I shall have to be discreet. I think I shall find that part rather hard. Oh, can you tell me something very secret, and then I can practise?'

Poppy fixed me with those grass green eyes, eager as a cuckoo on the first day of spring. I tried to think both of a secret, and one I wouldn't mind sharing. My only secret was Kit's dawn kiss and I didn't want to share that. It belonged to me alone—telling Poppy would dilute it somehow.

'Oh well,' she said with a shrug. 'Never mind. But if you think of something, be sure to let me know. I shall be gone three or four months.'

'So long?' I grimaced and looked away. First Kit,

now Poppy. I felt rather sorry for myself.

'Oh yes. Will is sure to miss me dreadfully,' she said happily. 'I feel quite desolate whenever I think about it. Do you think he'll weep and lose his appetite? I shall have to write him very passionate and very short letters.'

She was quiet for a few minutes and it took me a while to realise that she was staring at me with an intense expression.

'Elise, what do you know about sexual intercourse?'

I looked at her in surprise, absurdly flattered that she considered me so worldly. 'Why do you ask?'

'I thought I might make it with Will. Before I go away.'

'Oh,' I said, taken aback. When they thought I wasn't listening, Anna and Julian made a scurrilous joke about the repressed sexual desires of the British. Consequently, I believed that English people only had sex after they were married, and only then on Thursdays. It is funny to think how innocent we girls were in those days. Of course, we believed ourselves to be mighty sophisticated but really we were terribly naïve, however bohemian our parents.

'Well,' I said. 'My mother explained the . . . correct procedures. And according to Anna most operas revolve around sex. And singing. But really they're all about sex.'

Poppy frowned. A discussion of the finer opera plots was not really the information she wanted.

'And I read Julian's copy of Freud. That's full of sex,' I added, determined to be helpful.

I'd sneaked into my father's study and borrowed several volumes of Freud, anticipating a frisson of intrigue, similar to when I'd glimpsed the semi-clothed ladies with come-hither eyes, who were sold for a pfennig on picture postcards at the grimy stalls beside the Danube. I tingled when I imagined myself as one of those corseted beauties, with someone paying their penny to stare at me. The Freud books, on the other hand, were disappointing.

'And?' demanded Poppy. 'What did Mr Freud say? I really do need to know.'

I frowned with the effort of explaining. 'It's all about ids and egos and superegos. I think he puts his id, or is it his ego, into your superego and then you both experience sublimation. It's very complicated. And there were lots of things about the phallus.'

'Ah, yes,' said Poppy. 'I've seen those before. On horses and dogs. And once on a bull who was making intercourse with a cow. Well, if what cattle do is called intercourse that is. It looked angrier than that. I certainly didn't notice any ids or egos with the cows. But then, I wouldn't know what to look for.'

'No, me neither.'

'Well,' said Poppy, 'I suppose people got along all right before Freud explained things to them, so maybe we'll be all right.'

'Perhaps. But I rather wanted to be better than all right.'

Poppy raised an eyebrow.

'It's nice to be good at things,' I said, blushing and trying not to think about Kit. 'And I don't think Will would mind if you're a beginner. After all, everyone has to start somewhere,' I added kindly, repeating the phrase Mrs Ellsworth used whenever she taught me something new.

'I suppose if I sleep with Will, I shall be a floozy,' said Poppy, not unhappy at the prospect.

'I don't think so. Not if you love him. And besides, all the best heroines are floozies sooner or later. Eve. Floozy. Anna Karenina. Tragic Floozy.'

'Would you be one with Kit?'

I knew I ought to say no, I should not dream of it. Anna was rather less bohemian in moral matters affecting her daughters, forbidding Margot to go on holiday with Robert before they were married. I thought of my mother, small and furious, berating my sister, *'You shall not go gallivanting in Dusseldorf. Think of the poor aunts. They will die of shock.'* I felt a sharp pang. Anna would know exactly what advice to give Poppy.

Outside the cavern the light was fading into evening, dark clouds buffeted the shore. The black sea glittered, a slice of moon bobbing on the waves.

'Come,' I said, standing up and reaching for her hand. 'We should go back.'

* * *

The following morning, I slipped into the breakfast room as Mr Rivers lingered over his coffee. He studied his newspaper with a set frown, not noticing as I entered. I reached into my apron pocket, pulling out a handful of gold chains and set them down on his side plate. He glanced up, startled.

'Mr Rivers. This is to pay for the bribe. To get Anna and Julian out of Austria.'

He said nothing, only stared at the yellow gold spooled on the china, the colour of fresh butter.

'It was to pay for my ticket to New York. The

chains are quite valuable. Please sell them.'

He shook his head and pushed the side plate towards me, knocking over the marmalade.

'No. Keep your money. I shall do everything I can.'

I folded my arms behind my back.

'Take the chains, Mr Rivers. The money is not for you, it is for them.'

There must have been a note in my voice, as he gave a sharp nod and, folding the gold into his handkerchief, slid it into his pocket.

That night, as I lay in bed listening to the distant sea rumble against the pebbles on the shore, I worried the money from the chains would not be enough. I thought of the viola hidden beneath my bed. No one would publish Julian in Austria, but what about England? Mr Rivers read all his books, and if I translated them into English, then maybe a publisher would want them. I jumped out of bed, and rummaged through the stack of paperback novels on the chest of drawers. I chose one with an austere grey and black cover, deciding it looked suitably gloomy, and composed a letter to the publisher.

Dear Mr Editor,

I am the daughter of the famous Viennese novelist Julian Landau, described in the Vienna Times *as 'certainly the city's strangest writer' which I am sure you will agree is very a big compliment. By a stroke of magic fortune I have with me in England his latest manuscript. If you are interested, I can send it to you. It might take me a week or two, as it is presently hidden inside a viola for very safekeeping. I am most willing to*

take onboard his translation.
Yours etc.

Climbing back into bed, I was warm with hope, confident that Julian had sent with me the means to procure his own escape. As I slept, the song of the viola mingled with the rush of the tide.

* * *

If February was cold, March was quiet. I missed Poppy's chatter and I took my walks alone. I pounded across the hills or along the rain-lashed beaches with my sister's letters in my coat pocket, reading and re-reading until I was word perfect. I hated corresponding via letter—the conversation was too slow. I felt Margot and I were two old ladies, stuttering out our thoughts, with pauses the size of the Atlantic between each idea. I told her about the sale of the gold chains, but not about the novel in the viola. Perhaps I ought to have told her, but we are all wise with hindsight. It was my secret and unless the publisher summoned me to remove the pages from the viola, I chose to remain silent. She wrote eager letters guessing the value of the gold, and I replied, speculating on the number of weeks it would take for the visa to arrive. Sometimes I liked to sit at the pinnacle of Tyneford cap, the hardy hillside sheep grazing the slope below—the bells around their necks tinkling in the wind—and gaze at the blue clouds rushing across the sky, their shadows trawling the hill like great outstretched nets.

I perched on the low stone wall beside Flower's Barrow and read with growing disappointment the reply from the London publisher:

> *Dear Miss Landau,*
> *Thank you for the invitation to read Herr Landau's latest novel. While I am most intrigued by the notion of a novel smuggled inside a viola, I'm afraid there is simply little demand for German novels in England at the present time—even in translation. I am sure you understand.*
> *Thank you for considering us.*
> *Yours etc.*

March brought gales that hurled tiles off the stable roof, and sent Art up rocking ladders to nail them back into place. Snowdrops sprang up beneath the hedgerows and brown banks, and yellow and purple crocuses studded the lawns before Tyneford House, opening and closing in the sun like the mouths of hungry chicks. Spring arrived, causing the tulips to sprout in the terracotta pots on the terrace and blonde primroses to unfurl on the sunny banks. The fishermen took to their boats in droves—happy as the cackling coots that milder weather had returned. I watched the boats and birds from the cliffs or from my high roost on Tyneford cap. One afternoon, a month or so after Poppy's departure, I sprawled in my usual spot on the cap, watching with Art's binoculars as a rough-legged buzzard soared and then hovered, wings pulsing. I lay on my back, transfixed by the bird's black belly and vast outstretched wings, and lost all track of time. Then the church bells chimed three, and I shot up with a start. I was late. Binoculars slapping against my coat, I raced down to the house, skidding on stones and mud, scattering the bleating sheep as I ran. I arrived at the back of the house in twenty minutes, face bright red and glistening, shoes caked in muck. I paused in the driveway to catch my breath, bending over to stretch out the stitch in my side. As I straightened, I noticed a silver Wolseley gleaming beside the front door. Kit lolled beside it, smoking a cigarette. Without a thought, I bounded up to him and threw my arms around his neck.

'You're back. Thank goodness you're back.'

He chuckled and allowed me to embrace him, making no effort to disentangle himself. 'So you did miss me?'

I stood back. 'Well. It's been awfully quiet without you. Especially now Poppy's gone.'

Before he could reply, a slight figure in a tan-coloured Burberry raincoat came out into the driveway, putting up a small, gloved hand to shield her eyes from the sharp spring sunshine.

'Oh, that's still here,' said Diana, with a scornful glance in my direction. 'I thought it was fired.'

I balled my hands into fists and said nothing. I needed Mr Rivers to help me, not dismiss me for impertinence.

'Stop it, Di,' said Kit. 'Her name is Elise, as you jolly well know. Play nice.'

He leant forward and whispered in my ear, 'Sorry. Part of my penance. Being charming to Diana Hamilton. Taking her out to lunch and being gentlemanly. Tough act. But she's all right really.'

That I rather doubted. I excused myself, and disappeared into the house to prepare tea.

*   *   *

Now, in front of Kit, Diana was polite to me. She'd

clearly decided that to insult and ridicule the housemaid was not the way to endear herself (even if said housemaid was jumped up and frightful). During that first tea I decided, irrevocably, that Diana was not all right. She had not improved, whatever steel wool she had pulled over Kit's eyes. As I poured Earl Grey into china cups, Diana giggled. Not at me, but at some remark of Kit's. In fact, she never ceased giggling—she was like one of those rattling birds out on the marshes. Everything he said was a scream. She simpered and pouted, while I scowled and huffed and tried not to drop the biscuits. Kit could be quite amusing, but Diana was making herself ridiculous. Or at least, I hoped she was. I scrutinised him for his response, but Kit was staring lazily across the lawns to the sea.

'I'm glad to be home. I've missed you,' he murmured.

I wasn't sure if he spoke to the house itself, to Tyneford or to me.

*   *   *

As it had last summer, Kit's arrival woke up the household. We'd all become dreary and reconciled to our shabbiness over the dull winter, but Kit's presence rushed warmth into every corner. As well as Diana, he'd brought Juno and a couple of chaps from college. While she helped me wash up the tea things, Mrs Ellsworth complained that young Mr Kit couldn't go nowhere without a crowd. I said nothing, and dunked a floral teacup in the soapsuds, but I suspected that he was eager to avoid those long hours alone with his father. It was always better when there was an Eddie or a Teddy or a

George to prevent those awkward tête-à-têtes of mutual disappointment.

On his first evening at home, Kit lumbered into the great hall with Art and Burt, lugging half a tree among the three of them. Ignoring Mrs Ellsworth's cries of concern for the polished floor, or Mr Wrexham's fears that the chimney had not been swept these forty years, he stoked up a roaring bonfire in the massive stone grate. The chimney drew just fine, and the crackling hulk of oak sent tongues of heat rushing through the house. At Kit's insistence, we all gathered in front of the blaze, staff as well as ladies and gentlemen. Kit doled out glasses of pink gin to everyone and, as we sipped, the damp limestone plaster and spotted wallpaper was transfigured into snug magnificence. Even Mr Wrexham smiled and patted my arm. Mr Rivers and Kit brought out the old gramophone from the drawing room into the hall, and everybody, servants and society girls, danced to Cole Porter as the fire roared. The ladies and gentlemen danced on one side of the panelled hall and the staff on the other. I hesitated in the darkness beneath a portrait of a sallow-skinned chap in a frock-coat. I couldn't dance. Not here, not after last time. Kit bobbed with Juno, while Diana danced with Mr Rivers. I smiled at the spectacle and sniffed at my pink gin.

'Will you do me the honour?' said Mr Wrexham, with a kind smile.

I was so grateful, I could have wept. We moved to where Mrs Ellsworth stood up with Burt, and Henry bopped with May. It all felt rather jolly and twelfth-nightish. The telephone in Mr Rivers' library began to ring, and Mr Wrexham excused himself to answer it. He returned a few minutes later and confided something to Mr Rivers. Mr Rivers listened gravely, spoke a few words to the butler, who then glided over to the gramophone and lifted off the needle, so that the music stuttered into silence. There were disgruntled objections from the ladies and gentlemen, who continued dancing for a beat or two, until Mr Rivers held up his hand for quiet.

'My estate manager has telephoned. He has just heard on the wireless that Hitler has invaded Czechoslovakia.'

There was a pause, an intake of breath, and then an explosion of chatter. Diana hung onto Kit's arm while Mrs Ellsworth clasped May's pudgy hand, her face quite white. Mr Rivers slipped away to the library, and I followed him. He stood with his back to me, fiddling with the tuning on the wireless.

'Mr Rivers? Were you able to help us?'

He jumped as he heard my voice.

'Christ. Don't creep up on a man like that. It's uncanny.'

I shrugged. 'Mr Wrexham usually complains I'm a galumpher.'

He gave a tight smile and sat down in his battered chair, pouring the pink gin into a pot plant beside the window and helping himself to whisky from the decanter.

'It's not as easy as you might think, Elise. They really don't like your father's books in Austria, or in Berlin for that matter. The bribe is heftier than I could ever have imagined.'

I felt oddly calm. The world grew quiet around me, while at the same time I could hear the rhythmic tick-tick of the grandfather clock in the hall, a deep echo of the smaller one in our

Viennese apartment. I smelt Hildegard's cooking: roasting lamb fat and celery salt as her meatballs wrapped in white cabbage leaves sizzled in the oven. I listened to the twin clocks beating two sets of time, and heard my voice ask, 'But Mr Freud? They hated his books and they let him go.'

Mr Rivers sighed. 'Yes. But Mr Freud is very famous outside of Austria. Your father has fewer friends.'

I remembered Anna's pearls. 'I still have a necklace. I can sell it.'

Mr Rivers took a gulp of whisky. 'It won't do any good. I'm talking thousands of Reichsmarks.'

Before I could speak, the gentlemen surged into the library, Diana and Juno following in their wake, filling the room with bustle and noise.

'Shall we listen then, my good fellow?' said Eddie, though it may have been George. Kit thumped the wireless and the bells of Big Ben came over the airwaves.

'I feel quite sick,' declared Juno. 'I suppose there'll have to be a war now. One does think that they could sort it out between them without bringing us into it all.'

'Does anyone have a cigarette?' asked Diana, sinking onto the window seat.

I looked back at Mr Rivers and, seeing him swarmed with people, realised our conversation was finished. I didn't need to hear the news on the wireless. I slid out of the room and into the now empty hall. Mr Wrexham was clearing the empty glasses. He stopped when he saw me.

'It's past midnight. You may retire if you wish.'

I had not been asked to act as lady's maid to Diana and Juno on this visit. To our mutual relief—I suspected.

'Thank you, Mr Wrexham.'

I hastened along the servants' corridor and up the back stairs to my attic room. I lay in the darkness listening to the constant rush of the sea. Thousands of Reichsmarks. Thousands. I whispered the words aloud again and again, as though I could conjure such a sum out of the night. The house was still and full of sleepers. I padded through the silent hall and into the library. I scanned the bookshelves and, finding what I wanted, reached up and drew down *The Spinsters' Dowry* by Julian Landau, before creeping into the drawing room. The curtains were open and the moon filled the room with cold light, bright enough to read by. I sat cross-legged on the floor, the book open on my lap. It was not my favourite of Julian's novels and Anna actively disliked it, complaining it was unkind. That was why I wanted it with me tonight. With this book in my hands, I could hear my parents row. The three virgin spinsters were the great-aunts. Julian described them in cruel detail, down to the single hair sprouting from the round mole on Gretta's chin. Only in the book she was called Gertrude. Julian insisted that the aunts were transformed by fiction and Gretta, Gerda and Gabrielle (real life) had nothing to do with Gertrude, Grunhilda and Griselda (novel). Anna and the aunts remained unconvinced. When Julian attempted to justify himself over coffee and *sachertorte*, Gretta grumbled that she did not wish for her wart to be immortalised for eternity. After the aunts withdrew, dignity wounded, a fight echoed through the apartment. To Margot's and my tremendous delight, Anna threw a series of

Meissen plates at Julian. We cheered her on from round the nursery door, wondering if she'd succeed in hitting and killing him—'Do you think we shall be orphans? Will Mama wear lipstick in prison?' It was terribly thrilling.

I had understood Anna and the aunts' fury—they were not angered by Julian's lies but by his honesty. He ought not to have stolen from life, but tonight I was grateful he had. As I shivered on the floor in the drawing room of an English country house a thousand miles from Vienna, I could see my aunts in the pages of the book. They smiled up at me, offering me sugar biscuits and grumbling over the supercilious waiters at Café Sperl. I have no photographs of the aunts, and so they seem almost characters from a children's story—a clutch of creased fairy godmothers, fond of *linzertorte* and nieces—not quite belonging to the modern world. Yet they are preserved between the pages of Julian's novel like the crushed wings of a butterfly.

That night I read for hours, pretending I was among my family. Julian and Anna lazed on the sofa, Anna resting her blonde head in his lap.

'I wouldn't have come here, if I'd known you'd be stuck,' I said, frowning at them.

Anna smiled. 'What would you have done, little Bean? Sat and fretted with us?'

I shifted on the floor. 'We are all supposed to be in New York. It isn't supposed to happen this way.'

The vision of my mother was unchanged: the same tiny crease between her eyes, same half-smile.

'I hope the novel in the viola is about you and me and Margot. Only in the book we'll be much more glamorous. I'll be thinner and two inches taller. Margot will be just the same. Julian will sport a twirling moustache and you will wear ankle boots and smoke cigarillos. And Kit—'

'But we don't know Kit,' said Julian.

No, you don't, I thought and the mirage vanished like mist in sunshine. I would have to be up in a few hours to light the fires and clean the house. I struggled to my feet, and began to pace up and down the drawing room, trying to exhaust myself so that I could sleep. Perhaps I should start to clean now—then at least some of it would be done in the morning. I fished a handkerchief out of my pyjama pocket and started to dab at the picture frames. I worked my way round the mantelpiece, wafting the cloth at the miniature portraits, frocked ladies with high collars and lace caps, men in wigs and regimentals, a wide-eyed beauty with dazzling décolletage, her powdered wig set with pearls. I moved to the Turner seascape, ready to flick dust from its gilt edges, but the painting was gone. I blinked, and rubbed my eyes. Was it always here? I ached with tiredness and my mind felt doughy and unclear. Yes. The Turner hung on this wall, far enough away from the fire that it didn't get smoke damage, and out of the sunlight that streamed in through the southerly windows. Without a doubt, the painting had gone.

I sat on a baize sofa and stared at the empty wall. It wasn't like the bare walls in our Vienna apartment, when I thought of those I raged with unhappiness. This was different. Hope nudged inside me. The painting wasn't lost or stolen or re-hung in another part of the house. Mr Rivers had sold it. He was going to help us. Anna and Julian were coming to Tyneford.

CHAPTER SIXTEEN

Miss Landau

At six o'clock the following morning, I slipped into Kit's bedroom. It was warm enough that the gentlemen no longer had fires lit in their rooms—ladies such as Diana and Juno would insist upon them in blazing June. I was quite safe, but I locked the door just to be certain. The room held a sharp scent of sweat and cigarettes. Kit sprawled in the large white bed, a foot poking out from beneath the blankets, his blond head half hidden beneath a pile of pillows. I listened for a moment to the rhythmic sounds of his breath and tiptoed across to the window and peeked out across the striped lawn towards the hill. An early morning haar rolled down the valley, thick as smoke. The sun glowed through, a gold coin in a shroud. With a flick, I flung open the curtains wide and bright light spilt into the room, shining on the figure in the bed. I stepped back from the window, in case Mr Wrexham or anyone should happen to be walking in the gardens.

'Kit.'

He didn't stir.

'Kit.'

Nothing.

I sat on the bed, and reached out to touch a bare arm lightly dusted with pale hair. My fingertips brushed warm skin. 'Kit.' A hand clasped my wrist and drew me onto the bed.

'Fancy meeting you here,' said Kit, suddenly wide awake. He pulled me closer. 'This isn't very wise, you know. If I decided to be wicked, you couldn't really object.'

He scrutinised me for a moment and then yawned. 'Don't suppose you brought tea and aspirin by any chance?'

I ignored him and tried to sit up but he kept a firm grasp on my wrist and I was forced to turn my head, so that I was lying beside him, his face only an inch from mine.

'Kit. Tell me it's true. That Mr Rivers has sold the painting. That he's really going to help Anna and Julian.'

He released me, and propped himself up on the pillows and stared out over the green lawns.

'Well, it's not been sold yet. He wanted to make sure I didn't mind. My inheritance and what-not.'

'And do you mind?'

Kit didn't answer. He bent over me and kissed me on the lips, his fingers curving around the back of my neck, pulling me into him. And suddenly I wasn't thinking about Anna or Julian, only Kit. He bit my lip and I cried out, although it did not hurt. He smiled down at me.

'I love you, you know. I suppose I oughtn't. I ought to love Diana or one of those girls who's frightfully dull and frightfully rich. But I don't. I love you.'

I stared at him. No one apart from my mother had ever said those words to me. And I had always imagined that when somebody did, the words would be spoken in German, not English. To my ear, they sounded new. I'd never been to an English cinema and I never listened to Mrs Ellsworth's love-struck plays on the wireless. I'd read Kit's romance novels, but I'd never heard the words said aloud. The first time was when he said them to me.

'We'll get them here, I promise you, Elise,' he whispered. 'If I have to go to Austria myself and carry their bags, I will get them to Tyneford.'

He gazed down at me, blue eyes wide and guileless as a child. He was so certain and whenever I looked at him, I was certain too. I slid my hands into his golden hair and kissed him.

'I love you.'

I tried the words in English. They tasted strangely exotic in my mouth, and yet, in a way, detached from their meaning. I tried again in German.

'*I love you.*'

Kit laughed, a throaty chuckle. 'Say that again. I like it.'

Before I could, the door handle rattled.

'Mr Kit, sir. Would you be so good as to unlock this door?' called Mr Wrexham.

I sat up in horror, bumping Kit on the forehead in my haste.

'He knows I am here,' I hissed, springing off the bed.

Kit shrugged and reached for his silver cigarette case. 'Probably. Wrexham knows everything. Damn fine butler. Old school.'

He swung his legs out of bed and jumped up, grabbing a dressing gown from the back of the door. He glanced round to check where I was and seeing me lurking by the window smoothing my apron, he opened the door.

'Morning, Wrexham. Ah excellent, you brought tea. And aspirin, you really are a champ.'

The butler stepped into the room, holding out a tea tray, and stopped dead when he saw me.

Kit, apparently unconcerned, helped himself to the packet of aspirin, swallowing the pills dry. Mr Wrexham's face turned as grey as a winter's sky and he studied me without blinking.

'May I enquire as to Elise's presence?' he asked, recovering himself sufficiently to place the tray on the bedside table and pour Kit a cup of tea.

Kit took a noisy gulp. 'Yes. Well, if I'm honest, I woke up to find her here. Lovely surprise. Touch irregular, I know. But don't worry,' he added, seeing the old butler blanch. 'Nothing untoward happened. Well, nothing too untoward,' he concluded with a wicked smile in my direction.

I gave a short cry, and covered my mouth, turning to face the window. I did not wish to see Mr Wrexham's expression.

'Oh, it's all right, Wrexham,' said Kit. 'I love her, you know.'

'Perhaps, Mr Kit, you would be good enough to inform your father of this fact.'

The butler bent to scoop up a stray pillow and a fallen magazine from the bedroom floor. Kit crossed the room and settled into the battered armchair beside the window, looking slightly troubled for the first time since Mr Wrexham's interruption.

'Yes. Yes, I suppose I must.'

He shifted in his chair.

'Think I shall dress first, though.'

'Very good sir. Shall I draw you a bath?'

'Yes. Excellent.'

During this exchange, I had remained at the window, a few feet from Kit's chair. I was elated and mortified all at the same time. I wanted to cry, whether from joy or humiliation, I was not quite sure. It was clear that Mr Wrexham was not going anywhere, and so I decided that mostly I wanted to leave the room.

'I must clean downstairs,' I said. I did not think Kit would try to kiss me in front of the old butler, but I could not be sure. I could feel both men watching me as I fled, and was glad that I could see neither of their faces.

* * *

I avoided the breakfast room, not wanting to encounter either Mr Rivers or his guests, certain that the entire household must suspect something was afoot. I dusted the netsuke in the drawing room, taking them out of their glass cabinet and cleaning each piece in warm water before drying it and returning it to the appropriate shelf with shaking fingers. They were ugly things: grey ivory rats crawled over one another, tails knotted; fat warriors smirked. I washed the skirting boards with soap solution, and rubbed the dado rails with beeswax. I needed to keep busy; I couldn't stay still. When I thought about Kit, my fingers fluttered to my throat. I smiled. Perhaps I ought to worry about my possible dismissal and yet I was happy and untouchable. He kissed me. He loved me. Would we get married? I'd read all the romance novels stashed in the guest bedrooms, from *Lady Rose and Mrs Memmary* to the intriguing *Miss Buncle's Book* and the more troubling *Cheerful Weather for the Wedding,* but all the novels stopped at the crucial point: the wedding itself, and what came after remained terribly intriguing. I wished Margot were here to talk to. The information Poppy and

I had shared now seemed rather inadequate and I suspected that no books on Mr Rivers' shelves could offer practical assistance. My sister was not coy, and I knew she would deliver without a blush any information I required, between languorous pulls on her cigarette. I pictured her, sprawled upon the bed in the blue room in her elegant underwear, eating rose creams and offering advice on married life while surrounded by a haze of smoke. I would write to her, demanding detailed factual advice by return, but I did not want the cold page, I wanted her.

I tried to imagine Kit and me taking tea together on the terrace in summer, the climbing roses filling the air with their pervasive scent, as we discussed the unconscionably warm weather or perhaps the cricket. I giggled. Next, I imagined not leaving the room when he took his bath and sitting on the edge of the tub as I did with Margot—only this wasn't the same at all. I saw Kit lazing, naked, and smiling at me through the steam. What would I wear for such an occasion? A dressing gown? My underthings? Nothing at all? My cheeks flushed and I bit my lip. Yes, I decided, I could marry him very well.

* * *

Kit found me as I was sluicing the back steps by the stable yard. I was so busy scraping at the green moss on the stone that he was forced to shout.

'There you are. I've been looking for you all over.'

I stood up and brushed myself down, conscious of the layer of black-green slime beneath my fingernails.

'Come for a walk.'

I cast a guilty look at the bucket of filthy water and the half-cleaned steps.

'Oh, leave it. Do it later,' snapped Kit, grabbing hold of my wet hand and hurrying me out of the yard and along the path leading up the hillside. We didn't speak for a minute or two, breathless as we climbed the steep hill, slip-sliding over the damp ground. Fragile violets grew amongst the tangled grass stems, the first I had seen that spring, and I tried not to crush them underfoot. Kit walked swiftly, and I was soon panting to keep up, feeling my forehead moisten with sweat. As we reached the summit he slowed.

'Well, I spoke to him.'

I leant against the dry-stone wall criss-crossing the top of the hill. White clouds buffeted across the grey-blue sky. Kit came and stood beside me, a strand of damp hair sticking to his brow.

'What did he say?'

Kit shifted. 'Well. I sort of marched in there. Into the library. And I said "I love Elise". And he looked up at me and he said, "I know".'

' "I know"?'

'Yes. It's funny—I've only known myself since yesterday. I was almost sure when I left. And while I was away, I kept thinking about you. I'd be trying to do other things—dinner with the chaps, a game of tennis—and there you were. I started to wonder if I was in love. Then when I came back and you hurled yourself at me, beside the motorcar, I was certain.'

'I didn't hurl myself.'

'Oh yes. I'm pretty sure you did.'

I swatted him, half in anger and half in jest, and he caught my arm, tugging me against him. I smiled, snug in his arms, and thought, so this is happiness.

'And you smoked my cigarettes. I found one that was half spent. It smelt of you.'

Letting me go, Kit heaved himself onto the wall and helped me scramble up so that I perched beside him, our legs dangling. He gazed out towards the sea. It rippled in the distance, waves rushing the beach.

'It was odd. Father didn't want to know much about me. Already knew all about my grand passion. He was much more interested in you.'

'In me? Whatever for.'

'He wanted to know if you loved me. Asked me several times, if I was quite sure. He seemed rather anxious about it all. No.' Kit paused, searching the pale sky for the words. 'That's not right. Sad. He was sad.'

'Oh.'

I supposed Mr Rivers must be disappointed in Kit loving me. It couldn't be terribly good for his reputation. He probably wanted Kit to fall in love with a Diana or Juno or Lady Henrietta. Somebody with no chin and a large fortune and a wardrobe full of mink stoles. And a neat entry in the baptismal register of Some-shire.

We sat and listened to the birds, the swooping song of the skylarks, the chatter of the rock pipits as they parachuted to earth and the yaffle of a green woodpecker. The gorse dotted across the hillside was coated in sticky yellow flowers smelling sweetly of coconut. Kit was silent for a moment, then he fidgeted beside me, and said quietly, 'He doesn't want us to be engaged. Not yet.'

'Oh.'

My stomach twisted with uncertainty.

Kit smiled. 'Don't look so worried. He just wants us to wait.'

'Why?'

I found out many years later exactly what passed in the library between the two men. But on that spring morning in 1939, Kit described only part of their conversation, concealing what was said later. Over time I have pictured the conversation so often that sometimes I have to remind myself that I was not actually there and it is not a memory.

Despite it being barely ten o'clock, Mr Rivers poured two large measures of whisky, sliding one across the desk to his son.

'All right,' said Mr Rivers. 'I accept that you love her and she you. But come on, Kit. This is not what is supposed to happen. People like you and people like Elise. You're not supposed to marry.'

Kit recoiled. 'People like Elise? You mean Jews.'

'Yes,' answered his father, without apology.

'This isn't nineteen twenty. They're part of the set now,' said Kit, anger rising.

'Yes. They're welcome or, if we're honest, tolerated in almost any house in England. But when it comes to matrimony, they stick to their own kind. Their rules as much as ours.'

Kit shook his head. 'What nonsense.'

'Don't be such a schoolboy. Her father would be as furious as I am. And, it's not just that she's a Jewess. For God's sake, Kit. She's a housemaid.' Mr Rivers drained his whisky. 'I don't like it when people talk. Especially when it's about us.'

Kit gave a short laugh. 'You're as bad as the rest

of them.'

'Yes. I would like you to love a rich woman. I would like you to have something to pass down to your son. I have done my best, but Kit—Tyneford . . . we can't carry on as we are. The estate needs money.'

'So you want me to marry some girl I don't love, for her cash.'

Mr Rivers shook his head. 'No. I wouldn't wish that on anyone. Gone are the days, for better or for worse, when we married for England—to keep her land green and pleasant.'

Kit studied his father with cold curiosity. 'Did you love my mother? Or was it just her fortune?'

Mr Rivers stiffened. 'Don't you judge me. We did our duty. What everyone expected of us both. And that cash kept roofs on the village cottages, paid for Eton and Cambridge. It's why the limes on the avenue remain un-felled and the fields unsold.'

Mr Rivers' face softened in remembrance. 'I loved her in a way. She was a kind, sweet girl. A wonderful mother—she doted on you. I hope I made her happy. But did I love her with the passion of the poets? No. But we didn't expect to in those days.'

Kit stared at his father and felt his anger subside into sadness.

Mr Rivers sighed. 'This is a choice, Kit. If you marry Elise, then you must know that you will probably lose Tyneford—not this year, nor the next, but someday. Will you love her then, knowing that you gave up this place for her?'

'Of course,' replied Kit, with all the indignation of a young man in the flush of his first romance.

'I expected you to say nothing less.' Mr Rivers

gave a bitter laugh. 'No one would blink if you slept with her. Took her quietly as a mistress. Half the so-called gentlemen in England carry on discreet affairs. But I wouldn't let you do that to Elise.'

'And I wouldn't. I want to marry her.'

Mr Rivers gave a slow, tired smile. 'You're one and twenty. You don't need my permission but I would ask you to wait. Please, give it a year to be certain, for my sake. I've never asked much of you, Kit.'

Kit was silent for a minute and then nodded. 'All right. A year. But only because you ask it. I shan't change my mind.'

If I had known then the choice that his father presented to him, would it have altered anything? Would I have still agreed to marry him? I don't know. These things were so long ago.

Beside me on the wall, Kit blinked. I nudged him.

'Why does your father want us to wait, Kit?'

Kit took my hand. 'Come on, Elise. We must give him a little time. You're a Jew and you came here as a servant. It's nonsense to us but it matters to my father. It matters to all of them—the Lady Vernons, the Hamilton girls and despite appearances my father is still one of them.'

I bit my lip, hurt that despite everything—his admiration of Julian's books, selling the Turner, his kindness towards me—Mr Rivers saw me as marked by my Jewishness. It was worse than my humble position in his household—that was a mere flick of fate. Jew was in the blood.

'Have you even thought what your father would say?' asked Kit.

There had been plenty of mixed marriages

in Vienna, at least there had been before the troubles. They had been common enough to lose their exotic sheen. Julian argued over dinner with his mouth full of schnitzel that this was the future and one of the Good Things in This World. Well, this and excellent burgundy and publishers who didn't demand spurious changes to his manuscript or describe his work as 'obscure' and 'obtuse'. The 'obscene', he took as a compliment.

'Julian won't mind at all,' I said, after a moment's consideration. 'At least, I don't think he will. All his books are about perfect assimilation, and he's always talking about thoroughly modern marriages. So he ought to thoroughly approve. Also, I think he's an atheist.'

Kit frowned. 'It's possible a man might write one thing, but perhaps think something else when it comes to his daughter.'

I gazed at him blankly and he sighed and tried again.

'It's just, that, well, I'm not sure that a man's novels can be accurately read as a forecast to how he will react to his daughter's Christian suitor.'

I studied Kit and wondered whether this was something that he had thought all by himself, or if it was something that his father had voiced. It all seemed rather abstract without Julian here. Julian liked to argue for himself, preferring to surprise people with his opinion—usually the opposite of what they imagined him to think. He was so far away and Kit was right here beside me with his blue eyes and twitching smile and his scent of sandalwood and his particular blend of Turkish cigarettes. I was struck by a thought.

'You're not going to want me to convert, are

you?'

Kit laughed. 'Good God, no. I adore you as you are.'

'And you're sure that your father won't try to insist? Because I won't, you know. I can't.'

I thought in horror of the time I had peeked into the St Stephensdom, the cathedral in Vienna. It was pouring with rain and I had forgotten my raincoat and umbrella. I was clutching a sticky date pastry that would get spoilt, and I had ducked into the cathedral, looking for a dry corner to nibble my treat. A black robed priest grimaced when he saw me eating, and I stuffed it into my mouth before he could hiss at me. As I tried not to choke, I saw a grotesque marble statue of a man in agony on a white cross, trickling stone blood, his forehead torn by thorns, lips pursed, forever about to scream. And they thought we had done this? No wonder they hated us. Until I saw that statue and inhaled the sickly scent of burning incense, I had not realised how different the other girls in school were from Margot and me and the other Jews. I'd not eaten dates since. I shuddered as the cool March wind blew through the thin weave on my sweater.

'I won't. I can't.'

'Darling, I told you, no. And what about you? Do you want me to convert?'

Kit pulled a handkerchief out of his pocket and popped it onto his blond curls, like a makeshift yarmulke.

'Don't be silly. Of course not.'

'Well, then, it's settled, darling. We'll be thoroughly modern. Herr Landau will approve, so will Father. And we'll live happily ever after.'

'Just like in one of those romance novels.'

'Exactly. But with less taffeta.'

Kit leant over and kissed me, his long eyelashes fluttering against my cheek. I could kiss him all day and night. I supposed that this was what May and the dailies termed 'necking'. He took my hand, and traced his fingertips across my knuckles. I tried to draw away—my skin was coarse and chapped from hours spent scrubbing, and I was embarrassed. Gentlemen were supposed to marvel at their lover's remarkably smooth skin, not calluses and cracked nails. Violetta might have been a courtesan/whore but I was certain that she never had that particular problem—her hands were probably as soft as duckling down. I felt like an elderly Juliet with rough hands and thick ankles. Kit would make a splendid Romeo, even though I could picture him more easily idling with a cigarette and a gin cocktail than running a fellow through with his sword.

'Look, a dandelion clock. The first of the year,' said Kit, pointing to a white feathered flower nestling amongst the yellow dandelion scribbles that studded the green grass like a child's painting of a starry sky. He slipped off the wall and plucked it, offering it up to me.

'What o'clock?' he asked and blew, sending a volley of feathered arrows into the wind.

* * *

Kit and I might not have been engaged, but my life at Tyneford had shifted. Mr Wrexham enquired as to whether I wished to move to more commodious quarters, but I declined. I'd grown to love my attic room. Lying in bed at the top of the house, I dreamt that I sailed along on the lookout post upon the mast of a tall ship, and I had the best view of the endless sea, better than the captain himself. Mr Wrexham, though surprised, agreed that I may remain for the present in my attic chambers, but the morning after Kit's declaration, I became for the first time 'Miss Landau'.

Mr Wrexham summoned me into his study, and for once offered me a cup of tea, which so surprised me that I declined. The butler's face contracted and I realised, too late, that refusal had been a mistake. So, when he gestured to me to sit, I did so instantly, almost missing the chair in my haste. Manners always impeccable, he contrived not to notice. He perched on the chair opposite, back straight as one of the poplars beside the driveway, knees together, tails dangling behind him, white hands resting upon his black lap.

'This is a situation of some delicacy, Miss Landau. Mr Rivers has informed me that while yourself and Mr Kit are not presently engaged, such an event is highly likely,' he paused. 'This makes your present situation somewhat problematic. You can no longer continue as a maid, Miss Landau. But since you are not as yet engaged, we need to proceed with considerable tact.'

Mr Wrexham explained that my duties were to be undertaken by May and the dailies (Mr Rivers could not endure his future daughter-in-law washing his floors or making his bed a minute longer) but I was to assist Mrs Ellsworth with the running of the household, a more genteel task, that as far as I could tell involved the ordering of dinners and the endless arranging of flowers. I was not permitted to assist with actual cooking. My hands were to be smooth and untainted by work before a ring was slipped onto my finger.

'There remains the awkward matter of meals. Until the engagement is official and declared in *The Times,* it is not appropriate for you to take your meals with the family. But you can no longer eat in the servants' hall. It has been decided that you will take your repast in the morning room.'

I tried not to frown. 'Alone?'

'For the present, Miss Landau.'

'Very well, Mr Wrexham.'

He winced, ever so slightly.

'Madam, if I may be so bold. Circumstances have changed. If it pleases you, I am now "Wrexham".'

I shook my head. 'No. As you said, I am not yet engaged. I live in no-man's land. I take my meals alone. Until I am Mrs Rivers, you are Mr Wrexham.'

The butler did not smile but gave a slight nod. 'As you wish, Miss Landau.'

* * *

March drifted into April with a late frost, icing lacework patterns across the windowpanes and smudging the tides of yellow cowslips with white. The black tulips in the terracotta pots on the terrace were bejewelled, like ladies in sable coats dusted with crystal. The nights were clear and cold, and I stood on the single wooden chair in my attic room, peeking out of the window as the stars flashed upon the surface of the sea. Mr Rivers gave permission for me to wire the news to my sister, and did not complain when I sent a rapturous and lavish telegram to Margot.

EVERYTHING ALL RIGHT STOP BETTER THAN ALL RIGHT STOP SPLENDID STOP ANNA JULIAN COMING TO TYNEFORD STOP BURNT MY CAP AND APRON STOP KIT LOVES ME STOP YOU AND ROBERT MUST COME TO ENGLAND STOP BRING UMBRELLA STOP VERY DAMP HERE STOP

Diana and Juno departed for London, taking with them the last of Kit's college friends. Since Kit and I were not officially engaged, there was nothing to tell them, and Mr Rivers and the wily butler had contrived to keep me far away from the two young ladies during their last few days at the house. But the girls were shrewd when it came to matters of love and Diana, with the keen suspicion that she had been slighted, watched me with Gestapo eyes. On her final evening, I went upstairs to find her sitting on my bed. My drawers were open and the contents covered the floor in an untidy kaleidoscope of knickers, brassieres, blouses and gloves.

'Did you find what you were looking for?' I enquired, relieved that I no longer had to address her as 'your ladyship'.

Diana shrugged. 'No. I don't believe so. Those pearls weren't stolen, were they?' she added flatly, pointing to the fine string pulled from their hiding place inside my stocking.

'I'm afraid not. They're mine.'

'Pity,' she said without emotion.

I started to tidy things away.

'He ought to have been mine, you know,' she said.

I closed the drawer with a knock and leant back against the bureau. She was quite lovely—golden curls framing her heart-shaped face and a mouth like two curved rose petals.

'Yes. Perhaps he ought,' I said.

He's mine, I thought, and we both heard me say the words, even though I did not speak them aloud.

* * *

May arrived with apple blossom, bluebells on the cliffs, kisses before bedtime and thirty million pounds worth of Bank of England gold travelling in two warships to Canada for safekeeping. The cuckoos called from the dark woods, the Tyneford gardeners planted cabbages in neat rows, and the men debated when the call-up would be announced, while Mr Wrexham fretted as to the havoc such absences would inflict upon his meticulous staff plan. Each evening Kit and Mr Rivers discussed strategies for obtaining exit visas for my parents. While I did not dine with the men, I was permitted to join them afterwards and pour the coffee. Placing the gleaming pot back on the tray, and taking a square of bitter chocolate, I settled beside Kit as he lolled into me, resting his blond head on my shoulders.

'Let them say "no" to me in person,' said Mr Rivers, who had grown tired of the polite but ambivalent letters from the German embassy: '*We profoundly regret . . . humble apologies . . . minor delay . . . by Easter . . . before Michaelmas . . .*'

'I am tired of all this stalling. I've made an appointment at the embassy. I'll speak to them and see if we can't sort out this nonsense,' he said, confident in his belief that two reasonable chaps in a room together may quickly find an amiable resolution. I could not explain to him that German bureaucrats were neither reasonable nor amiable in the true British sense.

'I'll come with you,' said Kit.

'Yes, and I will too.'

I felt my palms itch at the possibility of looking the enemy in the eye—I'd see if I could make him flinch. I longed to do something to help Anna and Julian. I was exhausted by my impotence.

Mr Rivers frowned. 'Kit, come if you wish. Elise, it would be best if you did not. Your presence will not help matters.'

'They are my family.'

'And if you want to help them, then you will stay behind. I doubt if the embassy officials will even speak with you,' said Mr Rivers.

Frustration bloomed into anger. 'Because I'm a Jew. I am so tired of it. It's all I am anymore and I don't even know what it means. I eat pork and I hate God. But that's all I am to them. And to you, Mr Rivers. Elise mustn't marry Kit because she's a bloody Jew.'

The two men looked at me, shocked at my outburst. I supposed it wasn't how nice English girls behaved, and it certainly wasn't expected from reprieved housemaids. I knew I ought to burst into tears to lessen the effect of my rudeness but I was far too angry.

'I won't apologise,' said Mr Rivers. 'I am trying to do the best for your family. All I ask is that you both wait a short while. You are both very young.'

Now I did want to cry. 'I'm sorry. I'm so sorry.'

Excusing myself, I slipped outside into the

cool of the garden. Alone on the terrace, I was overcome with embarrassment and disgusted at how ungrateful I must appear.

* * *

Mr Rivers, however, did not bear grudges and he smiled at me as, slightly hesitant, I returned to the drawing room some time later.

'Come,' he said. 'Let us shake hands. Friends are allowed to quarrel.'

Solemnly we shook, and I settled myself on a footstool beside the fire.

'Now,' said Kit. 'Everything is arranged. We're going tomorrow. Is there anything you would like from town? Something for Mrs Landau, perhaps?'

Tears pricked my eyes, conscious that they were both being much kinder than I deserved. 'Well, if you're quite sure. Anna loves scented bath salts.'

Kit grinned. 'Expect I can stretch to that. Anything else?'

'Hildegard always used to fill her drawers with little sachets of rosebuds and lavender.'

'Consider it done. I shall go to Liberty's. They shall instantly pin me as a man in love, asking for such things.'

'And Mr Landau? What does he drink?' asked Mr Rivers. 'Wrexham keeps an excellent cellar. But if there is some continental spirit?'

I smiled. 'Thank you. You are both so kind. Julian is not particular. He likes any kind of red wine. He's not partial to spirits.'

Actually, he referred to the 'continental spirits' of schnapps or kirsch favoured by the great-aunts as 'old hen's poison'. I stretched before the fire, conscious of the generosity of the two men. I knew I was deeply lucky. Most girls in my position considered themselves fortunate to receive a kind word from the master of the house. Goodness knew, I did not deserve it. And yet with the exception of that night's outburst, I had noticed that the men were easier with each other when I was in their company. There was no awkward intimacy, no need to speak directly to one another; instead they could tell me about Tyneford, the history of the house and its previous inhabitants: grandmother Julie who was so terrified of dogs that she fainted upon seeing a fox on the hill; Uncle Max who preferred dogs to people, especially to his catty wife. With a comfortable third in the room, father and son appeared to take indirect pleasure in one another's company. They could talk without talking. Their dinners became shorter and shorter, until I had barely finished my lonely soup when Mr Wrexham came calling for me to come into the drawing room and pour the coffee.

'Shall we play a hand of cards?' Mr Rivers enquired.

Kit fidgeted and stretched. 'No. Not tonight.'

'Shall I make you some toast on the fire?' I suggested.

Kit snapped upright. 'Yes. Splendid.'

I rang the bell and asked Mr Wrexham to bring bread, butter and the toasting fork from Mrs Ellsworth's room. When he returned, I knelt before the simmering coals, piercing a thick slice of bread upon the prongs and held it out over the heat. The bread darkened to a golden brown, smouldering gently. The warmth made my cheeks rosy. Kit crept up behind me and crouched on the hearth, while

Mr Rivers fiddled with the gramophone, so that the room filled with the running peals of Chopin's Nocturne in F Minor.

'It's a little smoky in here,' I said, and Kit stood up to open the window.

A trickle of cool air flowed into the room along with the boom of the distant sea, a bass orchestra to accompany the Chopin. I looked at the firelight reflected on their faces and knew that I was forgiven, the quarrel already forgotten. I did not know then that this was one of the happiest moments of my life. I was warm and loved and as the music rippled around me, I knew the best was yet to come. But it is in our nature to be always looking away.

CHAPTER SEVENTEEN

BLACK DOGS AND WHITE GLOVES

June blazed into July. Dragonflies flitted across the village pond, their wings a shimmering, iridescent green, humming like miniature aircraft. Kit disappeared to Cambridge to take his exams and reappeared a fortnight later having passed with a respectable 2:2. Mr Rivers hid his disappointment behind a bottle of 1928 Veuve Clicquot. We sipped and toasted and I would have been content, if it wasn't for the ever present worry about my parents. Each morning, I paced the blue room, which had been prepared for their arrival: curtains freshly laundered, lavender bags sweetening the drawers, crystal scent bottles displayed upon the dressing table. I closed my eyes and imagined Anna stretched out on the bed in her cotton pyjamas waiting for me to bring her morning coffee, while Julian, robed in his dressing gown, scribbled in one of his leather notebooks beside the window. The minute they arrived, the last few months would be transformed into a game, everything simple and happy in hindsight; a fairy tale ending in a reunion and, in a year, a summer wedding upon the lawn. I wondered whether Margot and Robert would arrive in time for my sister to be maid of honour.

On the last day of July, Mr Wrexham came into the yard where I was helping Art brush down Mr Bobbin. He proffered a letter on his silver tray.

'Miss Landau.'

I seized it and tore it open.

Darling Bean,

The visa has come! It has come. I can't quite believe it, but here it is in my hands. We are coming. Really and truly. Your father is to line up and pay his exit tax (how we are to repay Mr Rivers I shall never know) and then we shall be with you. Tell me, what is Tyneford like at this time of year? You said the cooking is 'hearty'—is that the English word? I don't like offal very much, but I am sure I can get used to anything . . .

I read no more, but seizing Art and kissing the old man soundly, I raced into the house calling for Kit and Mr Rivers.

'The visa is here! They're coming!'

*　　*　　*

August 29th. Kit and I spread out a picnic rug on the lawns. He wanted to walk to the top of Flower's Barrow or go for a swim, but I wanted to read the newspapers and write my latest letter to Anna. I no longer posted them, as by the time they arrived Anna and Julian would have left, so I kept them in the viola case. I didn't want to forget anything when I told her about the last few months. I imagined her reclining in a cushioned deckchair beneath the oak tree's shade and reading my parcel of letters, chuckling softly and sipping iced tea.

I now read Art's *Daily Mirror* as well as Mr Rivers' copy of *The Times* and the papers were spread around us on the grass, weighted down with stones, and flapping like tethered gulls in the breeze. Kit rolled onto his back and shielded his eyes against the glare of the late summer sun.

'So? What does Mr Churchill say this morning?'

I rustled through the *Mirror.*

'No one knows what's going to happen abroad. Nor when the worst will happen.'

Kit opened an eye. 'Anna and Julian will be here any day.'

He'd finally caught my habit of calling them by their first names.

'Any day,' I echoed.

'Come, darling. There's no help in fretting. They'll be here before you know it.'

I turned to the *Mirror. 'All British ships are now under Admiralty control. From midnight on Saturday every British ship afloat came under Admiralty direction.'*

'Ah. Burt'll be tickled that *The Lugger* is now part of the navy,' said Kit, stroking the sun-darkened freckles on my arm. 'Come for a swim? It's so blasted hot.'

'No thank you. I'm going to stay here for a bit.'

'Suit yourself. If you fancy joining me, I'll be on Worbarrow beach.'

'All right,' I said, planting a kiss on his nose. 'I will. Give me an hour.'

I watched him as he strode down to the beach in his white tennis shoes. Long days spent outside in the sunshine had bleached his hair a brighter shade of gold, and his skin had ripened to a rich brown. I was tempted to abandon my papers and run after him. Kit was a muscular swimmer, cutting through the green waves with powerful strokes. Afterwards, he liked to stretch out upon the rocks in his shorts, glistening and lithe as an otter. Yes, I decided. The papers and Anna's letter could wait. I determined to fetch my bathing things from the house. I scrambled to my feet, flicking a scarlet ladybird from my blouse, and headed back to the terrace. There was the grumble of motorcar tyres on gravel, and then the thud-thud of two car doors closing. Mr Rivers was away across the hills for his daily walk, and Art never took the car without him. No guests were expected. My heart leapt. Anna. Julian. It had to be them. I ran to the side of the house, skidding on the loose stones, heart pounding in my ears like a timpani drum. I hurled myself round the corner, and stopped.

Anna and Julian stand in the driveway. A sound escapes from my lips and, for a moment, I think it is the cry of a gull and not my own voice. They are here. I say the words again and again, not quite believing them. Then I am buried in Anna's arms and ah, the spice of her perfume. And in the sunlight I see flecks of white in the blonde of her hair and Julian is thin, thinner than I've seen him before but it doesn't matter because they'll be fed gooseberry crumble until they're fat again. And I'm crying and I can't breathe and I'm making a mess on the pressed linen of Anna's collar.

'Darling, it's all right,' says Julian. 'Everything's all right now.'

I take his hand and lead them onto the terrace and we sit in the warm afternoon. A butterfly lands on Anna's lapel and she gazes down upon it benevolently. 'Be careful,' she says, 'or I shall get too fond of you and turn you into a brooch.'

I stare at my parents, and see that they are just the same: a little older and worn perhaps but otherwise unchanged. Anna smiles and her forehead creases. Julian stretches out his legs and I see to my delight that his socks don't match. There is too much to say, so we are silent and listen instead to the sea. Upon the water, a sailboat tacks and rushes towards the far side of the bay. I want to tell them everything: how Anna's drawers are full of lavender and that Mr Rivers has a special bottle of Château Margaux set aside to celebrate their arrival. I want them to meet Kit. I want Anna to love Kit. The scarlet geraniums in their terracotta pots are so bright—a bold, child's red, and I decide that I shall always have geraniums on the terrace and they will remind me of this moment. And I want to ask about the great-aunts but I can't because I am selfish and I don't want to spoil this feeling of happiness and I try to think of something to ask—anything to stop me thinking about the three old women left alone in Vienna—and I turn to Julian and I ask, 'What is the novel in the viola about?'

It all happened in a single tick of a pocket-watch. I stopped and blinked and I was alone on the driveway. The mirage of Anna and Julian had vanished, but I willed it to be them. I listened to the thud-thud of the car doors and saw that a police car was parked outside the house. But why had they come in a police car? Art would have picked them up from the station but it didn't matter, not now. The midday sun was blinding me; I shielded my eyes and scoured the driveway for my parents.

'Anna! It's me. Papa?' I called, unable to see.

'Miss?' said a voice, and I turned to see a uniformed constable standing beside the back door, round helmet clasped beneath his arm.

'Yes?' I answered, impatient.

'I understand that an Austrian maid is employed at this house.'

'Not anymore. Did you bring a couple with you? An Austrian couple? A fair-haired lady, very small, and a tall man with black hair and?—'

'Slow down, miss, I can't understand when yer talk so fast.'

The constable was joined by his partner, a round youth who sported what must have been his very first moustache, a grazing of brown hairs on his upper lip.

'Are you a British citizen, miss?' he enquired.

'No. I am Austrian. But it doesn't matter. Where is Anna? Where is Julian?'

'No one here but us, miss. I need you to come along now. No trouble. Just need you to come to the station.'

I made some feeble effort to object but, dazed with disappointment, I allowed myself to be hustled into the back of the police car. I was vaguely aware that I did not have my hat and coat. Anna always impressed upon me the importance of never venturing out in public without a hat. The young officer started the engine, and the motorcar rumbled across the gravel. Art came running in from the paddock, waving frantically at the car to stop, but the constable put his foot down and we surged forward. I turned and stared at Art, as he mouthed something at me through the glass.

*   *   *

They were very kind to me in the station. I was given cups of lukewarm tea and chocolate biscuits that I did not want and told to fill out endless forms. A plump secretary in an ill-fitting tweed skirt and a blouse that gaped to reveal a triangle of dimpled stomach, confided, 'Been told to round up all "enemy aliens" for assessment, we have. Not many continentals in these parts, so you is a bit of a novelty.' I said nothing and sipped at the sugary tea. Despair clutched at me with icy hands. If they were already rounding up foreigners in England, they would not be letting in any more. England's borders were closing with the inevitability of a clamshell at dusk. I barely noticed when Mrs Tweed led me to a cell and, muttering her apologies, asked a constable to lock me in. I did not care. I was glad it was cold. I was glad it smelt damp. A pain started to build behind my eyes, a piercing ache sharp as the knife Mrs Ellsworth used for boning quail. Bright lights flashed at the edge of my vision, blinding me. History happens somewhere else. Men march across Europe. Julian's books are hurled out of the window and moulder in the rain, words drifting in the puddles. Herr Finkelstein is beaten so hard that when he returns home to Esther, he spits his teeth out on the carpet like grains of sweetcorn. Even that is not large enough for history. History is the whole fleet of ships, not Burt's fishing-boat trawling for mackerel in the bay. Sitting on the floor of the cell I felt the brush of history along my arm. I saw two great black dogs chasing Anna and Julian across the fields at the top of the hill. Black dogs with white teeth and wide red jaws. They weren't dogs but wolves escaped from my old fairy tale book. Anna and Julian had to run run run. Kit would come and let me out but Anna and Julian had to run.

*   *   *

'This instant, I said. This instant!' I heard a familiar voice outside.

A moment later the cell door was unlocked and Mr Rivers entered. I ran over to him and hurled myself into his arms, and to my surprise discovered that I was crying, great shaking sobs that made my shoulders jolt. He pulled me close, whispering, 'Hush, Elise. Hush. You're safe. I promise they won't take you away.'

I tried to explain that it wasn't me but Anna and Julian, but found that I could not speak. Mr Rivers removed his jacket and wrapped it around my shoulders. I leant into him, trying to swallow my sobs, as he stroked the tears from my cheek with his thumb and kissed the top of my head.

'Shh. The car's outside. Let's take you home.'

I nodded dumbly, and then was sick upon his polished brogues.

* * *

I slept through the start of the war. The migraine lasted four days, and when I awoke I found myself in a strange room. It was absolutely dark. The bed felt soft and unfamiliar, and I smelt roses, sweet and sickly. I thought I should choke on roses and darkness, and I screamed. The door flew open, spilling yellow light into the room and Mrs Ellsworth appeared by my side and folded me into her bosom.

'All right, lovey. You've been awful poorly. Here, have a drink.'

She forced me to sip some lemon barley water, and I felt a little better, and rather silly for making such a fuss.

'I'm in the blue room,' I said, the light from the hallway falling on the curtains and wallpaper, making them shine like an evening sky.

'Yes, dear. Tired my old knees, scurrying up to the attic to look to you.'

I noticed the blackout blinds pinned to the windows. War.

'Have there been any bombs yet, Mrs Ellsworth?'

'No, miss. Not even in London.'

In a strange way, I was glad not to have missed anything. It was an odd feeling to go to sleep in peace and wake up in the midst of war, if not battle. Had the fighting started in Europe? Where were Anna and Julian? I felt a pain pulse behind my eyes and was glad of the blackouts.

'Oh, you gave the gentlemen a scare. When Mr Rivers came back from his walk and discovered you gone, he took the car and just left. Never seen him drive like that. Such a tearing hurry. I had palpitations that he'd crash!'

Mrs Ellsworth broke off to fan herself with her hand, as if to cool the memory.

'And when Mr Kit came back from the beach to find you vanished and the master off in the car. Well! We was all in a flummox, let me tell you. Then Mr Rivers storms in, carrying you in his arms he was. Mr Kit was all in a state. Didn't calm down till the doctor came and said it was a nervous attack. Mee-grain or something.'

Feeling guilty for even thinking it, I wished that I could remember Mr Rivers carrying me in and Kit beside himself with worry. It sounded quite charming, the way Mrs Ellsworth told it. If only I hadn't rather spoilt things by being sick on Mr Rivers' shoes. Violetta or Juliet or Jane Eyre would never have done such a thing. Nor Anna.

I winced and, curling onto my side, drew my knees up to my chin. When I was a little girl and I was ill, Anna would stroke my ears. I hated it. The sound was too loud and it tickled, and I always batted her away, but at that moment I wanted her to stroke my ears so much that I ached.

There was a gentle rap at the door, and I glanced up to see Mr Rivers in the doorway.

'You're awake,' he said, a slow smile spreading across his face.

'You can come and sit with her,' said Mrs Ellsworth, seeing him hesitate, unwilling to venture any closer without permission. 'I'm going down to fetch her a little supper.'

She bustled out and Mr Rivers pulled up an easy chair beside the bed. On impulse, he took my hand. He didn't speak for a minute. He made one or two attempts to start, and then finally spoke in a low voice, gripping my hand in both of his.

'Elise, I'm so terribly sorry. The war has started. All visas have been cancelled.' He squeezed my fingers so tight that it hurt. 'You are safe. I won't ever let them take you again. But Mr and Mrs Landau . . . they will not be allowed to enter the country. There is nothing I can do. We can only wait and hope for the war to be over quickly.'

I forced myself to breathe. 'Do you know where they are?'

He shook his head. 'I have a man in Paris. He will try to discover something.'

He reached out for the glass of water. 'Please, drink this. You're very pale.'

I took it and tried to drink, but my hands shook and the glass tipped over, spilling water on the bedcovers. Mr Rivers took it from me and, brushing my hair from my face, held the glass to my lips so that I could drink.

'Where's Kit?' I asked, as he replaced it on the bedside table.

'I sent him outside for some fresh air. He's been wearing a hole in Mrs Ellsworth's carpets with his constant pacing. I'll send him up to see you the moment he's back.'

He watched me in silence. I was too tired and miserable to be embarrassed, or wonder why he stared. I only knew that he looked as unhappy as I.

*   *   *

I felt the shadows draw around the house. They went up with the blackouts while I was sleeping, but when Mrs Ellsworth unfastened the blinds, the shadows remained. I had not realised that I had been living in Arcadia until it was time to leave. The horrid trick was that for the present we all remained, but the place shifted around us. The trees and lawns and shrubs were the same, and the house changed more slowly, but something was different. We did not know it then, but our lives at Tyneford had shifted key, and we were rushing towards the final movement, whether we were ready for it or not.

The following morning Kit bounded into my room laden with a breakfast tray. Mrs Ellsworth hovered in the doorway, suspicious that he would spill orange juice and marmalade all over her spotless carpet. He set it down with a wobble on the bedside table. Spoons clattered and the teapot rattled dangerously, and I reached out to catch the diving milk jug.

'You see, Flo? All's well,' he called to Mrs Ellsworth.

With a roll of her eyes and flick of her apron, she vanished. Kit sat on the edge of the bed. I wished I'd had time to brush my hair and wash my face. I couldn't imagine how dreadful I must look. I'd fallen asleep as soon as Mr Rivers left me the previous evening, and I'd not spoken to Kit since my adventure at the police station. He pulled me into him, wrapping his arms tightly around me.

'I'm so sorry,' he said, and his voice cracked. 'The minute the war's over, we'll find them. We'll go to Austria together. Or Paris, or Amsterdam. Wherever they are, we'll find them and bring them to Tyneford. I promise.'

I nodded dumbly.

'And they might still come.'

'Kit, no. Please.'

Nothing more must be said. Silence meant that it was not quite real. He loosened his hold, keeping his hands firm upon my shoulders. He caught my mood and scrutinised me, a faint smile playing on his lips.

'You look quite awful,' he announced with forced gaiety.

'Thank you,' I said, turning my head away.

'Yes,' he said cheerfully. 'Really dreadful. Hideous in fact. Good thing I'm hopelessly in love.'

He grabbed the breakfast tray and set it on the bed.

'I'm under strict instructions to make sure that you eat everything.'

I scowled, still cross with him, but I was hungry, so I took a spoon and attacked an egg.

'Ah, one moment at death's door and the next eating a boiled egg.'

He tried to kiss me, but I had a mouth full of yolk and I shooed him away.

'So cruel,' he sighed. 'Did Flo tell you that I was there every minute that you were poorly? I was most attentive.'

'Yes. You've been very kind. But I'm better now.'

I watched him over the top of my cup of coffee. It was such a relief not to have to drink that awful brown tea in the mornings anymore. I dunked a toast soldier in my egg.

The warm September sun spilt into the room. Kit unfastened the window and a breeze fluttered inside, carrying the scent of heather and the sea.

'Kit. Will you fetch me paper and a pen. I must write to Margot.'

'Darling, you can send a wire.'

I shook my head, regretting it as the pain cracked against my skull. 'No. Let her have another few weeks of hope and happiness. The letter will arrive soon enough.'

It has started and they have not come. We must hope they reached Paris. Kit swears he will find them at the end of the war. When I am with him, I believe him. You must too. Anna and Julian will come to Tyneford and so will you and Robert and your twelve children and we will drink lemonade and eat cucumber sandwiches on the lawns and the sun will shine.

* * *

'Mrs Ellsworth, I should like to work tomorrow,' I said a few hours later when she brought me up a pile of magazines and some lunch.

I needed to do something. Anything but lying here thinking. The housekeeper fussed around the bed, straightening the covers and picking at a non-existent mark on the blanket.

'When you feel better, you can order the dinners, and there's some linen you can help me sort.'

'No. I need to work.'

There was a trill of desperation in my voice, and Mrs Ellsworth stopped fussing and turned to look at me. For the moment the burning behind my eyes helped me, but when the pain subsided I must have work. Scrubbing the scullery, digging in the vegetable garden—I did not care.

'Has Henry joined up yet? Because he will, you know that,' I said, pleading. 'And the gardener's boy will go and May must do war work, and who knows if the dailies will stay. You and Mr Wrexham can't keep the house between the two of you.'

Mrs Ellsworth busied herself tidying the already neat scent bottles lined up on the dresser.

'Mr Rivers was very clear about you not washing any floors no more. It's not proper.'

I snorted. Until a few months ago, I'd been making his bed and folding his pyjamas.

'It's different now. I'll be called up to the labour exchange. Unless I'm doing essential work in the house and on the farm, I'll be sent away. I don't want to be in a factory. I want to stay here, but I must work.'

Mrs Ellsworth tutted softly. 'Mr Wrexham won't like it one bit,' she complained.

'Well, you tell him that if he won't let me, I'm going straight to the dairyman to offer my services for the milking of cows. In fact, I'm not sure that wouldn't be more fun . . .'

'No, no, miss. I'll tell him,' said Mrs Ellsworth, shooting me an anxious glance. 'But it'll never do. You're not to do any cooking. And you're not to set a foot in my kitchen.'

*　　*　　*

We sat before the hulking kitchen range, Mrs Ellsworth demonstrating the correct technique for the peeling of carrots. 'It'll be over by Christmas,' she announced, snatching the peeler out of my hands. 'Like this, stop scraping at it. Or spring at the latest,' she concluded, moving seamlessly between the prognosis of war and vegetable peeling.

'Such a to-do. And the digging up of all those potatoes for an air-raid shelter,' she snarled. 'What a waste! What's Mr Hitler want to bomb a potato patch for? He won't do very well in the war if he goes around bombing people's onions and taters.'

I did not try to explain. Mrs Ellsworth remained convinced that the Anderson shelter had to be dug in the potato patch because that was the most likely target of attack, rather than because the sheltered kitchen garden was the safest place.'All this disruption. Gives me the collywobbles.'

I said nothing, and let her rattle on. Mrs Ellsworth was tired. The kitchen boy, who it turned out was eighteen despite the skinny legs and pimples (or else taking the opportunity to escape the most horrid job in the house) joined up at the first instant and disappeared in the night. We never heard from him again. It meant that Mrs Ellsworth had a great deal more to do in the kitchen, and my helping became a necessity. Several of the farm boys volunteered early for service, not waiting for their call-up, and the dairyman required his daughter's assistance, which meant that we were down to one daily maid. Then Henry the footman joined up, and marched off for training in Wiltshire on the 12th of September, much to Mr Wrexham's disgust. 'One week's notice. That's the legal requirement,' the old butler complained, when the footman appeared in his parlour, dressed in his new green uniform, and handed back his once treasured footman's livery, now shoved into an unwashed bundle.

Henry shrugged. 'Don't pay me my last week's wages then. But it's not very patriotic of you. There's a war on, you know.'

Of course, Mr Rivers would not hear of Henry not being paid his last week's wages, and would have ordered the motorcar to take him to Dorchester, if it weren't for the rationing of petrol. Only essential journeys were to be taken by motorcar, but then Mr Rivers and Kit always seemed to prefer travelling with Art and Mr Bobbin, so there wasn't much difference. I listened to Mrs Ellsworth chatter and hum along to 'The Frog King's Parade' on the wireless. I liked being in the kitchen. It reminded me of home and hours spent getting in Hildegard's way as she baked *sachertorte* or diced steak for a *goulash*. The smells in Mrs Ellsworth's kitchen were different—pears, suet, sizzling bacon, kippers, scones and baked custard—but I liked them just the same. I'd just made my first fish and parsley pie and was feeling rather proud of myself. Mrs Ellsworth took it out of the oven with a hiss of steam, and placed it on the top of the cooker.

'Very good. Nice and brown. Go and wash, now. Mr Wrexham will ring the bell for lunch in five minutes.'

There was no use objecting. I hurried out of the kitchen and went to straighten my hair and splash water on my face. Despite the lack of staff, and the inordinate distance between kitchen and dining room, standards had to be maintained. The digging up of the potato patch and the disappearance of the under servants had disturbed Mrs Ellsworth, and she sought reassurance in the details of luncheon in the wainscoted dining room at one o'clock. Mr Wrexham, walking past the kitchen door with his laden tray and perfectly starched shirt, proved to her that England was mighty and indestructible. Wars might be declared, kitchen boys vanish to join the navy, blackout curtains smother the French windows, and previously reliable footman leave without notice, but lunch would be served at five minutes past one and the butler would wear white cotton gloves.

* * *

'Lulcombe Castle has been requisitioned by the army,' announced Mr Rivers. We sat taking tea on the terrace in the late afternoon. It seemed a lifetime ago that I had broken the porcelain teacup when serving the gentlemen. Today, Mr Wrexham carried the tray and I poured tea for three and spread butter upon the scones. It was warm for late September, the sky a watery blue unmarked by cloud, and only the purple leaves fluttering to the ground from the flowering plum showed it to be an autumn day.

'I offered Lady Vernon and the Hamilton girls refuge here while the Dower house is being prepared for the family.'

Mr Rivers paused, smiling at what must have been my stricken expression, while Kit shot me a sideways glance. I hated Diana and her aunt, Lady Vernon, terrorised me with her mastery of English subtext. Her words were unfailingly polite, but they were entirely separate from her meaning. On catching me one afternoon using my fingers to lift sponge cake to my mouth, she enquired, 'Miss Landau, would you care for a cake fork?' in a tone that clearly stated, 'You uncouth continental, my miniature pug has superior table manners.' Once on my way back from the sea, I passed her motorcar parked outside the Tyneford post office, and she called me over to remark upon my lack of hat. It had just blown off into the surf, and choosing not to place the dripping cloche on my head, I carried the sodden bundle in my hands. 'My dear!' she called, beckoning me over with a thin, gloved hand. 'No hat! Such daring. How I admire you. So self assured, you can walk around hatless!' Her tone conveyed that she would have sooner discovered me outside the post office quite naked than in my present state of semi-undress. I knew she detested me because of Kit. She considered him too poor to be a good match for one of her nieces, but she would have liked Diana to have had the opportunity of refusing him.

Mr Rivers gave me a wry smile. 'No, you're quite safe. She's not coming to stay. Though I fear we may have to invite them to dine rather more often than we might wish.'

'Let's hope that Tyneford's not requisitioned,' said Kit, licking jam from his finger and ignoring the scone.

'Yes, indeed,' replied Mr Rivers. 'But it doesn't seem terribly likely. There's no decent road and we're simply too far from the station. Besides, the house isn't big enough for an officers' barracks.'

'What about the schools? I heard Flo say that some of the country houses are being taken over by the London schools,' said Kit, lighting a cigarette.

Mr Rivers shook his head. 'We're too close to the coast. It's much too dangerous here. No point being evacuated from London into another danger zone.'

He folded his paper and placed it upon the table. 'Best thing we can do is help on the estate. Half the farm lads have already joined up, and the rest will get their call-up in a month or two. I've not driven a plough since I was a boy. I'm rather looking forward to it.'

I stirred my coffee with a silver spoon, watching the milk marble and then disappear. 'Mr Rivers, mightn't you be called up?' I asked, wondering whether I was being rude. The English were so strange about age.

'I rather doubt it. I'm over forty. So they would have to be pretty desperate.'

I smiled. He made it sound like he was an old man, which having seen him stride across the hills I knew was nonsense. I tended to agree with Anna—forty for a man was still perfectly youthful. Kit surveyed his father in silence for a minute, and then said with studied casualness, 'Will's joined the 2nd Dorsetshire. They sound all right. Thought perhaps I might too.'

Mr Rivers set his cup on the table. He turned quite white, almost as if he were struck by sudden seasickness. 'Not the army,' he said. 'I couldn't bear the army. You don't know what it's like. It's not some boyish adventure. It's hell.'

Kit took a long drag on his cigarette, trying to select words that would not further antagonise his father. 'It's different now. War is different. It won't be like it was for you.'

'You might be right, but please, Kit, no.'

Mr Rivers' eyes held a look that I had not seen before. A film of sweat coated his top lip. Kit reached out and brushed his hand, the first physical contact I had ever observed between them.

'All right. Not the army.'

Mr Rivers sat back in his chair and took a sip of tea, and his hand shook ever so slightly. He turned to me. 'Served for six months in 1918, when I was a year or two younger than Kit. God-awful. Hellish. Makes a mockery of the words one uses to describe it. All I can say is, it's something a man never wants his son to see.'

Kit proffered his cigarette case and Mr Rivers took one and struck a match, the only time I had ever seen him smoke. I toyed with the crumbs on my plate.

'My father's elder brother served for three years. He was killed at Flanders in 1917. Julian's first novel was about it,' I said.

Mr Rivers stared at me for a moment with an odd expression, then gave a short laugh. 'Fighting for the Habsburgs, of course.'

'Yes.'

Silence fell between us, as we sipped tea and nibbled scones and contemplated the fact that twenty-five years ago we'd been at war on opposite sides. A large white gull landed on a terracotta flowerpot and eyed the cake hungrily. Kit broke off a corner and tossed it onto the lawn. A moment later a flock of gulls descended onto the grass in a blizzard of white wings, the air filling with their hollow cries.

'The navy. It has to be the navy. If I'm to be away from Tyneford, I want to be at sea.'

* * *

A fortnight later, Mr Rivers and I stood in the driveway and watched as Art guided Mr Bobbin out of the yard, Kit seated beside him. The bus would take him from Wareham all the way to Hove and naval officer's training. We watched in silence as the horse lumbered along the green lanes. A fine drizzle began to fall, but we stayed watching, determined not to miss the last glimpse of our boy. I remembered Anna, Julian and Hildegard waving goodbye on the station platform, all resolutely not crying. The station hummed with hissing steam, baying porters, squalling babies and whispered goodbyes. I shivered and wrapped my woollen cardigan around my shoulders. An icy wind trilled through the eaves, carrying with it the comforting scent of wood smoke and peat. I imagined the sound to be the house itself calling some kind of farewell. At a bend in the track, Kit gave us a cheerful wave as he jumped down from the cart to open the first of the seventeen gates leading to the ridge and the world beyond Tyneford. Mr Rivers and I stayed as the figures became dots on the horizon, barely distinguishable from the stripped trees or the cattle scattered about on either side of the path. The cart inched along the top of the hill and then disappeared into the dark tunnel of trees, heading for Steeple, Wareham and a bus to another world.

'Mrs Ellsworth says the war will be over before Christmas,' I said. 'His training will take a while, so it's possible he'll never have to serve.'

'I hope Mrs Ellsworth is right. Shall we?'

He stood aside, allowing me to lead the way back into the house. I lingered in the quiet of the hall, listening to the whirr and tick of the death-watch beetles in the heavy beams overhead. A vase of brown tipped roses stood on the table, and a stray withered petal had fallen onto the surface. Any other day Mrs Ellsworth would have ensured they were instantly replaced—petals were barely allowed to drop before they were tidied away—but the instant of Kit's departure the house had assumed its forlorn air. The dying flowers left in their vase. A smear of polish on the parquet floor. The damask curtains beside the front door no longer appeared genteelly worn; they were shabby and old.

'I'll be in the library,' said Mr Rivers.

He strode away and I heard the door click shut and, a second later, the clink of the whisky decanter. I sat down on the bottom stair, resting my chin in my hands, and listened to the silence echo in the afternoon. I felt a long way from everyone I loved. I'd listened to Kit talk with the other boys, and they were all so eager to fight. 'Let us at him,' they clamoured, as though the minute they joined up they would be presented with a string of enemy soldiers ready for a good thrashing. I wished I could talk to my father. I knew he'd say something to comfort me, or at least make me smile. I hadn't spoken to Julian for two years, but if I went upstairs, I could break the viola and take out the pages. His novel lay there waiting for me to read.

In my old attic room, I retrieved the viola from its hiding place and sat with it on my knees, feeling the strange weight in its belly. I picked it up by the neck and held it aloft for a moment, ready to smash it down on the edge of the iron bedstead. And then, instead, I slotted it under my chin and, clasping the bow, drew it across the strings. For the first time in fifteen years I played the viola. I had not played since I heard the miracle of Margot's music. That was how the viola was supposed to sound, not the schoolgirl tunes that I could wrench from the strings. But this viola was different. It could only sound strange with the novel inside and I need not feel ashamed of my inability to produce music like my sister.

The tone was soft, as though the viola could only whisper. I tried a simple Mozart melody. It was thin and sad—the voice of a choirboy as opposed to the rich chocolate of an operatic soprano—and it suited me. Music isn't just notes; it's also filled with rests or measured silences. We wait during the pauses, listening to the possibility of music. I wanted to play into the gap left by Anna and Julian and fill up their silence, but their silence was not a rest. No black mark on the page told me when the sound would begin again. Their silence was not musical but a vacuum—a void where no sound can exist. I played another nocturne, but this time I could not hear the tune, only the pauses between the notes.

CHAPTER EIGHTEEN

THE ANNA

I went to bed early on New Year's Eve. Mr Rivers was obliged to attend a party held at Lulcombe Dower House by Lady Vernon, and while he'd insisted that I would be most welcome, we both knew this to be a polite lie. I remained at Tyneford, listening to the wireless in the library and eating candied figs in front of the fire, slipping away before Mr Wrexham could worry about whether or not to invite me to join the remaining servants for their glass of midnight sherry in the butler's parlour.

I kept off all the lights on the landing as well as those in my bedroom, and peeled back the blackout curtains and opened the window. It took my eyes a minute to adjust to the absolute darkness. It used to be that the odd light from the village glimmered in the night, or else the larger lights from distant Weymouth and Portland cast a yellow haze on the horizon. Now the darkness oozed about me. I curled up in an armchair and breathed the freezing air, so cold that my teeth tingled. It must have been nearly midnight but I couldn't see my wristwatch, and the church bells were silent—the law dictated that they were only to be rung in order to signal an invasion. All I could hear was the boom of the sea. By now it was an echo as familiar to me as the patter of my own thoughts. On the rare occasions when I had to venture into Dorchester or Wareham, I was struck by the quiet. The streets bustled and teemed but beneath the noise was a steady silence. I knew I could never live without the sea again; that was my music. At last I understood how Anna and Margot felt on the odd days when they could neither play nor listen to music.

Raising my whisky glass, I toasted my family and then Kit, knowing with happy certainty that wherever his ship sailed, he was thinking of me. Every few weeks, I received letters from him. (I kept them all these years and by now each one has grown worn around the folds from being endlessly re-read. They are filled with earnest nonsense, the sort of things that a boy writes to his sweetheart, but which somehow, when they are meant for you, never feel tired or clichéd or anything other than absolutely tender and true.)

I sat in the gloom and took out my bundle of letters and since it was too dark to read, recited them by heart.

Darling Elise,

King Alfred's is the name of the training ship. Though she isn't a ship at all, she's a converted school or something, but we're to pretend she's a ship. The front is the bow; we have a roll call to ensure we're all 'aboard' before lessons. I have lodgings in town but when we leave each evening we're off 'to sling our hammocks'. It's the naval way, rather odd at first but one does get used to it, and it has a haphazard poetry to it. When all this is over, we'll go down to Durdle Door one summer's evening and sling a hammock for two beneath the cliffs, and lie together and wait for a mermaid to come and comb her hair and flick her tail. Or else, we'll just drink sherry and get very drunk and I shall kiss you all the way from your toes to your knees and then the gap between your stockings and your smooth white thighs . . . I must tell you, my salute is very fine and I do look splendid in blue . . . I'm glad Burt taught me knots and the rules of the sea, makes one or two things easier, but I can't wait to actually get out on the water. Discipline and drill isn't too bad, rather reminds me of Eton, like being a schoolboy again only with the responsibility of other men's lives . . . Every night I dream of Tyneford and of you and you're dressed as a boy again and it might be wicked but I hold you and kiss you and this time no one stops me and I unfasten your bow tie and I lick that charming little hollow at the base of your throat . . . Ran exercises at sea today but it turned out to be nothing but an exercise in seasickness. Yes. It seems I get seasick. Never happened before on the fishing-boats or yachting but something about the larger vessels and the way they toss on the waves—oh God, I feel quite ill even thinking about it . . . We 'pass out' tomorrow and I don't feel in the least prepared . . . I had hoped for a destroyer but it wasn't to be. The corvette doesn't sound too bad. I wish I could tell you where I'm going but I don't know myself. I can tell you that I am terrified but so are all the chaps. Don't know what the regular crews are going to make of us wavy navy sods. Ah well, suppose it's a bit late to join the RAF now . . . Well, still seasick. I was ill all the way to ████████ but so were all the RNVR officers—green in every sense. But the regular navy chaps were jolly good about it; apparently sailors never make fun of seasickness, everyone's suffered at some point. The petty officer told me he still gets sick for the first two or three days aboard. I hope I shall find my sea legs before then. Especially if we're to go to ████████████ . . . Oh the Northern Lights! I wish you could have seen them, Elise. They were so bright, for a moment I thought they were a great battleship's flare—the entire horizon glowed with a greenish glare like a terrible dawn . . . We shall take a trip to ████████, you and I, and then sail a sedate launch around the ████████ I'll be the captain, and we'll have no one else. Perhaps for our honeymoon. What do you think? I think it will be splendid. We shall have boiled eggs and anchovies on toast (for you know quite well that I can cook nothing else) and dangle our feet in the ocean and swim naked and at night we will lie on deck and wait for the gleam of the Northern Lights . . . Oh God, can't write. So seasick, I could die. Why the navy? . . . Good chaps on board, I must say. Bit of a scare last night ██████████ . . . I wish I could be at Tyneford. I expect you're all freezing in this cold weather with the fuel rationing. Do you remember last winter when I brought in that chunk of oak and burnt it in the hall fireplace? I was in love with you but hadn't told you yet. I watched you dance with Wrexham, and I was actually jealous of the old man. I'm jealous of everyone who's near you at the moment when I'm not. I'm jealous of my father for he gets to see you every day and say 'please pass the marmalade' and see you every morning when you're flushed from your bath and only half awake—oh how one misses such precious banalities when away from home. We heard today that the destroyer ██████████ . . . When I'm back in Tyneford, I'm going to keep you to myself for a whole week. No one else may speak to you or go near you or touch you. If we were married, I should insist on you being naked the entire time but since we're not, I suppose I must make do with kissing you and perhaps I shall unfasten . . . It's a tradition in the navy to toast our wives and mistresses at midnight on New Year, so darling, know that wherever I am, I will be drinking to you . . .

love Kit

* * *

On New Year's Day, I walked across the cliffs to the Tilly Whim caves. I had helped Mrs Ellsworth prepare the Beef Wellington for dinner (a final treat before rationing commenced), peeled endless potatoes, sieved a quart of sloe gin, and after the heat of the kitchen I craved some fresh air. The sky was iron grey, and the dark sea writhed and crashed, white waves cresting before they reached the shore. Sleet began to fall, pockmarking the stone and seeping into my mackintosh, but I didn't mind. I'd learnt to relish the wind and cold slapping my cheeks, turning them bright as holly berries. I stalked along the cliff top path, passing above the sandy smear of Brandy Bay, and onto the limestone shelf at Tilly Whim. In the distance I could see the black shadows of the warships at anchor in Portland. I wondered if I were looking at a ship like Kit's. I wore a ruby cashmere scarf, a Christmas present from Mr Rivers, and took pleasure in its luxuriant brightness against the dull winter world. It was an item of such glamour that I could hardly believe it was mine. It was the sort of thing that Anna or Margot wore. I had not been expecting a gift, so gave Mr Rivers a book of Goethe's poetry that I had discovered in a second-hand bookshop in Dorchester and had intended to give to Kit. The gift was probably more suited to Mr Rivers anyway. Kit only really liked poetry that was either rude or made him laugh and preferably both at once.

The shelf of rock leading to Tilly Whim shone wetly, the limestone coated with a slick of freezing rain. The square mouths of the caves gaped as a lone white gull circled overhead, its cries drowned by the wash of the surf. A blur of movement caught my eye, and then a flash of red, bright as a fox's brush. But it wasn't a fox. It was Poppy. I ran towards her and then hesitated on seeing she was not alone. I lingered in the shadow of a rock, and spied several men in khaki greatcoats lugging boxes and tarpaulin drapes into the caves. There was an urgent furtiveness about them, like squirrels burying their hazelnuts on the lawns each September. After half an hour the men drifted away along the cliff, back up towards Lovell's Tower. Poppy loitered for a minute or two and then, pulling her wool coat around her, made to hurry after the men. I emerged from my hiding place and called to her. She spun around, hands fluttering to her throat in alarm.

'It's you! Goodness, Elise, you gave me a fright.'

She hurried over and hugged me quickly. I held her tight, reluctant to let go.

'Are you here to see Will?' I asked. 'Because he's joined the Dorsets.'

'I know. I saw him for an afternoon in Salisbury. He's waiting to ship. We strolled about the town and went for tea. Place was full of couples in uniform, all looking as miserable as us. Funny really, staring in your lover's eyes thinking, "When shall we meet again?" while eating buttered crumpets.'

'I wish you'd told me that you were coming home,' I said, picking a piece of moss from her hair.

She plunged mittened hands into her coat pockets. 'Ah, well. You see I'm not home. Not really. Secret war business.' She glanced over her shoulder, but her companions were already half a mile away, climbing the slope to the small tower. Her cheeks glowed with cold and excitement. 'Not really any point in your not knowing though, if you ask me.' She took a breath and then explained in a rush, 'We're dumping piles of ammunition and guns in hides around the coast. In case of the worst and invasion. Idea is that if it comes to it, locals will discover them and use 'em to fight the Germans. Bit pointless though, if no bugger knows where they are.'

I shrugged. 'Well, now I know.'

'Yes. But you mustn't tell anyone, else they'll be sure it's me and I shall be in awful trouble.' She coughed. 'Except if they invade. You can tell everyone then.'

I stared out across the sea, where wisps of mist drifted across the water like giant reams of silk from a vast spider's web. The sky had turned ink black and threatened snow. The stark trees on the horizon looked thin and cold, and the mouths of the caves were dark enough to swallow the last dregs of daylight. The breakers crashed against the shore, competing with the wind's howl. In the weird half-light I could imagine an armada of black ships sailing for England, their masts slicing through the mist. I saw men teeming upon the beach and crawling in their thousands up the steep cliffs, clawing the rocks with sharp nails and fever-bright eyes.

'I'll remember,' I said.

* * *

In February I picked snowdrops. They never lasted more than a day inside the house before wilting as though they really were beads of snow. Before breakfast, I set a vase of them upon the sideboard. That morning I'd received a letter from Margot, addressed to *Mrs Julian Landau, c/o Tyneford House*, sent when she still believed Anna and Julian were coming to Tyneford, and postmarked from

California last September. I'd opened it without hesitation, frantic for any word.

Darling Mama,

I am so pleased the visa arrived at last! Tell me how was your journey? No, never mind that, tell me about life by the sea. Has Papa been sea-bathing yet? I bet he looks very serious and never gets his hair wet. What do you think of England? Is it as green as the pictures and the food as terrible as everyone says?

And what do you think of Kit? Does he love Elise enough? I had thought at first that perhaps—well, never mind. I wish I were there with all of you. You must write and tell me EVERYTHING. I spoke to Robert about sailing to England but I suppose it might be dangerous if war's declared when we're at sea and we should really wait until after the war which must be declared soon but surely can't go on too long and oh I miss you all. Robert talks of going to Canada so he can fight when it starts but the University of course does not want him to go. And neither do I, even though I know I am being terribly selfish and that he should fight and then you will be safe and we can all go home.

Love to Elise and Papa.

Your daughter,

Margot

p.s. We went to the opera and saw The Marriage of Figaro. *The soprano who sang Cherubino was fat and sharp. But Robert wouldn't let me walk out, the beast.*

p.p.s. Still no sign of a baby. I hoped I would be

like you and fall pregnant on honeymoon. Your horrible tea didn't help at all. I made it exactly as you said (you wouldn't believe how hard it is to find dried marigolds here) but it was simply disgusting. It made me feel quite sick and I thought that perhaps it had worked but it was just the wretched marigolds.

I lowered the letter in surprise, pricked by hurt. Why hadn't Margot told me that she was hoping for a baby? Exiled from her confidence, I felt that she was further away than ever. Even as a girl she had never told me her secrets, hoarding her romances and whispering them to Anna behind the closed bathroom door. I listened with my ear to the keyhole and never heard anything more than the swish of water, or stray giggles. Even though she was far across the sea, Margot still made me feel like the little girl locked outside, ear pressed to the door. I was growing used to missing Anna and Julian. It was a constant ache, like an old injury, where the pain does not subside but one becomes accustomed to its presence. Reading Margot's letter, the pain throbbed and I felt a little dizzy. I missed Anna more than ever. All Margot's letters to me seemed empty and thin. I was not the pigtailed girl she'd said goodbye to all those years ago. Unlike Margot, I no longer dreamt about going home. Home in Vienna was gone. It existed before the war, in another time.

That morning, I felt hollow with hurt and worry. Kit's absence was more direct than my family's. I was used to seeing him, kissing him, walking with him every day. Several weeks had gone by without one of his letters. I supposed he must be somewhere far away, where the armed forces postal service could not function, but I wasn't sure whether I was concerned by his silence, or just annoyed. I slapped the flowers down so vigorously that the water slopped onto the polished cherry sideboard, and I had to mop it up with my sleeve before it stained. Mrs Ellsworth would not scold me but she'd rub at the mark with a cloth, her stooped back eloquent in reproach. I hoped Kit was missing me as much as I him. My sleeve was soggy and damp with the flower water. Did I really want Kit to be miserable? Surely it was more important that he was not too homesick while he was undertaking important war work. I propped up a snowdrop that was already starting to droop like the white head of a drowsy old man. No. It might be wicked, but I wanted Kit to be miserable. Just a little. A few tears at night perhaps—not so many that other officers would notice and tease him, but enough to demonstrate that his heart was a bit wounded. Three or four tears a night. Yes. That would be quite sufficient.

'Elise? What are you doing?' asked Mr Rivers.

Glancing down, I realised that I was flicking beads of water from a snowdrop stem all across the sideboard. Mr Rivers drew a handkerchief from his breast pocket and wiped away the mess.

'Join me for some coffee?' he said.

I sat down as he passed me a cup. A moment later Mr Wrexham appeared with a silver toast rack full of neat triangles, a dish of butter and another of marmalade. I reached for a slice, started to nibble it dry and then discarded it in disgust. Mr Rivers watched me in silence and then observed, 'You seem awfully fidgety.'

I did not tell him about Margot's letter. He felt bad enough. I'd overheard him remonstrating aloud when he thought no one was listening. *'If only I'd pushed them harder. One day. Even a single day.'*

He smiled at me. 'You'll hear from Kit soon, I'm sure.'

'Yes,' I answered, toying with the crumbs on my plate.

'I'm organising some repairs to a pair of old fishing-boats this morning. Since fish shan't be rationed, seems rather important to get all the boats in order. I want as many boats out in the bay as possible. You can help if you like.'

'Thank you,' I said, and forced a smile. 'I'd like that.'

An hour later we walked briskly down to the beach, where Art, Burt, a dozen of the village fishermen and a couple of boys too young for the army were all gathered in the ramshackle yard outside Burt's cottage. Two boats, about the size of *The Lugger* were propped up on stacks of bricks, with pieces of old carpet on top of the stacks to protect the hulls. The men circled the boats, peering closely, inspecting the keel here and the rudder there. They all seemed to be waiting for Mr Rivers' arrival before beginning work. Faint writing stencilled on the port side of one boat declared it to be *The Margaret,* but the name on the other had been rubbed away.

'They don't look too bad to me,' said Mr Rivers, after a careful inspection. 'That one needs a new tiller, and the keel on *The Margaret* needs repairing, and the rigging on each must be replaced, but I think we'll manage.'

There were grunts and nods of approval and the

men got to work. A pair of overalls was thrust into my hands.

''Ere are,' said Burt. 'Go an' put these arn. Can't do no dirty work in that slip o' a skirt. Be a ballywag o' a mess if yer tries.'

I slipped around the side of the cottage and quickly pulled them on, then returned to the throng. Burt grinned at me. 'Yer looks luverly, I must say. Jist needs a pipe.'

He chuckled loudly at his joke and gave me a piece of sandpaper and a chisel.

'Use him ter chip away at them barnacles and nasty weed. Her bottom must be smooth as a fish before she goes back in the drink. Jist do what the Miller boy is doin'.' He pointed to one of the boys whittling away at the muck with a knife.

For an hour I crouched beneath the boat, rubbing and scraping away at the weed welded to the paintwork, green as flecks of rain-soaked lettuce. The barnacles were small, hard warts and required the sharp chisel point to prise them away. All around me the men sanded or sawed small planks to replace the rotten pieces of timbers. Art and Burt climbed onto *The Margaret* and unscrewed the rusted fittings on the mast and the starboard rail, replacing them with salvaged ones. My arms cramped from work and I stood up to stretch and pace. The low winter sun peered from beneath a cloud, making the sea glitter. I squinted, shielding my eyes from the glare. In the far corner of the yard, Mr Rivers bent over a white sliver of wood, rubbing it smooth with a plane. He'd stripped to the waist, and leant into his work, the plane sliding to and fro, thin curls of wood dropping to the ground. I looked away.

‘’Ere, ’ave a drink,’ said Burt, offering me a flask of water.

Grateful, I took it from him, swallowing in gulps. Taking a lobster pot to use as a stool, I settled back beneath the spotted hull of the nameless boat and continued sanding. After a time Burt joined me, and we worked in companionable silence. He handed me the flask from time to time, but then once when I drank, it wasn’t water but rum. I nearly spat it out in surprise and Burt gave a low chuckle.

‘Aye. Needs a bit o’ a boost. A good tingle in yer veins.’

Mr Rivers and Art stood on the deck of *The Margaret* with coils of new rope, and began to feed them through the cleats, ready to rig the canvas sails, which lay in brown clouds beneath the mast. Placing a wooden handle in the jaws of the winch, Mr Rivers heaved while Art fed a line attached to the sail up the mast. The sail fluttered and flapped like a furious tethered bird, and the boat rocked on its makeshift platform. The noise was deafening, like claps of stage thunder, and I lowered my sandpaper to watch the two men wrestle with the wind. Mr Rivers left the winch to help Art, embracing the brown sail and reaching up with long arms to wrench it free. Suddenly it spilt along the boom, a great brown wing, half an eagle.

‘Champion seaman, Mr Rivers. Used ter race fer England when he wis a young man. Brilliant at yachtin’,’ murmured Burt in admiration.

I glanced at him in surprise and the old man smiled.

‘Aye. Doesn’t really understand yachtin’ myself. If yer is goin’ out arn the sea, might as well do a spot o’ fishin’. Sailin’ an’ no supper, seems a lot o' bother ter me.' He gave a tiny shrug. 'But Mr Rivers. Best yachtsman an' sailor. Better an' Kit. That boy's too impatient. Brave an' reckless. Dangerous that is. Sea is hungry fer foolish men.'

I put down my chisel and walked away. I didn't want to hear his doubts about Kit. Not now, when he was at sea. Behind me in the crumbling rocks, sand pipits had made nest holes, but they were abandoned, the owners far away in sunnier climes. The dwellings had an empty look, like cottages with unlit windows at dusk.

'Burt doesn't mean anything, Elise. He just worries about Kit. He's very fond of him,' said Mr Rivers.

He stood quietly beside me, watching the waves recede along the shoreline, the tide starting to turn.

'I don't like the silence,' I said. 'He always writes.'

'I know. But I am sure he's all right. Navy wires the families straight away if there's been a problem. Just up to something secret, that's all,' he said.

'Have you heard anything from your friend in Paris?'

He shook his head. 'I'm sorry. Nothing.'

He rested his arm lightly around my shoulders, and I leant into him. His skin was damp and he smelt of sweat and work. Suddenly we were both aware of his nakedness; he dropped his arm and I stepped away.

'Come. Time to paint,' he said, with a smile.

Everyone helped slick the bottom of the two fishing-boats with layers of anti-foul, aimed at repulsing the weed and barnacles and keeping the hull smooth and cutting through the water at a lick. The sun began to slide down the sky, until it was a round red chequer hovering above the horizon. The clouds flamed, bright as coals, and the sea shimmered pink, a miracle of watery fire.

'Needs ter 'ave a name. Smart boat like 'er needs a smart new name,' said Burt. 'Yer want ter name 'er?' he asked, with a grin in my direction.

'Are you sure?' I said, looking round the hoary faces of the fishermen, their beards daubed with red by the setting sun.

'Needs ter be the name of a woman,' added Art, scratching at a smear of paint on his forehead. 'It's tradition.'

I thought for a moment. There was only one possible name.

'*The Anna*,' I announced.

'Right yoos are,' said Burt, passing me the flask of rum.

I sprinkled a few drops over the bow, wetting her. '*The Anna!*' I shouted and the men grunted their approval. I gulped a sip of the rum and handed it to Mr Rivers. He drank, head thrown back. The sun dropped beneath the horizon and the pink sky dulled to grey. No lights appeared in the cottage windows, as blackout blinds were pinned into place. I thought of Anna and Julian. They'd be thrilled knowing there was a ship named for her. I wished I could launch *The Anna* that minute, and set sail to find them. I took the flask from Mr Rivers and swallowed another gulp of burning rum.

'Come,' said Mr Rivers, turning for home. I hurried to catch him, and together we strolled along the stone path in the early dark. I stumbled and he reached out to catch hold of my elbow, steadying me. Behind us, the slap of the sea and the laughter of the fishermen faded.

* * *

One March morning I woke early and padded downstairs in pyjamas and bare feet. It was soon after six and the daily housemaid had not yet started to clean the hallway. I unfastened the blackouts by the porch so that dawn light peeped in through the mullioned windows. The small drawing room was piled high with scraps of fabric and wisps of cotton filling floated out in the draught. The ladies in the village, marshalled by Poppy's aunts, had decided to make bed-jackets for wounded servicemen, and the yellow drawing room was declared ideal for this worthy occupation. The ladies descended upon us twice a week and sat round the fire and stitched, drank Mrs Ellsworth's plum wine, gossiped about the misery of war and the hideous inconvenience of the blackout and were very happy. My efforts were endlessly criticised and pulled apart, quite literally, to be re-sewn. In my opinion, the fact that my running stitch was not perfectly even would be the least concern of the corporal or private or captain who sat in bed clad in my mauve floral bed-jacket (recycled from a pair of old curtains—waste not, want not). It was an odd thing, making clothes for soldiers who were not yet wounded. The wearer of the ugly bed-jacket was presently preparing to ship off to France, or running exercises in a damp Wiltshire field, or drifting in the North Atlantic, in rude health. We sewed and prepared for future injury, ready to cosset our soldiers in beautifully stitched bedroom curtains, while they drilled with guns and bayonets and learnt to salute. It felt almost as though by making the wretched bed-jackets we were dooming them to months lying in the hospital, doing *The Times* crossword with one hand.

From the kitchen, I could hear the sound of May cussing as she tried to keep the vast black stove lit, so that Mr Rivers could have hot water for his morning bath. The range was ancient and as temperamental as a maiden aunt. I had spent hours fawning to its every whim, stoking it with coal, coke and kindling or simply pleading with it.

'Can I help?' I asked.

May was kneeling on the floor beside the range. She gave a shrug. 'If yer like. It's my last week anyways. Then Mrs Ellsworth will have to light the stupid fing herself.'

'Don't speak about Mrs Ellsworth like that. It's disrespectful.'

May snorted. 'Did you not hear me sayin' that I was off?'

I knelt beside her in my pyjamas, balling up old newspaper and feeding it into the stove. 'I thought you liked it here. Mrs Ellsworth is very fond of you.'

May had the grace to look a little guilt-stricken.

'Well. I has to do war work, doesn't I? Got a job in a factory in Portsmouth. Get my own money every week. No uptight old bugger to tell me what's what,' she said with a glance towards the butler's closed door. 'Dad wouldn't hear of a factory before. Said it wasn't nice. Girls in my family has always been in service. But it's my patriotic duty now, isn't it, and he can't say a word.'

The range finally lit, I stood up and brushed myself off.

'Don't you look at me like that, miss,' said the girl. 'You know what it's like. Why would anyone stay when they has got a choice?'

Knowing the miserable drudgery of the scullery maid's existence, I could not argue. 'I hope you'll be happy, May.'

As I walked down the corridor, I listened to Mrs Ellsworth in the store rattling jars and muttering to herself about the dwindling stock of jam. The back door opened with a slam, and the daily bustled inside with a blast of cool air and rustling parcels.

'Mornin',' she grunted, hurrying past me to start cleaning the house.

She looked more harassed each day as she attempted to undertake the work of three maids and a footman. With a sigh, I wondered how we would manage without May. I had beseeched Mr Wrexham to put away the dinner silver and china, and to use the plain luncheon set for both meals to keep down the amount of polishing, but he would not hear of it. 'The standard of a house is measured by its silver. What would the Ladies Hamilton think?' I thought that living in the Dower House, with the army teeming through Lulcombe Park, that they might tolerate luncheon silver. I was not sure that I cared; I was more concerned that our last daily might give her notice, exhausted by endless work. I tried to help the servants by stealth; dusting the china when Mr Wrexham was busy in the cellar, rolling out Mrs Ellsworth's pastry and setting it to blind in the oven, rubbing the beeswax onto the dining room table. Mr Wrexham was gratified by May and the daily housemaid's surprising efficiency, while the maids believed that Mr Wrexham had undertaken the work himself. I knew that this system of haphazard subterfuge could not continue.

The door to Mr Wrexham's pantry was open, and

I watched for a moment in silence as the old butler knelt by the grate, his elegant tailcoat covered by a white apron while he buffed his master's shoes to a gleam. The room was devoid of decoration, save for a faded photograph in sepia tones of Mr Wrexham with a young Mr Rivers and his bride. There were no pictures of Mr Wrexham's family. On the low table beside a lamp rested a calendar, each day tidily crossed out with blue ink as it passed. I glanced at the calendar. 6th of March.

'Oh,' I said.

Mr Wrexham looked around, a frown sliding across his face for an instant, before his features smoothed over once more. I knew he viewed my presence in the servants' halls as a violation of the green baize door.

'You may ring the bell in your room, should you require anything, miss,' he said, with mild reproach.

I ignored the reproof and continued to stare at the calendar.

'The date, Mr Wrexham. It's my birthday. I'm twenty-one today.'

* * *

'No argument, I'm taking you to lunch,' said Mr Rivers, propelling me across the driveway and into the waiting motorcar.

'But the petrol?'

'We've been saving the ration for months. And this is an essential journey. I'm taking you out to celebrate your birthday.'

He opened the door for me, and helped me inside.

'All right,' I said, sliding into the leather seat.

'Thank you. But it's really not necessary.'

He rolled his eyes. 'Good grief. I never realised how troublesome you can be.'

I said nothing. I saw myself dancing with Kit, my hair slicked smooth as a boy's. Kit dipping me, kissing me. I thought Mr Rivers knew exactly how troublesome I could be.

Art drove us to Dorchester. Mr Rivers and I did not speak much during the journey. He appeared busy with his thoughts, and trying not to knock into me as Art swung the Wolseley around the tight, hedged corners (Art was much more at ease driving Mr Bobbin than the smart motorcar). I was transfixed by the rushing green of the fields, punctuated around Lulcombe by the sage of the crawling army trucks and khaki tents that had sprung up across the parkland like giant molehills. We became stuck in a traffic jam of great army lorries outside Dorchester. They crawled towards us like dragons, the brown hedges brushing them on both sides. There was something ominous in the tick and growl of their diesel engines, and Art had to steer the car almost into a ditch in order to pass. Fifteen minutes later, he pulled up outside the Royal Hotel and, grumbling, lumbered around to open my door. Mr Rivers offered me his arm. 'Shall we?' he asked with a smile.

We drank champagne. An elderly waiter filled my glass and I looked at the bubbles rushing to the surface. Champagne always made me think of Anna. I was wearing the pearls she had smuggled into my luggage, and pretended that they were my birthday present. They felt tight around my throat.

'Do you not like champagne?' asked Mr Rivers, seeing I was not drinking. 'I can order something else, if you prefer.'

'Oh, no, thank you. It's lovely.'

I reached for the glass, and gulped down the liquid in a few swallows. There was a pleasant buzzing in my head. There was no linen on the table, only a waxed cloth that felt slightly sticky beneath my fingers. Mr Rivers ordered quail eggs and poached salmon and hot cucumbers and we ate a sort of trifle made with eggless custard for dessert. It tasted mainly of brandy and the buzzing in my ears built to a roar. The dining room was almost empty. A tired-looking man in army uniform lunched across from a woman with startling dyed-yellow hair, and in the far corner two old ladies in thick beige stockings sipped tea and gossiped beside the fireless grate. I couldn't help but think of Café Sperl or the Demel and the mirrored coffee houses of Vienna, where the towers of pastries and chocolates were reflected into infinity and neat waitresses in black and white glided between the tables, pouring creamy hot chocolate from polished silver jugs.

When we had finished eating, Mr Rivers ordered a cigar and a glass of port. Leaning back in his chair, he laughed softly.

'This is rather awful, isn't it?' he asked. 'Think we might have been better to have stayed at home, opened a bottle of the '23 Latour and let Mrs E. cook.'

I smiled. Mr Rivers did not know that it was usually me who now prepared his bourguignon or rhubarb sponge.

'No. It's lovely. Just the war's all. Makes it difficult.'

'Yes, well, if they're going to stay open, might as

well try to be a bit less grotty.'

He took a puff on his cigar. 'When Kit's home, we'll take a trip to London. I'll take you both to the Savoy and we can celebrate properly.'

At the mention of Kit we both fell silent, and at that moment I did not want to go back to the empty house. It was my birthday and I wanted to forget for an hour.

'Mr Rivers. Let's stay out a little longer, please.'

He looked at me in surprise and then he seemed glad. 'All right. Well. We could go to the pictures, I suppose.'

The Dorchester Picture Palace was showing *Rebecca.* Mr Rivers purchased two tickets, right at the back, and we tiptoed in, the main feature having already started. The auditorium was thick with smoke, and I stared at the screen through a yellow fog. We elbowed our way to our seats, stumbling over the tangles of embracing sweethearts who grumbled at our interruption. The seats at the rear were cramped and, as the airman sleeping beside me half sprawled onto my lap, I was forced to edge closer to Mr Rivers. I watched, enthralled, as the young Mrs de Winter fluttered through the house. The screen filled with the writhing sea and a timber boat bounced like a toy on the waves, and I shuddered, relieved Kit was aboard a proper ship. I had not been to the cinema in England, and I loved the ribald atmosphere—the audience cajoled and cheered the actors as though it was a live stage play. I belonged among them—squire, former housemaid/refugee, army officers, shop girls and WAAFs—we were just an audience, united by the story on the big screen. I forgot the world beyond the picture and I was happy.

We did not speak during the drive home. It began to rain and drops thrum-thrummed against the glass, while the motorcar roared through puddles, throwing up water as brown as milky tea. I must have fallen asleep, for the next moment we were drawing up outside the house. Mrs Ellsworth was waiting on the front steps. She clasped an umbrella with both hands, but it threatened to take off like a frightened bird. Filled with instant dread, I was opening the car door before it had even stopped. I hurled myself out, oblivious to the cascading rain, tore across the drive and ran up the steps, two at a time.

'It's Kit—' she started.

'Oh God, oh God,' I said.

I looked past Mrs Ellsworth into the gloom of the hall. Kit sat in a rather splendid wheelchair, his leg out in front, sporting my hideous hand-stitched mauve bed-jacket. 'Hullo,' he said. 'Happy Birthday.'

CHAPTER NINETEEN

WITCH-STONES

Kit was in plaster for six weeks. The cause of his injury was a source of considerable irritation to him. His ship had seen some brief skirmishes as part of an escort protecting merchant convoys in the North Atlantic from the wolf packs. Two officers had been injured and a midshipman killed by mines while running exercises, but Kit's broken ankle was more ignominious, caused by slipping on an icy deck during night watch off the coast of Norway. The ship's doctor set his leg, but on returning to Scapa Flow, Kit was transferred to land and sent home to recover. There was no room on the tightly packed corvette for an injured sailor.

Considering that he was usually quite content to lounge upon the sofa smoking endless cigarettes and devouring *Sporting Life,* he was an awful patient, always fidgeting and complaining that he was bored. I noticed that he smoked even more, if it were possible, and that he looked older. He had filled out a little, and necessarily confined to lolling in an armchair he lost that restless quick movement which always made him seem so boyish. He was in some considerable pain, and I think the cigarettes and morning whisky were ways of distracting himself. We sat for hours in the warm fug of the drawing room, the fire stoked to a furnace by Mr Wrexham, despite our protestations. I read novels aloud to entertain him, always the latest lurid romance—the more absurd the language of love, the more he liked them. Whenever my voice grew hoarse and I paused he'd wave impatiently, cigarette between his fingers. 'Well, go on.'

I laughed at him. 'You're unbearable. You read it.'

He shook his head and fixed me with a lazy smile. 'No. I like to hear you. Especially the wicked parts. They make you blush, you know.'

It was fortunate in some ways that Kit's injury forced a certain distance between us. In his letters, he had confided desires and breathless acts of love. At first they were fervent, schoolboy imaginings, the language one might expect of a love-struck gentleman who had once attended Sidney Sussex

College, Cambridge, but then, after a month or more onboard his ship, they grew coarser and more thrilling. I knew I ought to be shocked, or angry and repulsed. I was not. I was intrigued and baffled by these new words that my faithful German/English dictionary could not explain. The mysterious words were as exotic as the half-understood acts that they failed to describe. I was forced to imagine the pictures which these guttural, consonant clicking sounds represented. Unconstrained by meaning, my imaginings were frantic. Kit's descriptions of lovemaking might only have taken place in the pages of his letters, but I had read and re-read them, picturing them in the warm dark every night as I lay in bed, quite unable to sleep. We were both conscious of some shared intimacy, like adolescents the day after a kiss at a school dance, at once shy and eager.

'Read some more,' said Kit, stroking my cheek with his fingers.

'Later. My voice is all hoarse.'

'Your necklace,' he said, noticing Anna's pearls beneath the collar of my shirt.

'Do you like them? They were my mother's.'

He reached a hand behind my neck and drew me close, kissing me. As he let go, he unfastened another button on my shirt and traced the pearls with a finger, brushing the bare skin at my throat.

'They are very pretty.'

I let him kiss me and toy with the pearls. I was pleased that his attention was wholly upon me. The minute he returned to Tyneford, I knew that for the first time I had a rival. One much fiercer than Diana or Juno; a rival I had to accept and learn to live with for the duration of the war. Kit loved me, but his loyalty was torn between the two of us: *The Angelica* and me. He was glad to be home and to sit and chatter beside the fire, but it wasn't like before. A part of him yearned to be at sea. He hated being here while she was somewhere in the Atlantic, scouring the waters for U-boats and enemy destroyers. His shipmates risked their lives while he lazed on the sofa sipping cocoa and eating ginger biscuits.

'Tell me what it's like to be at sea,' I said.

Kit fell silent. He did not speak about life on the ship. He claimed his reticence was because of secrecy, but I suspected that it was simply easier. When onboard he needed to become another version of himself, Temporary Sublieutenant Rivers, and now at home he wanted to be Kit again. He did not wish to be one man, while speaking of the other. I did not push him, although later I wished I had.

When we were not reading together in the drawing room, or taking meals in the morning room, Kit liked to sit outside. He wheeled himself onto the terrace, discarding the tartan blankets Mrs Ellsworth insisted on tucking about him and, armed instead with a hipflask of brandy, he sat for hours with the old nursery telescope trained on the sea. To the gardener's dismay, he liked to propel himself across the lawn, the chair's wheels leaving two neat trenches. He sat at the end of the garden, where the line of bright grass cut into the blue horizon, and scrutinised the sea for ships. Mr Wrexham sometimes joined him, and the two men sat together, one head white as a laundered handkerchief, the other gold as harvest, passing the telescope back and forth between them. The butler carried out a low table and placed the portable wireless set upon it. Kit listened to it almost constantly, craning forward in his chair whenever the naval news came over the airwaves, as though he could get closer to the action. Whenever there was something about a Flower class corvette, his fists would clench, and he'd hold his breath. There was no mention of *The Angelica.*

The day Kit's leg was taken out of plaster, Poppy returned home for a few days' leave. She came straight to the house and joined us on the terrace where Kit was slowly limping up and down with the aid of a walking stick. It was near the end of April and a damp morning ripened into a warm afternoon, the bright lichen on the roof tiles yellow as sunshine. I paced beside Kit, hovering at his elbow, anxious as a mother house martin as her chick first takes to the skies. He swore in frustration.

'Fuck.' He banged his stick against the drainpipe. 'I'm like an old fucking man.'

I'd never heard him curse like this before, and halted for a second before helping him to sit on the wooden bench. Poppy leant against the wall, closing her eyes in the spring sun. 'Oh,' she said. 'Swear like a sailor now, Kit? Bit of a cliché.'

He smiled and pulled me onto his good knee, kissing my nose. 'Sorry, darling. Just not used to being a blasted cripple.'

'You're not. You'll be better before you know it,' I said, forcing myself to smile, conscious that as soon as his leg healed, he'd depart for *The Angelica.*

'How's Will?' asked Kit, changing the subject and looking at Poppy.

'I don't know. He sailed for France just before

you came home. He was all right, last I heard. Wrote asking me for scraps of French and to check that someone's looking after his plants and feeding that horrid cat. Don't think they're doing much. Training. Waiting for something to happen. Last I heard, only thing he'd shot was a rabbit.'

'Nazi rabbit, I hope?' said Kit.

Poppy smiled. 'No Nazis in sight. Not sure who all this waiting is worse for—us or them. And the post's been a bit ropey last few weeks.'

Her voice was playful, feigning unconcern, but I didn't believe it.

'I say, shall we call for some drinks? I know it's only teatime but I fancy something stronger,' she added, slumping into a chair.

I disappeared to ask Mr Wrexham for some wine, and when I returned with a bottle, the two of them were sitting in silence, huddled around the wireless.

'Denmark's surrendered,' said Kit, fixing himself a drink. 'God knows what's happening in Norway. Half the navy's probably up there.'

'What does it mean for France?' asked Poppy.

'I don't know,' said Kit, passing her a glass. 'The Western Front is going to have to open up sometime. Our boys are ready for them.'

* * *

This formed the pattern of the ensuing days. We lazed in the garden, warmed by gentle sunshine, listening to the wireless, often drinking rather too much wine, while the cuckoos called from Rookery Wood and the fishing-boats dawdled in the bay. I remember every day as a warm, unbroken blue.

It had the feel of the last weeks of the summer holidays, when school looms and yet belongs so completely to another world that one can scarce believe the sun-filled days of freedom could ever end. Lying on a picnic rug, I tried to count the newly ripened freckles on Kit's nose, and did not think it was possible to love him more than I did at that moment. I helped him with his exercises and his stride grew stronger as we spied our first spotted flycatcher alighting on the flowering plum. He discarded his stick the same day as a pair of holly blue butterflies flitted across a spray of irises. By the time the pale pink London pride bloomed in the rockery, he could walk smoothly with only slight pain. I tried not to wish Poppy away, but these were stolen days and I wanted Kit to myself.

I assisted Mrs Ellsworth with the cooking. She refused to listen to the Home Service with its constant news bulletins, complaining that it was 'stuffed to the gills gruesome', preferring the endless tunes playing on the Forces radio. She loved the cheerful wartime songs, and the kitchen echoed to the strains of 'Bye Bye Blackbird', 'All the Nice Girls Love a Sailor' and 'We're Going to Hang the Washing on the Siegfried Line'. She'd hum along as she curried parsnips and bottled elderflower cordial, breaking off to complain, 'Why can't they come up with such good tunes in peacetime? I don't know.'

When I returned to the garden, I found Poppy and Kit sitting in silence, elbows on the table, listening to the Home Service like an oracle. I felt a twist of jealousy and wished for the thousandth time that she would go.

Kit gave me a grim smile. 'Well, it looks like

Will's going to get a chance to shoot at more than rabbits. The fighting's begun in France.'

'He'll be all right, Poppy, I'm sure he will,' I said, making use of the platitudes that always irked me, suddenly filled with remorse at having desired her gone.

* * *

But my guilty wish was granted a day later. A telegram arrived for Poppy, summoning her immediately back to work—all leave cancelled—and the same afternoon Mr Rivers announced that he was going up to town for a week. We bade goodbye to Kit's father, and then drifted about the terrace hand in hand, suddenly unsure how best to make the most of this boon. Kit and I felt like children whose parents had gone out, leaving us to delicious freedom. From the wireless in the dining room came headlines about the formation of 'Local Defence Volunteers' and the 'fifth column tricks' in the Low Countries, but at that moment war seemed far away. The ancient gardener raked withered azalea blossoms from the lawn and a blue tit yanked a worm from among the lavender beds.

'Let's not dress for dinner,' said Kit.

'That's all? Your father's away and your best rebellion is not to change your shirt?'

Kit plucked a daisy and lobbed it at me. 'And what do you suggest?'

'We should get dressed up for dinner. In black tie. And drink champagne and cognac and get very drunk.' Then I remembered and shook my head. 'No. It's no good.'

'Why not? It's a splendid plan.'

'I've nothing to wear. Diana spoilt my only good dress.'

'I've an idea.'

Kit led me upstairs to one of the spare bedrooms. As a housemaid I had dusted and polished it every day, but since the war started and the staff disappeared from Tyneford, it had been shut up. All the furniture except a great mahogany wardrobe had been pulled into the middle of the room and shrouded in dustsheets. The grey curtains were closed and as Kit drew them back, a family of moths fluttered around his head. Batting them away, he unlocked the wardrobe and seized an armful of dresses.

'These belonged to my mother. Something here's sure to fit.'

I stepped back. 'Kit, no. I couldn't.'

'Why not? They're not doing anyone any good in here. And that would have annoyed her.'

'You don't remember what annoyed her.'

Kit shrugged. 'No woman can bear to think of a Parisian couture gown unworn.'

'Couture?'

Intrigue won over scruples.

* * *

I turned round in front of the mirror. The midnight-blue silk fell away from my left shoulder leaving it bare, and trickled in waves to the ground. A gold belt twisted below my waist and earrings shaped like leaves dangled from each ear. I thought of Kit's young mother pulling on this dress, checking her appearance, before descending the staircase to greet her guests. I wondered what Anna would say if she could see me. I didn't feel real.

Even Mr Wrexham colluded. He served us dinner on the best china, pouring us champagne, sliding back into the shadows so as not to overhear as Kit and I whispered and giggled. I did not feel like the future mistress of Tyneford, but a child playing tea parties who, as a treat, has been allowed to fill the toy pot with real tea and set out miniature sandwiches on the tiny plates.

After dinner, Kit and I slipped away onto the terrace. The blackouts were drawn and the only light in the garden was the glow of our cigarettes. I discarded my shoes and tucked my feet onto the bench, wishing I had scarlet polish for my toes. We passed champagne back and forth, sipping straight from the bottle. I tingled, thrilled by our decadence. I slid into his arms and we began to kiss, gently at first and then more eagerly. He stopped and unsure why, I tried to draw him back to me, but then I felt the warmth of his breath on my bare shoulder, and then the damp of his mouth on my skin. His fingers eased under the strap of my dress and as I felt his hand brush my breast, I heard myself wonder, as though from a distance, precisely how many of Anna's rules of etiquette I was breaking at that moment. He kissed me again and I kissed him back. I was drunk on champagne and on him. He pushed me down against the bench, and his fingers reached for the hem of my dress. I knew I ought to make him stop. It was what girls must do when young men got too fresh, too amorous, too delightful. I didn't want him to stop. I didn't want to disappoint Anna. I didn't want to be one of the fast girls in the chorus who made her sigh. I'd like to say that I considered the consequences, picturing myself as the deflowered heroine—Tosca, or perhaps Tess D'Urberville—but I was struggling to think very much at all. At that moment my body was utterly uninterested in the proper decorum expected from girls like me. Kit nudged my thighs apart with his knee and I heard the beautiful silk dress tear. That brought me back to myself and I tried to wriggle away but he held me firm, making a cage with his arms.

'Don't,' I said, pushing at him but he didn't seem to hear. Sweat glistened on his upper lip and he was now intent on reaching the waistband of my knickers. 'Don't,' I said again and shoved at him.

'I love you,' he whispered, but rather than encouraging me, his words made me cross and I elbowed him, hard. He recoiled and sat up, staring at me with a wounded expression.

'What's wrong?' he said. 'You wanted to make the most of having the place to ourselves.'

'Yes. But I don't want to do that. Not yet.'

I suddenly felt very childish, conscious that my finery was only borrowed.

'I'm wearing your mother's dress. And we've spoilt it.'

Kit shrugged. 'You could always take it off.'

'I most certainly cannot.' I heard Anna's voice coming from my mouth. My fingers flew to the pearl necklace heavy around my throat. I felt the cool disapproval of the two absent mothers. Adjusting my dress, I picked up my shoes and fled into the house, feeling hot tears prick my eyes.

* * *

When his father returned Kit grew restless. He

knew that somewhere others were busy with war, while he was reduced to planting cabbage seedlings or fishing for haddock with Burt. His leg was almost healed and he would not admit to any pain, desperate to be cleared for active service at the earliest possible moment. He prowled the garden, smoking, or disappeared down to the beach. He no longer insisted on my company. Somewhere a battle raged and *The Angelica,* small as she was, had her part and Kit was lost. I could not help wondering if things had gone differently, and I'd allowed him to make love to me, he might have confided in me more. In the years since I have had a long time to think about these things, and sometimes I still wonder. If the silk dress had not torn. If I had not been struck by a sudden pang of conscience. Is it possible that everything would have ended differently? But that is why the English invented gardens. When I find myself maudlin over such things, I prune the roses or attack the ground elder with renewed vigour.

A letter arrived from Margot, the first in months, the post having been hopelessly disrupted by the wolf packs. I imagined her missing letters sinking into the waves, and tried not to think of the ships missing as well. I read in the sunshine on the terrace, forcing myself not to rush, to savour every word.

I can't tell you how useless I feel marooned here in America. Have you had many bombs yet? Are you very frightened? I went to the cinema and heard on the newsreel the noise those blasted sirens make and they were quite terrifying, even in the movie theatre—I can't imagine what they're like when accompanied by planes and bombs. You must drink brandy for your nerves.

I wished I could tell her that we felt similarly useless on the quiet part of England's coast.

Spring here is beautiful. We have a lovely house now with a view of the harbour and a glimpse of the Golden Gate Bridge. I practise in a room with a view of the water, and as I play I think of you, gazing at the other side of another sea. I've been a little low lately. I am empty inside from missing all of you and I so want a family of my own and I know I should not worry about it not happening and that worrying only makes it more difficult and Robert and the doctor (who is terribly kind) both say the same thing but, Elise, it is very hard. Robert has bought me a dog, a beautiful golden retriever, to take for walks and dote upon. I have called him Wolfgang, Wolfie for short. You would love him. I remember how you used to plead with Anna and Julian to let you have a dog.

I wished my sister were at Tyneford so that I could comfort her. I knew that she'd always wanted to call her son Wolfgang. I pictured the two of us rambling along the ridge throwing sticks for Wolfie, laughing as the dog swam in the bay and then shook his coat all over us. It is interesting to note that in none of my fantasies did I tell her about the novel in the viola. Even though my sister longed for a word or a sign from our parents, I hoarded the viola to myself. It is too late now for regrets. Today will be a day spent in the garden. I shall plant the crocuses for next spring and try to think of other things.

One evening at the end of May I lingered in the drawing room after dinner with Kit and Mr Rivers. It was past eleven o'clock, the windows were tightly shut and the curtains drawn over the blackouts. It was too warm and I longed to open a window for some fresh air. Kit hunched on an armchair beside the empty grate, staring into nothing, while Mr Rivers pretended to read. I studied the household hints in *Woman's Own*, feeling terribly self-righteous and terribly bored. From the hall came the sound of the telephone. We all bristled, listening to the soft pad of the butler's footsteps and his low murmur. A few moments later the drawing room door opened and Mr Wrexham entered.

'Mr Kit. The telephone for you, sir, it's a Captain Graham Parsons.'

Kit leapt up and crossed the room in two strides. Mr Rivers and I lowered our papers and held our breath so we could eavesdrop. I craned forward in my chair and listened to Kit's voice, '*Yes, sir . . . certainly, sir . . . there is . . . twenty-four hours . . . yes, right away, sir . . . high tide . . . perfectly fit, thank you, sir . . . goodbye . . .*' and then the echo of his footsteps on the parquet floor. He came back into the drawing room, and I noticed that he was flushed with excitement, his eyes bright. He stood looking at Mr Rivers and me and leant against the wall, studying to appear nonchalant, but his lip twitched with a smile.

'I have orders. I am to commandeer a boat and sail her to Kent and then join a convoy to France.'

'Good God. Then it's true. The army's in retreat,' said Mr Rivers, discarding his newspaper.

'I suppose so. The captain didn't say. I'm to receive final orders when I reach Ramsgate.'

Kit perched on the edge of a sofa, then unable to settle, stood up and paced, circling the room. I caught his hand as he passed and forced him to a stop.

'When will you leave?'

'High tide. I'm to get the boat ready and sail for Kent as soon as she's ready.'

A sick feeling grew, and I gripped his hand so hard my knuckles turned white. Kit smiled at me, brushing a curl of dark hair behind my ear. 'Don't fret, darling. It's a relief to do something at last. I'll be back before you know it.'

I tried to smile but I did not release his hand. Despite everything that had happened to my family, Kit still could not imagine that sometimes people were parted for longer than they wanted.

'Go and change,' said Mr Rivers. 'Then we'll go down to the beach and speak to Burt. I presume that you wish to take *The Lugger*?'

Kit nodded. 'Yes. She's the nimblest of the fishing-boats. She's not the largest, but she's fast, and I know the quirks of her engine. That wretched outboard has blown up more times than I care to remember, and I've never not been able to fix her.'

Ten minutes later we were hurrying down to the cove, Kit dressed in his naval uniform and carrying his mackintosh. He looked handsome and older than before, clad in his long coat, the brim of his hat shadowing his eyes. I dug my fingernails into the fleshy part of my palms and wished I believed in God so that I could pray for his safe return. Mr Rivers had also changed into his work clothes, and I noticed a set of oilskins tucked under his arm. The night was cloudless and full of stars. An owl cried out in the dark and flew low across the pebbled beach, while the wind strummed the marram grass. I scrambled to keep up with the men's easy strides, and as we reached the beach I slithered across the rocks in my plimsolls. Burt's cottage windows were blacked out, but in the starlight a thin plume of smoke was visible as it curled out from the broken chimneypot. Kit knocked on the door, and a minute later it flew open. Burt blinked as he took in Kit standing on his front step in his naval trench coat and his lieutenant's cap.

'Burt, I need to commandeer *The Lugger*. I have to take her to France. Our boys are stranded on the beaches.'

Burt gave a slow nod, and then a half-salute. 'Aye, Officer. Well, yer told us before that *The Lugger* wis now part of His Majesty's navy. If the Admiralty needs her, then she mist go. Only wish I wis a bit younger an' a bit less creaky an' I'd sail with yoos.'

Kit strode across the darkened yard to the beach where the boat lay upon the pebbles under a blanket of tarpaulin. Mr Rivers helped him throw off the covering, and Burt joined them both, walking around the hull, scrutinising the paintwork with the flickering light of a match. Kit climbed onto the deck and started handing down coiled fishing-nets and lobster pots.

'She must be stripped of everything except essentials.'

I caught the nets and carried them into a corner of the yard.

'Are there any blankets?' called Mr Rivers. 'It'll be cold on the channel. And food. We need food in tins and at least three gallons of fresh water.'

'I'll go and ask Mrs Ellsworth,' I said, and turned to hurry back up the path to the house.

'There's plenty of time,' called Mr Rivers. 'Tide must turn. It's at the lowest ebb. We'll need to wait at least six hours until *The Lugger* can sail.'

I didn't care if there was time. I ran along the track as fast as I could—I wanted to spend every last minute with Kit. The moon cast a cold glow on the chalk path, white as bone. The night smelt sweetly of dog roses, which wove in tangles through the black hedgerows. I rushed past the tawny owl, now perched on a fencepost, his head swivelling to watch me with yellow eyes. I reached the back door, my breath coming in gasps.

'Mrs Ellsworth! I need blankets and tins of fruit and meat and custard and a flask for water . . . and dressings and bandages . . . and some brandy if you have it.'

She came bustling along the passage, her tanned forehead furrowed like plough lines across a field.

'Yes, yes, all right. Come in and close the door—you're letting out the light.'

I realised that in my hurry I'd forgotten about the blackout rules and light was streaming onto the cobbles in the yard. I slammed the door and followed her into the pantry. She thrust a sack into my hands.

'Fill this with tins from the bottom shelf. Take a dozen evaporated milk. Fruit pieces. Potted meat. And put in two tin openers. And spoons.'

Once I had packed the food, I dragged the sack to the back door. Wondering how on earth I was going to carry it all to the beach, I spied Art's wheelbarrow with relief. Mrs Ellsworth joined me in the yard, holding a pile of blankets and a picnic hamper, which she dumped on top of the wheelbarrow. I started to wheel it along the drive and back down the path to the bay. It clattered in the dark, and I was sure that I would wake every villager. I wondered how on earth the old smugglers managed. I supposed they didn't use wheelbarrows. It was heavy and kept sticking on the stones, but we returned to the beach within the hour. The men were checking *The Lugger*'s rigging and arguing over whether to take a spare sail.

'Can't sail into battle,' said Kit, arms folded across his chest. 'We'll use the outboard once we get near France.'

'But if the engine packs in?' asked Mr Rivers.

'Then we use the oars.'

'She's a devil ter row,' said Burt, shaking his head.

'Well, there'll be plenty of men. Some of them will have to help,' said Kit, determined.

'Right yer are,' said Burt. 'Take another set then.'

'What about flares?' asked Mr Rivers.

'Under bench in stern,' replied Burt.

Kit climbed down and came to stand beside me, draping his arm around my shoulders. 'Nothing more to do but wait for the tide.'

'Why don't you go back to the house and get yourself a few hours' sleep, sir?' asked Mrs Ellsworth.

Kit laughed. 'Couldn't sleep now. I'll stretch out on deck and rest,' he added, to mollify her. 'Come on,' he said, grabbing my hand and scooping up a blanket. 'You're always asking what it's like to sleep aboard a ship—come and find out.'

I allowed him to help me clamber onto the deck of *The Lugger.* He spread a blanket across one of the narrow wooden benches and lay down, tapping the space beside him. I hesitated for only a second before squeezing in next to him. He wrapped his arms around me and I felt his breath on the back of my neck. I was still cold and I gave a shiver. Kit wriggled upright.

'I'm sorry. Very ungallant. Here,' he removed his woollen trench coat, and laid it over us both. The tide was far out in the bay, and the water rushed against the rocks in the distance.

'It's not as comfortable as a Snottie's hammock,' he said.

'Snottie?'

'Midshipmen. We officers have the luxurious discomfort of a hard bunk in a broom cupboard and being flung onto the floor if the wind picks up. I've slung a hammock once or twice though, and magic things they are. Swing with the rhythm of the ship, sleep like a baby rocking in a cradle.'

'We'll try it when you get back,' I whispered. 'By Durdle Door. Like you said in your letter.'

We fell silent, conscious of the intimacies expressed in his letters and of the weeks squandered in Tyneford. He'd spent much of them wishing to be at sea and now that he was about to depart he brimmed with regret.

'I'm sorry, darling. It'll be different when I'm on leave. It was being out of action that made me act like such a cad.'

I twisted in his arms so that I could kiss him. His mouth was warm against mine.

'Elise,' he said, as he at last drew away. 'I want to marry you now. I don't want to wait anymore.'

I swallowed, feeling something lodge in my throat. 'Yes, all right.'

He brushed my cheek with his fingertips. 'Really? Yes?'

I tried to imagine the letter I would write to Anna . . . *Darling Anna, Today I married Kit. I wore your pearls.*

I brushed Kit's jaw with my lips. 'But,' I glanced down at my hands, too shy to look at him, 'even if we don't marry straight away. The things in your letter. We could try the things in your letter, even if we're not married. I won't stop you next time. If you like.'

'Yes, I'd like,' he said, his voice low. 'When I'm back.'

He pulled me tight and I squirmed against him and closed my eyes, listening to the crash of the sea. The tide was starting to turn. Each wave carried forward the moment of departure. I opened my eyes again, fighting against sleep in the warmth of his arms. Above the shadow of the trees nestling in the valley, I distinguished the sharp silhouette of the village church and the silent bell tower. The bells had not rung since the start of the war, not to mark the Sunday service, or the funeral of the Widow Pike, neither the quarter hour nor midnight. I wished that its silence marked the stopping of time; that until the bell tolled, Kit would remain lying beside me on the wooden bench, always waiting for high tide, never leaving. If the bell did not chime, then we could live always in the moment before parting and never part.

* * *

Dawn glowed all around. I had betrayed us both and fallen asleep. Mr Rivers sat on the bench opposite. He watched us, and in the second before he realised I was awake I saw that he was sad. He blinked and smiled, and the shadow passed away.

'Good morning,' he said. 'Mrs Ellsworth's cooking breakfast.'

Kit sat up and stretched, giving a great yawn. 'What time is it?'

'About four. Tide will be high enough in under an hour.'

'Jolly good,' said Kit, pulling me onto his knee as I sat up. He pressed his chin into the nape of my neck, and I felt the scratch of his bristles. The sea lapped several feet from *The Lugger*; in an hour she would be afloat. A few yards back, carefully positioned out of the reach of high tide, Mrs Ellsworth was frying bacon over a low fire. A handful of fishermen milled around Burt's yard, gulping tea from enamel mugs and discussing the weather in low voices. In the distance a slight figure dressed in tails walked steadily along the path leading down the beach. As he drew closer I realised it was Mr Wrexham, holding before him a basin of steaming water, a pristine linen towel draped across each wrist. A neat white apron was fastened around his waist. He bowed his head when he saw Kit and Mr Rivers.

'Good morning, Mr Rivers, sir. Mr Kit, sir. I trust you slept well, and were not too inconvenienced?'

'Splendid thank you, Wrexham,' replied Kit.

I thought I saw the butler's right eye twitch when he spied me perched upon Kit's knee, but I couldn't be sure.

'If I may?' inquired Mr Wrexham, offering up

the basin.

Mr Rivers took it from him, setting it upon the deck, and the next moment the butler was nimbly climbing aboard. Mr Rivers sat on the bench, keeping quite still, while Mr Wrexham draped the towel around his collar and, producing another smaller towel, laid upon it shaving tackle from his apron pocket. I watched with fascination as he soaked a flannel in the basin of water and then pressed it against Mr Rivers' face, the cloth steaming like early morning mist. From his pocket Mr Wrexham conjured a leather strop and a fearsome razor, which he snapped against the leather until the edge glinted. He whipped up a fine lather with soap and a shaving brush and painted it across Mr Rivers' chin and lip. This was masculine alchemy. I thought with a pang of Julian. His valet shaved him each morning and although I had often pleaded to watch my father told me in no uncertain terms that this was a moment of privacy for a man; a simple pleasure not to be spoilt by the presence of small girls. I wondered who shaved him now. In all his forty-six years, Julian had never shaved himself.

Mr Wrexham soaked the towel in the saltwater surf and then pressed the cloth against Mr Rivers' jaw. As the salt touched his skin, he winced, inhaling sharply.

'Good saltwater. Better than any cologne, sir,' said the butler.

Then he turned his attentions to Kit, repeating the entire process with fresh towels and brush. Neither gentleman appeared fazed that the butler had traipsed down to the beach, at no small inconvenience to himself, to attend to them in the open air. A British officer could not set sail without a proper shave.

'Shall I pack the shaving tackle up for you, sir?'

'Please, Wrexham,' replied both men.

The small boat was stripped to essentials, but clearly that included a razor. In my fascination, I had missed a crucial detail. Kit had not. He turned to his father in surprise.

'Your shaving tackle? You intend to sail to Kent?'

'If you will allow an old army so-and-so aboard. I know you can manage her single-handed, but you'll be devilish tired before you even get to Ramsgate. It's a fifteen-hour run.'

'I know,' said Kit, as though his father were questioning his judgement. 'I've checked the charts.'

'I'm sure you have,' said Mr Rivers evenly. 'Still, I would very much like to come.' He looked at Kit as if he were asking permission, his voice light, but I knew that it was not a question. He merely wished to give his son the illusion of choice.

The two men stared at each other, shoulders set firm. Kit gave a short nod, and they both relaxed.

'All right,' said Kit, 'I could do with the help, but I'm supposed to take aboard another wavy navy chap at Ramsgate.'

'Very well,' said his father. 'But if you're short-handed, I'm coming with you to France.'

I looked at the set of Mr Rivers' mouth and I knew, even if Kit didn't, that his father was going to France, regardless of wavy navy chaps. Mrs Ellsworth summoned us for breakfast and cut the argument short. The sun rose above the hills, glowing yellow gold like a gentleman's pocket-watch, and caught the sea pinks carpeting the cliff edge. The air filled with the yammer of gulls, while chiffchaffs warbled and flitted to and fro among the shrubs outside Burt's cottage. The smell of crisp bacon wafted in the morning breeze as Mrs Ellsworth handed round plates filled with hunks of bread and slices of marbled bacon and fried eggs. In the corner of the yard, Burt and Mr Wrexham were stringing odd-shaped stones along a fine piece of rope. The stones were large, misshapen pebbles with holes in the centre where they had been worn away by millennia of tides. The brothers carried the stones over to *The Lugger* and fastened the line around the bow, knotting it tightly around the base of two stanchions, so that the pebbles dangled in a loop at the front of the boat. Burt caught me watching and winked.

'Witch-stones,' he called. 'Ter stop witches catchin' a lift.'

I said nothing. I thought that German Stukas would be more of a danger than witches. Burt appeared to guess my thoughts and grinned. 'Aye. Well, better safe than sorry. An' don't have nothin' ter ward off Germans. Least we know that witches won't be no trouble.'

I could not tell whether he was teasing. I glanced from Burt to Mr Wrexham. The old fisherman was dressed in his usual coarse brown trousers and much-darned sweater, and a week's stubble, the colour of salt, sprouted on his chin. Mr Wrexham was immaculate in his black tails and starched shirt, but their eyes were the same shade of blue, and as they slung the witch-stones over *The Lugger's* bow, their limbs moved in unison, with the easy gesture of men used to casting nets and lives spent around boats. The butler was a fisherman still.

'It's time,' called Mr Rivers. 'Help to cast off.'

The water lapped around her hull, but *The Lugger* needed to be carried out farther into the surf, and the fishermen swarmed around her, indifferent to the water soaking their shoes. Grabbing hold of her sides, they heaved the small boat across the pebbles, shoulders bent to the task, wooden hull grinding against the stones. I waded out with them, drenching my plimsolls and stockings. Mr Rivers appeared beside me. He kissed me lightly on the cheek and took my hand in both of his.

'I'll bring him home, I promise. We'll see you in a few days. A week tops. I'll try and wire. But you're not to worry.'

I found that I was crying, and splashed my face with seawater to disguise the tears. Mr Rivers looked at me for a second, and then pulled me close.

'I am so sorry that I couldn't bring your parents to Tyneford. Sorrier than I can say. But I promise that I will bring Kit back to you.'

I felt the thundering of his heart through my thin blouse like the pulse of the waves. I thought he was going to speak again, but then he was letting me go, and he was wading through the water and swinging himself into the stern of the boat. I watched him, but he was busy checking the charts and did not see me. I brushed my eyes, and licked saltwater from the back of my hand. Anna. Julian. Now Kit and Mr Rivers.

Kit danced around the bow, holding the painter and swinging *The Lugger* about, so that her nose faced out to sea. Burt took the rope from him and Kit came over to say goodbye.

'Darling, I love you,' said Kit. 'And I will see you very soon. You know I have to go—it's Will stuck on those beaches.'

I nodded, my voice stuck in my throat. He kissed me, dipping me backwards towards the surf like we were a couple in a moving picture, and the fishermen cheered from the beach. I flushed with sudden anger; he was acting like a hero in some adventure flick, playing it up for the crowd.

'Kit, please. You must be careful. I like Will very much. But I love you. I'm selfish. I don't want you to die saving another girl's young man. If that makes me wicked, then I'm sorry, but you don't know what it's like to be parted from everyone you love. I was alone. Then I found you. I don't want to be alone again.'

He kissed me once more, but I knew he was impatient to be gone.

'Tosh,' he said. 'No one's going to die, darling.'

'Yes, Kit. Yes, they are. And if it's all right, I'd rather it wasn't you.'

I knew I wasn't being British. An Englishwoman would have kissed her boyfriend lightly on the lips, and said 'Darling, I'm quite fond of you, you know. Try not to get into any bother,' and then waved politely, perhaps concealing a stoic tear in her handkerchief and then make herself a nice cup of tea, and get back to darning socks. Well, I wasn't British, I was Viennese, and continental women say what they feel. I took a deep breath, and tried to ignore the fact that Kit was fidgeting with embarrassment.

'Everyone I love in England is about to climb into that wooden boat and disappear across the sea. Sail carefully because you sail with everything I hold dear on this funny, damp little island.'

(I am almost sure that is what I said. In the years since I have thought about that moment so often. If I did not, then it was what I wanted to say.)

Mr Rivers waved from the boat, and Kit cupped my face in his hands, kissing me gently.

'Goodbye, my darling.'

I remained in the surf watching as the small boat skirted the shore, before tacking towards the mouth of the bay and racing out into the open sea. The sun glinted off the bow and the brown sails soared across the waves like a peregrine falcon skimming for prey. In a minute the boat was toy-sized and in another it was gone. I turned around and trudged back to the beach, perching on one of the flat rocks beneath the cliff. I knew that I ought to feel proud, exhilarated by the bravery of the two men, but I did not. They were rushing off to France to save men stranded on the beaches, but their gallantry was muddied. Kit was excited by the adventure of it all. The danger and the daring thrilled him, even if he claimed that he only sailed for Will. I adored Kit, but I knew Burt had been right when he called him brave and reckless. Mr Rivers knew it too, and he went to France to make sure that his son came home.

CHAPTER TWENTY

A GULL ON THE HORIZON

I tried cooking with Mrs Ellsworth, but it was no good; I burnt the pastry, spoiling half the week's fat ration, and sliced into my finger while skinning a rabbit. I listened to the wireless for news, but the reports were vague and circumspect, careful not to compromise the ongoing rescue mission. Retreating into the small attic room (which I still thought of as mine despite my promotion to the blue room), I paced the bare wooden boards and pulled out the viola. I opened the little attic window, letting the salt air fill the room and drive away the sickly smell of damp and dust. Unfastening the instrument case, I took out the bow and a small clump of wax, which I warmed in my hands before brushing it softly along the bow hair. I slid the viola underneath my chin and pulled the bow across the strings. I played all afternoon—Vivaldi, Donizetti, Bing Crosby—not stopping for meals, nor to listen to the lunchtime news bulletin.

I spent the next few days either playing the viola or digging in the vegetable patch with old Billy. I tended the neat rows of lettuce seedlings, crushing up shells from the beach to drive off the slugs; sweat rolling off my forehead into the earth, I hacked furrows for a new crop of beetroot and chard. As I toiled, I heard the strange sound of the viola in my mind. It lodged inside my imagination like the sound of the sea in a dream, and I paced and hewed and dug and planted to its refrain. At dusk, I ambled down to the beach and sat with Burt on the lobster pots outside his hut. He packed his pipe with tobacco and we rested in amiable silence, watching the tide surge. The water rushed the beach, relentless in its constancy. At high tide it pounded the large flat rocks just beyond Burt's cottage, turning the pale grey stone into glistening black and the cracked slime into green velvet. At low tide, the water drew back to the edge of the bay, and the pebbles dried to gold and yellow and russet in the setting sun. I knew that somewhere far away the beaches echoed with guns and shellfire and the screams of Stukas and men, but here at Worbarrow the sea licked the shore and the only cries were those of the gulls.

The sun slid behind the horizon and Burt's pipe glowed in the darkness, like a second, red moon. There was the creak of footsteps on loose pebbles, and a fox streaked across the strand, the night air full of its sharp stink.

'Mustn't worry, missy. Squire'll keep young Mr Kit out o' trouble,' said Burt.

I reached for a smooth stone and sent it clattering across the beach.

'I want them both to stay out of trouble,' I said.

* * *

May turned into June and I sleepwalked around the house. I felt as if I carried a heavy string of witch-stones around my neck; two for Anna and Julian, and now two more for Kit and Mr Rivers. I was dull and slow and wanted only to sleep, but whenever I did, I dreamt of torn sails and churning, bloody seas. The newspapers printed photographs of weary and bedraggled men, dressed in khaki rags, limping off endless ships and pouring onto the quays at Dover and Portsmouth. The wireless reports and *The Times* insisted that they were 'tired but undaunted' and triumphant in defeat. Villages along the coast served twenty thousand rounds of sandwiches and thirty thousand cups of tea, and the nation was drunk with its daring rescue and the un-dashed spirit of its young men. I scoured the photographs for a glimpse of *The Lugger* or a snapshot of Kit or Mr Rivers, but of course there was nothing. I heard the click as rescued soldiers slipped their penny into the telephone callbox. I heard the shouts of other men's mothers and sweethearts and grandpas. One of the farm boys returned to Tyneford straight from Portsmouth, hitching a lift on the dawn milk cart. I instructed Mrs Ellsworth to send a bottle of celebratory port and a cigar to his father. I tried not to wish that it were Kit and Mr Rivers who had returned safely and not this unknown boy loved by strangers.

In my daze, it took me two days to realise that in their masters' absence the servants came to me for orders. The gardener wanted to know whether he ought to still plant sweet peas this year, or just shelling peas (I insisted upon sweet too, cheerful flowers being even more necessary during wartime) while Mr Wrexham ironed the newspaper and left it for me in the breakfast room each morning. When Mrs Ellsworth asked me for the dinner order, I informed her that I would eat whatever she was making for the servants.

'Mrs Ellsworth, we've enough cooking to do between us without making something special for me. The master's not here, and this does not constitute a slackening of standards,' I said firmly when I saw her ruddy cheeks blanch. 'While the Mr Rivers are away, I shall dine in the kitchen with you. It's silly having Mr Wrexham wait upon me in the morning room.'

The housekeeper scowled, and cleaned the already spotless kitchen table. 'Mr Wrexham won't agree.'

But Mr Wrexham did agree. The elderly butler was tired; he was undertaking the tasks of footman and valet as well as overseeing the household, and even for a man with the dignity of Mr Wrexham it was too much. The week before Kit and Mr Rivers left, I noticed that the firedogs had not been cleaned for a fortnight, while the evening silverware had vanished and we now used the luncheon silver at both meals. At first, I tried to reassure him, saying, 'This is very sensible, Mr Wrexham. We can bring out the dinner silver again after the war,' but while he said nothing at the time, the following evening the dinner silver reappeared, perfectly polished. The evening after that I surreptitiously wiped a black smear of polish off my knife and onto the napkin. In another week, the dinner silver vanished again, and this time I was careful not to say a word.

It was strange taking my meals with the servants again. Mr Wrexham and Mrs Ellsworth insisted on serving me first, rather than themselves as they had in the past when I was only a housemaid. It was cosy, if a little stifling, sitting in the kitchen before the great black range.

'May I offer you some wine, Miss Landau?' inquired the butler.

'No thank you. I am very happy with barley

water.'

We ate in silence. I was glad of the quiet, but felt guilty at the restraint my presence now inflicted on the company. After dinner Mrs Ellsworth refused to allow me to help with the washing up and I withdrew to the stillness of the library. I never sat in this room when Mr Rivers was present—it was his domain, and yet perhaps that was why at that moment it offered me some comfort. It was a man's room. Fumes from the whisky decanter mingled with the fusty aroma of the old books. His presence had seeped into the atmosphere and I could almost feel him, seated in his usual chair, half-watching me out of the corner of his eye. There was an hour until sunset and I sat with the doors and windows thrown wide. I perched on Mr Rivers' desk, idly playing with his binoculars—the pair he used when out walking or hunting so as to get a better glimpse of the peregrines or buzzards. I trained them on the sea and watched a gull drift along the horizon. I blinked. It couldn't be a gull. It was too far away to be a bird. I looked again.

It was a boat.

I dropped the binoculars and ran onto the terrace, shouting for Mrs Ellsworth and Mr Wrexham.

'A boat! A boat. Down to the shore.'

Without waiting to discover if they had heard me, I sprinted helter-skelter along the ragged path down to the sea. Dusk was drawing in and the shadows lengthened around me, tree outlines leered over the path and a thin smuggler's moon hung above the surf, a cut-out from a stage set. I heard the click and whirr of the evening crickets in the blue sea-grass like the tick from a thousand pocket-watches. As I reached the highest point on the path, I halted and peered into the distance, scouring the bay for the boat. Yes. There it was: a small dark sail flapping and not properly trimmed. I couldn't see how many figures were aboard. It crept along the mouth of the bay, turning in and hugging the black rocks. I scrambled down to the beach, skating on the scree. As I reached the strand, I saw that the fishermen were waiting, Burt and Art in their midst. They stood at the edge of the breakers, watching the fishing-boat sail closer and closer. Nobody spoke. It tacked and headed directly for us. I heard the crack of the wind in the ripped foresail, until I realised, a moment later, that it was the boom of my own heart.

'There's two of 'em,' shouted Burt.

And in the darkness I saw that he was right. Two silhouettes huddled on the deck, one beside the tiller and another sprawled over the main sheet. Burt's voice triggered something in the fishermen, and suddenly they were all wading into the sea, those who could swim slicing through the waves and rushing the small boat.

'Engine must 'ave packed in. Been sailin' fer hours, no doubt,' said Burt, frowning.

I ran into the shallows and stared as two, then three, then four men caught up with the boat and hauled themselves on board, and steered her onto the beach. Her hull ground across the pebbles as she beached, mast bent and unsteady. Kit sat at the helm, his greatcoat black with water and his hair plastered to his face, but he smiled at me. I breathed for the first time in five days. As Burt helped him climb out of the boat, I looked for Mr Rivers. He lolled on the deck, fingers gripping the main sail line, knuckles white. His face was grey, and there was a dark stain beneath his arm and a tear in his oilskins. I hauled myself onto the deck and scrambled over to him. I knelt beside him and slid my arm around his shoulders. As I brushed his cheek, I felt his skin, cool and damp.

'Go to the house. Tell Wrexham to call a doctor,' I shouted. The fishermen gazed at me, frozen with shock. 'Now!'

There was a scramble and I glimpsed Art sprint towards the shore.

'Brandy,' I called.

A bottle of something was thrust up to me, and I pressed it to Mr Rivers' colourless lips. He sipped feebly and opened one eye.

'Hullo you,' he said. 'This is pleasant.'

'Kit,' I called. 'What happened? Is he hurt?'

Kit sat on the beach, waves washing around him, too tired to move.

'Just tired. So tired. And a little piece of shrapnel.'

I lifted Mr Rivers' arm and examined the stain on his coat. I couldn't tell if the blood was his. The entire deck was reddened with bloodstains, and bullet holes pockmarked the sides. All the stanchions along the portside had been wrenched out of their mountings and dangled like loose teeth on snatches of skin. I closed my eyes as I pictured the desperate men swimming alongside, clawing *The Lugger* in their frenzy to climb aboard. The jib was in tatters, torn into strips for bandages, which now lay in seeping heaps, leaking reddish rivers across the deck. The only part of the boat that appeared intact was the necklace of witch-stones, draped around the bow, but in the darkness even they appeared tinged with blood.

'Lift him out and take him up to the house,' I said. 'And Burt, take Kit into your cottage and give him some hot food and dry clothes. Put him to bed by the fire.'

Two stout fishermen with muscles strong and lithe as eels slid their arms underneath Mr Rivers and, as though he weighed no more than a glittering fish, hoisted him up and passed him reverently down to another pair of waiting hands. I splashed beside them through the rushing waves to the shore.

'Carry him to the house, smooth as you can,' I directed, catching hold of Mr Rivers' hand and clasping it as the fishermen bore him across the beach to the cliff path. With the blackout in force it was now darker than the depths of the Tilly Whim caves. The moon and stars were veiled by cloud, but our eyes adjusted to the murk and we hastened along the chalk track, surefooted as the hares that streaked across the verges. The doors to the house had been thrown open, and I could hear Mr Wrexham and Mrs Ellsworth chattering anxiously. A feeble yellow torch beam wavered before the porch.

'Mr Wrexham! Over here,' I called.

The butler hurried towards us, shining the beam at Mr Rivers. Seeing his master's grey face, Mr Wrexham snorted in alarm, like a horse spooked by the wind, and I found myself speaking to him firmly.

'Mr Wrexham. Mr Rivers needs to be taken upstairs and put in a warm bed.'

The old butler continued to stare at his master and remained motionless, his lips parted in dismay.

'Wrexham,' I snapped.

The butler stiffened. He awoke from his stupor and began organising the fishermen and servants, herding them into the house.

'A hot-water bottle, Mrs Ellsworth, right away. And upstairs to the master's bedroom, please. No. Don't worry about your shoes,' he added as the fishermen paused in the hallway to discard their sand-encrusted hobnail boots. 'A posset, Art. Run down to the bungalow and ask the Miss Bartons to make up a posset. Bring it back here, soon as you can.'

I trailed after them, following them up the broad staircase and into Mr Rivers' own room. I lingered for a second on the threshold before entering; I had not been inside since I was a housemaid. Thick red curtains had been drawn and it reeked of leather and unfamiliar spices. Even on a June evening it was cold, and Mr Wrexham bent to strike a match to the kindling in the grate, before hastening to look for the doctor. Mrs Ellsworth bustled in, and hurried the fishermen out onto the landing.

'Thank you all very kindly. Now please go to the kitchen and wait there. There's a teakettle on the hob.'

There was a shuffle of feet and then a clatter as four pairs of hobnail boots descended the wooden stairs. Mr Rivers lay on the bed, skin as white as the linen sheets. Mrs Ellsworth hurried over and started to unpeel his sodden oilskins.

'You go and wait outside for the doctor, Miss Landau.'

I shook my head and crossed to the bed. 'No. It'll hurt him less if both of us do it.'

She clicked her tongue in annoyance, but

allowed me to help. With her sewing scissors, she sliced through his wet sweater and shirt. In the light of the bedroom, I could see that the blood beneath his arm belonged to Mr Rivers, seeping from a gash between his ribs. It looked red and inflamed around the edges.

'Will you fetch a dressing from my room, miss?' asked Mrs Ellsworth.

I looked at her, reluctant to leave.

'Please. I want to get him into his pyjamas. He'd not like you here,' she concluded, her voice gentle.

I nodded and slipped out of the room, running down the stairs to the housekeeper's room. When I returned a few minutes later with a dressing, Mr Rivers was tucked under the covers, and a handsome fire roared in the grate. I pulled up a chair beside the bed, and reached for his hand, grateful to discover that he was warmer than before. I felt a squeeze around my fingers.

'Elise,' he whispered.

'Yes, Mr Rivers.' I leant in close. 'Please don't talk. You're quite safe now. And Kit's safe too.'

'Yes,' he said. 'Yes. Kit's safe. I brought him back to you.'

I bent over the bed and kissed him.

'Thank you.'

I felt him seize my fingers beneath the blanket, squeezing so hard that my bones creaked. Then he released my hand and closed his eyes. I walked to the door, eager to hurry down to Burt's cottage and see Kit. My hand resting on the handle, I glanced back at Mr Rivers. His chest rose with shallow gasps and his fingers gripped the eiderdown. I couldn't leave him—not like this, his face tight with pain. I couldn't leave him with only the servants to care for him. I shut the door and settled into an easy chair, drawing a woollen blanket around my shoulders. Kit would understand.

'Mrs Ellsworth,' I said. 'I need to stay here with Mr Rivers. Please will you go down to Burt's cottage and check on Mr Kit? Make sure that he's resting. Tell him that I love him, but I must stay with his father.'

'Yes, miss,' she said.

As the door clicked shut, Mr Rivers opened his eyes and glared at me.

'Go. Go to Kit.'

'No. He's perfectly all right. Mrs Ellsworth will take excellent care of him, and so will Burt.'

He sighed, brow creasing. 'Shouldn't be here. Leave,' he added, with less resolve than before.

I ignored him and wriggled in my seat, feeling drowsy in the warmth of the fire. From downstairs I heard the distant thud and hurry of the household, but it felt far away, like listening to sounds underwater. Mr Rivers and I were cocooned in the sick room, sequestered from the rest of the house. The last time I had been ill, he and Kit had fussed over me like a couple of worried aunts, but the person I had craved was Anna. At home in Vienna she fed me honey-water and hummed the overture of *La Traviata*. Unlike most mothers, Anna couldn't sing to me when I was ill. Her operatic voice was simply too powerful even when she sang *pianissimo*, but humming *La Traviata*, the opera about the dying beauty, gave the sick room an aura of glamour. Margot complained that we were both morbid, but she was quite wrong. Imagining myself to be a wide-eyed beauty dying of consumption was my only solace when lying in bed feeling feverish and dreadful. I was not sure how much this game would comfort Mr Rivers, but I took his hand and hummed.

Some time later there was a knock at the door and the doctor entered. He smiled at Mr Rivers over the top of his spectacles.

'Dashing about the country, at your age. I don't know.'

'You'd have gone yourself, John, if you'd had a boat.'

'Yes. I probably would. Come, let's have a look at you.'

The doctor turned to me. 'Miss? Would you mind stepping outside while I examine the patient?'

'I'd prefer to stay.'

'Christopher?' asked the doctor.

'Yes, yes. She can stay.'

The doctor cast me an odd look, half curious, and half concerned. I lingered by the fireplace, my back to the room to give the men privacy. I wanted to turn so as to see the doctor's face while he examined him. I wanted to read in his expression what he saw, not wait for the platitudes, but I did not turn and I did not look. I closed my eyes and bit my lip and listened to the rustle of bedclothes, the unpeeling of bandages and then a sharp gasp from Mr Rivers as the doctor explored his wound.

'It's not deep, but it has a touch of infection. I expect you didn't even feel it at first with all the adrenalin.'

'No. There was so much noise and so many men so badly hurt. I didn't know I was hit. Not till we left Portsmouth.'

'Yes. Well. The infection would have set in after some hours. Why did you come back to Tyneford?

Why not stay in Portsmouth?' asked the doctor, talking to distract him from the pain.

'Kit. He wanted to go back. Make another trip once we'd set the soldiers ashore. But *The Lugger*'s engine was broken. Needed a part. Bastard Germans bombed the parts depot in Portsmouth. Kit thought Burt could fix her.'

I spun round and stared at Mr Rivers. 'He can't go back. He's exhausted.'

Mr Rivers smiled. 'Of course not. Do you really think Burt would fix her engine, even if he could?'

I studied Mr Rivers' tired face, the friendly creases around his blue eyes, and tried to still my unease. 'Yes. You're right.'

I came and settled back into the chair beside the bed, reaching for his hand once again, but I was glad that I had sent Mrs Ellsworth down to check on Kit. She wouldn't allow any nonsense. Mr Rivers relaxed and closed his eyes, and in a second he was asleep. The doctor stood behind me, and turning over Mr Rivers' wrist, took his pulse.

'Still a little fast. Fighting the infection. He's not too feverish, which is good, but we must be careful with him.'

I nodded and looked back at the still figure in the bed.

'He's easier with you here,' continued the doctor. 'I'd prefer it if you stayed with him,' he added, giving me another odd look.

'Of course I'll stay.'

'Christopher seems very fond of you.'

'And I am very fond of Mr Rivers,' I replied, my voice cold. The doctor would never dare such impertinence if Mr Rivers were awake. He chuckled and rummaged in his black leather bag.

'I'm going to put a poultice on the wound. He needs to rest and drink lots of fluids. Call me right away if there's any change.'

'I'd be happier if you would remain in the house,' I said. 'Mrs Ellsworth will prepare a room for you.'

The doctor laughed, a hearty rumble that made his shoulders shake. 'So, you started here as a housemaid? Good at giving orders now, aren't you?'

I felt my cheeks colour. 'I am sure that Mr Rivers would be most grateful.'

The doctor continued to chuckle. 'It's all right, I'm content to stay at your request, *Miss Landau*.' He gave me a little bow. 'I'll find Wrexham. Wonder if he's got any of that port open.'

As the doctor disappeared in search of the butler, I wrapped the coarse blanket around my shoulders and fidgeted, trying to get comfortable. Mr Rivers still gripped my hand, and it was growing numb. I laid my head on the edge of the eiderdown and closed my eyes, ignoring the tingling in my fingers. Behind me, I heard the creak of the door open.

'Miss? Are you awake,' whispered Mrs Ellsworth.

'Yes,' I said, sitting up, suddenly alert. 'Is Kit all right?'

'Yes, yes. Sleeping like a baby. Tucked him in myself, like I did when he was a little 'un. You can rest easy now.'

'Thank you.'

I allowed her to slip a pillow behind my head, and remove my shoes. She placed a bell by my hand.

'Just one little ring and I'll be here in a moment.'

'Thank you, Mrs Ellsworth.'

The next moment, I was asleep.

*   *   *

I opened my eyes as Mrs Ellsworth removed the blackouts. She kept the curtains drawn, but early morning light sneaked between the cracks, falling across Mr Rivers' face. He had lost the sickly grey colour, and his skin had almost a tan from the days spent at sea.

'Oh, he does look better,' I said, yawning and stretching my arms.

'Yes. And the doctor's been in. Took his pulse, says he's much better. Infection hasn't spread.'

I smiled with relief. 'I'm so glad. Is the doctor still here?'

'Yes, miss,' said Mrs Ellsworth. 'Wouldn't leave without seeing you first. Said he "didn't have the young lady's permission to depart."'

Mr Rivers began to stir. He opened his eyes and blinked.

'Elise.'

'Yes, Mr Rivers? How do you feel?'

'A trifle sore. But I'll be all right.'

Mrs Ellsworth smiled. 'You gave us quite a scare, sir. I'll get Mr Wrexham to bring up your breakfast.'

She tripped out, leaving us alone.

'You stayed,' said Mr Rivers. 'I told you to go.'

'Well, I didn't listen. I don't have to obey you anymore, you know. I'm not your maid.'

He managed a smile. 'Kit?'

'Is quite all right. Sleeping.'

'You want to go to him.'

I did not answer as it was not a question. I stood up and smiled at him.

'I'm so glad that you are feeling better.'

'Bring him back with you, if he's up to coming to the house,' said Mr Rivers.

'I will.'

I turned and walked out of the bedroom, sunlight streaming through the chinks in the curtain, feeling him watch me as I went.

* * *

The ground was drenched with dew, and my plimsolls were instantly wet. Rabbits hurtled through the long grass, white tails flashing in the morning light. In the distance I heard the roar of the sea, the pull and crash of the tide across the pebbles. The air held a chill, and while the sun sneaked between the clouds, the sky was dark and a black haze lined the horizon. The wind carried the metal scent of coming rain, and I wrapped my thin cardigan around my shoulders. I knew the telltale signs well enough by now to know that a summer squall was brewing. There was an eerie beauty in the smoke-dark clouds rolling across the water, while the waves far out in the bay peaked with foaming white horses. Black cormorants skimmed the shallows like shadow birds. The yellow buttercups scattered across the grass verges seemed like stars in the half-light. I smiled and hurried towards the beach and Kit. I remembered the promise I'd made the night before he sailed and I felt a flutter of anticipation in my belly. I thought of his letters and my blood fizzed in my veins, suddenly electric.

I can see it now as vividly as a moving picture. Kit is waiting for me beside a small skiff. 'Come on, hurry up,' he calls, eager to dodge the coming squall. Panting, we push the boat out into the shallows, shoving away from the beach with an oar. Kit heaves up the canvas sail, wobbling for a second in the swell. I hold the tiller and steer her, Kit's fingers covering mine. The tide races and carries us out to the mouth of the bay and we tack around the coast, seeing the black rocks of Kimmeridge loom before us. I want to ask Kit if he was very frightened at Dunkirk but I am silent. I notice a scratch above his eye and along his cheek. The sky turns grey and it begins to mizzle. My dress is thin and I shiver, and Kit wraps his arms around me to keep me warm. He tugs me down onto the floor of the boat. It is damp and smells of stale fish. He starts to kiss me and I am crying. The sail flaps wild in the wind and the boat rocks like a cradle on the tide. I unfasten my dress with steady fingers and lie back on the ropes coiled at the bottom of the boat. All I see is Kit and all I hear is the crack of the loose sail. I love you, I tell him, and draw him down on top of me. The coil of ropes digs into my back. This time I do not ask him to stop.

I have imagined it so many times that sometimes I have to remind myself that it is not true. That it happened to some other Elise in another version of this story. In my memory there are a myriad of Kits spinning in the sunshine like the gaps between the leaves, and who is to say that one of them did not find his way home to peel off my stockings. I wanted to see it here in words. As I write it becomes as real as anything else.

But what happened is that I stood alone on the beach. A thin plume of smoke filed out of Burt's cottage chimney, while the old fisherman perched on his usual lobster pot, filleting mackerel ready to smoke in the inglenook for breakfast. He looked surprised to see me, but gave a friendly nod.

'Won't shake yer hand missy,' he said. 'Got fish guts up to my elbows. I stinks like the sea.'

'Is Kit still asleep?' I asked.

Burt frowned, deep creases furrowing his brow.

'Nope. 'ee weren't 'ere when I woke up. Thought Mr Kit had garn up ter the big house ter see yoos an' the squire.'

I shook my head. 'No. He's not at the house.'

'How long has he been gone?' I asked, hearing my voice grow thick and strange.

'Since dawn. Sun wakes me, blackouts or no,' said Burt, rising to his feet, gutted fish slithering to the ground in a brown bloodied trail.

'But he couldn't go,' I insisted. '*The Lugger* needs repairing. I saw her. She couldn't sail. And the engine. You didn't fix the engine.'

'Course not.' Burt shot me an angry glance. 'Locked up tool shed too. Jist in case. But it's no matter—as you say, *The Lugger* couldn't sail ter Swanage much less ter France.'

Rain spots began to pelt the sand and mottle the pebbles along the beach. The sea growled and thrashed against the shore. Burt marched around the side of the cottage to a series of wooden sheds half-concealed beneath the cliffs. I followed close behind as he hurried to the furthest shelter, a haphazard boathouse. One door was missing, rotted away years before, while the other was thrown back, dangling from its hinges. Burt took a step towards it and gave a short cry. I peered inside the shed. It was empty. Neat tracks led down to the shore.

'*The Anna*,' he cried. 'He's taken *The Anna*.'

CHAPTER TWENTY-ONE

My name is Alice

Brave and reckless. Brave and reckless and I loved him. I rushed out into the water, the cold slapping my ankles, then my thighs as I waded deeper and deeper. Why had he gone? To save Will and others like him? For an adventure? I needed him to come back. I'd lost everyone else. I wished I'd stayed with him, watched him all night. I wouldn't have let him leave. The cold water reached my stomach and I gasped. I couldn't see anything out in the bay. Not *The Anna*. Not any boat. The rain battered the sea and drenched my hair. From the shore I heard Burt yelling at me to come back. Why? Kit had come back and then he'd left again. He didn't even say goodbye. But then, what could he have said? I would have pleaded with him not to go. I ducked down under the surface, the saltwater stinging my eyes and nose, my hair brushing my cheeks like fronds of seaweed. I scooped up a handful of pebbles and rising out of the water, hurled them back into the sea. I screamed his name—*Kit! Kit! Kit!*—as though some supernatural force would carry my voice to him and the moment he heard it he would sigh and turn the boat around, and before that black cloud reached Lovell's Tower—no, before that grey-bellied gull alighted on the rock stack in the bay—I'd see the small wooden boat racing across the water towards me. My throat hurt from shouting, but there was no boat. The cloud hurtled past Lovell's folly on the cliff and the gull vanished behind the rocks. I crashed my way through the surf to the far edge of the bay. The yellow cliff of Worbarrow Tout bookended the beach, the sharp ridge running up a hundred feet, a snub-nosed lookout point rising above the water like the snout of a sea-monster. My clothes and shoes dripped as I crawled across green rocks greased to a slick by waves and rain. Sharp barnacles sliced my fingers and shins, and blood streaked my skin. I clawed my way up the haphazard path to the pinnacle of the tout, breath coming in rasps. I stood at the very edge of the cliff, watching the water tumble and break below me on three sides. The water was as black as the rocks and sky. I searched the horizon. Empty.

I looked out towards Lulcombe Cove with its neat cobbled causeway and cluster of stone cottages, and then further west towards the jutting strip that linked Portland to the Dorset coast. Hulking ships glowered in the channel, black smoke puffing from funnels small as cigars from this distance. Beyond the curve of Worbarrow Bay lay the outside world. In its way, Tyneford was as separate from the rest of England as the Isle of Portland. The valley and the coomb and the barrows and the black woods belonged to a more ancient world. The war happened elsewhere. I felt its sorrows in the silence from my family, and the slow disappearance of the young men one by one into the armed forces. For those of us left behind, life continued much as before: the servants grumbled over the inconvenience and we had to churn our own butter from the milk on the farm, and without elastic our stockings slithered down our knees, but the changes were irksome, not yet catastrophic. We all felt the war at night in the utter darkness and in the hush of the church bells, but the wireless reports referred to another world. Tyneford hardly seemed to belong to Europe, and if we only stayed here, hidden in these hills and vales, we would be safe. I watched the storm front crawl along the horizon, rain rushing the breakers and I saw Kit disappear into the outside world. He surrendered himself to the unknown, to that noisy, smoke-filled other place.

Rain streaking my face, I turned and retreated down the path to where Burt waited on the beach. The water fell in lines, spouting from the sky like the pump in the yard, but through the downpour I saw that he clutched something, a jagged necklace of giant teeth. Blinking, I realised that Burt held before him the string of witch-stones, and in the weird gloom of the June storm they appeared brushed with red-brown blood. The wind crackled in the long sea-grass and I felt a twinge of dread, cool and light as the brush of a feather, crawl along my spine.

* * *

'How could he have taken it?' repeated Mr Rivers. 'I don't understand. *The Anna*'s too heavy for one man to sail.'

Mr Rivers sat in the leather armchair in his bedroom, still dressed in his pyjamas. Mrs Ellsworth and I lingered by the window, feigning calm.

'Christ, Wrexham. Help me dress,' he commanded.

The old butler stepped forward. 'Sir. Please,

if you will permit the impertinence. I believe the doctor said that sir should rest.'

'Wrexham. There is an indignity in learning one's son has rushed back to battle while one is wearing Simpson's striped pyjamas. I should very much like to dress.'

'Very good, sir.'

The butler retreated into the dressing room and began to open and shut drawers. Mr Rivers' face assumed the same ghastly hue as it had the previous evening.

'Well? Will someone tell me how Kit managed to take her?'

'Jack Miller has gone,' I said, leaning against the windowsill. 'His parents noticed him missing this morning. The two of them managed to drag her down to the beach together.'

'Good God. Well, I suppose we'll find out more when Jack Miller comes back in a day or two,' said Mr Rivers, closing his eyes for a minute. When he opened them again, he realised that we were both watching him. 'Kit will send the boy home. He's only seventeen. Kit won't let him sail to France.'

* * *

Mr Rivers was right. Two days later, Jack Miller returned to Tyneford on the morning milk cart. I was sitting in my old attic room perched on a tower of cushions, gazing out of the sloping window at the horizon. Dawn fired across the water, while in the distant farmyard a chorus of cockerels crooned. From the house below, I heard shouts.

'Elise! Miss Landau! The Miller boy is back.'

I pelted down the attic stairs and then the grand

staircase. Mrs Ellsworth and the daily maid lingered in the hall. Mr Wrexham pointed to the library.

'The master is interviewing the boy inside, miss.'

I pushed open the door. Mr Rivers leant against his desk, while the youth stood before him, cap clasped in his hands, head bowed. Both glanced towards me as I entered.

'I jist wanted ter help Mr Kit,' insisted the boy, kicking at a piece of mud on his boot.

'It's all right,' said Mr Rivers. 'You're not in any trouble. We just want to know what happened.'

Jack Miller looked over at me, his eyes watery green as a spring tide.

'Not much ter tell. After we left Tyneford, we sails ter Portsmouth an' refuels. Then we gits on ter Dover. Thousands of boats there wis. Big ships spewin' black smoke an' lil paddle-steamers like them ones in Swanage fer day-trippers. An' corvettes, an' destroyers an' even a battleship. All of 'em packed wi' soldiers. Port and quays wis brown wi' men. Thousands and thousands of 'em. Never seen ser many souls in all my life.'

Mr Rivers gave a curt nod. 'Yes. I saw it for myself at Portsmouth. What happened when you got to Dover?'

'Well, Mr Kit, he knows where he wis going. Finds a motor launch wi' a man with a hat and stripes on his shoulder an' says 'ee needs a chap ter sail wi' him back ter France. Mr Kit tells him that I'm too young—I try ter argue but 'ee won't listen. Half an hour later, two blokes come on board *The Anna* and takes over from me at the 'elm, an' I'm put back on their rowing boat and sent back ter shore. A chap gives me a rail ticket and I gets a train back ter Wareham, and 'ere I am.'

'Thank you, Jack,' said Mr Rivers. He strolled over to the windows and gazed across the smooth lawns. 'Nothing more to do. Wait. Hope.'

I didn't reply. My life was spent waiting and hoping. Anna. Julian. Now Kit's name was added to the echo inside me.

'Miss Landau?' asked the boy.

I jumped, lost in my reverie.

'Yes?'

'Mr Kit talked about yoos all the time. Not soupy nonsense, like. But said yoos was a right special girl. He's going ter marry yoos the minute 'ee gits home—I know cos 'ee invited me ter the weddin' an' all. Wis really bothered about all the upset that 'is going away would cause yer. An' 'ee wrote yer a letter. Made me promise ter give it ter yoos right away like.'

A letter from Kit. It made all the difference. Suddenly his going away didn't seem so absolute. There was news. A message. Our story could continue. I felt a smile twitch at the corner of my mouth. The boy reached into his trouser pocket, pulling out various scraps of paper. He grinned awkwardly, then fumbled inside his jacket.

'Jist a minute, miss. Know 'ees 'ere.'

Mr Rivers turned his back to the window and studied the boy as he emptied his pockets onto the desk.

'Take your time, Jack,' he said. 'Don't worry about making a mess. Lay everything out on the blotting pad.'

'Yes, sir,' said the boy, reddening. 'Ah. 'ere we go. Got 'im.'

He passed me a scrap of paper. My hands trembling, I unfolded it.

‘Oh,’ I said, voice shaking. ‘It’s just a receipt for fuel.’

‘No. No. Turn ’im over. Note’s on the back,’ said Jack.

I flipped it over, but the reverse was blank.

‘Shit. Shit,’ said the boy. ‘Must ’ave slipped out my pocket. I chucked out the wrong un. Mr Kit’ll ’ave ter tell yer hisself what ’ee wanted ter say.’

‘Yes,’ I repeated. ‘He’ll have to tell me himself.’

I don’t remember leaving the room. I suppose I spoke to Mr Rivers and we shared some comforting platitudes of mutual concern. I remember disappearing up to the attic chamber and slipping the blank receipt into the viola case, alongside the letters I wrote to Anna. There were now so many letters in there that they spilt out every time I opened the case, jamming in the hinge and sliding across the floor. It was such a cruel joke: a cacophony of letters to those I loved, and now a single, blank reply.

* * *

Days passed. Hours. Weeks. Minutes. The rags of time. The sun rose and fell. Shadows skirted the banks of the hill, growing and shrinking. Scarlet strawberries ripened in the fields. Climbing roses bloomed along the stone at the front of the house. Yellow petals rained upon the ground, turned brown and rotted away. Will returned. Mr Churchill declared the Dunkirk rescue a triumph. Only twenty-five little ships lost. Names not released. Sweet peas and mint flowered in the kitchen garden. Nightingales trilled in the heath. Poppy came back to Tyneford and spent days traipsing along the beaches with Will and I couldn't bear to speak to them. Their happiness choked me. Mr Rivers drank alone in his library. I spied an otter in a freshwater stream trickling down to the sea. In the darkness a nightjar called from the jasmine outside my window. I paced along the beach in bare feet, feeling the pebbles grind beneath my toes, and padded down to the surf. The water foamed around my ankles, still cold enough to make me gasp.

'Kit!' I shouted his name. 'Anna. Julian. AnnaJulianKit!'

Their names mingled into fathomless sound, separated from all meaning. I reached into my mind for bad words, terrible words. I needed to curse. I needed words that would cut my tongue as I spoke them.

'Fuck. Hate. Cock. Shit.'

None of them was wicked enough. I remembered the first time I'd come to the beach to rage at the sea. I closed my eyes, waiting for him to join in the game. It was a silly joke, and in a moment I would hear his voice, *'Oh, is it a private game?'*

'Testes. Cockles.' I hurled the words at the waves, but there was only silence, and the grind and roar of the tide drawing back along the strand.

* * *

If there was only something: a body, wreckage from the boat. But there was nothing. The sea swallowed him up like Jonah into the whale. Then one night, a month after he disappeared, I heard music outside my window. I wasn't asleep, merely writhing under the hot blankets, seeing his face in the dark. I had taken down the blackouts, suffocating in the warm

July heat, and the glass was open to the drifting fiddle music and men's voices. I slid out of bed and leant on the sill. The fishermen stood in the darkness; ten of them singing a lament, as the strings rippled.

Our boy 'as gone ter sea
An' sails o'er the green waves-o,
Bright 'ee were an' fair and young.
'Ee has no grave, no grassy mound
Jist the green waves-o.
We'll hear 'is voice in the gulls
An' in the smashin' of the tide
But we'll see him no more.
Fer our boy 'as gone ter sea.
An' sails o'er the green waves-o.

* * *

There was a crack of shutters as Mr Rivers opened the doors from the drawing room and stepped out onto the terrace. He had not gone to bed, and he stood in his white shirt, a ghost against the stone wall. I slipped downstairs through the darkened hall and drawing room to join him outside. The summer night was warm and reeked of flowers: jasmine, honeysuckle and old china roses. He stood quite still, his skin like marble. I listened to the lament, licking away salt tears.

'They sing this when a fisherman is lost at sea,' said Mr Rivers. 'They know Kit is dead.'

No one had said the word 'dead' aloud. I whispered it in the dark when I could not sleep. I had turned it over and over in my mind in every language I knew, but the moment Mr Rivers uttered the word, I knew in my soul that it was true.

Kit is dead. Kit is dead. Kit is dead.

I tried it aloud.

'Kit is dead.'

'Yes,' he replied. 'Kit is dead.'

We listened to the fishermen, who sang their melancholy song again and again. They retreated into the shadows at the edge of the lawn and then tripped away down to the sea, their voices mingling with the far-off crash of the tide. I don't know how long we stood there in the darkness, side by side, not touching. We wanted comfort but only one man could give it and since he could not, we wanted none. I missed Anna and Julian and Margot and I grieved for Kit. I would not marry him and we would not make love and he would not grow old. I must age and my skin crease and dark age spots appear on my face and hands, and my hair turn grey then white, and I would speak with the slow-steady patter of age, but he would stay young, always a beautiful man-boy with blue eyes. I wondered that I did not shatter and break apart or blow away like a dandelion clock in the wind. I imagined myself hurling china and storming through the house, smashing vases and silver and clocks in my fury, but I did nothing. I stood silent in the dark.

The death of Kit was the death of Tyneford, even if I did not know it then. From that day the dust would never quite be swept away. The browning petals that fell from the vase of garden roses always remained on the table in the hall; even Mrs Ellsworth did not care to tidy them. Mr Wrexham stopped fretting that the war prevented him from ordering wine to lay down in the cellar. There was enough for twenty years and after then—what did it matter? The church bells could not toll to mark the death of the son and heir and future squire, but we heard it just the same. We thought back of the great mackerel catch in the bay—would it have been a day of such happiness and abandon if we had known that it was our last?

Mr Rivers broke the silence. 'I read that they are interning German and Austrian women. I have done my best to keep you safe, but I want you to change your name. To something English.'

I looked at him. His face was pale and his blue eyes appeared black in the darkness. His shirt was crumpled and the top buttons undone. Despite Wrexham's morning ministrations, a dark shadow lined his jaw and above his lip a muscle ticked, making him seem wolfish in the gloom. On his breath I smelt the stench of cigars and whisky.

'I like my name.'

It linked me back to Anna and Julian. My father had cried when my sister changed her name on her wedding day. He claimed it was too much champagne and happiness but I knew better.

Mr Rivers grimaced. 'I did not ask if you liked your name. I asked if you would change it.'

He hissed the words at me, eyes glinting. He seized my wrist and tried to pull me closer, but half-frightened of him I wrenched free and backed away along the wall. He closed his eyes, trying to gather himself, but his voice was firm and low. 'Change your damned name.'

I felt the emptiness grow inside me, gobble up all my flesh and blood into nothingness. I imagined myself to be perfectly hollow. I would never be Mrs Kit Rivers. What did my name matter anymore? I hadn't noticed Mr Rivers slip inside, but now he reappeared clutching the whisky decanter and a pair of glasses. He set them on the table and motioned me to sit. He sloshed liquid into each glass, slid one across to me, and raised his own.

'To him,' he said.

'To him,' I replied.

We drank, and I felt whisky burn my throat and tears sting my eyes. I blinked them back.

'There has been a Rivers in Tyneford House since 1610,' he said matter-of-factly. 'But all things come to an end. Kit has no cousins. The entail will simply die out with me. The world is changing and this is the way of things.'

His voice was calm but his hand shook like a branch in the wind. He had almost finished his second tumbler of whisky and I realised that he was well on the way to being very drunk.

'Well?' he said, turning to face me, eyes bright with alcohol. 'What shall we call you?'

I shrugged. 'My middle name is Rosa.'

'No,' he banged his fist down on the table. 'Something English. So they won't take you away.'

He drained his tumbler and poured himself another.

'Drink,' he commanded, pointing to my half-full glass. 'Elsie. That's quite like Elise, but a good old-fashioned English name.'

I winced and shook my head. 'Absolutely not. My sister called me that and I hated it.'

He laughed, a low unfamiliar sound. 'Then how about something after your parents? Anna is nice and English. Or, if you want to be named for your father, Julia is pretty.'

'No. We only name children after the dead. It

carries their memory forward. To name a child after someone living brings bad luck, even death.'

Mr Rivers fell silent and I realised with a pang of guilt that he was thinking he had given his own name to his son.

I glanced around the garden. It was shrouded by night-time shadows, a breeze rustled through the fig tree overhanging the terrace and I imagined that I heard a low thrum from the soil, earthworms churning beneath the surface. Stray stars poked through the mantle of cloud and I could distinguish the pale tufts of sheep scattered about the hillside. I licked my lips and they tasted of salt. Nothing had changed and everything had changed. At once, I knew my name.

'Alice,' I said firmly.

I was Alice through the Looking Glass; I had fallen into a topsy-turvy world, where everything looked the same but was the other way round. I longed to wade out into the breakers on the shore, where the pounding of the waves overwhelmed the noise in my mind. I felt sick standing still. It was as though the quiet meadows and stone ground shook and tossed like the green sea.

'Alice. Alice Land,' repeated Mr Rivers, testing out my new name like an unfamiliar dish. 'Yes, all right. It sounds well enough. Expect it'll take a bit of getting used to.'

I closed my eyes and wondered if he could see the piece of me break away. I felt myself cleave in two: Alice and Elise. I smiled; it was a little death. Part of me had died with Kit, the part of me that dreamt of marriage to her sweetheart and picnics on the lawn, and a wedding with Anna in her black silk and Julian in his dinner jacket, and me taking the novel out of the viola and lying in a hammock with Kit by Durdle Door, and allowing him to peel off my stockings one by one and run his fingers along my smooth, plump thighs, and drifting on a boat with him at dusk—both of us naked and me trailing a lazy toe in the water and letting him kiss my belly and throat and breasts and the pleasure of languid summer days. It was easier if I was no longer Elise. Another girl, one whom I used to be, had dreamt of those things. Now, my name is Alice.

CHAPTER TWENTY-TWO

Run, rabbit, run

The August sun raged and the rugged Dorset cattle huddled beneath the spreading trees, seeking shade. The sheep fared better, shorn by the travelling gangs of shearers and left comically bald, soft sprouts of new wool appearing patchily across their backs. The hedgerows wore the thick gloss of high summer, the brambles studded with white flowers and tight, green berries. The countryside carried on just the same without Kit. Nothing in nature cared for him: not the larks laughing as they alighted in clouds from the mulberry bushes, nor the fork-tongued adder basking open-eyed on the sandy heath. And yet, despite nature's indifference, both Mr Rivers and I sought our solace out of doors.

My skin ripened, and I was as lean and strong as one of the roe deer galloping across the hilltop. My parents would not recognise me with my new name and close-cropped hair as I criss-crossed the meadows, watching the sheep. I had taken over from the shepherd's boy, the latest to receive his commission. The shepherd, Eddie Stickland, was as old and weathered as the salt-lashed hazels on the cliff, and as he climbed the sloped meadows the wind blew him sideways like a leaf curl.

Tending the flock it was as if nothing had changed: the seasonal rhythms were as steady as the grinding of the sheep as they chewed the tough hill grass. But that August in 1940, the war came to Tyneford. We no longer sat at the edge of the conflict, concerned about distant battlefields in foreign lands. I spent several evenings sitting on the steps of the shepherd's hut watching the planes. The hut was a small painted caravan perched on the top of the hill like a bowler hat. The only light was a torch with the regulation layers of paper stuck over the lamp, but aware of the severe shortage of batteries, I was loath to even turn it on. I heard the growl of aeroplanes flying low across the channel. I hadn't learnt yet to distinguish whether they belonged to 'us' or 'them' or both. A fine haze covered the sea, so that the noise of explosions and the rat-a-tat of gunfire was strangely bodiless, an invisible battle behind the mist. I expected that nearby Portland must be getting hit, or else a small war seethed out at sea. The sheep grazed, nonchalant and oblivious. They hid during a thunderstorm and yet this, being somehow outside nature, remained beyond their reckoning. As the sun vanished beneath the horizon, stars began to emerge one by one, as though a celestial Mrs Ellsworth was busy with her taper and candles. The hillside was quiet, filled only with the huffing of the sheep and the far-off rustle and snuffle of a badger or hedgehog, while out at sea came the steady patter of guns and the whine and bang of shells. I sat in the growing darkness and listened.

I heard gunshots. Not the pounding of distant artillery but a gun being fired close by. Had a fifth columnist broken cover or the Home Guard cornered a spy? Curiosity overcame fear and I hurried along the spine of the hill to the steep path leading down the cliff and emerged onto the beach. The night was cool and the beach so still that at first I thought it deserted. Perhaps I had been mistaken, and the sound had been a trick of the tide, or a farmer scaring a fox from his chickens. I padded along the rocks trying to get the panorama of the bay. Then I saw him. On the edge of the surf stood a man holding a revolver. As I watched, he cocked it and fired it into the waves.

'I'll kill you. I'll kill you all,' he shouted, aiming the gun again at some invisible enemy.

I recognised the voice. It was Mr Rivers. I scanned the water again, but there was nothing there—neither man nor boat. He raised the gun and squeezed the trigger but the chamber was empty. He felt in his pocket for more bullets and I sprinted to him, trying to grab his arm before he had time to reload. He spun round, raising the gun again. On seeing it was me, he lowered it. 'Alice,' he said. 'They're coming. I heard them coming and I won't let them have him.' Then growing angry, he turned on me. 'I could have hurt you, stupid girl.'

He staggered and aimed the empty revolver again at the sea. I tugged on his arm and he shook me off, casting me into the water. He fumbled with a bullet and, terrified he would injure himself or me, I shoved him as hard as I could. We both fell into the surf. He remained sprawled in the water, making no attempt to get up. I sat beside him and smelt the alcohol on his breath. He did not resist as I prised the revolver from his grasp.

'I am a little drunk, Alice,' he said, lying back in the shallows, letting the waves lap around him, soaking the fine wool of his suit.

'Very drunk,' I corrected, remaining beside him. 'And where did you get the gun?'

'It's mine. I'm leader of the auxiliaries in these parts. I'm to head the resistance and keep out the invaders. Very hush-hush.'

'You weren't being terribly hush-hush just then.'

'No. I suppose not. Pity. You didn't suspect a thing till now. Went training for a week in Wiltshire and told you and Kit that I was going to London.'

I looked at him in surprise. 'You weren't really in town?'

He shook his head. 'Neither of you even asked why I was going. You were both so pleased to have me gone and be alone.' He smiled. 'It's all right. Don't look so guilty. I remember what it was like to be twenty-one and in love.'

'What were you shooting at just now?' I asked, changing the topic.

'I don't remember. I heard planes. I thought . . . I don't know.'

On the horizon a ship blazed and grey flakes of ash wafted ashore and landed on our skin like a dirty snow shower. I did not offer him any empty words of comfort, just sat with him and watched the ship glow.

'Did shooting at the sea make you feel any better?'

'No. My family is still dead.'

He stated this as a mere fact without any hint of self-pity. It was odd but I'd never really thought about Mrs Rivers as being Mr Rivers' wife, I'd always thought of her as Kit's mother.

'Do you miss your wife as well as Kit?'

Mr Rivers sat up, the water licking around his feet. 'No. It's so long ago. It was a sad and awful thing. But not like this.'

I watched the burning ship and wished the flames could burn inside me too, cauterise the wound. I was as lonely as I had been during my first days at Tyneford. No. I stopped myself. This was a lie. I missed my family, hating the silence that war had brought, and I wanted Kit so badly that my ribs hurt. In the stories I told to myself, I was always the heroine, the dying soprano with the waspish waist, adored and mourned by her desolate admirers—but fate had left me alive and in excellent health. It was the hero who had gone. And yet, I shared my loneliness. I knew that Mr Rivers' pain must be worse than mine. No father should bury his son; human hearts were not made for such grief. I had Mr Rivers' friendship, and if I loved Kit I must help soothe his father, make his pain a thing he could bear.

* * *

I made small changes to the running of the house. It would never be the same and it was useless to pretend otherwise. I did not want Kit's room to become some sort of ghastly mausoleum. In Vienna, when the great-aunts lost their mother they preserved her things in tissue paper, not even taking the hair out of her comb, or emptying the tea from her cup. They never used the room, even though she'd been dead ten years before I was born, and the aunts—slotted beside one another on the sofa like books on a narrow shelf—could certainly have done with the space. Margot and I were afraid to go into our great-great grandmother's room, terrified that her ghost lay inside, perfectly preserved within a rustle of tissue paper. I would not let this happen to Kit. Children would not be scared of visiting his room, as though he were some brittle, yellow-toothed phantom. Mrs Ellsworth bristled at what she perceived to be my lack of sentimentality.

'Barely cold in his grave and you're turning out his things. What would he think, miss?'

I gave her what I hoped was a hard stare.

'Mrs Ellsworth, Kit doesn't have a grave. And since he's dead, he doesn't think at all. He certainly doesn't need three very handsome, navy blue Guernsey sweaters. Burt, on the other hand, I'm sure could find use for them.'

Mrs Ellsworth bustled out, grumbling about 'the heartless girl'. Whose 'Hunnish tendencies' were only buried after all.

I sat down on Kit's bed. The room contained the scent of his ever-present cigarettes, that unique Turkish blend. He'd left his silver cigarette case and I helped myself. A box of matches lay beside the framed photograph of his mother and one of Kit, taken on the morning of his twenty-first birthday. Kit and his mother had died at almost the same age, and in the photographs side-by-side on the dresser they appeared more like brother and sister. At least I remembered Kit. He had not disappeared so absolutely from the world as Mrs Rivers. I lit my cigarette and inhaled the scent of Kit. If we ever had visitors, I would direct Mrs Ellsworth to make up this room. It must be done—we could not shut him away in a closed-off room.

I made my way downstairs. During the last few months I had remembered how to dawdle. The hectic dash of the housemaid was in my past, and I knew from Diana and Juno that the English upper classes believed an idle saunter to be an important distinction of rank. Only the middle classes risked a jog. I couldn't care less about rank, but I found it hard to hurry. My limbs were weary and cumbersome, and I was always tired. The only time I had energy was when I was striding across the hills and fields and through the damp summer woods.

Mr Rivers was in the morning room, drinking a cup of coffee. He did not sit, but lingered beside the long windows, gazing across the lawn at the downy clouds drifting along Tyneford Barrow. Usually he took his breakfast early, sometimes so early that I wondered if he'd been to bed at all.

'Good morning, Mr Rivers.'

He turned towards me but avoided meeting my eye. 'I am sorry about last night. I would be grateful if—'

'I shan't say a word—you must know that.'

He nodded and then said briskly to change the subject, 'We're haymaking again today.'

All week from my perch upon Tyneford cap, I watched him driving the farm horses across the fields below, his shoulder bent against the beast's neck, cajoling, shouting, or else standing behind the vast rolling rake that gathered up the grass in wide green stripes. Now, in the elegant morning room with its cheerful yellow paper and breakfast china, he lurked in his work clothes; his Savile Row suit replaced by coarse trousers, hobnail boots and a plain white shirt. The sunlight caught his face, and I saw a growth of dark stubble upon his jaw. I wondered why Mr Wrexham had not shaved him. The butler-valet certainly would have baulked at laying out such an ordinary wardrobe for his master.

'I must go,' said Mr Rivers.

He placed his cup on the table, and left the morning room. I knew he avoided the house at mealtimes. Neither of us could help staring at the empty chair. He now took his lunch out in the fields, bread and cheese and a flask of beer, as though he really were one of the common labourers on the estate. The farmers avoided eating with him—he was the squire after all—and I knew he did not correct them, as he desired no company. Most evenings he stayed out so late that I had already dined before he returned. I knew it was because he couldn't bear the formality of the dining room. It belonged to another time. I resolved on speaking to Mrs Ellsworth.

* * *

'I have never heard of such a thing, not in my forty years of service,' she said, clattering the wooden rolling-pin down on the kitchen table and flipping over her pastry. Little flurries of flour billowed across the surface, forming drifts beside the butter dish.

'But Mrs Ellsworth, his son is dead,' said Mr Wrexham in a quiet voice. He pulled out a chair and sat beside the whistling range. 'Our duty is to serve their comfort. The practices and customs of our profession are to attend the comfort of the household. If, as Miss Land says, the needs of the master are best fulfilled by serving him dinner in the kitchen, then it must be done.'

I looked at him with gratitude. 'Thank you, Wrexham.'

'My pleasure, miss. I take it that you would prefer to inform Mr Rivers of this alteration in present arrangements?'

'Yes. And,' I hesitated, 'I shall tell him that it is at Mrs Ellsworth's request. I shall explain that now with so few servants, it will make things very much easier.'

'Very good, miss,' replied Mr Wrexham with a slight nod.

Mrs Ellsworth coughed in annoyance. The butler stiffened and his eyes narrowed. 'My dear Mrs Ellsworth, in this one instance it is required that you feign an incapacity that we all know is, in truth, a gross misrepresentation of your remarkable capabilities. But this is what must be done to serve the master of this house.'

He looked past us both, fixing on some indefinable point in the distance.

'The son and heir is dead. We must serve the last master of Tyneford with our very best, until the end.'

* * *

I walked through the valley carrying Mr Rivers' lunch. He'd left in such a hurry that morning he'd forgotten to take it with him, and despite her irritation Mrs Ellsworth handed me a neat wax paper parcel to deliver to him in the fields. It was a warm August day, and I wore my broad-brimmed straw hat and a short-sleeved summer dress, enjoying the sensation of the sun warming my bare arms. Everything had sprouted lush and green, the grass speckled with pink willow herb and ugly nubs of figwort. A family of wrens patrolled beside the path, churring at me, while a pair of clouded yellow butterflies landed on the dry-stone wall. It was hot work rambling through the valley bottom in the midday sun, and I was grateful when I spotted Mr Rivers. He stood upon a large wooden cart hitched to a team of working horses. The cart was piled with hay, and Mr Rivers stooped with his pitchfork to gather the dry grass into higher and higher peaks, as a pair of youths, barely men, tossed up more towards the cart, which Mr Rivers caught on the prongs of his fork. I paused at the edge of the field, leaning against the flint wall, and watched them. I remembered the haymaking during my first year in Tyneford when the new tractor had been used. Now, with petrol rationed, they had reverted to using the great shire horses. There was a steady rhythm to their motions, like the elegant whir and tick of the movement inside a clock; the back and forth of the boys throwing up armfuls of hay and Mr Rivers receiving them with the inevitability of a pendulum. I felt a sense of peace as I watched, a congruity of time like the bud and fall of leaves on an oak tree. Men had been haymaking in these fields, in exactly this way, for more than a thousand years. Birth and death, rain and sun, were simply part of the rhythm. One of the boys glanced up and saw me. He mumbled something to Mr Rivers, who stopped and beckoned me over.

'I brought your lunch,' I said.

'You can set it down over there in the shade. On the wall, out of the way of the rats.'

I shuddered at the mention of rats, and the boys laughed.

'An' he wis telling us that yoos are a country girl now an' all.'

I felt myself grow prim. 'Well? No one likes rats.'

'Stanton does,' said one of the boys, a fair-haired youth, his cropped head almost the same colour as the downy dandelion clocks. He pointed at the small spaniel rolling in the cut grass, blissful as a pup.

'Come. More to be done,' said Mr Rivers, returning to work.

'We needs some of them land-girls,' muttered one of the boys as he bent over his shovel.

I set down Mr Rivers' lunch and returned to the cart. 'I can help.'

They surveyed me dubiously.

'I'm as strong as any land-girl. Besides, they're all pasty things from the city.'

'Fine.' Mr Rivers tossed me a rake. 'Use that to tidy the stray pieces of grass into rows.'

I caught it in my fist and started to comb through the loose strands that the horse-drawn rake had missed. Within a minute, the sweat rolled down my forehead and into my eyes. My cotton dress clung to my back. I could feel the muscles in my stomach and shoulders ache but I kept doggedly to my task, pulling the cut grass into neat lines. Here and there were strewn sundried wild flowers—camomile, buttercups and stinging nettles that prickled my bare legs. I found a lilt to my work, a rippling dance and saw in my mind the Brueghel landscapes in the Vienna galleries. I was like one of the peasant girls in those paintings, and I hummed a snatch of Beethoven's 'Pastoral' Symphony. My arms burnt with tiredness, but I lost myself in the pulse of the work. From beneath the broad brim of my sunhat, I glimpsed Mr Rivers, shovelling, catching, shovelling, and I knew the physicality of the labour helped him too. The calm was pierced by a bark and a high-pitched scream, as the spaniel snapped its jaws round a fat, black rat and shook. The unfortunate prisoner squealed, a horribly human sound, its rope-like tail flicking back and forth in the dog's jaws. Then quiet. The spaniel abandoned its victim beneath a hedgerow. The tiny corpse twitched and was still. The boys chuckled, and I reddened, realising I'd dropped my rake in horror.

'Enough,' snapped Mr Rivers. 'Break for lunch.'

The boys downed tools and ambled across to the far side of the field and the shade of a spreading oak. I hesitated, watching Mr Rivers.

'Come. You can share with me. Mrs Ellsworth packs enough for half the village.'

I sat beside him on the stone wall, taking the proffered bread and cheese. We ate in silence. My face was sticky with sweat, husks of grass clinging to my skin, and I sported painful blisters on my palms. I glanced over at Mr Rivers' hands. His nails were encrusted with dirt and his once soft, gentleman's hands had grown coarse. His skin had toughened from the work and blistered no longer. Apart from the empty, cadaverous look in his eyes, he looked healthy, a man in his prime exuding strength. He tossed scraps of bread to the spaniel which careered through the meadow in joyous pursuit. Clearing my throat, and studying to appear casual, I explained about dinners in the kitchen. He nodded absently, and said nothing. I wriggled, the stones of the jagged wall digging into me.

'So you'll come back tonight before supper?' I asked.

'Yes. I'll come,' he said, and turned to look at me.

I was suddenly self-conscious about the husks congealed in my hair and the seed cases stuck to my skin.

'Alice,' he said, and I stiffened, still unused to my new name. 'Why don't you grow your hair again?'

I shrugged and looked away, unable to meet his steady gaze. 'I can't. Not anymore.'

Elise was the girl who had hair reaching down her back in a black python plait. Alice's hair was bobbed below her ears, strands tickling the base of her neck, but cool and swishing as she raked in the field or walked along the sun-soaked hillside, watching the sheep in the swell of the afternoon.

'That was before,' I said, not managing to explain.

'I like it this way too,' he said. 'Just makes you look older.'

I smiled. 'I am older, Mr Rivers.'

* * *

We toiled for hours, until day mellowed into evening, and the chirping of the birds was replaced by the whining of the gnats and the whir and tick of the crickets in the uncut grass. My eyes stung and itched from the pollen, and I gave my nose a surreptitious wipe with the back of my hand. The men had inched around the field, the cart steadily gobbling up the lines of hay, but the lengthening shadows told me it was growing late.

'Mr Rivers,' I called. 'I'm going back to the house. I need to help Mrs Ellsworth with the dinner. You'll be back before eight?'

From his position on top of the hayrick, he gave me a wave and resumed his task. I watched for a second and then turned for home. I dawdled along the dry valley bottom, tracing the route of the underwater stream, noting the dark green marsh grasses, fed from below. The sea glittered like a thousand mirrors, while a pair of fishing-boats bobbed in the mouth of the bay. In the distance I heard the growl of an aeroplane engine. It was odd. The bombers usually came at night, but the onslaught had increased over the last couple of weeks—Swanage, Portland, Weymouth and even Dorchester had been pounded, and I supposed day raids were bound to start. The papers no longer listed all the details—there were too many, and they didn't want to give the Germans confirmation of what they had hit. Sometimes as I sat on the bottom rung of the shepherd's hut, I saw the planes swoop along the valley below, engines screaming, wing tips appearing to brush the sloping fields on either side.

The engine noise grew deafening, and I clapped my hands over my ears. I looked up, and saw not one but two Messerschmitt fighters dive out of the sun, wings and snouts mustard yellow, black crosses daubed beneath their wings. Fury bubbled in my throat. How dare they fly here? Under these English skies men and horses trawled the meadows, gathering hay for the winter. The skies belonged to the sparrow hawks and greylag geese, not these dirty machines with their stuttering roar. The

Messerschmitts rushed closer and closer, hurtling along the valley so low that their yellow bellies seemed to brush the blackthorn scrub. I was not frightened but angry. Hate pooled in my stomach like indigestion and I clenched my fists, fingers stiff with rage, and stooped to pick up a lump of flint. I drew my arm back and hurled it towards the first plane as it skimmed the valley.

'Get out! Get out!' I shouted.

The pebble curled in an arc, and I felt a moment of exhilaration and triumph—I'm going to hit it! I'm going to get the bastard! A second later, the pebble fell to earth and landed impotently. I swore and bent to find another pebble. In my fury, I did not notice that the engine note had changed, and that one plane had soared in a loop and was now rushing back along the valley towards me. I watched for a moment as the black nose and yellow snout rushed at me, more interested and angry than afraid, until suddenly, as it neared me, the ground exploded with machine-gun fire. I was paralysed, open-mouthed with rage and surprise. Then I started to run. I ran faster than I had ever run in my life. The plane sprayed the valley with bursts of bullets. The hills rattled with gunfire and the staccato roar of the engines. It was a game. Just a game. I was its run, rabbit, run. I couldn't feel my legs—I was a blur, a sweating, running thing. I was nothing. I was a hurry of speed and fear. I heard that silly hit of the previous summer playing in my mind—*Run Rabbit Run . . . here comes the farmer with his gun, gun, gun.* Bullets. Running. The purple head of a thistle flew off, decapitated. I was aware of everything and nothing. Only running. The record played round and round, my mind a spinning turntable. *On the farm every Friday it's rabbit pie day. So run rabbit run rabbit run! Run! Run!* My tennis shoe came off. I did not slow. I sprinted, conscious of my skin slicing open on the sharp rocks and pricked by the nettles, but I couldn't feel the pain, numb with adrenalin.

The woods. Run to Tyneford Great Wood. Reach the woods. Hide among the trees and I am safe. I am Kit, running, running across the hills, fast as a roe buck. The tree shadow. Closer. Bullets clattering against the flint, strafing the eweleaze. *Bang! Bang! Bang! Goes the farmer's gun.* A fence falls. Sheep running. I can't look to see if they're dead. Something red. Blood on wool. Nearly at the trees. If I reach this hazel, that post, then I'll be safe. I'll live. *Run rabbit run run run! Don't give the farmer his fun fun fun!* I run into the wood. The planes growl above the trees. It's angry, I can hear it. It's driven its rabbit into cover. I fall into the leaf litter, warm and damp and smelling of earth and mould. It's firing into the tree canopy. Bullets and twigs and leaves rain onto the forest floor. I'm on my hands and knees. I'm on my feet again and I'm running, running. The mud and muck flies up around me as the bullets spray, sometimes so close I have to breathe to check that I'm still alive. I am all fear and running. The big tree. I see the big oak tree. It has white arms and it beckons to me out of the green dark. I run to the tree and the arms grab me and pull me down, down into cool dark and quiet.

* * *

'You're safe,' soothed Poppy. 'Quite safe.'

I lay in the gloom, listening to the quiet. Nothing moved. The beetles and ants and woodpeckers held their breath. The wind hummed through the ash leaves, and a larch rustled. Then a wood pigeon cooed, a rook cackled and shrieked, and the forests crawled to life once again.

'How can you be sure they won't come back?' I asked.

''Spect they're out of ammo for one thing. Less than ten seconds worth of solid gunfire. Not much fuel left either.'

I sat up, picking leaves and moss from my hair, and an enterprising earwig from my cotton brassiere.

'He played with me, Poppy.'

'Here, drink this, you'll feel better.'

I grabbed the bottle from her and downed a hefty gulp of what turned out to be Scotch.

'You don't seem very hysterical,' said Poppy, looking rather disappointed as I tipped out stones from my remaining tennis shoe. 'I must say, I was looking forward to slapping you. It's what you do with hysterics. Are you sure you're not feeling even a little peaky?' she asked with a hopeful smile.

'No.'

I took another swig of Scotch and surveyed my surroundings. We sat in what appeared to be an earthen cave, roots tangled above our heads. A bright hole of daylight led back to the wood, and a torch was slung from a root on a piece of string, angled to illuminate the recesses of the cave. Black guns glinted.

'Best not look,' said Poppy. 'Top secret and all that.'

'Bit late now.'

I remembered the guns that I'd seen her hide in the Tilly Whim caves and Mr Rivers' revolver. I wondered if Poppy and Mr Rivers were part of the same resistance group, but honouring my promise to Mr Rivers, I did not enquire.

'So, you have these hides all round the coast?' I asked instead.

'Yes. Just in case.'

'I want to help. Whatever you're doing, I want to be part of it.'

Poppy shifted and wouldn't meet my eye. 'Can't, I'm afraid. British nationals only. We really are Top Secret you know. You're not supposed to be down here, 'specially not since you're an enemy alien, but seemed the right thing to do, since otherwise you would have been shot and all.'

I crawled over to the disc of daylight and elbowed my way out into the wood. Dusting off my filthy dress as best I could, I stood up and glared down at her.

'Enemy alien? How could you?'

Poppy flushed. 'I'm sorry. It's beastly. It's not me, it's the wretched government.'

'Just be quiet,' I snapped. I kicked at the tree with my shoe and balled my fists. I was so angry I could spit. Without saying goodbye or thank you, I turned and walked away. It was not fair. I wanted to join the fight.

I hobbled along the path, searching for my dropped plimsoll. An evening breeze drifted in from the sea and licked across the valley. The sheep grazed and curlews floated across the sky. I found my shoe and slipped it on. A flotilla of red admiral butterflies flitted around a patch of clover and, at the far end of the valley, the last combs of hay lay in curving lines. A pastoral idyll once again. Something glinted in the grass. I bent and scooped it up between my fingers—a fat bullet, glossy as a slug. On the hill at a distance from the rest of the flock, one of the sheep lay motionless. I clapped my hands and shouted. It did not move. Squinting, I realised it must be dead. I ought to send a message to the shepherd. The ewe was freshly killed—no use wasting good mutton. I noticed that at the far end of the field there fluttered a row of crimson flags, like a bleeding scratch across the skin of the meadow. I wondered what they signified. I suspected Poppy knew, but she probably wouldn't tell me, even if I asked.

When I reached the house, Mr Rivers was prowling the terrace.

'Good God,' he said, hastening towards me. 'Are you hurt?'

I was too exhausted to receive his concern with any grace. 'No. Just in need of a bath.'

He tried to take my arm as I passed. 'Alice, I heard gunfire.'

I shook him off. 'Please. Leave me be. I'm quite all right. Tell Mr Stickland one of his sheep is dead.'

I hurried into the house and up the stairs before anyone else could accost me. My terror had subsided. I was angry and exhausted and helpless. They'd shot at me and there was nothing I could do. In a few hours they would be back and the darkness would growl with enemies, metallic and sinister. Soon the horizon would simmer red, as Swanage or Portland or Dorchester burnt. I unbuttoned my frock and paced the room in my underwear. I waited for the stillness to be torn apart by an aeroplane's roar. I didn't really rest anymore. Not since Kit died. I saw him in my dreams; he was exactly the same as before, but even in my sleep I knew he was dead. In the mornings, when I woke, my grief choked me, thick as smoke. When I was a child, I imagined that if my parents died, or Margot, that I would die of grief; I'd cleave in two like an elm tree in a lightning strike. But I didn't die. I was hollowed out, scraped clean inside. I imagined myself to be like an empty Russian doll, filled with black nothing. Sometimes when I paced beside the sea, the shingles washed as the waves rushed and withdrew, I wondered whether I ought to slip into the tide. I could fill my pockets with pebbles and wade out beyond the black rocks, beyond the peak of Worbarrow Tout, until the saltwater trickled down my throat. It seemed a quiet, easeful death. Perhaps Kit waited for me beneath the waves, as he did in my dreams. It was an idle thought, brought on by misery and the sad call of the sea. That afternoon, when the Messerschmitts had chased me, I only wanted to live. I had not thought for a second that I ought to embrace death and join Kit. As I ran, sweating and feral with terror, I discovered that I was greedy for life. My instinct to live was as desperate as that of a bloodied rat caught in a dog's jaws.

* * *

Mr Rivers and I ate dinner in the kitchen, while Mr Wrexham waited upon us, resplendent in his white cotton gloves and pristine tails. Behind us, the ancient stove smoked and grumbled. I liked the kitchen; its warmth and the smells of simmering fat and carbolic soap, the clatter and bustle of Mrs Ellsworth, all reminded me of home. I sipped at my wine and toyed with the mashed potato. Mr Rivers frowned.

'Alice, what happened this afternoon? Are you all right?'

I recalled Mr Rivers mad with rage firing his gun. Determined not to incense him again, I spoke with studied calm. 'There was a Messerschmitt. It let off a few rounds in the valley.'

'Was it shooting at you?'

His voice was low, but contained a coldness that I did not like. I reached across the table for his hand.

'I am fine. Please. If you get cross, then I shall be upset.'

A muscle pulsed in his jaw, but he said nothing more on the topic.

After dinner, Mr Rivers and I remained in the kitchen by silent consent, reluctant to return to the muffled stillness of the drawing room. The decay had been creeping in, year on year, but in the sunshine of Kit's presence we had not noticed. We'd revelled in the faded grandeur, like children enjoying the romance of a dustsheeted castle in a story. Now, in our unhappiness, Mr Rivers and I winced at the house's shabbiness, like a husband who realises his bride has grown fat. I imagined the house to be mortified by her present state and spent hours attempting to restore her beauty, but there were not enough maids to keep her properly clean, and even with my help the skirting boards and dado rails were grey with dust, the parquet scratched and unpolished.

Mrs Ellsworth placed candles on the scrubbed

oak table and, after securing the blackouts, vanished into the housekeeper's room. Mr Wrexham poured his master's port and withdrew, leaving us alone listening to the gurgle and tick of the stove. Mr Rivers had not dressed for dinner, understandable now that we dined in the whitewashed cosiness of the kitchen, but it nonetheless marked a final alteration in the customs of the household. He'd removed his outdoor boots but that was his only concession. He leant back on the wooden chair, stretching out his legs, workman's shirt unbuttoned at the throat. His clothes were stained with dirt and he smelt of hay and sweat. Reaching into his pocket, he pulled out a box of matches and lit a cigar. The incongruity made me laugh.

'Mr Rivers, you look like you ought to be packing your pipe with ha'penny tobacco, not smoking cigars from Jermyn Street.'

He ignored my teasing and exhaled smoke, which drifted in blue curls up to the rafters. 'Why do you call me Mr Rivers?'

'Why shouldn't I?' I asked, with a smile. 'You want to change your name too?'

'No. It's an old name. One of England's best,' he said with a touch of the old pride. He reached for a saucer and let the ash fall from his cigar. 'Why won't you call me by my Christian name? Why won't you call me Christopher?'

I studied the table. 'I can't,' I said, unable to look at him. 'Kit was Christopher. I can't call you by his name.'

He inhaled sharply. 'He was named after me. I was Christopher first.' His voice held a note of anger.

I knew I hurt him, but I could not help it. 'Not to me.' I met his gaze, unblinking. 'I don't want to think of him when I speak your name.'

He glanced up at the high window where a strand of honeysuckle tap-tapped against the glass, and sighed.

'My second name is Daniel. Can you call me Daniel?'

He strode over to the range, opening the furnace and poking the coals so that crimson sparks flew out into the room. He had not shaved for several days now, and even in the firelight, I could see a thick layer of bristles covering his jaw.

'Daniel, are you intending to grow a beard?' I asked.

He turned round in surprise, running a hand across his chin.

'No. Just haven't had Wrexham shave me for a day or two.'

'Well, tomorrow, you must let him.'

He turned away from me and gave the furnace another vicious prod, so that a nugget fell out of the grate and landed on the flagstone where it smouldered. He stared at the glowing coal, complaining under his breath about 'wretched, bloody women'.

'Yes, well you should be grateful. It is I who keep you civilised.'

He smiled and sat down. 'Do you want a cigar? Kit once told me that you smoked. He was mighty impressed.'

I laughed. 'Good. That was why I did it.'

He took the cigar from his mouth and passed it to me. I sucked, trying not to cough. He watched me steadily, and did not look away. I noticed his eyes were a remarkably bright shade of blue, and that one was darker than the other. No one else knew this. It was the kind of information that only mothers or lovers cherished, and his mother was dead; so was his wife, and his son. So this little detail belonged solely to me.

'You're thinking of Kit,' said Mr Rivers, interrupting my reverie.

I flushed. 'Yes,' I lied.

CHAPTER TWENTY-THREE

Red flags

The following morning a letter arrived from Margot, the first since Kit's death.

> *I don't know what to say. Everything I try sounds clumsy and useless . . . I wish I could find you a* sachertorte *like the ones from the Sacher Hotel. I used to get a slice for you when you cried when you were small and I know it can't possibly help you now but I want to get it for you all the same.*
>
> *They sell them here in 'continental bakeries' but they're nothing like the real thing which I suppose we shan't have again—not unless they exile the pastry chef with the secret recipe. Do you remember when you were little and you used to think that the hotel was named after the cake and not the other way round? Hotel Chocolate Cake . . . I imagine sometimes that we are still sitting there, younger versions of ourselves after an opera or concert, eating* sachertorte *with*

cream and chattering about the sharp soprano and the sweating tenor with his droll pocket-handkerchief.

I shall write a letter to 'Margot and Elise c/o Hotel Chocolate Cake, Vienna' and it will reach that Elise and another Margot and none of this will have happened. One day after the war we'll go back there and we'll talk about how the second violins got away from the rest of the orchestra in the scherzo and think of nothing but music.

A year ago, Anna sent me the recipe for a horrible tea which the aunts made for her when she wanted a family (though I am slightly at a loss as to why she sought this kind of advice from three maiden aunts). It tastes awful and yet I drink it every morning—not because I believe it will do me any good but because it was the last piece of advice that she gave me. I find myself hoarding all my memories of Anna and Julian, reciting them again and again, terrified in case I forget something.

Reading my sister's letter, I saw my own fears reflected. Our parents had disappeared. Were they hiding in the French countryside, Anna disguised as a pink-cheeked peasant, or concealed by friends in Amsterdam? I preferred to imagine cheerful adventures for them than voice the other possibility.

Needing to be distracted from my own thoughts, I walked down to the bay in search of Poppy. As I approached the shingle, I saw that it teemed with people. Three strange men dressed in labourers' overalls addressed the fishermen clustered beside the boats outside Burt's cottage. Wooden boxes littered the beach. The fishermen leant against the boats, arms folded across their chests and eyes narrow with suspicion. A bearded fisherman spat and then slouched off, dismissing the stranger with a curt wave as he tried to pursue him. At the back of the crowd, seated on a lobster pot, I spied Poppy. Easing my way through the throng, I settled beside her.

'Home Guard,' she said, pointing to the three strangers, before I'd even had a chance to ask. 'Mr Rivers asked them to get the fishermen to mine the bay. Stupid idea if you ask me. Excellent way to kill a lot of perfectly good mackerel. Come on.'

She scrambled to her feet and tugging my arm, led me away from the group.

'Best let them get on with it. Won't want our interference,' she said, hauling me off along the strand.

I jogged to keep up with her. The sun warmed the cliffs and they glowed golden brown, tempting as freshly baked biscuits. Crimson poppies studded the coarse sea-grass sprouting in tufts along the top, while sand martins zoomed in and out of tiny holes quarried from the sandstone face. We walked to the far end of the beach, where Flower's Barrow loomed above the valley and the bay. A steep path crawled up the precipice and, without breaking step, Poppy started to climb. In five minutes we reached the top and she pulled me onto the grass ledge. Sprawled on the ground, I closed my eyes, catching my breath.

'Come on. No time to nap,' said Poppy.

Grumbling, I dusted myself off and hurried after her.

'Where are we going?'

'Will,' she replied, as though this were enough of an answer.

We headed along the ridge. Below us the fields were spread in a haphazard patchwork, as though stitched together by a careless seamstress. At the bottom of the coomb, where the hillside flattened into wide meadows, Mr Rivers and the boys were finishing the haymaking. The school had been emptied of children for the last day, and boys in short trousers and girls in wellingtons and faded summer dresses rushed through the meadows gathering up armfuls of dry grass and moulding them into mountainous peaks. Their shouts mingled with the spaniel's barking and drifted up towards us on the wind. Mr Rivers tossed the dog a stick and it scrambled in pursuit, ears flapping in ecstasy. Under the wide sky, Mr Rivers appeared at ease. Then, as if he sensed me watching, he paused and glanced up at the hill, shielding his eyes from the sun. I hurried on, embarrassed, and hoped he had not seen me.

Poppy waited at the next stile, sitting contentedly on the wooden bar, tap-tapping with her sandal.

'He won't be the only one,' she said. 'By the end of the war, there will be lots more.'

'Doesn't make it any easier.'

'No,' she said slowly. 'I just meant, he will survive this.'

'What does that even mean?' I snapped. 'That he will carry on breathing and spreading butter on his toast and speaking on the telephone. I don't want him to survive. I want the possibility of happiness. Not moments of pleasure like a square of chocolate or a hot bath. Happiness.'

I stopped talking, no longer sure whether I spoke

of Mr Rivers or myself. Poppy watched me.

'You will. Both of you. It gets easier, and then it gets worse again as you realise it's getting easier and you feel guilty.' She paused, seeing my puzzled expression, and smiled. 'My parents. When I was ten. Why did you think I lived with my aunts? Ma and Pa died in a fire while taking a holiday in a hotel in Blackpool. They went to see the lights. The aunts think holidays are very dangerous. I've never been allowed to take one, certainly not to a northern seaside resort.'

'I'm sorry,' I said. 'I didn't know.'

Poppy shrugged. ''S all right. Long time ago. Let's go and find Will. He has only two days leave left and he's spending it fencing.'

When we reached Will he was splitting timber with an axe and wedge, slicing the wood apart so that it lay on the grass, gleaming in the sunshine. Behind him a new fence curled up to the top of the hill, pale struts slotted neatly into round upright posts, like pieces of a giant jigsaw. Two small boys lay stretched out on their stomachs, pinning chicken wire to the base of the post with a hammer. They scarcely looked old enough to be out without their mothers, let alone fixing fences, but they worked steadily, neither glancing up at Poppy or me. Will let his axe fall into the grass and, placing a thick arm around Poppy's waist, pulled her into him and kissed her. I looked away, suddenly self-conscious, and tried not to think of Kit.

'Well?' demanded Poppy, shoving him away affectionately.

Will shrugged. 'Not too much longer, I 'spect. Rest of the afternoon, anyhoo.' He thrust his hands into his pockets and scowled. 'Don't like these wretched fences. Too quick. Not thought out. Nothin' like a good stone wall. Some things is supposed ter be slow. If yer goin' ter cut up hillside, yer got ter do it right, an' that takes time.'

I glanced across the hill and saw the flint walls running across the hillside like stone rivers. In the warmth of the morning sun they shone bone white, speckled with flecks of jet—as much part of the landscape as the swaying grass or wind-battered hazel.

'What's wrong with the old wall?' I asked.

'Army's creepin' in,' replied Will, pointing to a row of red flags between the wall and fence. 'Keep takin' more an' more farmland fer their trainin'. Barely sev'n hund'erd acres left. Be fencin' the beach soon enuff.'

Poppy kicked at a daisy and gave a sharp snort. 'Fencing? Ha! Mines more like. Soon the beaches and the barrows will be crawling with barbed wire and machine-gun posts.'

Will bent to pick up the axe. 'Nuff jibber-jabber. Can do nothin' 'bout it. Leave it to the yows ter bleet an' blether. Yoos twos goin' ter help?'

Poppy tossed me a stout mallet and, following her lead, I started to beat a thick wooden post into the earth. The cattle and sheep dawdled about us in the cowleaze, oblivious to the new fence, the red flags or the prickle of change that I felt running up my arms with each beat of the mallet. From the army camp on the Lulcombe estate, just beyond the brow of the hill, came the rat-a-tat of gunfire and the mosquito whine of shells. The animals ignored the noise; the fat summer lambs flicked their tails and danced among the dandelions, while the cows chewed the cud and blinked away the buzzing flies.

* * *

When I arrived home that evening, I heard raised voices on the terrace. It was almost seven and I expected to find Mr Rivers alone, drinking his whisky in the last glow of the afternoon. On the walk back I'd filled my sunhat with blackberries, ready to bake into a pie, and I quietly set them down beside the garden gate before venturing across the lawn. Mr Rivers stood on the terrace, while Lady Vernon and Diana Hamilton perched uneasily on the upright garden chairs. None of them saw me approach.

'I am sorry,' said Lady Vernon. 'I only wished to say that I am so very sorry.'

Mr Rivers spun to face her. 'Everyone is sorry. What good to me is sorry? Hang your sorry.'

Lady Vernon winced but her serene society smile did not waver. Diana studied her neat little hands folded in her lap, as Mr Rivers started to pace the terrace. I stood at the edge of the lawn, in the shadow of the walnut tree, and waited, unnoticed.

'Perhaps he will come home,' said Lady Vernon. 'It is possible he was taken prisoner. Many were.'

'No. He is dead.'

Mr Rivers came to a halt beside her chair. He watched her with steady eyes, forcing her to look at him. For a moment, her glass expression cracked and a look of pity flitted across her bulldog face. For a moment, I did not hate her.

'Will you have a memorial service?' she asked softly, twisting the gold wedding ring on her pudgy finger.

'No. I remember. Alice remembers. That is

enough.'

He turned away from her and stared absently out towards the bay.

'It is usual in these cases—' she began.

'Damn what is usual. What world is it that the murder of a man's son is usual?'

She smoothed over his outburst with a practised social smile. 'I'm perfectly happy to take on the organisation.'

In two strides he was beside her chair, a hand on either armrest. He towered over her, eyes cold with fury. To her credit she did not flinch, nor even lean back in her chair, but sat upright, her back finishing-school straight.

'Don't turn me into one of your projects!' he hissed. 'If you are idle then knit socks for soldiers, or repaper your damn drawing room.' He straightened, fists trembling, and with visible effort succeeded in controlling his temper. 'I'm going up to change. Ring for Wrexham if you require refreshments. Good night.'

He strode away into the gloom of the house. I slipped out of the shadow and came up the terrace steps.

'Well,' tutted Lady Vernon, shocked as a bantam hen disturbed in her egg laying. 'Well.'

'I told you we shouldn't have come,' said Diana, nostrils flaring with displeasure when she saw me.

'Good evening, Lady Vernon. Lady Diana,' I said, forcing a smile. 'I'm sorry for Mr Rivers' behaviour. He is not himself.'

This was not true. He was absolutely himself. He was simply not the person he had been before. Neither of us were; but unlike me he did not even look the same, with his unkempt hair, stubbled chin and coarse workman's clothes. His eyes had an empty, feral look, which proclaimed him to be a man beyond the restraint of civility. I wondered that neither woman had noticed it, and cursed them for provoking him. A child could tell them that this man was no longer a gentleman—any rudeness they had brought upon themselves. Both women studied me with unconcealed displeasure. Diana's lip curled in contempt. That it was left for me to apologise made it worse—the fact it was necessary at all was awful, a violation of social niceties; that the apology came from me, the Kraut-Yid and usurping maid, was unbearable. Lady Vernon rose and gave me a curt nod.

'Good evening, Miss Land, or whatever it is you're calling yourself today. I shall walk through the park in this pleasant weather. Diana?'

She nodded at the girl, but Diana shook her blonde curls.

'No thank you, Aunt. I shall join you in a minute.'

Lady Vernon's eyebrow twitched in surprise at Diana choosing my company over her own, but she made no comment and swept down the terrace steps into the garden. I turned and watched Diana, waiting for her to speak. She stared at me, to see if I would be first to break the silence. I sighed. I just wanted her gone.

'Would you like some tea, Lady Diana?'

'Are you asking as my hostess or as the maid?' she inquired, gazing at me with her large violet eyes.

'What do you want, Diana?' I asked, leaning against the back of a chair.

She settled into her seat, smoothing the cotton

print of her yellow summer dress, carefully chosen to bring out the creamy pink of her skin. She smiled at me through the thick veil of her lashes.

'People talk, you know,' she said.

I said nothing and scratched at a piece of moss sprouting between the paving slabs on the terrace with my plimsoll. Diana watched me for a second and then tried again.

'Why do you stay here?'

I snorted in surprise. I had never considered leaving.

'Because I must.'

She gave a coy smile. 'Why? You're not a servant anymore. You're not engaged to Kit. I'm sorry, darling, but you never reached "death do us part". There's no reason at all to stay.'

Anger heated my cheeks. 'Mr Rivers. Daniel. I stay for him. I cannot possibly leave him.'

Diana simpered in triumph. 'Daniel? Who is he? Christopher Rivers? A pet name. How adorable!'

'I'm sure your aunt is wanting you,' I said, my Austrian accent growing stronger with my rage.

Diana dismissed my feigned concern with a wave. 'Oh, she's quite all right. She'll be simply fascinated. As I said, people *love* to talk—especially about love. The more scandalous the better.'

'Please leave,' I said, abandoning any pretence of civility.

Clapping her hands with pleasure and laughing happily, Diana stood. 'It's too delicious. Obscene. But delicious.'

She leant forward and planted a cool kiss on my cheek, ignoring my distaste. 'Goodbye. Thank you for a charming afternoon.'

When she had gone I sat on the step, resting

my chin in my hands. I didn't care what people said. Perhaps it was obscene. Did such things even matter anymore? What I'd said was true: I had to stay. Mr Rivers needed me.

* * *

That night as I lay awake listening to the sea rush in the dark, I did not think about Kit but Mr Rivers. Was Diana right? I climbed out of bed and rummaged through the drawer in my dressing table until I found the Liberty-patterned notepaper Mr Rivers had purchased for me on his last trip to London. Tucking one leg beneath me, I wrote to my sister.

> *Do you think my staying here shocking? I hope you don't. I think it would be very unfair if you did. You were always kissing Robert in public even after you were married (and no one likes to see married people kiss their own spouses) so I don't believe that you're entitled to disapprove.*
>
> *I can't help wondering what Anna and Julian would think. The great-aunts would never approve of my staying in the house unchaperoned, but then the aunts rarely do, disapproval being one of their chief pleasures in life, along with a whiff of scandal and toasted marzipan squares. Anna probably has an opinion on such matters—she has one on most things. I know she is against a woman removing her hairpins and shaking out her hair in front of a man with whom she does not intend to fall in love, and she is decidedly for rosewater being sprinkled on underthings. You know how I*

listen to Anna (always looking over my shoulder before adjusting a single hairpin), but this is not like those things.

Do you remember Herr Aldermann when his wife died? We watched him shrivel. He went from being a fat man who wobbled with laughter as he wiped the chicken schmaltz from his jowls, to a husk. He shuffled into our apartment for supper, drank his schnapps and shuffled back to his empty house. I don't want Mr Rivers to shuffle. At the moment, he is angry. He rages at the world, but his fury will cool to despair and I must be here. I don't want him to turn into an old man who doesn't care to pick up his feet as he walks or lets the grease stay on his chin.

You understand why I cannot leave, whatever they say, don't you, Margot?

The wind huffed through the leaves outside my window, making them patter against the glass like raindrops. I was restless and sticky with unease. In the night I listened to the creak of floorboards in the library below, and knew that it was the sound of Mr Rivers pacing up and down. When later I fell asleep, I heard him in my dreams, walking restlessly, footsteps echoing in the dark.

* * *

Will's leave ended and it fell to Poppy and me to finish the fence. The small boys who had helped were summoned back to school to practise reading and arithmetic, and so Poppy and I were alone on the hillside. August was fading into September. We had that melancholy feeling that accompanies the last days of summer; the sunshine had lost its ferocity and I wished I could catch handfuls of it in my fists to preserve until next year. The fields, stripped during haymaking, looked bald and yellow, and only snatches of ragged robin and frog orchids were left at the edges. We worked in shirtsleeves—me in an old pair of shorts that I'd discovered at the back of Kit's cupboard. I'd taken to wearing his old clothes. It irked Mrs Ellsworth, who fretted that my appearing in Kit's blue school shorts would strike a blow to Mr Rivers' heart. I'd remonstrated with her—'His heart is broken whether I stain my only good dress mending fences or wear Kit's old things.' In truth I didn't care about ruining my clothes; I liked wearing Kit's belongings—they smelt of him. Anything taken from his wardrobe was infused with that scent of sandalwood and cigarettes. I'd almost smoked the last of Kit's Turkish blend and had decided to order some more from his place in Jermyn Street, when silently the store in his room was replenished; the slim silver case refilled. Of course it was Wrexham. The butler had recognised the paraphernalia of my grief, and quietly seen that it was taken care of.

I lay on my stomach in the grass, feeling the blades scratching my skin, removing stray pieces of flint from the dry ground. Poppy passed me a trowel and I hacked at the earth, creating a small hole for the next fencepost. The sheep milled around us, bleating amiably, oblivious to our work and the sinister flutter of the creeping flags. Poppy hammered cross sections into place, nails pursed between her lips. A kite soared above us, its red wings flashing in the afternoon sun. From the cliffs a kittiwake called, its shrill cry piercing the steady boom of the waves. Lulcombe camp was silent, but we could see green army trucks crawling across the hill like armoured beetles, and soldiers the size of lead toys marching in steady formations in the empty fields. The ancient stone castle crouched over them, an oversized model, and I imagined that it smiled, content to watch battles played out in its shade once again.

Poppy straightened, stretching her arms above her head, revealing a triangle of freckled midriff. She'd used the last of her hair elastics, and there were no more to be had, so she'd used a smooth stick to pin up her tumble-mane of hair. The effect was striking, and if she chose to sunbathe on the rocks I couldn't help thinking that the fishermen would mistake her for a pale-skinned mermaid. She dug her hand into her pocket and reached out a couple of pear drops, tossing one to me. I sucked on it, satisfied for a minute to close my eyes in the sunshine and taste sugar on my tongue. This was how I lived now, savouring the pleasure of an odd moment, always trying not to think. So it took a few seconds for me to register the staccato roar of the Messerschmitt. I sat upright, almost crashing my head against the bottom rail of the fence. Poppy perched on her haunches, alert as a March hare, every part of her listening. I felt bile rise and burn my throat, sweat prickle the back of my knees. No. I willed myself to calm. I hadn't survived his attack just to die in the meadow grass a few weeks later.

'It's all right,' said Poppy. 'Look.'

She pointed to a white bobtail of a cloud and I saw a Spitfire drop out from behind it. The afternoon exploded into gunfire. First from the Spitfire: the rattle and crack of bullets. A howl as the Messerschmitt engine screeched and the plane arced around. The Spitfire gave chase and I laughed out loud.

'Get the bastard! Get him,' I shouted, gleeful in my revenge.

There was a grace and an unreality to the fight. I'd spent hours and days on the top of this hillside, watching birds of prey. I'd seen a hawk attacked by a flurry of black crows, which swarmed the larger bird in a dark storm of wings as it made desperate attempts to escape. I'd seen a peregrine swoop and snatch songbirds out of the sky, catching a lark into silence. This aerial game was no more real than the bloodied battles of birds, and I felt oddly distanced as I watched them weave among the clouds. It was hard to imagine that inside each cockpit lurked a young man, filled with sweat and terror and fighting to the death with the tenacity of any buzzard or falcon. The hill echoed with gunfire, and tracer rounds strafed the blue sky. Vaguely, I wondered that they didn't pierce the clouds and cause a storm of pellets and rain.

'He must be low on fuel,' observed Poppy, shading her eyes as she studied the Messerschmitt with her steady green gaze.

I stared at the yellow-nosed plane hurtling towards the bay, only to be fired upon by the Spitfire and forced to loop back inland, and tried to feel pity at the pilot's choice: fire and death, escape and drown. I felt none. Like any cornered animal, the Messerschmitt was desperate. It would break its wing to get away, even if that meant death in any case. Escape. Nothing else mattered. The Spitfire was in no hurry; it had enough fuel and was on home ground, and seemed almost leisurely as it soared and rattled its guns, dodging the bullets of the other plane with casual ease, staying behind a cloud here, dancing through the sky with balletic grace. Then it came. High above us, but close enough that we saw the burst of fire, like flames from the mouth of a dragon, the Spitfire lined up in perfect position behind the enemy, and spat a stream of tracer rounds. The Messerschmitt fell from the sky, a flaming phoenix, engine stuttering into silence. The Spitfire lingered to watch for a moment and then vanished into the evening glow. Poppy and I climbed onto our half-finished fence to watch the descent of the wounded plane. Out of the wreckage floated a white parachute, as smooth and unhurried as a seed case from a dandelion; it dawdled on the breeze, wafting towards the ridge of Tyneford Barrow. Poppy jumped off the fence and grabbed my hand.

'Run,' she said.

Hauling me beside her, she took off along the hillside. My lungs burnt and my eyes streamed in the wind, but I didn't slow or stop. We had to find him. I blinked and envisioned the pilot freed from his parachute, wielding his handgun and shrieking as he fired upon us. I picked up the pace, so that for once Poppy trailed behind me. I bounced from stride to stride, remembering how Kit used to run across the hills and realising how effortless it was. The sun was getting lower now, a glowing disk sinking beneath the horizon and I squinted as I scoured the bare hilltop for a sign of the parachute. Smoke. A flash of white.

'There,' I said, pointing to a wind-rushed field.

We sprinted across the barrows, up and down the waving ridges, slowing with caution as we reached the gate leading into the field. Wreckage from the plane blazed and the air stank of burning fuel. Smoke billowed in thick plumes like a thousand chimneys and a slick of grey began to coat my skin. Poppy and I held hands by silent accord. We spoke in whispers.

'Do you see him?' she asked.

'No. Let's get closer.'

I crept towards the gate, keeping her fingers firmly clasped in mine, and wished we had thought to bring either the mallet or hammer to use as a weapon. I hoped the airman was unconscious or dead.

'They wear British uniforms in case they crash. And they speak perfect English,' hissed Poppy. 'You have to stamp on their feet really hard to see which language they swear in.'

'Well, we know he's a Nazi, don't we? So there's no need to go stamping on his foot, unless we want to.'

A cry cut through the air. It was a note of fury and hate. Feral rage and fear pooled in my stomach. We dropped over the gate and slid through the grass, grateful for the mask of smoke as we edged across the field. A figure loomed in the murk, towering over the fallen silk of the parachute and clutching a pitchfork. With the flames from the plane licking the sky behind him, he looked like the devil himself. I felt a scream build in my throat and willed myself not to turn and run. The figure turned to look at me.

''Ullo. Caught myself a Nazi,' said Burt. 'Makes a nice change from cod.'

* * *

The prisoner sat in the dining room at Tyneford House. He dabbed at a gash on his forehead and vomited into a bucket Mrs Ellsworth had placed beside his boots. His face was smoke-blackened and his eyes bloodshot and furious. He looked incongruous in the sunlit dining room, clad in his tan sheepskin jacket with the small Nazi insignia on the sleeve. The Wedgewood shepherds and shepherdesses watched him with staunch disapproval from the mantelpiece, and I wondered that the falcon and adder grappling on the dusty coat-of-arms didn't cease their fight to leap off and savage him. Burt lingered in the doorway, still clutching the pitchfork. Poppy stood flat against the wall, her hands folded behind her back. Mr Rivers was perfectly relaxed, no more concerned than he would be with a tedious dinner guest. He sat across from the pilot on one of the upright dining room chairs, removing the cartridges from the German's service revolver with practised ease.

'Safer like this, don't you think?' he said pleasantly.

The pilot looked at him with steady hate, and then leant over and retched into the bucket. Mr Rivers pulled Kit's cigarette case from his pocket, offering it to the pilot. He took one and allowed Mr Rivers to light it, without a word of thanks.

'I'm afraid you're going to have to stay here for an hour or two, till they can send an army chap to fetch you,' said Mr Rivers. 'You'll be quite comfortable. No one will hurt you. When you're feeling better, you may have some food.'

The man said nothing, just drew on his cigarette.

'Alice?' said Mr Rivers, without turning to look

at me. 'Will you translate? In case he's ignorant rather than ill-mannered.'

I stepped forward, resting my hand on the back of Mr Rivers' chair.

'Herr Pilot, someone from the army will come. Until then, you must stay here. You will be kindly treated.'

The German sat up and stared at me, his mouth slightly agape.

'You are Austrian.'

'Yes. I was born there.'

He continued to stare, as though disbelieving his own ears. He touched the wound on his forehead, as though unsure if I was a mirage caused by the blow. Swallowing, he licked dry lips and his eyes flicked around the room, meeting for a moment Mr Rivers' cool gaze. Apparently satisfied that he was not dreaming, he focused upon me once again.

'Where in Austria, Fraulein? I am from the Tyrol.'

I smiled despite myself. In all my imaginary meetings with captured Nazis, I had not considered making small talk. I hesitated, deciding whether to answer. I gave a small sigh.

'Vienna. I was born in Vienna.'

He gazed, unseeing, out of the window. *'The most beautiful city in all of the world. Pretty enough for heaven.'*

'Yes,' I agreed, staring at him. He was a Nazi but this man who had fallen out of the sky was speaking in my mother tongue. He understood Vienna. I hated him and yet we shared something. For a moment I was crippled with homesickness. I wanted the army to take their time in coming to collect him, so I could spend the afternoon talking with him about the Café Sperl and listening to the

band in the park of the Belvedere Palace, or which cake was better, the chocolate at the Sacher or the *linzertorte* at Hotel Bristol. In a way, he was more my countryman than Mr Rivers or Mrs Ellsworth or Poppy or Burt could ever be. But he would also burn my father's books in the street and force me to wash faeces off the pavement and make Anna and Julian leave the beautiful apartment in Dorotheegasse and sell the grand piano and—I blinked.

Mr Rivers glanced at me and then at the pilot, but said nothing. His German was passable, but I knew we spoke too fast for him to fully understand.

'*Ah, the mountains of the Tyrol. Snow in winter. Edelweiss in summer,*' said the pilot, letting the ash fall from his cigarette onto the dining room rug. '*I don't suppose I shall see them for a while.*'

'No.'

I replied in English, uncertain if he was asking for my pity, but his face was blank and I realised that he merely thought aloud. He had sandy hair, a snub nose, and his eyes were a greenish blue. Blood congealed on his forehead from the cut and in the sunlight I thought I saw a glimpse of white bone. I felt sick and swallowed. He dabbed feebly at his gash with the compress, the cotton pad congealing brown and red. Unaware of what I did, I found myself stepping forward and reaching for the cloth. Then I stopped dead and shoved my hands into my pocket. I would not touch him. I backed away, feeling my lip curl in horror at the thought of his proximity, and retreated behind Mr Rivers' chair.

The pilot eyed me curiously, intrigued as to my obvious revulsion. I could sense him wondering and, as the fog of pain and shock cleared from his mind, considering why an Austrian girl would be living in an English country house. Any moment and he would know. He was a logical man and first he eliminated other possibilities. He scrutinised my left hand for a wedding ring.

'*Fraulein?*'

I did not reply; I would not help him.

'*He is your husband?*' he asked, nodding towards Mr Rivers.

I flushed and shook my head.

He gave a tiny, satisfied nod. Then there was only one reason for my presence. I heard him say the word in his mind. *Jew.* I heard it as loud as if he had shouted, '*She lives here in exile because she is a Jew.*' It would have been better if he had spoken it. His silent condemnation enraged me. How dare he? He was the traitor. He was the one who had chased me through the fields like a run-rabbit as he fired upon me with his machine-gun and made the woodland floor leap with bullets and the sheep on the meadow explode with a belly full of blood. He silenced my mother's singing and her letters, kept my sister far away across the sea, and he trapped my father inside the viola. He chased me all the way from Austria across the ridge of green English hills and now sat here in the sunlit room taunting me. I read hatred in his silence. He said nothing, so I heard everything. I crossed the room again, but this time I did not flinch from touching him. I drew my arm back and hit him across the face. I felt his jaw crack, all the way up my arm. My palm stung and I was glad. His hand went to his cheek, a streak of red on his fingertips where my thumbnail had caught his skin. No one spoke. Not Mr Rivers. Not Poppy or Burt. The pilot looked at me in surprise.

'You shot at me,' I shouted. *'You.'*

He shook his head. *'No, Fraulein. I did not shoot you.'*

'It was you. I know it was you.'

I trembled, whether from anger or remembered fear I neither knew nor cared. Mr Rivers grabbed my wrist to steady me, but I shook him away. I was entitled to a moment of crazed fury. There was a fleck of blood under my nail. Nazi blood, the same colour as any other. In my dreams I'd imagined them to bleed black like witches. I felt the violence beneath my skin, and the hair on my arms prickled. I thought of the night fox with his hackles raised in the dark, and knew that a savage part of me wanted to kill this man. Wanted to bite and tear and claw and bleed him more than a petty thumbnail scratch. I walked out of the room and slammed the door shut, leaning for a second against it, and listened to the hammer and thud of my own heart and the hushed voices on the other side.

I lay in the semi-darkness of my attic room, cradling the battered viola case and did not move until I heard the rumble of tyres on the gravel driveway below. I listened for the sound of boots on stone and, a few minutes later, the snarl of the engine as the army truck drove away, and I knew he was gone.

CHAPTER TWENTY-FOUR

'We thank you kindly for not smoking in the bedrooms.'

The WAAFs arrived in March with the thaw. They came as the daffodils erupted on the banks in golden clouds and the tart spring wind carried the scent of green things. I watched from my bedroom window as they clattered across the drive in a hurry of suitcases, woollen stockings and mouths painted Woolworths red. They chattered and smoked and filled the hall with unrepressed laughter and whispered confidences. I came down to greet them, noticed the fragrance of 'ashes of roses' mingling with too much cheap violet perfume and smiled. We'd been stupid with grief for too long, numbed by winter cold and unhappiness. The house needed these girls with their romances, pencilled eyebrows and cheerful noise. The girls hushed as they saw me. I shook hands with each in turn. 'Hullo. I'm Alice Land. If you need anything at all, you've only to ask me or Mrs Ellsworth.'

The housekeeper had retreated in annoyance into her kitchen, irritated by the war forcing upon us more guests than we had bedrooms for, but I knew she would relent in the face of all the happy chatter. There were fifteen girls and I'd had to squeeze four into each of the guest rooms and, for the first time since I'd been at Tyneford, all the maids' rooms were full. All except my little attic. As I'd gone up to put fresh sheets on the bed and air the room, I'd realised that I couldn't bear anyone else to sleep there. The WAAF girls could manage perfectly well and I decided they would probably prefer to share rooms in the cold house. Spring always arrived late to Tyneford, and despite the blossom dusting the hedgerows like duckling down, the wind hissed through the gaps in the brickwork and, without coal to keep them going, the log fires stuttered into ash after dark. A layer of ice coated the inside of the windows most mornings. I shepherded the girls upstairs, enjoying the bustle of noise and footsteps. As I ushered the last few into Kit's old room, I heard whispers behind me and a giggle. A girl called Maureen had seized the photograph resting on the dresser.

'He's a dish,' she said, admiring the picture of Kit. 'When's he home on leave?'

'Bet he's a smasher in uniform,' said Sandra, a stout girl with brown eyes and mousy hair dressed in a permanent wave.

I resisted the urge to tear the picture out of their hands. 'He won't be coming home. And if Mr Rivers is a bit short with you, well, that's why.'

Maureen replaced the photograph and the chatter dulled for a moment. She gave a small sigh that sounded almost like disappointment.

'That's a right shame,' murmured Sandra, struck by the waste of such a handsome young man and clearly feeling cheated out of a romance.

'Yes. Every woman fell in love with Kit,' I said, noticing with a smile that they still did. 'It'll be a squeeze in here, but I'm sure you'll manage. Dinner will be served at seven in the kitchen. Please don't be late. And if you would give me your ration books, Mrs Ellsworth will take care of them.'

The girls handed me beige ration books with

military obedience, and then those who did not have to get ready for their shift sprawled across the double bed and the low camp cots set out on the floor.

'And I must ask you not to smoke in the bedrooms.'

They promised me most politely that they wouldn't dream of it, and I retreated to the doorway and watched as they set to, making up their faces and thumbing through Diana's old copies of *Vogue* and this month's *Woman's Own* with eager shrieks. I saw Margot and me laughing as we prepared for a party, me eyeing her enviously as she slipped into gorgeous lace underwear or a pair of Anna's handmade high-heeled shoes, neither of which would have fitted me. Withdrawing, I closed the door and made my way downstairs. As I buttoned up my coat, ready to walk down to the farm, Mr Wrexham appeared in the hall, holding out a large brown package.

'This arrived in this morning's post. From America, I believe, Miss Land,' he announced, as delighted as if he had fetched it from California himself.

I opened the parcel to reveal a large cardboard box, stuffed with presents all carefully wrapped in shredded newspaper. I reached in and pulled out a vast bar of Hershey's milk chocolate. Attached to the silver paper was a letter. Discarding the chocolate, I tore open the envelope.

Darling Bean,

I hope this package reaches you. We hear nothing in our newspapers except how terrible things are in England. Our newsmen have you starving in the streets with no stockings and nothing to eat but radishes and potatoes and worst of all—no music! I hope you like the records (if they've reached you unbroken). I am sure you said that Mr Rivers had a gramophone. This music is all the rage here. All the young things dance to it (and old things too—no one can help it)—it's called 'Jitterbugging'. It's not Dvorak or Mozart or Strauss but do you know?—it's swell. And you remember little Jan Tibor? Well, he's here in America and he's a conductor. He's gaining a reputation. I've put in his first recording—he was always sweet on you, he'd like to think of you listening.

And, I was not sure whether to send it or not, but I found in a second-hand record store one of Anna's recordings, La Traviata *with the Vienna Philharmonic.*

I delved inside the parcel, drawing out several records. In a plain cardboard wrapper, I discovered Anna's. I couldn't listen to it any more than I could read the novel inside the viola but I was glad Margot had sent it. One day, I would listen. My rummaging was interrupted by excited voices. I glanced around and saw half a dozen of the WAAF girls dressed in their uniforms, all ready to go on shift.

'Oh! Records! From America,' said Sandra, actually jumping from foot to foot, as she saw the package lying on the table.

'May I?' asked Maureen, reaching for the box.

'Of course.' I smiled at her and she pulled out a record.

'Glenn Miller, Billie Holiday and, oh dear, this one's broken.'

I took it from her, holding the two snapped sides together so as to read the label: 'My sister and I'.

'Never mind,' said Sandra. 'It's the Tommy Dorsey Orchestra with Frank Sinatra I want to hear. And look, it's perfect.'

She held up another for me to admire.

'Can't we have a dance here?' asked one of the girls.

'Oh yes, please,' added Maureen and Sandra, their faces shiny with hope.

I paused, glancing at Mr Wrexham, both of us wondering what Mr Rivers would say. There was a cry of delight and then an awed hush fell over the assembled girls as Sandra pulled a small cardboard tube from the box.

'It's Elizabeth Arden,' she whispered, in reverent tones. 'Cherry red.'

'There's been none in England for two years,' murmured Maureen, and for an awful moment I thought she was going to cry.

'Come on,' said Sandra, fixing me with a hard stare. 'You simply must have a party now.'

* * *

The WAAF girls were right—we ought to hold a dance at the house. There had been more laughter and brightness in a single morning in their presence than through the entire winter. Mr Rivers might grumble but it would do him good. And all those new things did deserve a bit of a celebration. Margot had even sent me four pairs of nylon stockings and a new set of silk underwear, all wrapped up in cream tissue paper. The paper was almost as precious as the luxuries themselves—packing paper, even in the finest stores, was now quite illegal. Last month Mrs Ellsworth caught the bus back from Wareham holding two kippers by their tails, having forgotten to take her own newspaper to wrap them in.

I finished Margot's letter and had half-memorised it before I left to clean out the hens. As I sprinkled fresh straw around the clucking bantams, I recited it in my mind.

Playing makes worrying about Anna and Julian a little easier. I imagine that I'm playing for them. That you are all in the front row in some concert hall here in California or else we're at Frau Finkelstein's again and I'm giving a recital as you sit squeezed together on one of her overstuffed pink couches. The great-aunts are there too and trying to disapprove of my performing in public, but then, when I finish the Schubert, I look at Gretta and see she's wiping a surreptitious tear from her long nose. Everything I play, I play for Anna and Julian. I know it's nonsense but I imagine that they can hear me somehow, even if it's only in their dreams. One day I shall play for you all in a great concert hall. When the British have won the war and we are all back in Austria again, I shall play at the Opera House. You will all be seated in a box, Anna in her arctic fox fur, pretty as ever, and Julian will be white haired and handsome, and you, Elise, shall lead the standing ovation! It will all be grand, and afterwards we'll go to the Sacher for dinner and neither you nor Anna will tell me the bits I played wrong. For now, my only audience is Wolfie. The dog sits beside me while I play—if I shut him outside for a minute he whines and thuds the door with his nose until I let him in. I'm sure it's because I named him after Mozart. I don't believe that golden retrievers are music lovers in general.

I hummed snatches of *The Magic Flute* to the cockerel, and tried to imagine returning to Vienna. I was glad that playing the viola helped Margot. I wore my worry like an old woollen jumper; it scratched and irked me, but I pulled it on every morning nonetheless, finding it almost comforting in its familiarity. I did my best to imagine being without it, but I couldn't.

It was the final lines of Margot's letter that I heard over and over again. I tried not to think about them, to think of something, anything, else, but they echoed inside me like a distant voice on the wireless.

Write soon, my darling. And kiss your Mr Rivers for me.

Kiss your Mr Rivers . . . your Mr Rivers. Margot was quite wrong. He was not my Mr Rivers. He was not anybody's. I would not pass along my sister's love to him like one would to a father. But she did not mean like a father.

After feeding the chickens, I trudged through the mud-steeped ground leading to the eweleaze. The rams had served the ewes during the winter and I expected the first lambs at the beginning of April. On the high ground, patches of frost lingered in the shade and a bank of primroses lay half-buried in ice. I hastened up the slope, grateful to be wearing my new slacks. Mrs Ellsworth had run them up for me to wear while working outside, and they were so much more practical than skirts or frocks. The material had been recycled from Kit's old sailing trousers and lined with one of his silk shirts. Mrs Ellsworth had ceased to complain at my perceived lack of sentimentality, finally throwing herself into the 'make-do-and-mend' spirit with religious fervour. She listened to the *Kitchen Front* broadcasts on the wireless every morning without exception, and for a fortnight she insisted on grinding up the eggshells so as to recycle the grit for the chickens to peck at, until I persuaded her that there was no shortage of either grit or dirt in the countryside.

As I reached the top of the hill, Mr Rivers was already stuffing hay into slotted feed bins as sheep milled around him, bleating and pawing at the frozen ground. The ewes were big with lambs, and grunted with the effort of moving, grateful to tear at mouthfuls of hay. Mr Rivers surveyed them critically.

'Not long now,' he said.

'No. About a month. Maybe less for the pure-bred Dorsets.'

He nodded and then pointed to a hunched shape along the ridge. 'Lost one in the night. Bloody dogs. From the army camp, I expect. Must have been scared off or it would have spoilt the lot. Bloody lucky really. The other girls seem all right. Still, she was having triplets. Criminal waste.'

A ewe nibbled my fingers, hungry for salt. I pushed her away and started to refill the salt lick container, trying not to look at the mauled carcass sprawled twenty yards away.

'Your sister sent you a package?'

I nodded. 'Yes. And a letter.'

'Any news?'

'Not really. This and that. And she sends you her–' I paused, reaching for the right word. *Regards*. Far too cold. *Best greetings*. Not even decent English. Ought I to kiss him from her? Margot was always so good at this. A kiss bestowed by her would be the perfect blend of tenderness and sisterly gratitude. I realised that I was colouring with embarrassment, and Mr Rivers studied me with an odd expression.

'Are you all right?' he asked.

'Yes. Yes. Margot sends you her . . . best.'

'And send her my warmest regards when you reply.'

Warmest regards. Of course, that was the correct expression.

'Yes, I shall,' I said, but I was thinking that if I ever kissed Mr Rivers, I wanted it to be from me, not my sister. I seized the container of salt and turned away so that he would not see my face.

'Art's got hold of some paint. I'm going to patch the barn this morning,' continued Mr Rivers, helping me pour the salt crystals.

'I'll help, just as soon as I've checked the fence to see how the dog got in. I might walk down to the army camp, have a word.'

He gave a curt nod and then tucked my scarf back into my coat from where it had come loose, and brushed stray flecks of salt off the wool and from my cheeks. His fingertips were coarse on my skin.

'There,' he said with a smile, satisfied.

We'd fallen into an easy rhythm over the last months, working contentedly side-by-side. We didn't chatter like the WAAF girls, or even talk as I used to with Kit. In fact we were mainly silent, but I liked his company. I liked it better than my own. He started to walk down the hill.

'Don't be long,' he called, 'I shall be glad of your help. And don't let those army buggers give you any gyp.'

I laughed. 'Don't worry. I shan't. And Daniel, I think we ought to have a dance up at the house. For the WAAF girls. It's terribly dull here for them. I shall invite some of the "army buggers" too.'

Mr Rivers smiled. 'Whatever you want, Alice.'

* * *

That afternoon, I felt rather pleased with myself. The officers at Lulcombe camp were delighted to be invited to a dance the following week. They also promised to discover the offending dog and shoot it. I felt no regret for the doomed animal, not after seeing the mutilated ewe—meat was scarce enough without such wanton waste. I hurried back to the house to collect my and Mr Rivers' lunch as usual. The wind had picked up and the daffodils trembled beneath the lime avenue, while the taut barbed wire fence hummed a melancholy tune. My skin had turned red, battered by the cold, and I was looking forward to the prospect of warming myself by the kitchen range for a few minutes before venturing out on the windswept hill in search of Mr Rivers. I paused in the hall, unfastening my gloves, when I noticed one of the WAAF girls standing on the bottom stair, watching me. I hadn't seen her among the others this morning, and I turned to her with a friendly smile, holding out my hand.

'Hullo,' I said. 'Alice Land.'

'Yes. I know who you are,' she said.

Instantly, I lowered my hand. 'Juno.'

'Yes. I didn't think you'd be terribly pleased to see me.'

I didn't reply. She looked well, dressed in her smart green uniform, strawberry blonde curls slick beneath her little cap. I despised her: elegant, perfectly at ease and superior. Then, very deliberately, she stepped down from the bottom stair. Since she was a good few inches shorter than me, when she spoke she was forced to look up at me.

'I am sorry,' she said. 'Just so sorry about Kit. It's simply too awful. I don't know how you bear it.'

'Thank you.'

She gazed up at me with violet eyes, a shade softer than her sister's, and I realised that they brimmed with water.

'I don't want your tears,' I said.

'Oh they're not for you,' said Juno. 'Just because you got him, doesn't mean the rest of us didn't care frightfully about him too.'

Her snappish reproof made me dislike her a little less.

'Yes. You're quite right. I'm sorry,' I said.

'No. Don't be.' She sat down on the step. 'I joined the WAAFs after Kit died. Felt so helpless sitting at home, listening to Diana complain about not having enough sugar in her tea.'

I snorted. 'Yes. I can imagine, joining up would seem better than that.'

To my surprise, Juno laughed. 'I'm not like her, you know. I realise it probably seemed that way. Diana's a cow to everyone.'

Before I could reply, a huddle of WAAFs burst into the hallway, sweeping Juno up in their midst.

‘Come on up and see where we’re staying! It’s the most amazing old place.’

I watched them lead her away. Juno giving no indication of ever having been at Tyneford before and allowed the other girls to revel in the pleasure of showing round the newcomer. She gave suitable murmurs of excitement.

‘I’m afraid all the good beds have been bagged,’ confided a black-haired girl, ‘so you’ll have to sleep on a put-you-up.’

To my amazement, Juno made no complaint.

* * *

After a week, I had almost forgotten that I had known Juno before. The war had reversed our roles once again, and she slotted into the new ways at the house with apparent ease. It had taken Mr Rivers two days to recognise her, and when he did, it was without pleasure or grace.

‘Oh it’s you,’ he remarked, wandering into the kitchen in his work clothes one evening as the girls ate spam hash around the large table. A battery of forks were lowered, as fifteen pairs of eyes turned to gaze at him. Mr Rivers did not notice, and continued to frown at Juno. ‘Don’t bring your aunt up to the house. I’ll only shout at her again.’

Juno shook her curls. ‘No, Mr Rivers. My aunt doesn’t know I’m here.’

I believed her. I rather suspected that the other WAAFs had no idea that it was Juno’s aunt who owned the splendid castle over the hill. Only the day before I had overhead her telling Sandra that she needed ‘the lav’ rather than ‘the loo’. From time to time I might doubt the outcome of the war, but I knew with utter certainty that the naming of the water closet was the most important marker of class among British women. Juno, I realised, wished to cast off her aristocratic heritage and appear lower class.

On Saturday it was Juno and Poppy who helped Mrs Ellsworth and me prepare the house for the dance. We pushed the furniture against the walls and stacked the more fragile chairs in the morning room. Juno wrapped the netsuke and china bells in rags for safekeeping. Poppy put on the gramophone to 'get us in the party spirit' but really it was so that we didn't have to talk. All of us remembered the last party in these rooms and none of us wished to discuss it, so we listened to the loud, honeyed songs of Cole Porter. Poppy chewed her scarlet plaits and Juno sniffed. In a minute someone was going to cry. I rolled my eyes.

'That's it. No more maudlin. We're getting drunk,' I declared.

I marched over to Juno, took the silver bell out of her hand and rang it with enthusiasm. A few minutes later the old butler appeared, looking a little startled. We hardly ever rang any more, and he had clearly been taken by surprise, for although his expression remained inscrutable, there was a tiny smudge of polish on his nose.

'Wrexham. Could you bring us a bottle of—I don't know? What do you like?'

'Gin and orange?' suggested Juno.

'No,' I said firmly. 'You might be trying to fit in or become a socialist or something, but this is not a public bar. Besides, we don't have any orange. Not even the artificial kind.'

'Pink gin,' said Poppy.

'Yes. What a good idea. Three cocktail glasses, please,' I said.

'There's no ice, miss,' said Mr Wrexham.

'I know that. It doesn't matter. We're going to get sloshed.'

'Very good, miss,' replied the butler, and withdrew.

Half an hour later we were giggling like old chums and taking it in turns to swing in pairs around the stacked chairs. I clapped and wiggled in time as Juno and Poppy danced across the threadbare Persian rug, Juno playing the man and Poppy kicking her heels with deft clicks. I laughed, cheering them on as Poppy leant back in Juno's arms, her face as grave as a rabbi at a funeral. The music stuttered into silence, and the girls turned to me. 'Find another. Stick it on, quickly,' said Juno.

'Something romantic,' called Poppy.

'All right, all right.'

I drained my cocktail glass, and thumbed through the other records.

'This one. It has to be this one,' I announced, putting the vinyl on the turntable, and setting the gramophone needle. '"Amapola (Pretty Little Poppy)".'

There was a crackle, then Jimmy Dorsey's orchestra began to play a lilting dance and, after exchanging a glance, Juno and Poppy started to tango across the drawing room. I leant against the wall, keeping out of their way and giggled as Juno caught the simple lyrics and began to croon them to Poppy, '*Amapola, the pretty little poppy . . . must copy its endearing charm from you.*'

My shoulders shook with laughter and I clapped them on as the beat changed and their tango fell apart.

'Switch!' called Poppy, and the two girls traded places, with Juno now dancing the girl's part as they shuffled into a ragged swing.

As I watched them dancing, I couldn't help remembering the outrage Kit and I had caused when we'd waltzed together in this very room. The dinner suit I had worn that night remained untouched in Kit's old wardrobe. It was the one item I would not give up to 'make-do-and-mend'. Juno kissed Poppy's cheek, and wound her long hair around her wrist with mock solemnity. No society matron would scowl at the two of them dancing—it was schoolgirl fun. In Vienna, I had taken my first waltz lessons with Margot; the great-aunts instructing us while Anna played the piano and rolled her eyes, biting her lip so that she didn't laugh every time I stamped on Margot's toes.

'You seem far away,' said a male voice.

I turned and saw Mr Rivers standing beside me.

'They look like they're having fun,' he said, with a smile. 'Shall we? Or do you also only dance with girls?'

'I suppose I could make an exception.'

I allowed him to lead me onto the woollen rug, which formed the centre of the dance floor. He placed my arms around his neck and we started to dance. I had never danced with him before and, having kicked my shoes off some half hour earlier, it struck me once more that Mr Rivers was very tall.

'If we're to do this again, we shall have to find you some heels,' he said, resting his chin on the top of my head.

We swayed in easy silence; he was a good partner, steering me firmly, his hand resting on the small of my back. Unfortunately, I was dizzy with gin and I tripped over the edge of the rug, stumbling into him.

'I thought Viennese girls were supposed to be good at this,' he teased.

I frowned. 'Yes, well. I've had a good deal of gin and not much practice.'

The music finished and we paused in the middle of the drawing room. I began to step away from him but he stopped me, keeping my arms locked around him. Without the music, it was not a dance but an embrace. I rested against him, feeling the warmth of his body and the steady rise and fall of his chest. His chin was covered in only the barest shadow and I realised with relief that he was allowing Mr Wrexham to shave him once again. I allowed my cheek to rest against him. I glanced over at Poppy and Juno and saw that they lingered by the gramophone, conscientiously studying the records and trying not to notice us.

'Shall we try a waltz next?' he asked. 'I'm old fashioned.'

'No,' I said too quickly and flushed.

The last waltz had been with Kit.

For a moment, nobody spoke. Mr Rivers looked down at me, but I could not tell whether he was angry or just sad.

'Let's try another of the American records. I want to jitterbug,' said Poppy. 'Get some practice before the others arrive.'

Mr Rivers frowned, and this time when I moved away he did not stop me.

'I don't even know what that is,' he complained.

'It's like a swing but sort of made up,' said Juno. 'We have to try it. It's very modern.'

‘And you can’t possibly not join in because Juno can’t partner both of us at once,’ said Poppy, placing her hands on her hips and giving him an owlish stare, remarkably like Mrs Ellsworth’s.

Mr Rivers’ grim expression broke into a smile. He laughed and shook his head. ‘No of course not. Well. Let’s have at it then.’

Poppy sloshed a good slug of gin and a dash of bitters into my empty glass and handed it to Mr Rivers.

‘Think you’d better have this first. Make it a good deal easier, I expect,’ she said.

I thought he was going to object, but Mr Rivers shrugged and downed the gin all at once with barely a shudder. I’d forgotten how much he drank. Poppy refilled the glass. He drained it again.

‘Now you won’t notice when Elise gets it wrong and steps on your toes,’ she said with approval.

Mr Rivers shook his head. ‘No, but she might notice if I stand on hers.’ He turned to me. ‘Can we not find you some shoes?’

‘Why don’t you take yours off too?’ I asked. ‘Then you won’t be so horribly tall.’

He hesitated, as though considering the propriety of such a request, and then sat down on the edge of the sofa and removed his brogues, revealing a pair of much darned grey socks. Juno wound up the gramophone and the music started to growl ‘A Chicken Ain’t Nothin’ But a Bird’. Mr Rivers stared at me for a second, and then pulled me into a swing. He swung me round and round and I kicked up my heels, shrieking with laughter, trying not to collide with Poppy and Juno. We twisted and shook, and I giggled and slid across the polished floorboards in my stockings while

Cab Calloway crooned in the corner: *'a chicken's a popular bird . . . you can boil it roast it broil it cook it in a pan or a pot, eat it with potatoes, rice or tomatoes but a chicken is still what you got . . .'*

'Oh God,' called Poppy, breathless from dancing, 'I wish I'd got a chicken. And I don't mind how you cook it.'

'Yes, it's making me hungry,' complained Juno. 'I can't concentrate on jitterbugging. I can only think about roast chicken.'

I frowned, rubbing at the stitch in my side. 'Margot really shouldn't have sent us this one at all—not unless she was going to post an actual chicken at the same time. Though, I did think that one of the cockerels has been looking a bit seedy the last few days. If he gets worse—'

Mr Rivers seized my hand and swung me round again. His face glowed from alcohol and exercise and I saw that he was happy. I didn't want the music to stop. I wanted it to keep on playing its tunes, however silly, and I wanted Mr Rivers to keep on smiling. I hadn't seen him laugh like this since before. I danced towards the gramophone, pulling him with me, so that he objected, 'Who's leading whom?' and tried to haul me back towards the far end of the room, making me turn and turn until I grew dizzy and saw colours blur and flash.

'No. The music mustn't stop,' I cried, a frantic note in my voice, and reached for the gramophone handle.

I knew if it stopped, the spell would be broken and we would return to our regular dreary selves. As long as the music played, he would be happy and we wouldn't think, only drink and laugh and dance.

*   *   *

I lay in bed, humming Cole Porter and Vera Lynn and Tommy Dorsey. The party had been a huge success. Even Wrexham's foot had started tapping as he hovered in the hallway, guarding the refreshment table from the hungry fingers of flushed dancers. He actually smiled as he reproved Maureen and Sandra with a 'may I assist you?' as they reached for the spam fritters without serving spoons. I danced all night since there were not enough girls to partner the men. I had intended to be terribly grown-up and act as a sort of chaperone to the WAAFs, but the gin and laughter made me forget all my good intentions. It seemed churlish to refuse the barrage of sweet-faced young men who begged for a dance. There were so few girls that frequently I did not make it to the end of a song before switching partners halfway across the floor. No one seemed to mind, and the drawing room and panelled hall echoed with music and friendly shouts of 'may I cut in?' and the pounding of boots on the parquet floor. Of course none of us knew then that this was the last party at Tyneford House. Had we known, it would have spoilt our jitterbugging and lessened the laughter, but we did not so the house reverberated with joyful clatter and the lights beamed behind the blackouts.

I only danced one number with Mr Rivers that night, but I knew he watched me and I was glad. He gallantly refused to dance again, not wanting to deprive any soldier of a partner, so patrolled the floor, offering glasses of burgundy and port, which most of them had not tasted for years. Wherever he was—discussing Churchill with the commanding officer, the shortage of boots with a second lieutenant, or lingering beside the fireplace—I knew he looked for me among the dancers. I was easy to find: the men were a sea of khaki and most of the girls elected to wear their smart WAAF green, so I rather stood out in my new pink cashmere and scarlet lipstick. The sweater now lay, neatly folded, on the wicker bedroom chair. It was the first day since the war began and Kit had died that I had been almost happy. It was fleeting and, even while I laughed, I knew the feeling could not last. But during those hours, I enjoyed moments of pleasure strung together like beads along a string, so that they formed something like happiness. It was neither content nor ease, but it was something and I was glad.

After the last revellers left for Lulcombe and I had finally gone up the stairs to bed, I lingered on the landing, listening to the bass chime of the grandfather clock resonate midnight through the now empty hall. I found myself remembering that other clock, ringing out in the Vienna apartment all those years ago. Mr Rivers joined me and we stood together in silence, listening until the bells ceased and the only sound was the steady tick-tick of the minute hand, the heartbeat of the old house. I reached for his hand and he took mine between his fingers, raising it to his lips, brushing my knuckles briefly. He stepped towards me and opened his mouth, and my own heart hammered as I waited for him to speak. But then he said nothing. He only leant forwards, tucking a stray curl behind my ear and stooped to kiss me on the cheek. I half turned, and he caught the soft edge of my mouth. When he straightened, his eyes black in the darkness, I saw a tiny smudge of crimson in the corner of his mouth. My lipstick. Cherry red. Margot's gift. I had kissed him after all, and not from her.

That night I did not dream. I did not see pale faces in the dark. I dreamt of neither Anna nor Kit. I only slept.

*   *   *

Voices outside my bedroom. A muffled shout and a cry. I woke suddenly and reeled up in bed, lost for a moment. The blackouts were down and I could not tell whether it was night or day. Shouts drifted down the stairs and hurried footsteps drummed outside my door. I darted out of bed and onto the landing in my faded cotton pyjamas. Rubbing the sleep from my eyes, I saw WAAF girls scurrying in their nighties and dressing gowns, curlers tangled in their hair. I was bleary and dazed, my head throbbing from the gin, and I blinked and blinked until I realised it was not my vision that was blurred but smoke billowing down the stairs. I sprinted across the landing and hammered on Mr Rivers' door.

'Mr Rivers! Daniel! Wake up. Fire.'

Not waiting for him to open it, I rushed inside. He was already half out of bed and pushed past me onto the landing teeming with girls.

'Downstairs!' he bellowed. 'All of you, outside.'

The girls stopped scurrying, turning to stare at him.

'Now. Out.'

They didn't wait to be told again, and in a flap of dressing gowns and a thump-thump of bedroom slippers they hurried down the stairs and filed out through the porch. Excited chatter drifted in through the vast front door. I didn't follow them, but headed up the narrow steps at the far end of the landing that led up to the servants' attic. Thick smoke streamed down, floating into the great hall, filling it with dark clouds, black as any storm. Through the shouts and the fog, I was dimly aware of Wrexham appearing in the hall below and calling up to Mr Rivers. I had only one thought: the viola. It lay upstairs besieged by fire. It must not burn. I'd lost Kit. Anna and Julian had disappeared into silence. The novel in the viola was all I had left and I would not lose it. The words would not burn before being read.

As the two men debated what was to be done, I slipped up the attic stairs, unseen. The smoke was thicker than the densest sea fog and my eyes streamed, hot tears coating my cheeks. I reached into my pocket and pulled out a grimy handkerchief, placing it in front of my mouth and nose, breathing in rasps, trying not to choke. In a second, I was utterly disorientated. I fumbled in total darkness like a blind man. I had to go on. I had to find the viola. In my mind, I heard it calling to me. It sang with Margot's distinctive tone but it sang Anna's melody, *Für Elise.* The music trickled along the narrow landing, mingling with the smoke-haze so I imagined that it was music I saw drifting in the darkness. *Elise.* My father called out to me. He always fretted about losing a manuscript. We teased him for writing on yellow copy paper and the stash of pages locked in the desk drawer but he was right—oh he was right and I had failed him. *Elise!* His voice grew stronger now. I was close. The attic door loomed out of the smoke. I reached out to touch the door handle but hands wrenched me back. Strong arms grabbed me and hoisted me up. I sprawled over a set of broad shoulders. I kicked and screamed and sobbed but I was carried away from the small wooden door and away from the viola. *Elise. Elise.* The voice grew louder. I yelled and struggled but I was blinded by smoke. I wanted to see. Hands laid me down on the ground. The smoke thinned. I sat up and found myself cradled in Mr Rivers' arms.

'Alice,' he said, half shouting. 'What the hell were you thinking?'

His face was red with rage and terror. I pushed him away with all my strength and escaped back to the attic stairs. He caught me and gripped my arms.

'Alice! What is it? What are you doing?'

'The viola.'

I coughed and choked, spitting black stuff onto the floor.

'My father. His last novel. In the viola.' I twisted in his arms and looked into the tight face gazing down at me. 'I have to save it.'

Mr Rivers studied me for a second, then he gave a nod and he was gone. I scrambled after him but Mr Wrexham blocked my way.

'Miss Land, please. If it is possible, he will find it.'

For a moment I toyed with the idea of pushing aside the old butler, but I leant back against the wall, sliding down to sit on the floor. In the distance, I heard the church bells ringing. *Invasion! Fire! Fire!* I saw villagers leap from their beds, ready to hurry down to the shore with broom-bayonets, only to see the manor ablaze. I screwed my eyes shut and willed his safe return.

'He mustn't be hurt. I should have gone,' I said,

covering my face with my hands.

'The master will be careful,' replied Mr Wrexham, trying to chivvy me onto my feet. 'We should wait outside. It's not safe here.'

I wrenched away. 'I won't go without him. Leave if you like.'

The butler coughed not with smoke but annoyance, and settled down beside me. We waited for days. Years. A hundred. Then a thousand more. Smoke. Then footsteps. Coughing and choking. Mr Rivers half ran, half fell down the stairs. He clutched the viola case.

*   *   *

The fire was out before the engine arrived from Dorchester. The WAAFs gathered in excited huddles on the lawn, drinking cups of tea in the dark and chattering to the firemen who, their conventional services not required, dedicated themselves to the soothing of maidens' nerves.

Mr Rivers and I remained alone in the house. I told him about the novel in the viola. He listened in silence, his brow creased with concentration. I sat with the case in my lap, stroking the battered leather. When I had finished, he reached for it, glancing to me for permission. I nodded and he unfastened the clasp, opening the small, coffin-shaped case to reveal the rosewood viola. He picked it up, holding it as carefully as a newborn chick, weighing it in his hands.

'So it's inside?' he asked.

'Yes.'

'And you've never tried to take it out?'

'I thought about it, but I'd have to break the

viola.'

We huddled in the drawing room, wrapped in horsehair blankets and through an illicit hole in the blackouts watched dawn creep up over the hills. Mr Rivers leant forwards and brushed my face with his fingertips.

'You've singed your eyelashes,' he observed, his voice harbouring only the faintest tinge of accusation.

'They'll grow back,' I said with a shrug and edged closer towards him.'What's the novel about?' he asked, gesturing to the viola.

I smiled. 'I have no idea. I often wonder. I like to believe that it has a happy ending.'

CHAPTER TWENTY-FIVE

I LIVE NOT WHERE I LOVE

The following day those WAAFs who weren't on the morning shift bustled around in droves, organised into cleaning battalions by Mrs Ellsworth. They listened with bowed heads to her battery of scolding, none admitting who had disobeyed the neat signs entreating 'no smoking in the bedrooms' and tossed a careless cigarette into the wastepaper basket. Hammering came from the roof as Art dangled from a ladder, trying to shore up the new hole. The girls trudged around in filthy overalls, clutching pails of brown water, hardly daring to hum last night's tunes under their breath. A thin layer of ash and soot like black snow coated the great hall and landing, streaked the panelling and smattered the tops of the dado rails. The paintings in the hallway had aged a hundred years and stared out through Tudor gloom. I didn't offer to help with the clean-up but closed the door to my bedroom and settled down at the desk.

Ever since the last night in Vienna I had hoarded Julian's novel, but after the fire I resolved on telling Margot about it. Nearly losing the viola frightened me. If it had been destroyed, I knew that she would never forgive me.

I can only say that I'm sorry. I know I've been selfish, but perhaps if you are honest you'll see that you would have done the same thing.

On my last night in Vienna, Julian gave me the carbon copy of his latest novel, hidden inside your old viola. I've kept it safe. I've not read it, I promise. I always thought that Julian would take it out and read it to us himself, and it would be like old times. Anna would laugh in the right places, while you and I would laugh a little in the wrong ones, and he'd huff and grumble and nothing would have changed.

But last night there was a fire. Mr Rivers saved the viola. The novel is still inside. But, if it had gone without either of us reading it, without your knowing about its existence, I knew, well, I knew that you would not forgive me.

So, I'm telling you now and I hope you will not be too angry. I wanted something that was mine and no one else's. You have Robert, and whatever you think, he is not my Mr Rivers. Please don't write straight away but wait a little and try to understand.

I sealed the envelope and took it downstairs to place on the tray in the hall. I wondered how long it would take for the letter to reach her. Weeks. Months. I might have to wait half a year for her reply. I was apprehensive of her anger. Margot did not rage but nurtured her resentment. When we were children, she had a doll with real hair which I'd trimmed, believing it would grow back. Margot had refused to utter a single word to me for an entire fortnight. As Margot entered adolescence her silences lengthened. When I'd dared describe Robert as 'a pleasant young man' (it being our sisterly code for dull) her quiet anger had taken six weeks to subside. She'd only allowed me to be a bridesmaid when Anna intervened. I dreaded to think how long her silence would last over this.

* * *

Despite the fire, more WAAFs arrived to stay at the hall. There was no use in objecting or saying that we had nowhere to put them. Any complaint might lead to the house being requisitioned, and we'd already heard the horror stories from Juno of statues at Lulcombe daubed with lewd graffiti, stucco ceilings ruined by dry rot and pistol shot. The ancient beech avenue had been felled for firewood during the arctic January, despite Lady Vernon's impassioned pleas. There was even talk of her being made to surrender the Dower House. So we made not a word of complaint, but quietly removed the furniture from the dining room, stored it in the rapidly emptying wine cellar, and turned the room into a makeshift dormitory. The girls who slept there actually felt themselves quite fortunate since, unlike the bedrooms, it possessed a radiator.

By summer the house teemed with WAAFs and Mrs Ellsworth was forced to surrender a portion of her kitchen to a forces cook, while the ancient servants' hall was brought into use as a cafeteria. Mrs Ellsworth wandered through the house for several days clucking miserably, 'I don't know if I'm living in a boarding school or a barracks.' Yet the girls were in general so gay and good-natured that they soon won her round—sharing homemade cures for dressing corns, or lighting the kitchen boiler at four on their way out for the early shift, so that for the first time in years Mrs Ellsworth could laze till dawn. They even lent her a spare tin hat to use as a most effective bathing cap. Gaggles of them marching down to Lulcombe camp for duty was a thrice-daily sight. Burt left shining mackerel in baskets for two dozen breakfasts, and Mr Wrexham offered tips on the buffing of endless black shoes. Soon we were perfectly accustomed to their presence, and could not imagine life being different.

I watched the weeks and then the months slip by without a letter from Margot. Every morning and afternoon I checked the tray in the hall for letters. It was always overflowing with post for the WAAFs but there was never anything for me. My unease steadily grew. Was she too irate to even write? Was she punishing me with silence? Then, one day in early June, just as the buttercups were starting to spill across the meadows, a letter arrived from California. Sitting on the terrace in the morning sunshine, I tore open the envelope and for a moment my heart soared—she was not angry—and then I saw the date, '6th March, 1941'. My own letter could not have reached her before she had written this. I closed my eyes and saw two ships pass in the Atlantic, each carrying a letter across the sea.

I am expecting a baby. You must write and suggest some names. I don't know what to call him, if he's a boy. I always thought I'd call my son Wolfgang. But when I gave up hoping for a baby, I called the dog Wolfie, instead.

I hate being so far away from all of you. Shall you like being an aunt? I suppose it shan't make much difference since you won't even see the baby for years, maybe. I'm sorry for being so miserable. Or at least I'm sorry for writing about it. I know I ought to keep it to myself especially with such a 'happy event' on the way, but I am a little frightened and I never thought Anna wouldn't be with me and now . . .

Oh Elise, I can't imagine her as a grandmother. She isn't nearly old enough. Julian could growl like a proper grandpa but Anna would be more like a fairy godmother than a grandmama. Sometimes I worry that she will never even see the baby and that I can't imagine her old because . . . but no. Robert tells me I'm not to say such things, that it's bad for the baby but how can I stop when years go by and we hear nothing?

I felt the sunshine warm upon my cheeks. So, I was to be an aunt. I experienced a tug of excitement. Perhaps I could knit the baby something—I was rather tired of making socks for soldiers. I remembered soon after Margot and Robert married, Anna and I lingering over breakfast on the balcony. I can see it now: the table laid with a white cloth, a scattering of crumbs from our bread rolls, the red geraniums in the flowerpot. 'I don't mind whether it's a boy or a girl,' said Anna, 'as long as the child's musical.' I frowned, hurt, and Anna reached out, catching my hand. 'Oh my darling, I couldn't care less about your prowess. It's simply that music is all Margot really understands. I think having her for a mother will be easier, if the child is also a musician.' She gave me an arch smile. 'Naughtiness, baby will learn from her aunt.' I said nothing, sipped my coffee and pictured the baby belonging to Margot and Anna's coterie of musicians, sharing in that language from which I was inevitably excluded.

Reading Margot's letter all those years later, nothing was how we'd imagined it to be. A goldfinch alighted on the garden wall, the sunlight catching the bright feathers on his head, and started to warble. I wondered if the baby would be able to sing, or if she'd be like me. It didn't matter. Anna was wrong. Margot wouldn't mind if the baby wasn't even a music lover. Though she'd probably still name him Amadeus if he were a boy or Constanze for a girl.

*   *   *

On a cool afternoon in early October, I decided to take a walk along the bluffs. Harvest and haymaking were finished and I was savouring a brief lull before the ploughing started. It was one of those days when the sea battled against the wind and the roar and crash of waves smashing into the black rocks was drowned out by the wind screaming along the cliff path. My ears ached with cold, and blown by the gale I lurched and stuttered towards the precipice like a drunkard. It was safer low to the ground so I crouched, fingers grasping at the hawthorn and thistles to steady myself. The earth smelt of loam and heather. From this height, the curve of the bay below appeared as if it had been scooped out of the land, the honeyed cliffs as smooth as the inside of a clay cup spinning on a potter's wheel. The sea washed the beach, white sheets of water rolling up and down, coating the pebbles with layer after layer of rushing white foam. It was wild up on the cliff, and as the light began to fade I was almost frightened. When I looked back down at the beach, I saw the figure of Mr Rivers standing in the surf.

I scrambled down the steep path to the beach and hesitated, watching him from a distance, before calling out, 'Mr Rivers! Daniel.'

He turned and waved, and I ran across the strand towards him, my feet grinding into the pebbles. As I approached, I saw to my surprise that he was not dressed in his usual outdoor work clothes but one of his pre-war suits. His brogues were sluiced by the tide and I frowned at the spoiling of good shoe leather.

'What are you doing?' I asked, catching his elbow and drawing him further up the beach.

'It's finished,' he said.

I frowned. 'What's finished?'

'Tyneford.'

His face was pale and dark circles shadowed his eyes. Between clenched fingers, he clasped a letter. 'They're taking over the house. The village. Everything. We have to leave by Christmas.'

He stepped back from the shore and walked a

few paces up the beach. The wind roared through the trees and made the dune grass sing. I chased after him, easing the letter from his hand.

Dear Mr Rivers,

In order to give our troops the fullest opportunity to perfect their training in the use of modern weapons of war, the army must have an area of land particularly suited to their special needs and in which they can use live shells. For this reason you will realise the chosen area must be cleared of all civilians.

It is regretted that, in the National Interest, it is necessary to move you from your home. Everything possible will be done to help you, both by payment of compensation, and by finding other accommodation for you if you are unable to do so yourself.

The date on which the military will take over this area is 19th December, and all civilians must be out of the area by that date.

The Government appreciate that this is no small sacrifice which you are asked to make, but they are sure that you will give this further help towards winning the war with a good heart.

C. H. MILLER Major-General i/c Administration
Southern Command

I read it through twice and then, hands shaking, returned it to Mr Rivers.

'They gave it to me first,' he said tonelessly. 'A day's courtesy. The rest of the village will get theirs tomorrow.'

I started to speak but he shook his head.

'There's nothing to be done. I've been to see the Major-General. It's quite decided. Everywhere from East Lulcombe to Kimmeridge is to be cleared of civilians.'

I felt myself reel. The sound of the sea crashed through me, drawing out my breath with the tide.

'No,' I said. 'No.'

I loved this place. I loved the wildness and the saltwater cracking against the black rocks and the greylag geese crying overhead and the sea pinks reaching over the cliff tops and the adders basking on the heath, the song of the fishermen and the rainbow bellies of the mackerel, the silent church and the glimpse of Portland in the mist and the way the weather was as changeable as a Mozart opera—one moment sunny and warm, gulls laughing in the bay, and the next rain pockmarking the waves. I loved the wooden fishing-boats dawdling in the bay and the sweep and rush of water in the dark. Here, I had loved Kit. I loved him swimming among these rocks and filching cockles in that tide pool and running along Flower's Barrow. Here we met and fell in love. He stays in Tyneford in the echo of the sea upon the shore and–

'How can we leave him?' I pleaded.

Mr Rivers sighed. 'He's gone, Alice. He left us first.'

I shook my head. 'No. Kit is in Tyneford. This is the only place we've known together. We shared these pebbles and this sea.'

Mr Rivers took my hand and drew me down beside him. 'Then it's right you should leave. That we should both go. Each of us needs to start somewhere new. Try to live a little again. He died. We didn't.'

He reached his arm around me and pulled me tight into his side.

'You're young, Alice. You should have a sweetheart. Those wretched WAAFs have endless boyfriends. You should too.'

I began to sob, and he rocked me gently.

'His life was tragic. Yours oughtn't to be.'

'But I don't want to leave this place. This valley. This bay.' I wiped my nose on my sleeve. 'I was lost and then I was home.'

'I know,' he said. 'It casts a spell over you. There's something about the place. I was born here, so were my father and my grandfather. I thought my grandchildren would grow up playing in these woods.' He sighed again. 'But the war has changed everything. It would have changed eventually—it's just happening all at once in a rush and we're not ready for it.'

He gave a bitter laugh. 'We were all so worried about the damn invasion and losing the place to the Nazis. I joined the auxiliaries for Christ's sake. And the invasion came anyway.'

'Even your gun couldn't keep them out.'

We both fell silent, remembering the night on the same beach and Mr Rivers shooting at the void. He plucked a golden pebble off the ground and sent it skimming into the waves, where it bounced again and again across the surface before finally sinking into the grey water. As it vanished, sadness overwhelmed me, cold as the October sea.

'Perhaps it's good for us. It's not right . . . this . . . you and I,' he said as I rested my head on his shoulders, and I shuddered, not knowing whether this was a return of the old propriety or a reference to our mutual grief. He continued, 'Sometimes I feel that it will be a relief to get away from here—from the house, which is, honest to God, falling down about our ears, and away from all the memories. There are so many everywhere that sometimes I choke on them.'

I was crying silently now, and he wiped away my tears with his thumb.

'Don't cry, Alice. Please, don't cry. They say we can return at the end of the war. As soon as it's all over we can all come back. The old life can start again, if you like.'

I smiled and stroked his hand but we both knew that this was the end of Tyneford.

* * *

Five hundred years lay in packing boxes. Mrs Ellsworth received the news well, filling only one pocket-handkerchief with her tears. Mr Rivers would not dismiss the staff; they had homes with him, if they wanted them. Art was to tend the garden, and Mrs Ellsworth determined to keep house for the evicted squire—the thought of Mr Rivers boiling his own egg was a travesty too far. Yet to Mr Rivers' surprise and regret, Mr Wrexham declined. He received the news standing up in the library, refusing the offer of either a brandy or a seat. He was silent for a moment.

'I am much obliged for the generous offer, sir. But I am not in the first flush and perhaps this is a suitable juncture for me to consider my retirement. I think I might live with my brother in a quiet spot by the sea.'

He crossed to the window and adjusted the curtain sash, which had caught and creased. Once it was smooth, he turned back to Mr Rivers. 'Is there anything else, sir?'

Privately, I wondered what had made the old butler choose to leave the Rivers' family services. I couldn't imagine that fishing with Burt held such an appeal. Perhaps the servant could not bear to see Mr Rivers in such reduced circumstances, or perhaps he considered that once he left, Mr Rivers was no longer the master of Tyneford House. Or else, it was simply the end of the old world as he had forecast all those years ago, and he chose not to cling to it, but to withdraw with his customary dignity. He would slide out of our lives with the same discretion with which he left the gentlemen to their port after a good dinner.

The house itself seemed forlorn. Every creak of wood was a reproach and the wind sighed through the eaves at night. Mrs Ellsworth ceased entirely to polish the parquet and dust gathered in drifts behind doors, while Mr Wrexham uttered not a word of complaint. I decided that it was better we left—a sharp goodbye—rather than watch the slow decay increase each year; the guttering fall off the west gable and not be replaced, the attic roof collapse, dry rot in the ancient panelling, the damp steal up from the cellar into the great hall. We could remember the house as she had been, luminous and proud, lights in every window and storm lanterns flickering across the lawns. In memory she remained a great English country house, always ready to receive her guests as their motorcars drew up outside, chauffeurs opening doors and ladies strolling up to the porch in a hurry of fur coats. In our minds it would always be summer as we took tea on the terrace, the scent of bluebells from Rookery Wood drifting like smoke across the lawns.

My own future was uncertain. Each night after dinner I retired to the library with Mr Rivers. His calendar sat on his desk, leering at me. Another day gone. And another. I wanted to turn it face down, as though that would pause time. Anna and Julian would never see this place. Neither would Margot. Mr Rivers buried himself in arrangements; he had a house on the other side of Kimmeridge Bay, and he supervised the removal of the most precious things: paintings of the ancestors, photographs of Kit and the smaller pieces of furniture. Everything else would have to be packed in the cellar and locked away.

'Alice,' he said, looking up from his desk, 'what are you going to do?' He paused and swallowed. 'You know that you cannot come with me. Other places are not like Tyneford. People would talk. I don't care about me—they can say what they like about me, but not about you.'

I didn't like to tell him that people already talked.

'Don't worry,' I said brightly. 'I shall be fine. I'll become a land-girl. There's a farm at Worth Matravers short of hands.'

Mr Rivers frowned. 'Yes, I know it. Nigel Lodder's place. He's a good man.' He looked at me sharply. 'I want you to check with me first. I don't want you going just anywhere.'

I shrugged. I was leaving Tyneford; it didn't seem to matter much where I went. 'Fine. But you must come on my Sunday off, and take me out for tea.'

He tried to smile and make his voice light. 'Yes, of course. I'll take you to the Royal Hotel in Dorchester for stale scones and margarine.'

I bit my lip and looked away. I imagined not seeing Mr Rivers every day. We would not work side-by-side anymore, catching lame ewes or mending foxholes in the fence. With an uncomfortable twist in my stomach, I realised that the dab of lipstick I applied each evening before dinner was for him. I wasn't sure which I minded most, leaving Tyneford or leaving Mr Rivers.

*　　*　　*

Unable to bear the melancholy of departure any longer, I agreed to go for a picnic with Poppy. I hadn't really wanted to go, preferring to mope about the farm or wander among the hilltop sheep feeling sorry for myself, but Poppy was insistent. Grumbling under my breath, wishing she'd let me pine in peace, I trudged down to Worbarrow Bay. The day was bright, the autumn sun glimmering on the sea, as dry leaves fluttered onto the beach, masquerading as shells. A squadron of cormorants flew in formation across the pale sky while a lone tern perched on the pinnacle of the tout, filling the air with its yelping cry. A cormorant broke formation to dive into the waves and snatch a flapping fish. I snorted—it would take more than a War Office decree to ban all Tyneford residents. I picked my way along the beach, staying away from the dunes where barbed wire lay in coils. Inside one of the concrete pillboxes nestled into the cliff, I saw a flash of binoculars and waved at the WAAF girls concealed inside. I scanned the bay for Poppy, spying her just beyond Burt's cottage. Thrusting my hands into my pockets, I hurried over. She'd laid out a tattered woollen rug on the beach and set on top of it a covered picnic basket.

'Hullo,' she said. 'I hope you're hungry. And thirsty.'

She lifted the tea towel covering the basket to reveal a feast of pastries, and to my amazement, a forest of beer bottles. I gaped in awe. Britain had been short of beer for more than a year.

'Where on earth?'

'Wrexham,' she said with a smug smile. 'He found a stash in the cellar when he was making space for the furniture. It's Kit's last brew.'

She looked at me narrowly. 'Don't go sentimental. I'm drinking it. Kit would never waste good beer.'

I retrieved a bottle from the basket and uncorked the stopper. 'He certainly wouldn't.'

To my surprise, I saw Will strolling along the beach towards us, his arms full of driftwood. He was dressed in his army uniform, trousers rolled up above his calves and feet bare. He grinned when he saw me and, setting the wood down in a heap, collapsed beside us on the rug.

''Ullo, Alice. Yer can be the first ter wish us congratulations. We jist got married. This here is a weddin' breakfast.'

Poppy shot me a shy smile. 'And I'm having a baby. It's why we got married really—Will thought it would be tidier. And I suppose now we're leaving Tyneford, perhaps it is for the best,' she said, her words tumbling out all in a rush.

I kissed Poppy, hugging her tightly, only releasing her so that I could shake Will's hand.

Happiness rolled off them in dizzying waves.

'I'm so pleased for you both. And pleased for me—I can be aunty to a baby close by. I shall spoil him horribly, I'm telling you now.'

I raised my beer, toasting them. Poppy pried a bottle from Will and took a hefty swig. 'Yes,' she said. 'New beginnings.'

I raised an eyebrow. 'Are you sure that you should? Now you're in the family way.'

'Tosh,' said Poppy. 'Beer's good for baby. Shall we swim before eating?'

'It'll be freezing.'

'Invigorating.'

She was already stripping off, discarding her knitted sweater and wriggling out of her green slacks, as Will lounged back on the rug, watching with quiet approval. I hesitated for a moment, and then began to peel off my coat and unbutton my blouse. Poppy was already splashing into the waves in her grey underwear, shrieking at the cold. Her skin was blue-white and her red hair a vibrant waterfall tumbling to her waist. Her long limbs retained the thin gawkiness of childhood, but her freckled belly was slightly swollen. I wondered if her baby would have red hair.

'Come on!' she yelled, and I raced in after her, my mind washing clean at the crash of cold. My skin tingled and I screamed. I dove under the surface, choking with ice, my eyes and mouth filling with saltwater. I was empty, every thought numbed. I shivered and retched with cold. The tide poured through me, sluicing away conscious thought. I snorted stinging salt and treaded water, free for a few moments from myself. Then I broke the surface, gasping for air. Poppy giggled on the beach as Will towelled her blue skin. He waved at me to get out. I sprinted from the surf and caught the towel he tossed me, and started to rub myself dry, teeth chattering.

Burt appeared on the beach. He crouched beside the pile of driftwood logs, blowing gently on a rustle of burning newspaper. He grinned when he saw me.

'Well that were right stupid,' he said.

'Invigorating,' I replied.

He chuckled, and sat back on his heels as the logs began to crackle and hiss. He spat on his hands and wiped them on his trousers, leaving a trail of charcoal. Pulling on my slacks and sweater I knelt next to him, warming my hands over the blaze. Poppy, no longer blue, snuggled in beside me and handed me a piece of cold rabbit pie. I chewed and stared at the bonfire, hypnotised by the flames. He and Will hummed an old melody, *'Let us sing together for to pass away some time . . . for my heart's within her, though I live not where I love.'*

I joined in the chorus, and then stopped, prodding the fire. 'Well, that was my last swim in Worbarrow Bay,' I said.

'None o' that magpie chatter,' said Burt, clapping his hands. 'If yer eats rabbit pie when yer is moanin', yer belly'll be groanin'.'

Poppy looked at him narrowly. 'I've never heard that one before.'

'Nope. That's cos I jist made him up. Sounds right enuff though.'

'We won't be so far away,' said Will. 'An' all this coast is washed by the same sea. Everywhere has a bit o' Tyneford, if yer think about it.'

Poppy planted a kiss on the tip of his nose and lazed back on the blanket.

‘Knew it were comin’,’ said Burt. ‘That we’d be ousted.’ He gave a guilty grin. ‘It’s my fault, if yer wants ter know the truth of it.’

We stared at him with blank faces.

‘Well. Everyone were talkin’ ’bout hin-vasion. Hin-vasion this. Hun-vasion that. Well. I don’t want no Hitlerin’ Nazi bastards in Tyneford vale. So, I does what a man must. I went up ter Tyneford Barrow an’ got proper drunk. An’ then proper starkers. I walked buttock naked along the long barrow and the short barrow and Flower’s Barrow an’ I shouted out ter them ol’ English kings what lie buried there that if they doesn’t want Nazi boots clatterin’ about on their noggins that they better do something. Keep out them bastarding Jerry-Huns. Keep Tyneford free.’

He paused and poked the fire with a stick, so that vermillion sparks flew out of the blue driftwood flames. The light shone on his hoary bristles, turning them rosy red.

‘Only I reckon I wis a bit too heffective. My shoutin’ and prayin’ or whatever, worked a bit better than I expected. Them kings of the barrows kept out Hitler, but they’ve gone an’ buggerin’ chucked us out too.’

A nugget fell out of the bonfire in a flurry of sparks, and Burt stamped on it crossly.

‘Should a stuck ter witch-stones. Strung ’em along a bit o’ twine from ’ere ter Dover. That would o’ done the trick wi’ out unforeseen consy-quinces.’

We stared at him in silence, even Poppy for once speechless.

‘Well, them army chaps say we can come back at the end of this here war. An’ I don’t see that Hitler feller lasting much longer. An’ wi’ a bit of pleadin’ and maybe a little sacrifice . . .'

Here Poppy interrupted. 'A sacrifice? Don't look at me.'

Burt gave her a withering glare. 'When do yoos think this is? It's 1941 not the Middle Ages. An' fat lot a good yoo'd be as a sacrifice in yer current state, madam.'

Poppy scowled and Burt chuckled. He gave a luxurious stretch, his bones creaking like the burning driftwood. 'Anyway, wi' a bit o' luck the army and them ol' kings and what-not will let us back ter Tyneford.'

'Yes,' I said not looking at him. 'With a bit of luck.'

*   *   *

The letter from Margot arrived on the first of November. It was the first day of winter and as I walked back to the house from the eweleaze, the air was thick with wood smoke. It puffed from the towering chimneystacks of the great house, curling up to meet the clouds. The air crackled with rooks. The light faded from grey to black, and in the dark I heard the bleat and shuffle of the distant sheep on the hillside, the wash and crack of the tide against the shore.

The house was quiet. The WAAFs who were not on shift had vanished to a dance at the army camp, and the stillness was like old times. I lingered in the panelled hall listening to the death-watch beetle rattle and tick. I had unpeeled my gloves, unwrapped my scarf and was halfway across the room before I saw the cream-coloured envelope resting on the hall table. I'd like to say that I had some premonition, that the paper scalded my fingers and I dropped it or, as I reached out to touch it, that the wind screamed and a bird dashed itself against a windowpane, but there was nothing. Such things only happen to gothic or operatic heroines. I only felt a twinge of pleasure when I saw the handwriting. I studied the postmark: San Francisco, September, 1941. I felt a thrill of excitement and wondered whether Margot's baby was a girl or a boy. I hoped my package had reached her in time. These pleasant musings were quickly followed by a nudge of apprehension—supposing Margot was still angry with me?

* * *

I ran, no, I walked down the servants' corridor. The smell of damp. My tongue stuck to the roof of my mouth. I called for Wrexham but my voice belonged to a stranger and did not come from my own lips.

'Champagne, Wrexham. Champagne.'

He appeared in the doorway of his parlour and gaped at me. He clutched a pair of Mr Rivers' boots encased in mud, and lowered them as he stared, his gaze lingering on the letter dangling between my fingers. I stamped my foot.

'Champagne. I need goddamn Champagne.'

He flinched. 'Yes, miss.'

'Please bring it upstairs. I'm running a bath.'

* * *

The water howled and shrieked in the pipes, loud as a steam train. Fuck the black line. Fuck water rationing. I was going to fill this bath right to the top. Lose myself in scalding water; drink champagne like I was back in Vienna. Anna's voice drifted up the stairs. I must have put on her gramophone record but I didn't remember. I could pretend it was Anna herself singing downstairs. Anna. Anna. I crouched on the bathmat and listened as her song curled upwards, her voice filling the air like the scent of warm chocolate. In my hand I clutched Margot's letter.

Dearest Elise,
I received a letter from Hildegard. Oh, Elise. Anna died on New Year's Day . . . Typhoid in the ghetto . . . Robert kept the letter from me until I'd had my baby . . . On September 5th I had a little girl. She weighed five pounds and ten ounces and she has dark hair like you. I have named her Juliana to remember both parents.

The water reached the top of the bath, slopping against the sides. The electric lights flickered. I grasped the champagne bottle and opened the foil, easing out the cork with my fingers—it shot up like an anti-aircraft bullet and ricocheted off the mirror, leaving a mark in the condensation on the glass. I took a swig and closed my eyes. *Anna . . . Typhoid. Juliana. To remember both parents.* Margot knew that Julian was dead. Even if he still breathed, he was dead. He would not live without Anna. He loved us, Margot and me, but he loved Anna best. If my father was not already dead, I knew that somewhere he waited to die. I closed off the taps and the room was quiet save for the groan and gurgle of the pipes.

Dearest Elise . . . Anna died on New Year's Day.

What had I done on New Year's Day as my mother lay dying? I couldn't even remember. That day had passed unmarked, unremembered. I leant back against the bath, and thought of my last night in Vienna—Anna, Margot and me gathered in the bathroom before the party, drinking champagne, rose-scented bath salts lacing the steam. Anna lying in the bath, laughing and singing, while Margot lounged in her silk chemise smoking a cigarette and, unseen by the others, Julian in the doorway, crying.

I took a gulp of cool champagne, the bubbles tickling my throat, and turned back to the letter.

I was angry about the novel in the viola. You should have told me. If something had happened to it and I hadn't read it . . . you're right, I don't think I could have forgiven you. But none of that matters now. You must take the novel out of the viola and you must write it down word by word and send it to me. Send the first pages tomorrow. We still have one conversation left with Papa, Elise.

Margot knew we would never speak to our father again. We could no sooner imagine Julian without Anna than we could daylight without the sun. Julian would disappear. I took another gulp of champagne and addressed my sister.

'All right, Margot. I'll take it out. But don't you see—as long as the novel stays in the viola, unread, the story isn't finished. And it can't be finished. It can't.'

I glanced towards the old viola case propped against the windowsill. I knew I had to open it. I had brought it into the bathroom knowing I must, and yet I stayed leaning against the bath. Taking a long drink of champagne, I crawled over to the case and pulled it onto my lap. I wished I could remember the words to a prayer; it should probably be Kaddish but anything would do. The strains of Anna singing one of Violetta's arias from *La Traviata* seeped through the floorboards as though she sang her own lament. I unfastened the case, drawing out the viola. The letters I'd written to Anna and never sent cluttered the lining and in my fury I hurled them across the room. They fluttered to earth like scribbled doves, landing on the floor and in the sink and in the bath, where they floated, the ink running in black rivers, dripping into the water.

I took a deep breath and willed my thundering heart to slow. I'd found a knife and I eased the edge of the blade beneath the face of the viola. The glue sealing it to the sides was too strong and I could not find a hold. I swore and shoved the knife inside the f-holes, jamming my fist down on the handle. With a crack the face splintered and broke. The bridge snapped and the strings dangled loose like dislocated fingers. For a moment I stared at the smashed viola in horror, and then I snatched at the first page, drawing the paper to the f-hole, trying to prise it from the viola without tearing it on the splintered wood. With a surgeon's concentration, I pulled it out. I sat for a second with the thin sheet on my lap, and then I started to read.

Blank.

The page was blank. I turned it over and held it up to the light. Nothing. I sighed—he must have put a blank page on top to protect the manuscript. I slipped my fingers back inside the viola and grasped another page and tugged it up through the f-holes. Heart pounding in my ears, I studied the page. Blank.

No longer caring whether I ripped the pages, I yanked out a clump of paper. I held them up, scrutinising each one for a stray word, the faintest trace of brown ink. Blank. Blank. I cast them aside, letting the sheets drift around the bathroom, mingling with my letters to Anna. The room filled with paper, but the only words were mine.

I tore out more and more pages, knocking aside the tuning struts inside the viola with another crack. Every single sheet was empty. Was it the salt air? Had Julian made some mistake and inserted a void copy into the viola? Had I left it too long and allowed the ink to fade? No. I closed my eyes. Julian was already dead. His words had disappeared with him. I imagined at the moment of his death the pages inside the viola turning white, the words unwritten.

But Margot? She would never understand. She would believe it my fault. I had stolen the last conversation with our father.

* * *

I did not close the blackouts. I sat in the bath and drank and drank and stared at the silent moon. A crescent moon. A stage moon. A moon I had seen in the Opera House, as Anna sang Cherubino or Violetta or Lucia and I cried hot proud tears and clapped until my palms stung red. The bathwater scorched my skin. It hurt and I smiled in relief, needing the pain. Through the wine-fuelled dullness, I heard rapping on the bathroom door, Mrs Ellsworth's voice.

'Miss Land? Miss.'

I shut my eyes and sank under the water, letting it wash over my face and hair. If only it was cold—then it could empty my mind like that last swim on the beach. I could be as blank as Julian's pages.

*   *   *

The water was no longer hot, only warm. I stared at the peeling flock-print wallpaper and a smear of toothpaste beside the sink. Condensation dripped down the windowpane.

*   *   *

The tepid water grew cool. Then cold.

'Miss Land. I'd be most obliged if you would open the door,' said Mr Wrexham.

'Alice, dear,' called Mrs Ellsworth. 'Please let me in.'

I did not move, just drained the champagne bottle and sank under the water once more.

*   *   *

I shivered in the cold bath, knees tucked up beneath my chin. If only I could cry. It would be better if I could cry. Hammering on the bathroom door. Mr Rivers' voice calling to me.

'Alice. Alice, unlock this door, or I shall come in myself.'

I did not move. The sound of a key clicking into a lock. The door opened and then closed again.

'Alice,' he said. 'Alice? What is it, little one? What has happened?'

I sat in the bathtub and stared up at him. All around the bathroom lay sheets of carbon-copy paper. They littered the floor and clung to the damp windows and drifted in the bathwater along with my sodden letters. In the corner of the room lay the broken viola. Everywhere pages spilt out onto the ground, yellow as old bone. I pointed to Margot's letter, propped upon the soap dish. 'They're dead. They're both dead.'

He knelt beside the bath and I saw his eyes were wet with tears.

'Don't cry,' I said. 'You're not allowed to cry. I can't, so neither can you.'

He swallowed. 'All right. I shan't.'

He slid his hand into the water and recoiled. 'It's cold. Get out before you catch a chill.'

I sat quite still, somehow unable to move. He watched me for a second and then crouched over the tub, sliding his arms beneath mine and lifted me out, setting me down on the floor. I stood before him naked, making no attempt to cover myself. I shivered and my skin prickled, nipples blown to beads. Beneath my feet I felt crumpled pages. I looked at him without flinching and his breath quickened. He stooped to pick up a towel and offered it to me. When I did not take it, he began to dry me, rubbing the fabric across my skin.

'I'm so sorry,' he said.

I backed away.

'Don't. Don't you see, Daniel? Everyone is dead. No one is left who loves me. Not like Anna loved me. Not like—'

Kit's unspoken name lingered in the air between

us. I looked at him and it was a challenge. I dared him to look at me. I dared him to say it and save us both. He stood and walked across to me.

'Not everyone who loves you is dead.'

* * *

I lay on his bed where he had carried me, my hair still damp from the bath. The room smelt of him. A red wine decanter, half full, rested on the dressing table and beside it a photograph of Kit as a laughing boy. Daniel's jacket was slung over the back of a chair and the wind shrilled from the empty grate. He lay fully clothed beside me, close but not yet touching. He leant over me muttering, 'I'm much, much too old for you.'

'Yes,' I agreed. 'Definitely too old. It's obscene. You're how old? Seventy-five? A hundred?'

He laughed; a low chuckle in his throat. 'Old enough to know better.' He bent to kiss me. 'Alice. Elise.'

I held him back and shook my head. 'No,' I said. 'Elise has gone. With you I am only Alice.'

'All right then Alice, but I'm still going to kiss you.'

Daniel was only the second man I had kissed in my life. His lips tasted of salt and suddenly I realised I was crying. His face was slippery with my tears and my mouth stung with saltwater. I remembered that Passover long ago and I heard Julian's voice: *A man who has experienced great sorrow and then has known its end, wakes each morning feeling the pleasure of sunrise.* But it had not ended. I felt sorrow and pleasure rushing at me all at once and I could not breathe and I knew that if Daniel stopped kissing me I should dissolve into a blank, like the novel in the viola, but he did not stop. His fingers trailed down my cheeks to my breasts and the soft skin of my belly and I unfastened his shirt with steady hands and pressed my lips against the rough grey hair. I felt his mouth on my thigh and then his tongue, delicate as a snake's. I was breathless as though from running as he pushed my knees apart and then he wrapped himself in me, a tangling of limbs and loves and lives. As he moved inside me, I felt a sob build in my chest and I cried out. I broke apart and he held me. I was new and warm and naked. I lay in his arms and I understood. I am two women and I love two men. Elise will always love Kit and Alice loves Daniel. This was not the life or the love I had expected but it was love all the same. We must leave Tyneford, but we would not leave alone.

CHAPTER TWENTY-SIX

The Novel in the Viola

I am Mrs Rivers after all. Alice Rivers. Our wedding photograph sits on my dressing table, and next to it is the photograph of Kit and me, taken the summer we were engaged. I am happy in both pictures.

I don't remember very much about the wedding itself. It was before we left Tyneford, but I wouldn't marry in the church, so it took place in Dorchester register office. It was a bright December day, the ground carpeted in frost thick as snow, while shining icicles hung from the trees. I wore Anna's pearls and Mrs Ellsworth made me a corsage with greenery from the garden. Daniel and I waited our turn, queuing along a linoleum corridor filled with soldiers and their sweethearts. We had no guests. A young lieutenant and his soon-to-be bride acted as our witnesses. I forget their names now. We ate our wedding breakfast in the kitchen at Tyneford, Wrexham insisting on serving us the tinned asparagus omelette in his white cotton gloves and Mrs Ellsworth dabbing her eyes. We gave champagne to the WAAFs but I did not drink, as champagne made me think of Anna.

The only cloud was Margot. She did not answer my telegram. She did not wire or write. I knew she blamed me for the blank novel. For the next three years I sent her long letters and presents for the baby, pleading with her to understand but she never replied. After the war, my letters were returned, stamped 'no such person, address unknown' and I no longer wrote.

I have had so much time over the years to think about our rift. At first I believed she was angry and unable to forgive me. Once we stopped writing to each other we receded from one another's lives. The conversation had faltered, and after a while neither of us knew how to begin again. And yet, I also wonder if the silence was something else. We had lost almost every part of our old lives. I became Alice and I suspect that Margot similarly became another version of herself. We were the only things tying one another to our lost family and it was simply easier to try and forget, to hide the past in silence and busy ourselves with the present. I thought of her often. I could not eat her favourite rose creams or listen to Berlioz's viola concerto.

And, as I grew older, I thought more and more about my niece, Juliana.

* * *

I always hoped that we would be allowed back to Tyneford, and we were, one last time. The Ministry of Defence decided that the land was essential for armed forces training and informed us that they were compulsorily purchasing the entire estate. Tyneford would no longer belong to the Rivers family, even in name. We returned one afternoon in early March 1963. A light wind blew from the east, and a fine film of drizzle obscured the vista of the bay. I was glad of the rain. I was not sure I could have borne to see it dazzle in the sunshine. We parked some distance down the now gravelled road, and walked the last mile to the village. I didn't see the houses at first; the trees had crept forward and embraced them in a mass of spring green as though they wanted to pull them deep-deep inside the woods. Cottages lurked among silver birch, hazel and tangles of blackthorn like drawings in a fairy tale. Everything was green—the springy moss clinging to the boughs of the trees, the bright lichen spotting the bark and the leaf shadows on the stonework. We walked closer, and saw that the roofs had caved in and the timber upper floors rotted away so that fireplaces sprouted from halfway up the walls. Fingers of ivy poked through the stonework and forget-me-nots trembled between the flagstones. The walls were pockmarked with bullets, some of which had rusted and bled during the rain, leaving brown-red smears.

From the village we walked up to the house. The

army had pulled down the Tudor wing some years before, and it stood half naked, the bare timbers exposed to the daylight like ribs. We picked our way inside; the doors had long since been wrenched from their hinges. The hall was open to the sky and it rained onto the stone floor, the parquet having been stripped out and shipped away to America by GIs years before. The drawing room held the reek of fox, and I saw that one had made his lair in the great fireplace. He hadn't noticed us and dozed on, his scarlet brush poking out between the discarded fire irons.

Hand in hand, Daniel and I wandered onto the terrace and looked out over where the garden used to be. All that remained were the stone steps leading down to the lawns. The lawns themselves had reverted to meadow grass and weeds tore through the lavender and thyme borders. Then the sun slunk out from behind a cloud, casting a watery light across the valley and catching a treasure-hoard of golden daffodils and the red flash of a kite's wing. The song of a Dorset warbler punctured the stillness, and in a shaft of pale sun I glimpsed clusters of buttery primrose speckling the path leading to Flower's Barrow.

We walked down to Worbarrow Bay in silence, scouring the beach for Burt's cottage. It had slunk back into the strand, pebbles washed away in the tide so that only a tumbledown pile of brown and white stones remained. There were no boats in the bay, but the gulls shrieked and a black cormorant dabbled and fished. As the sun sank into the sea and dusk gathered on the hills, we left the shore and walked back to our car, knowing we intruded upon the stillness. Mankind did not belong here anymore.

* * *

The next journey home happened later, in the autumn of 1984. We stood in the hurry of the Vienna Westbahnof, knocked by suitcases and the jostle of other people's farewells. Daniel took my hand. 'Are you all right, darling? Shall I get you some water?'

I shook my head and held onto the crook of his arm. I glanced up at the station clock. Eleven fifty-nine. The train would arrive in one minute—at least in Austria they ran to time. I couldn't bear even a minute's delay. My heart thundered in my ears and I forced myself to breathe. I gripped the viola case even tighter. Twelve o'clock. There was the shriek and stutter of a train pulling up to the platform. Doors slammed open. Luggage was handed out and a flurry of travellers hurried towards me. Standing on tiptoe, I peered through the crowd for her—a slim girl with blondish hair, doubtless very smartly dressed. People rushed me on both sides, and I swivelled and stared but could not see her. The crowd thinned and I choked back a sob. How could she miss the train? How could she?

'Elise.'

I turned around. I saw not a girl of twenty but a woman with white hair standing before me. The green eyes were the same. She smiled and I stepped forward into her arms, the viola case sandwiched between us.

'Margot. Margot,' was all I managed for a minute or two. 'I forgot. It's been so long, I was looking for a girl.'

She gave a short laugh. 'You'll make me wish I'd dyed my hair.' She appraised me with that look of old, head tilted to one side. 'You're just the same.'

I flushed as though I were still nineteen. 'Yes, well, I was thinner for a while in between.'

Margot laughed. 'I didn't mean that.'

There was so much to say and it hadn't been said for so long that we stuttered on small talk. I admired her brooch; she liked my ring. We spoke in English, and silently I marvelled at her American accent, those glamorous vowels. Our husbands had discovered one another and discussed the weather and the inconvenience of foreign travel. After a few minutes Margot interrupted.

'Is this the viola?'

I nodded, my mouth dry. 'Yes. I had it mended and re-strung.'

I offered it to her, and she took it in silence. She swallowed and then opened her mouth as though to speak, but said nothing. It was suddenly very quiet in the station, as though the din had been smothered and Margot and I stood alone on platform twelve.

* * *

From outside, the Opera House looked almost the same, an island of light in the middle of the *Ringstrasse*. Men in black tuxedos and women in long dresses swarmed up the steps to the colonnade. A rope of lanterns glimmered above the bronze statues poised on the first floor loggia, the light pooling about them like halos. Above us, a pair of winged horses reared, heads thrown back, metal manes streaming. Daniel and I edged forwards, absorbed into the throng, and I listened to the once familiar chatter, the air humming with the excitement of opening night. I'd been here so often with Julian and Margot and the trio of aunts—Gretta fussing over whether she'd forgotten her opera glasses and wouldn't be able to spy on her friends (she liked to be able to give Anna a minute report of the audience's reaction; a single yawn in the balcony was noted and divulged). Gerda used to hurry us, tripping over the train of her old-fashioned skirts. Poor Margot was always quiet and a little pale, imagining too clearly her mother's nerves. Julian and I, not being musicians ourselves and never having known the terror of performance, merely simmered with pride. Anna was going to sing! Our Anna. But that was many years ago and Anna had not sung here for a long time. I glanced at the grey and white heads in the crowd and wondered if any of them remembered her.

Daniel and I lingered outside in the cool of the loggia, he wondering at the exquisite frescos of *The Magic Flute* and I listening to the car horn concert from the street below. We were both strangers here. My home was the Vienna of 1938, not this shrieking modern city. I was relieved to speak in English. I was not forced to have waiters and the maître d' sneer at my museum German. Daniel sensed my reluctance and it was he who told the taxi driver the name of the hotel and ordered our *linzertorte* and coffee. I could wear the mask of a British tourist, an Englishwoman able only to stammer and smile, ordinarily ignorant.

I watched the crowd, spying at last Margot and Robert. They came over to us and the men exchanged pleasantries, while I watched Margot, noticing that she was quiet and a little pale. Catching my eye, she smiled. The five-minute bell summoned us to our seats, and then somehow the four of us were sitting in the auditorium. I found that I was shaking and Daniel reached out to squeeze my hand. It was not an Opera House but a palace, a cathedral to music—crimson and gold and bright with light. The audience clapped and hushed. I fidgeted and fanned myself with the programme, almost hearing Gretta's goose-hiss of disapproval. The lights dimmed and the theatre filled with familiar faces. There in the stage box was Herr Finkelstein, still thrilled at being mistaken for the balding Baron, and Frau Goldschmidt sweating in her fur, but refusing to surrender it to an unknown fate in the cloakroom, and there, at last, was Julian, leaning forward in his seat, listening. He scarcely seemed to breathe, taut with anticipation. We clapped the conductor, and then little Jan Tibor strode onto the stage. Only he wasn't little Jan any longer. This was no phantom, but a slight, white-haired man with that hush of authority possessed only by dictators, lion-tamers and conductors. He beckons the soloist onto the stage and out strolls Anna. She looks exactly as she did when I last saw her—a beautiful woman of forty-five—but in her hand she clasps a viola. This is not Anna. This is my niece, Juliana.

I glance down at the programme open on my knee.

World Premiere
The Novel in the Viola: Concerto in D minor for Viola and Orchestra
Music: Jan Tibor

Conductor: Jan Tibor
Viola: Juliana Miller

This music belongs to my family. Little Jan Tibor, who used to feed lettuce to the tortoise and played parlour concerts for the aunts, making Anna's piano sing and cry out in pleasure at its own beauty, has written this for us. I inhale with the orchestra and the world pauses on the upbeat: then the baton lash and sound swirls. Green and blue waves of strings whirl and soar. A flute, clear as a water trickle, is echoed in a deeper stream of cellos and then, at last, Juliana's viola, deep and sweet and rich as honeyed wine. Her music fills my ears and lungs. The *allegro* moves into the waltz and I am dancing at the Opera Ball with Kit as Anna sings and I am dizzy with champagne and there is the tinkle of breaking glass. Jan conducts the orchestra with taut fury, pulling from them a spiralling kaleidoscope of sound and Juliana bows higher and higher and then, on the edge of the precipice, Jan holds them back with a twist of his finger and soothes the strings into sighing *diminuendo*.

Now the slow movement. The audience waits. This is what they've all come to hear. Juliana sets down her Stradivarius and picks up a small rosewood viola. The audience scrutinises this pedlar's fiddle—a collective wrinkling of noses. It's more suited to a schoolroom or a subway than the grand Opera House. Jan raises his baton and brings it down in a whiplash and it begins, a melody muted and strange, a song of a white page.

Concerto in D Minor

63
mp
67
mf
f
mp
71
subito p
75
mp
mf
79
f
mf
83
f
p
Leggiero
f
94
mp
mf
mp
p
mp
101
mf
mp

I reach for my sister's hand and listen to my niece draw music from the strings. She sings of the novel inside the viola and its unwritten story. Only I know that the novel in the viola is not blank. I dried the pages and before I sealed them back inside, I filled them one by one with my story. Those pages are covered in words and the novel in the viola is now a palimpsest. After the concert tonight, I shall write the last page and slip it into the viola.

Somewhere a clock ticks backwards and midnight is un-struck. Juliana plays and plays and it is every time at once. Burt is fishing in *The Lugger* on the Danube at dawn, and Mrs Ellsworth and Hildegard bake a game pie together in the small kitchen of our old apartment. And always I love two men.

* * *

Tonight I shall dream of Tyneford House. As I lay down to sleep, I shall see the house as it was that first summer. The dog roses tangled around the back door. The horse in the stable yard. Teeth grinding grinding. The scent of magnolia and salt. And then I shall wake inside my dream. I am Elise again. Alice rests and everybody lives. My hands are white and smooth, unmarked by age spots. I stand on the lawn and listen to the call of the sea, the knock of sailboats in the bay. I run down to the beach. My feet are sinking into the pebbles and the water slaps the shore. The sun shines and there is a boy on the beach. An English man-boy. He stands in the white surf. He waits for me there, smiling always smiling, and he waits to kiss me. I taste saltwater on my tongue. Saltwater—tears and a journey. And above it all, the crash of the sea.

AUTHOR'S NOTE

The village of Tyneford is based upon the ghost village of Tyneham on the Dorset coast. People lived in Tyneham and Worbarrow Bay for more than a thousand years, but even during the 1930s it was a remote and secret place, far away from either main roads or rail and its lanes separated from the outside world by a series of wooden gates. The Elizabethan manor was celebrated as one of the most beautiful in England: an exquisite house hewn from golden Purbeck stone. Life in the valley continued virtually unchanged for millennia: men fished for mackerel in the bay, women worked in the fields or the great house owned by the Bond family, who had been in possession of the estate for several hundred years.

Then, in the midst of the Second World War, everything changed. The War Office requisitioned the entire estate for military occupation. A letter was sent on 16th November 1943 informing the villagers that their homes were to be taken and they had one month to leave. Most presumed they'd be back after Christmas and planted up their vegetable gardens in readiness for their return. In any case, Churchill promised that their homes would be returned at the end of the war. The villagers pinned a note on the door of the church as they departed, asking the army: 'Please treat the church and houses with care; we have given up our homes where many of us lived for generations to help win the war to keep men free. We shall return one day and thank you for treating the village kindly.'

The army (British and American) did not treat the village kindly. They used the cottages as target practice, shelling the walls and firing at the windows. The ancient lime avenue was felled and a fire started in the medieval west wing. But worse was to come. At the end of the war, Churchill reneged on his promise: the village was not returned, but instead requisitioned permanently. The people never came home and the cottages decayed into ruins. The Elizabethan manor was partially demolished during the 1960s and remains in a restricted military area, far away from curious eyes.

Tyneham is now a 'ghost village'. The army permit access to certain parts of it during the year, and it is a strange and melancholy place—somewhere that has haunted me since childhood. I have always wanted to fill it with people again, even if only in my imagination, and show it as it might have been. While many of the places are real, the people of Tyneford are imaginary—although I am indebted to Lilian Bond's elegiac account of her childhood in the great house.

Despite the sadness of Tyneham's history, the place is unique. So many villages along the Dorset coast bear the marks of modern life, while the landscape around Tyneham remains unchanged. It has never been subject to intensive farming methods, either during the 'dig for Britain' campaign or afterwards, and remains a period landscape from the 1940s with small, hedged fields. The cottages lie in ruins, but in many ways the army's occupation has preserved as much as it has destroyed. During a damp August afternoon, I saw a peregrine falcon and a nightingale as well as countless wild flowers. Abandoned by man, it has been reclaimed by nature.

Elise Landau is inspired by my great-aunt Gabi Landau, who, with the help of my grandmother Margot, managed to escape Europe by becoming a 'mother's help' for an English family during the late 1930s. Many refugees, particularly young girls from affluent, bourgeois households, escaped this way on a 'domestic service visa'—swapping cosseted and comfortable lives for the harsh existence of English servants. Like Elise, Gabi was desperately homesick and missed her sister Gerda, who emigrated to the United States. The two women did not meet for more than thirty years, and when they were reunited—on the Liverpool docks—they did not recognise one another.

ACKNOWLEDGEMENTS

I am hugely grateful to everyone at Sceptre: my wonderful editor Jocasta as well as Lucy, Nikki, Alice, Jason, Alix, Charlotte, Ruth, Carole, Sophie and Sarah who designed the gorgeous cover. James went above and beyond, agreeing to be shaved by a Mayfair barber wielding a cut-throat razor in the name of research, while Kate allowed me to stuff her viola full of paper. Sotheby's kindly helped me establish the value of a Turner in 1939, and Lisa Curzon generously shared her memories of working in service as a young refugee in 1938. Thanks to Jeff Rona who composed the Viola concerto, to Neel Hammond who performed the viola part so beautifully and to Michael Glenn Williams who devised the piano accompaniment (to listen to the music go to www.natashasolomons.com). Thanks always to my agents Stan and Elinor, to my parents, Carol and Clive, and to my husband and collaborator, David.